W9-CMI-920

Once Upon a River

Also by Diane Setterfield

The Thirteenth Tale
Bellman & Black

Once Upon a River

Diane Setterfield

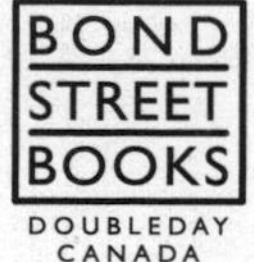

Library and Archives Canada Cataloguing in Publication

Setterfield, Diane, author
Once upon a river / Diane Setterfield.

Issued in print and electronic formats.
ISBN 978-0-385-66332-8 (hardcover).—ISBN 978-0-307-36794-5 (EPUB)

I. Title.
PR6119.E88O53 2019 823'.92 C2017-907585-3
C2017-907586-1

This book is a work of fiction. Names, characters, places, events and incidents are either the product of the author's imagination or are used fictitiously. Any resemblance to actual persons, living or dead, events, or locales is entirely coincidental.

Jacket design by Alex Merto
Jacket illustration © two cranes on the edge of a pond (w/c on paper),
indian school, (17th century) / musee guimet, paris, france / bridgeman images;
© swans, 2007 (oil on canvas), wright, liz (b.1950) / Private collection / Bridgeman Images

Printed and bound in the USA

Published in Canada by Bond Street Books,
a division of Penguin Random House Canada Limited

www.penguinrandomhouse.ca

10 9 8 7 6 5 4 3 2 1

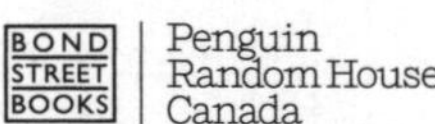

To my sisters, Mandy and Paula.
I wouldn't be me without you.

Along the borders of this world lie others.
There are places you can cross.
This is one such place.

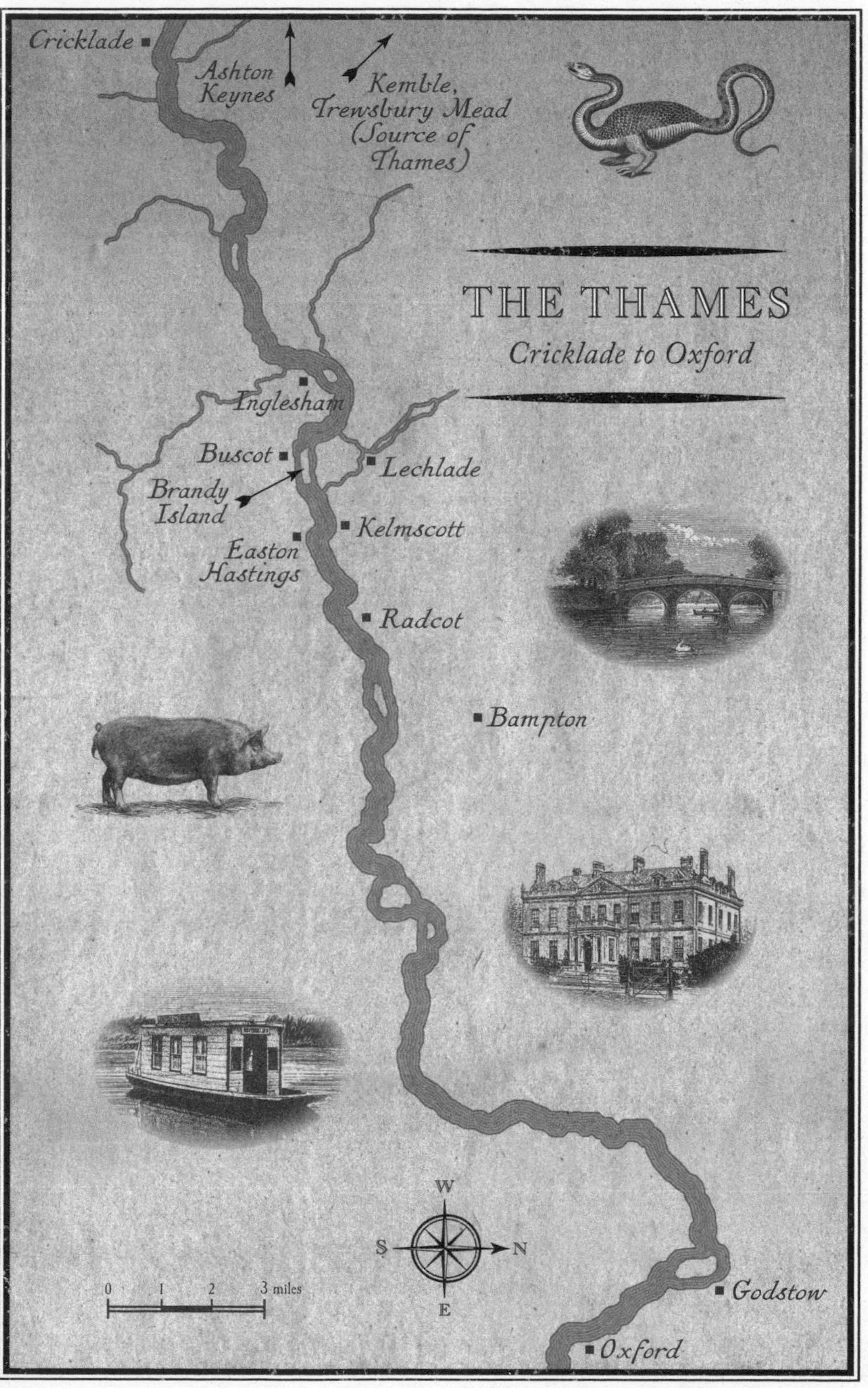
THE THAMES
Cricklade to Oxford
Cricklade
Ashton Keynes
Kemble, Trewsbury Mead (Source of Thames)
Inglesham
Buscot
Lechlade
Brandy Island
Kelmscott
Easton Hastings
Radcot
Bampton
W
S
N
E
0 1 2 3 miles
Godstow
Oxford

Part 1

The Story Begins . . .

THERE WAS ONCE an inn that sat peacefully on the bank of the Thames at Radcot, a long day's walk from the source. There were a great many inns along the upper reaches of the Thames at the time of this story and you could get drunk in all of them, but beyond the usual ale and cider, each one had some particular pleasure to offer. The Red Lion at Kelmscott was musical: bargemen played their fiddles in the evening and cheesemakers sang plaintively of lost love. Inglesham had the Green Dragon, a tobacco-scented haven of contemplation. If you were a gambling man, the Stag at Eaton Hastings was the place for you, and if you preferred brawling, there was nowhere better than the Plough just outside Buscot. The Swan at Radcot had its own specialism. It was where you went for storytelling.

The Swan was a very ancient inn, perhaps the most ancient of them all. It had been constructed in three parts: one was old, one was very old and one was older still. These different elements had been harmonized by the thatch that roofed them, the lichen that grew on the old stones and the ivy that scrambled up the walls. In summertime day-trippers came out from the towns on the new railway, to hire a punt or a skiff at the Swan and spend an afternoon on the river with a bottle of ale and a picnic, but in winter the drinkers were all locals, and they congregated in the winter room. It was a plain room in the oldest part of the inn, with a single window pierced through the thick stone wall. In daylight this window showed you Radcot Bridge and the river flowing through its three serene arches. By night (and this story begins at night) the bridge was drowned black, and it was only when your ears noticed the low and borderless sound of great quantities of moving water that you could make out the stretch of liquid blackness that flowed outside the window, shifting and undulating, darkly illuminated by some energy of its own making.

Nobody really knows how the tradition of storytelling started at the Swan, but it might have something to do with the Battle of Radcot Bridge. In 1387, five hundred years before the night this story began, two great armies met at Radcot Bridge. The who and the why of it are too long to tell, but the outcome was that three men died in battle – a knight, a varlet and a boy – and eight hundred souls were lost, drowned in the marshes, attempting to flee. Yes, that's right. *Eight hundred souls.* That's a lot of story. Their bones lie under what are now watercress fields. Around Radcot they grow the watercress, harvest it, crate it up and send it to the towns on barges, but they don't eat it. It's bitter, they complain; so bitter it bites you back, and besides, who wants to eat leaves nourished by ghosts? When a battle like that happens on your doorstep and the dead poison your drinking water, it's only natural that you would tell of it, over and over again. By force of repetition you would become adept at the telling. And then, when the crisis was over and you turned your attention to other things, what is more natural than that this newly acquired expertise would come to be applied to other tales?

The landlady of the Swan was Margot Ockwell. There had been Ockwells at the Swan for as long as anyone could remember, and quite likely for as long as the Swan had existed. In law her name was Margot Bliss, for she was married, but law was a thing for the towns and cities; here at the Swan she remained an Ockwell. Margot was a handsome woman in her late fifties. She could lift barrels without help and had legs so sturdy she never felt the need to sit down. It was rumoured she even slept on her feet, but she had given birth to thirteen children, so clearly she must have lain down sometimes. She was the daughter of the last landlady and her grandmother and great-grandmother had run the inn before that, and nobody thought anything of it being women in charge at the Swan at Radcot. It was just the way it was.

Margot's husband was Joe Bliss. He had been born at Kemble, twenty-five miles upstream, a hop and a skip from where the Thames emerges from the earth in a trickle so fine that it is scarcely more than a patch of dampness in the soil. The Blisses were chesty types. They were born small and ailing and most of them were goners before they were grown. Bliss babies grew thinner and paler as they lengthened, until they expired completely, usually before they were ten and often before they were two. The survivors, including Joe, got to adulthood shorter and slighter than average. Their chests rattled in winter, their noses ran, their eyes watered. They were kind, with mild eyes and frequent playful smiles.

At eighteen, an orphan and unfit for physical labour, Joe had left Kemble, to seek his fortune doing he knew not what. From Kemble there are as many directions a man can go in as elsewhere in the world, but the river has its pull; you'd have to be mightily perverse not to follow it. He came to Radcot and, being thirsty, stopped for a drink. The frail-looking young man with his floppy black hair that contrasted with his pallor sat unnoticed, eking out his glass of ale, admiring the innkeeper's daughter and listening to a story or two. He found it captivating to be amongst people who spoke out loud the kind of tales that had been alive inside his head since boyhood. In a quiet interval he opened his mouth and *Once upon a time* . . . came out.

Joe Bliss discovered his destiny that day. The Thames had brought him to Radcot and at Radcot he stayed. With a bit of practice he found he could turn his tongue to any kind of tale, whether it be gossip, historic, traditional, folk or fairy. His mobile face could convey surprise, trepidation, relief, doubt, and any other feeling, as well as any actor. Then there were his eyebrows. Luxuriantly black, they told as much of the story as his words did. They drew together when something momentous was coming, twitched when a detail merited close attention, and arched when a character might not be what he seemed. Watching his eyebrows, paying attention to their complex dance, you noticed all sorts of things that might otherwise have passed you by. Within a few weeks of his starting to drink at the Swan he knew how to hold the listeners spellbound. He held Margot spellbound too, and she him.

At the end of a month, Joe walked sixty miles to a place quite distant from the river, where he told a story in a competition. He won first prize, naturally, and spent the winnings on a ring. He returned to Radcot grey with fatigue, collapsed into bed for a week, and at the end of it got to his knees and proposed marriage to Margot.

'I don't know . . .' her mother said. 'Can he work? Can he earn a living? How will he look after a family?'

'Look at the takings,' Margot pointed out. 'See how much busier we have been since Joe started telling his stories. Suppose I don't marry him, Ma. He might go away from here. Then what?'

It was true. People came more often to the inn those days, and from further away, and they stayed longer, to hear the stories Joe told. They all bought drinks. The Swan was thriving.

'But with all these strong, handsome young men that come in here and admire you so – wouldn't one of those do better?'

'It is Joe that I want,' Margot said firmly. 'I like the stories.'

She got her way.

That was all nearly forty years before the events of this story, and in the meantime Margot and Joe had raised a large family. In twenty years they had produced twelve robust daughters. All had Margot's thick brown hair and sturdy legs. They grew up to be buxom young women with blithe smiles and endless cheer. All were married now. One was a little fatter and one a little thinner, one a little taller and one a little shorter, one a little darker and one a little fairer, but in every other respect they were so alike that the drinkers could not tell them apart, and when the girls returned to help out at busy times they were universally known as Little Margot. After bearing all these daughters there had been a lull in the family life of Margot and Joe, and both of them had thought her years of child-bearing were at an end, but then came the last pregnancy and Jonathan, their only son.

With his short neck and his moon face, his almond eyes with their exaggerated upward tilt, his dainty ears and nose, the tongue that seemed too big for his constantly smiling mouth, Jonathan did not look like other children. As he grew, it became clear that he was different from them in other ways too. He was fifteen now, but where other boys of his age were looking forward impatiently to manhood, Jonathan was content to believe that he would live at the inn for ever with his mother and father, and wished for nothing else.

Margot was still a strong and handsome woman, and Joe's hair had whitened, though his eyebrows were as dark as ever. He was now sixty, which was ancient for a Bliss. People put his survival down to the endlessness of Margot's care for him. These last few years, he was sometimes so weak that he lay in bed for two or three days at a time, eyes closed. He was not sleeping; no, it was a place beyond sleep that he visited in these periods. Margot took his sinking spells calmly. She kept the fire in to dry the air, tilted cooled broth between his lips, brushed his hair and smoothed his eyebrows. Other people fretted to see him suspended so precariously between one liquid breath and the next, but Margot took it in her stride. 'Don't you worry, he'll be all right,' she would tell you. And he was. He was a Bliss, that's all. The river had seeped into him and made his lungs marshy.

It was solstice night, the longest night of the year. For weeks the days had been shrinking, first gradually, then precipitously, so that it was now dark by mid-afternoon. As is well known, when the moon hours lengthen, human beings come adrift from the regularity of their mechanical clocks. They nod at noon, dream in waking hours, open their eyes wide to the pitch-black night. It is a time of magic. And as the borders between night and day stretch to their thinnest, so too do the borders between worlds. Dreams and stories merge with lived experience, the dead and the living brush against each other in their comings and goings, the past and the present touch and overlap. Unexpected things can happen. Did the solstice have anything to do with the strange events at the Swan? You will have to judge for yourself.

Now you know everything you need to know, the story can begin.

The drinkers gathered in the Swan that night were the regulars. Gravel-diggers, cressmen and bargemen for the most part, but Beszant the boat-mender was there too, and so was Owen Albright, who had followed the river to the sea half a century ago and returned two decades later a wealthy man. Albright was arthritic now, and only strong ale and storytelling could reduce the pain in his bones. They had all been there since the light had drained out of the sky, emptying and refilling their glasses, tapping out their pipes and restuffing them with pungent tobacco, and telling stories.

Albright was recounting the battle of Radcot Bridge. After five hundred years any story is liable to get a bit stale, and the storytellers had found a way to enliven the telling of it. Certain parts of the tale were fixed by tradition – the armies, their meeting, the death of the knight and his varlet, the eight hundred drowned men – but the boy's demise was not. Not a thing was known about him, except that he was a boy, was at Radcot Bridge, and died there. Out of this void came invention. At each retelling the drinkers at the Swan raised the unknown boy from the dead in order to inflict upon him a new death. He had died countless times over the years, in ways ever more outlandish and entertaining. When a story is yours to tell you are allowed to take liberties with it – though woe betide any visitor to the Swan who attempted the same thing. What the boy himself made of his regular resurrection is impossible to say, but the point is, raising the dead was a not infrequent thing at the Swan, and that's a detail worth remembering.

At this telling, Albright conjured a young entertainer, come to distract the troops while they awaited their orders. Juggling with knives, he slipped in the mud and the knives rained down around him, landing blade-down in wet earth, all but the last one, which fell plumb into his eye and killed him instantly before the battle had even begun. The innovation elicited murmurs of appreciation, quickly dampened so the story could continue, and from then on the tale ran pretty much as it always did.

Afterwards there was a pause. It wasn't done to jump in too quickly with a new story before the last one was properly digested.

Jonathan had been listening closely.

'I wish I could tell a story,' he said.

He was smiling – Jonathan was a boy who was always smiling – but he sounded wistful. He was not stupid, but school had been baffling to him, the other children had laughed at his peculiar face and strange ways, and he had given it up after a few months. He had not mastered reading or writing. The winter regulars were used to the Ockwell lad, with all his oddness.

'Have a go,' Albright suggested. 'Tell one now.'

Jonathan considered it. He opened his mouth and waited, agog, to hear what emerged from it. Nothing did. His face screwed tight with laughter and his shoulders squirmed in hilarity at himself.

'I can't!' he exclaimed when he had recovered himself. 'I can't do it!'

'Some other night, then. You have a bit of a practice, and we'll listen to you when you're ready.'

'You tell a story, Dad,' Jonathan said. 'Go on!'

It was Joe's first night back in the winter room after one of his sinking spells. He was pale and had been silent all evening. Nobody expected a story from him in his frail state, but at the prompting of his son, he smiled mildly and looked up to a high corner of the room where the ceiling was darkened from years of woodsmoke and tobacco. This was the place, Jonathan supposed, where his father's stories came from. When Joe's eyes returned to the room, he was ready and opened his mouth to speak.

'Once upon a—'

The door opened.

It was late for a newcomer. Whoever it was did not rush to come in. The cold draught set the candles flickering and carried the tang of the winter river into the smoky room. The drinkers looked up.

Every eye saw, yet for a long moment none reacted. They were trying to make sense of what they were seeing.

The man – if man it was – was tall and strong, but his head was monstrous and they boggled at the sight of it. Was it a monster from a folk tale? Were they sleeping and was this a nightmare? The nose was askew and flattened; beneath it was a gaping hollow, dark with blood. As sights went, it was horrifying enough, but in its arms the awful creature carried a large puppet, with waxen face and limbs and slickly painted hair.

What roused them to action was the man himself. He first roared, a great bellow as misshapen as the mouth it emerged from, then he staggered and swayed. A pair of farmhands jumped from their seats just in time to grab him under the arms and arrest his fall so that he did not smash his head on the flagstones. At the same time, Jonathan leapt forward from the fireside, arms outstretched, and into them dropped the puppet with a solid weightiness that took his joints and muscles by surprise.

Returning to their senses, they hoisted the unconscious man on to a table. A second table was dragged forward so that the man's legs could be rested upon it. Then, when he was laid down and straightened out, they all stood around and raised their candles and lamps over him. The man's eyes did not flicker.

'Is he dead?' Albright wondered.

There was a round of indistinct murmurs and much frowning.

'Slap his face,' someone said. 'See if that brings him round.'

'A tot of liquor'll do it,' another suggested.

Margot elbowed her way to the top of the table and studied the man. 'Don't you go slapping him. Not with his face in that state. Nor pouring anything down his throat. Just you wait a minute.'

She turned away to the seat by the hearth. On it was a cushion, and she picked it up and carried it back to the table. With the aid of the candlelight, she spotted a pinprick of white on the cotton. Picking at it with her fingernail, she drew out a feather. The men watched her, eyes wide with bewilderment.

'I don't think you'll wake a dead man by tickling him,' said a gravel-digger. 'Nor a live one either, not in this state.'

'I'm not going to tickle him,' she replied.

Margot laid the feather on the man's lips. All peered. For a moment there was nothing, then the soft and plumy parts of the feather shivered.

'He breathes!'

The relief soon gave way to renewed perplexity.

'Who is it, though?' a bargeman asked. 'Do anyone know him?'

There followed a few moments of general hubbub, during which they considered the question. One reckoned he knew everybody on the river from Castle Eaton to Duxford, which was some ten miles, and he was sure he didn't know the fellow. Another had a sister in Lechlade and was certain he had never seen the man there. A third felt that he might have seen the man somewhere, but the longer he looked, the less willing he was to put money on it. A fourth wondered whether he was a river gypsy, for it was the time of year when their boats came down this stretch of the river, to be stared at with suspicion, and everybody made sure to lock their doors at night and bring inside anything that could be lifted. But with that good woollen jacket and his expensive leather boots – no. This was not a ragged gypsy man. A fifth stared and then, with triumph, remarked that the man was the very height and build of Liddiard from Whitey's Farm, and was his hair not the same colour too? A sixth pointed out that Liddiard was here at the other end of the table, and when the fifth looked across, he could not deny it. At the end of these and further declarations, it was agreed by one, two, three, four, five, six, and all the others present that they didn't know him – at least, they didn't think so. But looking as he did, who could be certain?

Into the silence that followed this conclusion, a seventh spoke. 'Whatever has befallen him?'

The man's clothes were soaking wet, and the smell of the river, green and brown, was on him. Some accident on the water, that much was obvious. They talked of dangers on the river, of the water that played tricks on even the wisest of rivermen.

'Is there a boat? Shall I go and see if I can spy one?' Beszant the boat-mender offered.

Margot was washing the blood from the man's face with deft and gentle motions. She winced as she revealed the great gash that split his upper lip and divided his skin into two flaps that gaped to show his broken teeth and bloodied gum.

'Leave the boat,' she instructed. 'It is the man that matters. There is more here than I can help with. Who will run for Rita?' She looked round and spotted one of the farmhands who was too poor to drink much. 'Neath, you are quick on your feet. Can you run along to Rush Cottage and fetch the nurse without stumbling? One accident is quite enough for one night.'

The young man left.

Jonathan, meanwhile, had kept apart from the others. The weight of the drenched puppet was cumbersome, so he sat down and arranged it on his lap. He thought of the papier mâché dragon that the troupe of guisers had brought for a play last Christmastime. It was light and hard and had rapped with a light *tat-tat-tat* if you beat your fingernails against it. This puppet was not made of that. He thought of the dolls he had seen, stuffed with rice. They were weighty and soft. He had never seen one this size. He sniffed its head. There was no smell of rice – only the river. The hair was made of real hair, and he couldn't work out how they had joined it to the head. The ear was so real they might have moulded it from a real one. He marvelled at the perfect precision of the lashes. Putting his fingertip gently to the soft, damp, tickling ends of them caused the lid to move a little. He touched the lid with the gentlest of touches and there was something behind. Slippery and globular, it was soft and firm at the same time.

Something darkly unfathomable gripped him. Behind the backs of his parents and the drinkers, he gave the figure a gentle shake. An arm slid and swung from the shoulder joint in a way a puppet's arm ought not to swing, and he felt a rising water level, powerful and rapid, inside him.

'It is a little girl.'

In all the discussion around the injured man, nobody heard.

Again, louder: '*It is a little girl!*'

They turned.

'She won't wake up.' He held out the sodden little body so that they might see for themselves.

They moved to stand around Jonathan. A dozen pairs of stricken eyes rested on the little body.

Her skin shimmered like water. The folds of her cotton frock were plastered to the smooth lines of the limbs, and her head tilted on her neck at an angle no puppeteer could achieve. She was a little girl, and they had not seen it, not one of them, though it was obvious. What maker would go to such lengths, making a doll of such perfection, only to dress it in the cotton smock any pauper's daughter might wear? Who would paint a face in that macabre and lifeless manner? What maker other than the good Lord had it in him to make the curve of that cheekbone, the planes of that shin, that delicate foot with five toes individually shaped and sized and detailed? Of course it was a little girl! How could they ever have thought otherwise?

In the room usually so thick with words, there was silence. The men who were fathers remembered their own children and resolved to show them nothing but love till the end of their days. Those who were old and had never known a child of their own suffered a great pang of absence, and those who were childless and still young were pierced with the longing to hold their own offspring in their arms.

At last the silence was broken.

'Good Lord!'

'Dead, poor mite.'

'Drowned!'

'Put the feather on her lips, Ma!'

'Oh, Jonathan. It is too late for her.'

'But it worked with the man!'

'No, son, he was breathing already. The feather only showed us the life that was still in him.'

'It might still be in her!'

'It is plain she is gone, poor lass. She is not breathing, and besides, you have only to look at her colour. Who will carry the poor child to the long room? You take her, Higgs.'

'But it's cold there,' Jonathan protested.

His mother patted his shoulder. 'She won't mind that. She is not really here any more, and it is never cold in the place she has gone to.'

'Let me carry her.'

'You carry the lantern, and unlock the door for Mr Higgs. She's heavy for you, my love.'

The gravel-digger took the body from Jonathan's failing grip and lifted her as though she weighed no more than a goose. Jonathan lit the way out and round the side to a small stone outbuilding. A thick wooden door gave on to a narrow, windowless store room. The floor was plain earth, and the walls had never been plastered or panelled or painted. In summer it was a good place to leave a plucked duck or a trout that you were not yet hungry for; on a winter night like this one it was bitter. Projecting from one wall was a stone slab, and it was here that Higgs laid the girl down. Jonathan, remembering the fragility of the papier mâché, cradled her skull – 'So as not to hurt her' – as it came into contact with the stone.

Higgs's lantern cast a circle of light on to the girl's face.

'Ma said she's dead,' Jonathan said.

'That's right, lad.'

'Ma says she's in another place.'

'She is.'

'She looks as though she's here, to me.'

'Her thoughts have emptied out of her. Her soul has passed.'

'Couldn't she be asleep?'

'Nay, lad. She'd've woke up by now.'

The lantern cast flickering shadows on to the unmoving face, the warmth of its light tried to mask the dead white of the skin, but it was no substitute for the inner illumination of life.

'There was a girl who slept for a hundred years, once. She was woke up with a kiss.'

Higgs blinked fiercely. 'I think that was just a story.'

The circle of light shifted from the girl's face and illuminated Higgs's feet as they made their way out again, but at the door he discovered that Jonathan was not beside him. Turning, he raised the lantern again in time to see him stoop and place a kiss on the child's forehead in the darkness.

Jonathan watched the girl intently. Then his shoulders slumped and he turned away.

They locked the door behind them and came away.

The Corpse without a Story

THERE WAS A doctor two miles from Radcot, but nobody thought of sending for him. He was old and expensive and his patients mostly died, which was not encouraging. Instead they did the sensible thing: they sent for Rita.

So it was that half an hour after the man was placed on the tables, there came the sound of steps outside and the door opened on a woman. Other than Margot and her daughters, who were as much a part of the Swan as its floorboards and stone walls, women were a rare sight at the inn, and every eye was upon her as she entered the room. Rita Sunday was of middle height and her hair was neither light nor dark. In all other aspects, her looks were not average. The men evaluated her and found her lacking in almost every respect. Her cheekbones were too high and too angular; her nose was a bit too large, her jaw a bit too wide, her chin a bit too forward. Her best feature was her eyes, which did well enough for shape, though they were grey and looked at things too steadily from beneath her symmetrical brow. She was too old to be young, and other women her age had been crossed off the list of those suitable for appraisal, yet in Rita's case, for all her plainness and three decades of virginity, she still had something about her. Was it her history? Their local nurse and midwife, she had been born in a convent, lived there till adulthood and learnt all her medicine in the convent hospital.

Rita stepped inside the winter room of the Swan. As if she were not aware of all the eyes upon her, she unbuttoned her sober woollen coat and slid her arms out of it. The dress beneath was dark and unadorned.

She went directly to where the man lay, bloodied and still unconscious on the table.

'I have heated water for you, Rita,' Margot told her. 'And cloths here, all clean. What else will you want?'

'More light, if you can manage it.'

'Jonathan is fetching spare lanterns and candles from upstairs.'

'And quite likely' – having washed her hands, Rita was gently exploring the extent of the gash in the man's lip – 'a razor, and a man with a gentle and steady hand for shaving.'

'Joe can do that, can't you?'

Joe nodded.

'And liquor. The strongest you have.'

Margot unlocked the special cupboard and took out a green bottle. She placed it next to Rita's bag and all the drinkers eyed it. Unlabelled, it bore the signs of being illegally distilled, which meant it would be strong enough to knock a man out.

The two bargemen holding lanterns over the man's head saw the nurse probe the hole that was his mouth. With two blood-slicked fingers she drew out a broken tooth. A moment later she had two more. Her searching fingers went next into his still-damp hair. She explored every inch of his scalp.

'His head injuries are just to the face. It could be worse. Right, let's first get him out of these wet things.'

The room seemed to start. An unmarried woman could not strip a man's clothes from him without unsettling the natural order of things.

'Margot,' Rita suggested smoothly, 'would you direct the men?'

She turned her back and busied herself with setting out items from her bag, while Margot instructed the men in the removal of his clothes, reminding them to go gently – 'We don't know where else he is injured yet – let's not make it worse!' – and undid buttons and ties with her maternal fingers where they were too drunk or just too clumsy to do it. His garments piled up on the floor: a navy jacket with many pockets like a bargeman's but made of better cloth; freshly soled boots of strong leather; a proper belt, where a riverman would make do with rope; thick jersey long johns; and a knitted vest beneath his felt shirt.

'Who is he? Do we know?' Rita asked while she looked away.

'Don't know that we've ever set eyes on him. But it's hard to tell, the state he's in.'

'Have you got his jacket off?'

'Yes.'

'Perhaps Jonathan might have a look in the pockets.'

When she turned to face the table again, her patient was naked and a white handkerchief had been placed to protect his modesty and Rita's reputation.

She felt their eyes flicker to her face and away again.

'Joe, if you would shave his upper lip as gently as you can. You won't make a perfect job of it, but do your best. Go carefully around his nose – it's broken.'

She began the examination. She placed her hands first upon his feet, moved up to his ankles, shins, calves . . . Her white hands stood out against his darker skin.

'He is an out-of-doors man,' a gravel-digger noted.

She palpated bone, ligament, muscle, her eyes all the while diverted from his nakedness, as though her fingertips saw better than her eyes. She worked swiftly, knowing rapidly that here, at least, all was well.

At the man's right hip Rita's fingers inched around the white handkerchief, and paused.

'Light here, please.'

The patient was badly grazed all along one flank. Rita tilted liquor from the green bottle on to a cloth and applied it to the wound. The men around the table twisted their lips in little expressions of sympathy, but the patient himself did not stir.

The man's hand lay alongside his hip. It was swollen to twice the size it ought to be, bloodied and discoloured. Rita applied the liquor here too, but certain marks did not come away, though she wiped once and again. Ink-dark blots, but not the darkness of bruising, and not dried blood. Interested, she raised the hand and peered closely at them.

'He is a photographer,' she said.

'Blow me down! How do you know that?'

'His fingers. See these marks? Silver nitrate stains. It's what they use to develop the photographs.'

She took advantage of the surprise generated by this news to work around the white handkerchief. She pressed gently into his abdomen, found no evidence of internal injury, and worked up, up, the light following her, until the white handkerchief receded into the darkness and the men could be reassured that Rita was safely back in the realm of decorum again.

With his thick beard half gone, the man looked no less ghastly. The misshapen nose was all the more prominent, the gash that split the lip and ran up towards his cheek looked ten times worse for being visible. The eyes that usually endow a face with humanity were so swollen they were tight shut. On his forehead the skin had swollen into a bloodied lump; Rita drew splinters of what looked like dark wood from it, cleaned it, then turned her attention to the lip injury.

Margot handed her a needle and thread, both sterilized in the liquor. Rita put the point to the split and drove the needle into the skin, and as she did, the candlelight flickered.

'Anyone who needs to, sit down now,' she instructed. 'One patient is enough.'

But nobody was willing to admit to the need to sit.

She made three neat stitches, drawing the thread through, and the men either looked away or watched, fascinated by the spectacle of a human face being mended as if it were a torn collar.

When it was done, there was audible relief.

Rita looked at her handiwork.

'He do look a bit better now,' one of the bargemen admitted. 'Unless it's just that we're used to looking at him.'

'Hmm,' said Rita, as if she half agreed.

She reached to the middle of his face, gripped his nose between thumb and index finger and gave it a firm twist. There was a distinct sound of gristle and bone moving – a crunch that was also a squelch – and the candlelight quivered violently.

'Catch him, quick!' Rita exclaimed, and for the second time that night the farmhands took the weight of a fellow man collapsing in their arms as the gravel-digger's knees gave way. In doing so, all three men's candles fell to the floor, extinguishing themselves as they dropped – and the entire scene was snuffed out with them.

'Well,' said Margot, when the candles had been relit. 'What a night. We had best put this poor man in the pilgrims' room.' In the days when Radcot Bridge was the only river crossing for miles, many travellers had broken their journey at the inn, and though it was rarely used these days there was a room at the end of the corridor that was still called the pilgrims' room. Rita oversaw the removal of her patient and they laid him on the bed and put a blanket over him.

'I should like to see the child before I go,' she said.

'You will want to say a prayer over the poor mite. Of course.' In the minds of the locals, not only was Rita as good as a doctor, but given her time in the convent she could stand in for the parson at a push. 'Here's the key. Take a lantern.'

Back in her hat and coat and with a muffler wrapped around her face, Rita left the Swan and went to the outbuilding.

Rita Sunday was not afraid of corpses. She was used to them from childhood, had even been born from one. This is how it had happened: thirty-five years ago, heavily pregnant and in despair, a woman had thrown herself into the river. By the time a bargeman spotted her and pulled her out, she was three-quarters drowned. He took her to the nuns at Godstow, who nursed the poor and needy at the convent hospital. She survived long enough for labour to commence. The shock of almost drowning having weakened her, she had no strength left to give birth and died when her belly rippled with the strong contractions. Sister Grace had rolled up her sleeves, taken a scalpel, sliced a shallow red curve into the dead woman's abdomen and removed from it a living baby. Nobody knew her mother's name, and they would not have given it to the child anyway – the deceased had been triply sinful, by fornication, the act of self-murder and the attempt at killing her baby, and it would have been ungodly to encourage the child to remember her. They named the baby Margareta, after Saint

Margaret, and she came to be called Rita for short. As for her surname, in the absence of a flesh-and-blood begetter she was called Sunday, for the day of the heavenly Father, just like all the other orphans at the nunnery.

The young Rita did well at her lessons, showed an interest in the hospital, and was encouraged to help. There were tasks even a child could do: at eight she was making beds and cleaning the bloodied sheets and cloths; at twelve she carried buckets of hot water and helped lay out the dead. By the time Rita was fifteen she was cleaning wounds, splinting fractures, stitching skin, and by seventeen there was little in the way of nursing that she could not do, including delivering a baby all by herself. She might easily have stayed in the convent, becoming a nun and devoting her life to God and the sick, were it not for the fact that one day, collecting herbs on the riverbank, it occurred to her that there was no life beyond this one. It was a wicked thought according to everything she had been taught, but instead of feeling guilty, she was overwhelmed with relief. If there was no heaven, there was no hell, and if there was no hell then her unknown mother was not enduring the agonies of eternal torment, but simply gone, absent, untouched by suffering. She told the nuns of her change of heart, and before they had recovered from their consternation, she had rolled a nightdress and a pair of bloomers together and left without even a hairbrush.

'But your duty!' Sister Grace had called after her. 'To God and the sick!'

'The sick are everywhere,' she had cried back, and Sister Grace had replied, 'So is God,' but she said it quietly and Rita did not hear.

The young nurse had worked first at an Oxford hospital, then, when her talent was noticed, as general nurse and assistant to an enlightened medical man in London. 'You'll be a great loss to me and the profession when you marry,' he said to her more than once, when it was plain a patient had taken a shine to her.

'Marry? Not me,' she told him every time.

'Why ever not?' he pressed, when he had heard the same answer half a dozen times.

'I'm more use to the world as a nurse than as a wife and mother.'

It was only half an answer.

He got the other half a few days later. They were attending a young mother, the same age as Rita. It was her third pregnancy. Everything had gone smoothly before, and there was no particular reason to fear the worst. The baby was not awkwardly positioned, the labour was not unduly prolonged, the forceps were not necessary, the placenta followed cleanly. It was just that they could not stop the bleeding. She bled and she bled and she bled until she died.

The doctor spoke to the husband outside the room while Rita gathered up the bloodstained sheets with efficient expertise. She had lost count of the dead mothers long ago.

When the doctor came in, she had everything ready for their departure. They stepped out of the house and into the street in silence. After a few steps she said, 'I don't want to die like that.'

'I don't blame you,' he said.

The doctor had a friend, a certain gentleman, who called frequently at dinner time and did not leave till the next morning. Rita never spoke of it, yet the doctor realized she was aware of the love he felt for this man. She appeared to be unperturbed by it, and was entirely discreet. After thinking things over for a few months, he made a surprising suggestion.

'Why don't you marry me?' he asked her one day between patients. 'There would be no . . . you know. But it would be convenient for me, and it might be advantageous for you. The patients would like it.'

She thought about it and agreed. They became engaged, but before they could marry he fell ill with pneumonia and died, too young. In the last days of his life he called his lawyer to alter his will. In it he left his house and furniture to the gentleman, and to Rita a significant sum of money, enough to give her modest independence. He also left her his library. She sold the volumes that were not medical or scientific, and had the rest packed and taken upriver. When the boat came to Godstow, she looked at the convent as she passed and felt a surprising pang that called to mind her lost God.

'Here?' the boatman asked, mistaking the nature of the intensity on her face.

'Keep going,' she told him.

On they went, another day, another night, till they came to Radcot. She liked the look of the place.

'Here,' she told the bargeman. 'This will do.'

She bought a cottage, placed her books on the shelves, and let it be known among the better households of the area that she had a letter of recommendation from one of the best medical men in London. Once she had treated a few patients and delivered half a dozen babies, she was established. The wealthier families in the area wanted only Rita for their arrivals in the world and departures from it, and for all the medical crises in between. This was well-paid work and provided an adequate income to round out her inheritance. Among these patients were a number who could afford to be hypochondriacs; she tolerated their self-indulgence, for it enabled her to work at very low rates – or for nothing at all, for those who could not afford to pay. When she was not working, she lived frugally, read her way methodically through the doctor's library (she neither thought of him nor referred to him as her fiancé) and made medicines.

Rita had been at Radcot for nearly ten years now. Death did not frighten her. In those years she had tended the dying, witnessed their demise and laid out the dead. Death by sickness, death in childbirth, death by accident. Death by malice, once or twice. Death as the welcome visitor to great age. Godstow's hospital was on the river, so naturally she was familiar with the bodies of the drowned.

It was death by drowning that was on Rita's mind as she made her way briskly through the cold night air to the outbuilding. Drowning is easy. Every year the river helps herself to a few lives. One drink too many, one hasty step, one second's lapse of attention is all it takes. Rita's first drowning was a boy of twelve, only a year younger than herself at the time, who slipped as he sang and larked about on the lock. Later was the summer reveller who mistook his step from a boat, received a blow to the temple on the way down, and his friends were too drunk to come effectively to his aid. A student showing off jumped from the apex of Wolvercote Bridge on a golden autumnal day, only to be surprised by the depth and the current. A river is a river, whatever the season. There were young women, like her own mother, poor souls unable to face a future of shame and poverty, abandoned by lover and family, who turned to the river to put an end to it all. And then there were the babies, unwanted morsels of flesh, little beginnings of life, drowned before they had a chance to live. She'd seen it all.

At the door to the long room, Rita turned the key in the lock. The air seemed even colder inside than out. It outlined a vivid map of passages and cavities behind her nostrils and up into her forehead. The chill carried the tang of earth, stone and, overwhelmingly, river. Her mind sprang instantly to attention.

The feeble light from the lantern faltered long before it reached the corners of the stone room, yet the little corpse was illuminated, shimmering with a glaucous gleam. It was a peculiar effect, caused by the extreme paleness of the body, but a fanciful person might have thought the light emanated from the small limbs themselves.

Aware of the unusual alertness that stirred in her, Rita approached. She judged the child to be about four years of age. Her skin was white. She was dressed in the simplest of shifts that left her arms and ankles bare, and the fabric, still damp, lay in ripples around her.

Rita automatically initiated the convent-hospital routine. She checked for breathing. She placed two fingers against the child's neck to feel for a pulse. She peeled back the petal of an eyelid to examine the pupil. As she did all this, she heard in her mind the echo of the prayer that would have accompanied the examination in a chorus of calm, female voices: *Our Father, which art in heaven . . .* She heard it, but her lips did not move in time.

No breathing. No pulse. Full dilation of the pupils.

The uncommon vigilance was alive in her still. She stood over the little body and wondered what it was that had set her mind on edge. Perhaps it was nothing but the cold air.

You can read a dead body if you have seen enough of them, and Rita had seen it all. The when and the how and the why of it were all there if you knew how to look. She began an examination of the corpse so complete and so thorough that she entirely forgot about the cold. In the flickering light of the lantern, she peered and squinted at every inch of the child's skin. She lifted arms and legs, felt the smooth movement of joints. She looked into ear and nostril. She explored the cavity of the mouth. She studied every finger- and toenail. At the end of it all, she stood back and frowned.

Something wasn't right.

Head on one side, mouth twisted in perplexity, Rita went through everything she knew. She knew how the drowned wrinkle, swell and bloat. She knew how their skin, hair and nails loosen. None of this was present here, but that meant only that this child had not been in the water very long. Then there was the matter of mucus. Drowning leaves foam at the edges of the mouth and nostrils, but there was none on the face of this corpse. That too had its explanation. The girl was already dead when she went into the water. So far, so good. It was the rest that disturbed her. If the child had not drowned, what had happened to her? The skull was intact; the limbs unbeaten. There was no bruising to the neck. No bones were broken. There was no evidence of injury to the internal organs. Rita was aware how far human wickedness could go: she had checked the girl's genitals and knew she had not been the victim of unnatural interference.

Was it possible that the child had died naturally? Yet there were no visible signs of illness. In fact, to judge from her weight, skin and hair, she had been exceptionally healthy.

All this was disconcerting enough, but there was more. Even supposing the child had died of natural causes and – for reasons impossible to imagine – been disposed of in the river, there should be injuries to the flesh made after death. Sand and grit abrade skin, stones graze, the detritus on the river's bed will cut flesh. Water can break a man's bones; a bridge will smash his skull. Wherever you looked at her, this child was unmarked, unbruised, ungrazed, uncut. The little body was immaculate. 'Like a doll,' Jonathan had told her when he described the girl falling into his arms, and she understood why he had thought so. Rita had run her fingertips over the soles of the girl's feet, around the outer edge of her big toe, and they were so perfect you would think she had never put foot to earth. Her nails were as fine and as pearlized as those of a newborn. That death had made no mark on her was strange enough, but nor had life, and that, in Rita's experience, was unique.

A body always tells a story – but this child's corpse was a blank page.

Rita reached for the lantern on its hook. She trained its light on the child's face, but found it as inexpressive as the rest of her. It was impossible to tell whether, in life, these blunt and unfinished features had borne the imprint of prettiness, timid watchfulness or sly mischief. If there had once been curiosity or placidity or impatience here, life had not had time to etch it into permanence.

Only a very short time ago – two hours or not much more – the body and soul of this little girl had still been securely united. At this thought, and despite all her training, all her experience, Rita found herself suddenly in the grip of a storm of feeling. Not for the first time since they had parted company, she wished for God. God who, in her childhood years, had seen all, known all, understood all. How simple it had been when, ignorant and confused, she could nonetheless put her faith in a Father who enjoyed perfect understanding of all things. She had been able to bear not knowing a thing when she could be sure that God knew. But now . . .

She took the child's hand – the perfect hand with its five perfect fingers and their perfect fingernails – laid it in her open palm and closed her other hand over it.

This is wrong! All wrong! It should not be so!

And that is when it happened.

The Miracle

BEFORE MARGOT PLUNGED the injured man's clothes into the bucket of fresh water, Jonathan went through his pockets. They gave up:

One purse swollen with water, containing a sum of money that would cover all kinds of expenses and still stand them all a drink when he was feeling better.

One handkerchief, sodden.

One pipe, unbroken, and a tin of tobacco. They prised open the lid and found the contents to be dry. 'He'll be glad of that, at least,' they noted.

One ring, to which were linked a number of dainty tools and implements over which they puzzled – was he a clock-mender? they wondered. A locksmith? A burglar? – until the next item was drawn out.

One photograph. And then they remembered the dark stains on the man's fingers and Rita's idea that he might be a photographer, and this seemed to lend weight to it. The tools must be something to do with the man's profession.

Joe took the photograph from his son and dabbed it gently with his woollen cuff to dry it.

It showed a corner of a field, an ash tree, and not a lot else.

'I've seen prettier pictures,' someone said.

'It wants a church spire or a thatched cottage,' said another.

'It don't seem to be a photograph *of* anything exactly,' a third said, scratching his head in perplexity.

'Trewsbury Mead,' said Joe, the only one to recognize it.

They didn't know what to say, so they shrugged and put the

photograph on the mantel to dry and went on to the next and last item to come out of the man's pockets, which was:

One tin box, in which was a wad of small cards. They peeled off the top one and handed it to Owen, the best reader of them all, who raised a candle and read aloud:

Henry Daunt of Oxford
Portraits, landscapes, city and country scenes
Also: postcards, guide books, picture frames
Thames scenes a speciality

'She was right,' they exclaimed. 'She said he were a photographer, and here's the proof of it.'

Then Owen read out an address on Oxford's High Street.

'Who will be going to Oxford tomorrow?' Margot asked. 'Anybody know?'

'My sister's husband runs the cheese barge,' a gravel-digger suggested. 'I don't mind going to her house tonight and asking him.'

'Barge'll take two days, won't it?'

'Can't leave his family worrying about him for two days.'

'Surely he won't be going tomorrow, your sister's husband? If he did, he wouldn't be back in time for Christmas.'

'The railway, then.'

It was decided that Martins would go. He was not wanted at the farm tomorrow, and he had a sister living five minutes from the station at Lechlade. He would go to her house now, to be on hand for the early train. Margot gave him the fare, he repeated the address till he knew it, and set off, with a shilling in his pocket and a brand-new story on his tongue. He had six miles of riverbank along which to rehearse his tale, and by the time he got to his sister's house he would have it to perfection.

The other drinkers lingered. Storytelling of the usual kind was over for the night – who would stop to tell a story when one was actually happening? – and so they refilled their tankards and glasses, relit their pipes and settled on their stools. Joe put his shaving things away and returned to his chair, where from time to time he discreetly coughed. From his stool by the window, Jonathan kept an eye on the logs in the fire and surveyed the level of the candles. Margot prodded the river-wet clothes into a bucket with an old paddle and gave them a good swirl, then she put the pan of spiced beer back over the stove. The fragrance of nutmeg and allspice mingled with tobacco and burning logs, and the smell of the river receded.

The drinkers began to talk, finding words to turn the night's events into a story.

'When I saw him in the doorway there, I was astonished. No, astounded. That's what I was. Astounded!'

'I was stunned, I was.'

'And me. I was stunned *and* astounded. What about you?'

They were collectors of words, the same way so many of the gravel-diggers were collectors of fossils. They kept an ear constantly alert for them, the rare, the unusual, the unique.

'I reckon I was *dumbfounded*.'

They tried it out for flavour, weighing it on their tongues. It was good. They gave their colleague admiring nods.

One was new to the Swan, new to storytelling. He was still finding his feet. 'How about *flabbergasted*? Could I say that?'

'Why not?' they encouraged. 'Say flabbergasted, if you like.'

Beszant the boat-mender came back in. A boat could tell a story too and he'd been to see what it had to say. Everybody in the inn looked up to hear.

'She's there,' he reported. 'All bashed in along the saxboard. Graunched something terrible and taking in water. She were half under. I've left her upturned on the bank, but nothing can be done. 'Tis all over for her now.'

'What do you suppose happened? Was it the wharf that he went into?'

He shook his head with authority. 'Something came smashing down on the boat. From above.' He brought one hand down powerfully through the air and crashed one palm against the other to demonstrate. 'Wharf, no – boat'd be bashed in from the side.'

The drinkers now talked themselves up- and downstream, furlong by furlong, bridge by bridge, setting the damage to man and boat against every danger. All were rivermen of one kind or another – if not by profession then by long association – and every man had his say as they tried to work out what had happened. In their minds they smashed the little boat into every jetty and every wharf, every bridge and every millwheel, upstream and down, but none was right. Then they came to Devil's Weir.

The weir had great uprights of solid ash at regular intervals across the river, and between them were wide expanses of wood, like walls, that could be raised or lowered according to the flow. It was customary to get out of your boat and drag it up the slope that was made for the purpose, in order to go around the weir and then re-enter the water on the other side. There was an inn on the bank, so most of the time you could count on finding someone to give you a hand in exchange for the price of a drink. But sometimes – when the boards were up and the boat was nimble, when the river was calm and the boatman very experienced – then a man might save himself a bit of time and steer through. He would have to align his boat carefully, not take it askew, then he would need to pull in his blades so as not to break them against the great uprights, and – if the river was high – he would need to duck or else throw himself flat on his back in the boat to avoid knocking his head on the weir-beam.

They measured all this against the man. They measured it against the boat.

'So is that it?' asked Joe. 'It was at Devil's Weir he came to grief?'

Beszant picked up a fragment of wood, matchstick-sized, from a little pile. Black and firm, it was the largest of the splinters Rita had extracted from the forehead of the injured man. He tested it against his fingertip, felt the residual firmness of the wood despite the long contact with water. Most likely ash, and the weir was built of ash.

'I reckon so.'

'I've taken Devil's Weir myself more than once,' a farmhand said. 'You too, I reckon?'

The boat-mender nodded. 'If the river's in the mood to let me, yes.'

'Would you attempt it at night?'

'Risk my life to save a few seconds? I'm not such a fool.'

There was a sense of satisfaction at having settled at least one aspect of the night's events.

'And yet,' Joe wondered, after a pause, 'if it was at Devil's Weir he came to grief, how did he get from there to here?'

Now half a dozen small conversations broke out as theory after theory was proposed, tested and found wanting. Suppose he had rowed all the way after the accident . . . With those injuries? No! Then suppose he drifted, lying in the boat between life and death, until at Radcot he came to his senses and . . . Drifted? A boat in that cock-eyed state? Negotiating obstacles in the dark all by itself and letting in water all the while? No!

Round and round they went, finding explanations that fitted one half of the facts or the other half, that supplied a what but not a how, or a where but not a why, until all imagination came to an end and they were no nearer an answer. How had the man not drowned?

For a while the only voice to be heard was that of the river, and then Joe coughed lightly and gathered his breath to speak.

'It must be Quietly's doing.'

Everybody glanced towards the window and those near enough looked out, into the soft, flat night in which a span of swiftly moving blackness shone with a liquid gleam. Quietly the ferryman. All knew of him. From time to time he featured in stories they told, and some swore they'd met him. He appeared when you were in trouble on the water, a gaunt and elongated figure, manipulating his pole so masterfully that his punt seemed to glide as if powered by an otherworldly force. He spoke never a word, but guided you safely to the bank so you would live another day. But if you were out of luck – so they said – it was another shore altogether that he would take you to, and those poor souls did not return to the Swan to lift their pint of ale and tell of their encounter.

Quietly. Now that would turn it into another kind of story altogether.

Margot, whose mother and grandmother had spoken of Quietly in the months before they died, frowned and changed the subject.

'It'll be a sorry awakening for that poor man. To lose a child – there is no heartbreak like it.'

There was a murmur of agreement and she went on: 'Why would a father take a child out on the river at this time of night, anyway? In winter too! Even if he were alone it was foolish, but with a child . . .'

The fathers in the room nodded, and added rashness to the character of the man who lay senseless in the next room.

Joe coughed and said, 'She were a droll-looking little maid.'

'Strange.'

'Peculiar.'

'Odd,' came a trio of voices.

'I didn't even know it was a child,' a voice said wonderingly.

'You weren't the only one.'

Margot had been pondering this all the while the men had been talking of boats and weirs. She thought of her twelve daughters and her granddaughters and admonished herself. A child was a child, dead or alive.

'How did we not see it?' she asked, in a voice that made them all ashamed.

They turned their eyes to the dark corners and consulted their memories. They conjured the injured man to stand again in the doorway. They reinhabited their shock, considered what there had not been time to consider as it happened. It had been like a dream, they thought, or a nightmare. The man had appeared to them like something from a folk tale: a monster or a ghoul. They had taken the child for a puppet or a doll.

The door opened, as it had opened before.

The drinkers blinked away their memory of the man and saw this: Rita.

She stood in the doorway, where the man had stood.

The dead girl was in her arms.

Again? Was it time's error? Were they drunk? Had they lost their wits? Too much had happened and their brains were full. They waited for the world to right itself.

The corpse opened its eyes.

The girl's head swivelled.

Her gaze sent a wave through the room so strong that every eye felt its ripple, every soul was rocked on its mooring.

Time went unmeasured, and when the silence was at last broken it was Rita who spoke.

'I don't know,' she said.

It was an answer to the questions they were too stunned to ask, an answer to the questions she could scarcely form herself.

When they found that their tongues were still in their mouths and still working, Margot said, 'Let me wrap her in my shawl.'

Rita put out a warning hand. 'Let her not be warmed too quickly. She has come this far in the cold. Perhaps she should grow warm by slow degrees.'

The women laid the child on the window seat. Her pallor was deathly. She was unmoving; all but her eyes, which blinked and looked.

The rivermen and the cressmen and the gravel-diggers, young men and old, with hard hands and reddened fingers, grimy necks and rough chins, sat forward in their seats and gazed with soft yearning at the little child.

'Her eyes are closing!'

'Is she dying again?'

'See her chest rise?'

'Ah! I see it. And now it falls.'

'And rises again.'

'She is falling asleep.'

'Hush!'

They spoke in whispers.

'Are we keeping her awake?'

'Shuffle aside, will you? I cannot see her breathe!'

'Now do you see her?'

'She breathes in.'

'And out.'

'In.'

'Out.'

They stood on tiptoe to lean forwards, peer over shoulders, squint into the circle of light from the candle that Rita held over the sleeping girl. Their eyes followed her every breath and, without knowing it, their breathing fell in time with hers, as if their many chests might make a great pair of bellows to inflate her little lungs. The room itself expanded and contracted with her respiration.

'It must be a fine thing to have a little child to look after.' It was a bony cressman with red ears who spoke, in a longing half-tone.

'Nothing finer,' his friends admitted wistfully.

Jonathan had not taken his eyes off the girl. He edged across the floor until he stood beside her. He extended a hand uncertainly and at Rita's nod laid it gently on a strand of the girl's hair.

'How did you do it?' he asked.

'I didn't.'

'Then what made her come alive again?'

She shook her head.

'Was it me? I kissed her. To wake her, like the prince in the story.' And he brought his lips to her hair to show Rita.

'It doesn't happen like that in real life.'

'Is it a miracle?'

Rita frowned, unable to answer.

'Don't go thinking about it now,' his mother said. 'There's a great many things hard to fathom in darkness that set themselves straight in the light of day. The little mite needs to sleep, not have you fidgeting around her. Come away, I've got a job for you.'

She unlocked the cupboard again and took out another bottle, set a dozen tiny glasses on a tray, poured an inch of liquor into each.

Jonathan handed one to everybody present.

'Give one to your father.' Joe didn't usually drink in winter and when his lungs were bad. 'What about you, Rita?'

'I will, thank you.'

As one, they raised the glasses to their lips and swallowed in a single gulp.

Was it a miracle? It was as if they had dreamt of a pot of gold and woken to find it on their pillow. As if they had told a tale of a fairy princess and finished it only to find her sitting in a corner of the room listening.

For close on an hour they sat in silence and watched the sleeping child and wondered at it. Could there be any place in the country more interesting tonight than the Swan at Radcot? And they would be able to say, *I was there.*

In the end, it was Margot who sent them all home. 'It's been a long night, and nothing will do us more good now than a bit of sleep.'

The dregs in tankards were drained and slowly the drinkers reached for their coats and hats. They rose on legs unsteady with drink and magic, and shuffled over the floor towards the door. There was a round of goodnights, the door was opened and one by one, with many a backward glance, the drinkers disappeared into the night.

The Story Travels

MARGOT AND RITA lifted the sleeping child and worked her sleeveless shift over her head. They wrung out a cloth in warm water and wiped the river smell away, though it still lingered in her hair. The child made a vague sound of contentment at the touch of the water, but did not wake.

'Funny little thing,' Margot murmured. 'What are you dreaming of?'

She had fetched a nightdress she kept for visiting granddaughters, and together the women fed small hands and arms through the sleeves. The girl did not wake.

Meanwhile, Jonathan washed and dried the tankards, while Joe concealed the night's takings in the regular place and swept the floor. From a corner he dislodged the cat that had slipped in unnoticed earlier in the evening. Offended, it stalked out of the shadows and made for the hearth, where the embers were still glowing.

'Don't go thinking you can settle here,' Margot told the animal, but her husband intervened.

'It's deathly out. Let the creature stay, the once.'

Rita settled the child on the bed in the pilgrims' room next to the sleeping man. 'I'll stay here for the night to keep an eye on them,' she said, and when Margot proposed bringing in a truckle bed, 'The chair will be all right. I'm used to it.'

The house settled.

'It makes you think,' Margot murmured, her head at long last on the pillow, and Joe muttered, 'It does, that's for sure.' They shared their thoughts in whispered voices. Where had they come from, these unknown people? And why here, to their own inn, the Swan? And what precisely was it that had happened tonight? *Miracle* was the word Jonathan had pronounced, and they tested it on their own tongues. They were used to it in the Bible, where it meant impossible things that happened an impossibly long time ago in places so far away from here that they might as well not exist. Here in the inn, it applied to the laughably improbable chance that Beszant the boatmender would ever pay his slate in full: now that would be a miracle all right. But tonight, at winter solstice in the Swan at Radcot, the word had a different weight.

'I shan't get a wink of sleep for puzzling over it,' Joe said. But miracle or no, they were tired and so, with the long night more than half over already, they blew out the candle. The night closed over them and almost immediately wonderment came to an end.

Downstairs, in the pilgrims' room where her patients, man and child, were asleep side by side on the bed, Rita sat awake in the armchair. The man's breath was slow and noisy. The air entering and leaving his lungs had to make its way past swollen membranes, through passages filled with drying blood whose paths had been altered and reset in the past hours. It was no wonder it made a sound like the teeth of a saw on wood. In the silences where his breath tipped from in to out, she could hear the insubstantial flutter of the child's breath. Behind them both, in the background, the breath of the river, an endless exhalation.

She ought to sleep, but had been waiting to be alone to think. Methodically, dispassionately, she went over it all again. She watched herself perform the routine checks, noted all the signs she had been trained to look for. Where was her mistake? Once, twice, three times she went through it all in close detail. She found no error.

What then?

Since her learning was of no use, she looked to her experience for elucidation. Had there ever been an instance when she had been unsure whether a patient was dead or alive? It was commonplace to say that a person was at death's door, as if there were some real line between life and death and a person might stand upon it for a time. But she had never in such circumstances had any difficulty in discerning which side of the line the patient was on. No matter how far illness had progressed, no matter how great the weakness, a patient was alive until the moment of death. There was no hovering. No in-between.

Margot had sent them all to bed with the encouraging thought that enlightenment would come naturally with the dawn, a sentiment Rita shared with regard to other kinds of trouble, but this was different. The questions in her mind related to the body, and the body was governed by laws. Everything she knew told her that what she had experienced *could not happen*. Dead children do not come back to life. There were two possibilities: either the child was not alive – she listened: there it was, the delicate breath – or she had not been dead. She considered again all the indications of death that she had checked. Waxy white skin. Absence of breathing. Absence of pulse. Pupil dilation. She revisited the long room in memory and knew she had checked each of these things. Every indication of death had been present. The fault was not in her. Where was it, then?

Rita closed her eyes the better to focus. She had decades of nursing experience, but her knowledge did not end there. She had spent long evenings studying books intended for the use of surgeons, had memorized anatomy, had mastered the science of the apothecary. Her practical experience had developed these pools of knowledge into a deep reservoir of understanding. She now permitted the evening's experience to be placed alongside what she knew. She did not chase after explanations or make effortful attempts to connect thoughts. She simply waited, with a growing thrill of trepidation and exhilaration, until the conclusion that had been carefully preparing itself in the depths came to the surface.

The laws of life and death, as she had learnt them, were incomplete. There was more to life, more to death, than medical science had known.

A door opened, beckoning her towards new knowledge.

Again she missed God. She had shared everything with Him. From childhood she had gone to Him with every question, doubt, delight and triumph. He had accompanied every advance in her thinking, in action He had been her daily collaborator. But God was gone. This was something she was going to have to work out by herself.

What to do about it?

She listened. The breathing of the girl. The breathing of the man. The breath of the river.

The river . . . She would start there.

Rita laced up her boots and buttoned herself into her coat. In her bag she groped for something – it was a slim tin box – and dropped it into her pocket before creeping quietly outside. Around her lantern flame the chill darkness expanded vastly, but she could make out the edges of the path. She stepped off it and on to the grass. As much by feel as by sight, she made her way to the riverbank. The cold air sidled through her buttonholes and the stitches of her muffler. She walked through the warm steam of her own exhalation, felt it lay itself as wetness on her face.

Here was the boat, upturned on the grass. She pulled off a glove, and her cautious fingers found jagged edges of wood, but then a solid part; she placed her lantern there.

She took the box from her pocket and held it for a moment between her teeth while – ignoring the cold – she gathered the folds of her skirt and tucked a bunch of hem into the same pocket so that she could crouch without getting her dress wet. Before her was the dark shimmer of the river. She reached forward and down till she felt it nip viciously at the flesh of her fingers. Good. Opening the tin, she removed from it a glass-and-metal vial with complications impossible to see in the dark. By feel, she immersed the tube in the freezing water and counted. Then she rose and, with all the care her numb fingers could muster, closed the tube in its case for protection, and without bothering to straighten her dress made her way as swiftly as she could back to the inn.

In the pilgrims' room she held the tube as close to the lantern as was necessary to read the gauge, then took a notebook and a pencil out of her bag. She wrote down the temperature of the water.

It wasn't much. But it was a start.

She eased the child off the bed and settled her gently on her lap, in the chair. The little head nodded to rest against her chest. *I won't sleep now*, she thought as she arranged the blankets to cover herself and the child. *Not after all this. Not in this chair.*

As she prepared herself to sit out the night, with scratchy eyes and an aching back, her namesake came to mind. Saint Margaret who consecrated her virginity to God and was so determined not to marry that she bore the pain of torture sooner than become a wife. She was the patron saint of pregnant women and childbirth. In her early days at the convent, washing the filthy, bloodied sheets, laying out the bodies of the women who had died in childbirth, Rita had been rather relieved that her own future was as God's bride. She would never be sundered by a child emerging from her belly. God had left her, but her commitment to virginity had never wavered.

Rita closed her eyes. Her arms folded around the child, whose sleeping weight rested heavily against her. She felt the rise and fall of the girl's breathing, and measured her own inhalations so that as her chest fell, the child's expanded; as the child's fell, her own filled the space. An obscure pleasure took hold of her; she sought drowsily to identify it, name it, and couldn't.

An idea came floating towards her in the dark.

If she doesn't belong to this man. If nobody wants her. She could be mine . . .

But before she had time to register her own thinking, the sound of the river, endless and low, filled her mind. It nudged her from the solidity of wakefulness, carried her on to the current of the night where, without awareness of what was happening, she drifted . . . drifted . . . into the dark sea of sleep.

All were not sleeping, though. The drinkers and the storytellers had some way to walk before they found their beds for the night. One of them turned away from the river on leaving the Swan and skirted the fields to find his way to the barn two miles off where he slept with the horses. He regretted that he had nobody waiting for him, nobody he could shake awake and say, 'You won't believe what's just happened!' He pictured himself telling the horses what he had witnessed that night, saw their large unbelieving eyes. *Nay, they will say*, he thought, and *That's a good joke, I'll remember that*. But it wasn't horses he wanted to tell; the story was too fine to be squandered on animal ears. He turned off the direct path and made a detour to the cottages by Gartin's fields where his cousin lived.

He knocked.

No one answered, so the story made him knock again, a full-fisted hammering.

In the adjoining cottage, a window was flung up and a woman put her head out in her nightcap to remonstrate with him.

'Wait!' he said. 'Hold your scolding till you know what I have come to tell you!'

'Is that you, Fred Heavins?' She peered in the direction the voice was coming from. 'Drunken stories, I shouldn't wonder!' she grumbled. 'As if I haven't heard enough of those to last me a lifetime!'

'I'm not drunk,' he said, offended. 'Look! I can walk in a straight line, see?' He placed foot in front of foot with elaborate ease.

'As if that proves anything!' she laughed into the night. 'When there is no light to see by, any drunk can walk in a straight line!'

The argument was interrupted by the opening of his cousin's door. 'Frederick? What on earth is it?'

Simply, with no embellishments, Fred told what had happened at the Swan.

Leaning out of the window, the neighbour was drawn in, at first unwillingly, to the story, then she called to someone behind her.

'Come, Wilfred. Listen to this!'

Before long, Fred's cousin's children were shaken out of their beds in their nightgowns, and the neighbours on all sides were roused too.

'What is she like, then, this girl?'

He described her skin, as white as the glazed jug on his grandmother's kitchen windowsill; he told of her hair, that hung in a dead straight curtain and was the same colour dry as wet.

'What colour are her eyes?'

'Blue . . . Blueish, at any rate. Or grey.'

'How old is she?'

He shrugged. How was he to know? 'If she was by my side she'd come up to . . . about here.' He indicated with his hand.

'About four, then? What do you reckon?'

The women discussed it and agreed. About four.

'And what's 'er name, this girl?'

Again he was stumped. Who would have thought a story needed all this detail, things he had never considered while it was happening?

'I dunno. Nobody asked her.'

'Nobody asked her name!' The women were scandalized.

'She was drowsy, like. Margot and Rita said to let her sleep. But her father's name is Daunt. Henry Daunt. We found it in his pocket. He's a photographer.'

'So he's her father, is he?'

'I'd've thought so . . . Wouldn't you? It was him brought her in. They arrived together.'

'Perhaps he was only taking her photograph?'

'And they both half drowned, taking a photograph? How do you make that out?'

There was a general hubbub of conversation between the windows, as the story was discussed, its missing pieces identified, attempts made to fill them in . . . Fred began to feel left out of his own tale, sensed it slipping from his grasp and altering in ways he hadn't anticipated. It was like a living thing that he had caught but not trained; now it had slipped the leash and was anybody's.

He became aware of a persistent, urgent whisper. 'Fred!'

A woman was beckoning him to a lower-floor window at the next-door house. As he approached she leant forwards, candle in hand, yellow hair escaping from her nightcap.

'What does she look like?'

He started again with the white skin and the nondescript hair, but she shook her head. 'I mean, *who* does she look like? Does she look like the fellow?'

'The state he's in, I'd say there ain't nobody on earth looks like him.'

'Has he got the same hair? Limp and mousy?'

'His is dark and wiry.'

'Ah!' She nodded meaningfully and left a dramatic pause while she gazed at him. 'Did she *remind* you of anyone?'

'It's funny you should ask . . . I had the feeling she reminded me of someone, but I can't think who.'

'Is it . . . ?' She beckoned him closer and whispered a name in his ear.

When he stood back from her, his mouth was open and his eyes wide.

'Oh!' he said.

She gave him a look. '*She* would be about four now, wouldn't she?'

'Yes, but . . .'

'Keep it under your hat,' she said. 'I work up there. I'll let them know in the morning.'

Fred was called then by the others. How did the man, the girl and a camera fit in a boat small enough to go under Devil's Weir? He explained there was no camera in the boat. So how did they make the fellow out to be a photographer if he had no camera? Because of what was in his pockets. What was in his pockets, again?

He gave in to demand, telling the story once and again, and the second time he put more detail in, and the third time he anticipated the questions before they arose, and by the fourth time he had it just so. He left out the idea planted by the neighbour with the yellow hair. Finally, an hour after he arrived and frozen to the core, Frederick took his leave.

In the barn he told the story once more, in a mutter, to the horses. They opened their eyes and listened unsurprised to the beginning of the story. By the time he was halfway through they had returned to sleep, and before the end, so had he.

Back at his cousin's cottage was an outbuilding, partly concealed by shrubs. Behind it, a pile of old rags with a hat on top organized itself into a man, albeit a scruffy one, and struggled to its feet. He waited to be sure that Frederick Heavins was out of the way, and then set off himself. Towards the river.

*

As Owen Albright followed the river downstream to reach the comfortable house he had bought in Kelmscott when he returned from his lucrative adventures on the sea, he didn't feel the cold. Usually the walk home from the Swan was a time for regret – regret that his joints ached so badly, that he had drunk too much, that the best of life had passed him by and he had only aches and pains ahead of him now, a gradual decline till at the end he would sink into the grave. But having witnessed one miracle, he now saw miracles everywhere: the dark night sky his old eyes had ignored thousands of times before tonight unfolded itself above his head with the vastness of eternal mystery. He stopped to stare up and marvel. The river was splashing and chiming like silver on glass; the sound spilt into his ear, resonated in chambers of his mind he'd never known existed. He lowered his head to look at the water. For the first time in a lifetime by the river, he noticed – *really* noticed – that under a moonless sky the river makes its own mercurial light. Light that is also darkness; darkness that is also light.

A few things came home to him then – things he had always known but that had been buried under the days of his life. That he missed his father, who had died more than sixty years ago when Owen was still a boy. That he had been lucky in life and had much to be thankful for. That the woman waiting for him at home in bed was a kind and loving soul. And more: his knees didn't hurt as much as usual, and there was an expansiveness in his chest that reminded him of how it had been to be young.

At home, he shook Mrs Connor's shoulder before he had even undressed.

'Don't go thinking what you're thinking,' she grumbled. 'And don't bring the cold in with you either.'

'Listen!' he told her. 'Just listen to this!' And the story spilt out of him, the girl and the stranger, dead and alive.

'What you been drinking?' Mrs Connor wanted to know.

'Hardly a thing.' And he told her the story all over again, because she hadn't grasped it.

She half sat up to see him properly, and there he was, the man she had worked for for thirty years and shared a bed with for twenty-nine, and he was still dressed, upright, a torrent of words pouring from him. She couldn't make sense of it. Even when he had finished speaking, he stood there as if under a spell.

She got out of bed to help him off with his clothes. It wasn't unknown for him to have such a skinful that he couldn't manage his buttons alone. He wasn't staggering though, nor did he lean on her, and when she unbuttoned his breeches she discovered him full of the kind of vigour that a drunk man is unlikely to sustain.

'Look at you,' she half chided him, and he embraced her with a kiss the like of which they had not shared since the early years of their time together. They rolled and tumbled in the bed for a little while, and when they were done, instead of turning over and going to sleep, Owen Albright kept her in his arms and kissed her hair.

'Marry me, Mrs Connor.'

She laughed. 'Whatever's got into you, Mr Albright?'

He kissed her cheek, and she felt his smile in the kiss.

She was nearly asleep when he spoke again. 'I saw it with my own eyes. It was me that held the candle. Dead, she was. That was one minute. And the next – alive!'

She could smell the breath from him. He wasn't drunk. Mad, perhaps.

They slept.

Jonathan, still dressed, waited till he heard silence in the Swan. He let himself out of the upstairs room and came down the external staircase. He was underdressed for the weather, but he didn't care. He was warmed by the story he held in his heart. He took the opposite direction from Owen Albright, turned upstream and walked against the river. His head was alive with ideas and he walked rapidly to deposit them with the person who would surely want to know all about it.

Arriving at the parsonage at Buscot, he rapped loudly at the door. There being no answer, he rapped again, and again, until he was knocking without cease, with no regard to the lateness of the hour.

The door opened.

'The parson!' Jonathan burst out. 'I must speak to the parson!'

'But Jonathan,' said the door-opener, a figure clad in a dressing gown and nightcap, who was rubbing his eyes, 'It is I.' The man took off his nightcap, displaying an untidy mass of greying hair.

'Oh. Now I know you.'

'Is someone dying, Jonathan? Is it your father? Have you come to fetch me?'

'No!' And Jonathan, who wanted to explain that his reason for coming was the very opposite of that, fell over his words in his rush to tell, and all the parson could understand was that nobody was dead.

Sleepily, he interrupted. 'You cannot rouse people from their sleep for no reason, Jonathan. This is no night for a boy to be out – too cold by far. You should be in bed yourself. Go home and sleep.'

'But Parson, it is the same story! All over again! Just like Jesus!'

The parson saw that his visitor's face was white with cold. His up-slanting eyes were running and the tears were freezing on his flat cheeks. His entire face was illuminated with the pleasure of seeing the parson, and his tongue, always too big for his mouth so that it sometimes got in the way of his speech, was resting on his lower lip. Seeing him, the parson was reminded that Jonathan, for all his goodness, was incapable of taking care of himself. He opened the door wide and ushered the boy in.

In the kitchen, the parson heated milk in a pan and placed bread in front of his guest. Jonathan ate and drank – no miracle would get in the way of that – and then told his story again. The child that was dead and came to life again.

The parson listened. He asked a few questions: 'When you thought to come here, were you in your bed and had been sleeping there? . . . No? . . . Well, then, was it your father or Mr Albright that told the story of this child in the inn tonight?' When he had ascertained that the event – extraordinary and impossible, as Jonathan described it – had some basis in something that had actually happened, and was not the boy's dream or a tall tale told by some drinker, he nodded. 'So, in fact, the little girl was not dead at all. But everyone thought she was.'

Jonathan shook his head vehemently. 'I caught her. I held her. I touched her eye.' He mimed the catching of a heavy bundle, the holding of it, then the gentle fingertip.

'A person might seem dead after something terrible has happened. That is possible. To appear to be dead, but in fact only be in a – a kind of sleep.'

'Like Snow White? I kissed her. Was it that that woke her up?'

'That is just a story, Jonathan.'

Jonathan considered. 'Like Jesus, then.'

The parson frowned and was lost for words.

'She was dead,' Jonathan added. 'Rita thought so.'

That was a surprise. Rita was the most reliable person the parson knew.

Jonathan gathered up the breadcrumbs and chewed them.

The parson rose. It was more than he could take in.

'It's cold and it's late. Sleep here for what remains of the night, eh? Here's a blanket, look, on this chair. You're worn out.'

Jonathan wanted something else. 'I'm right, aren't I, Parson? It's like Jesus, all over again?'

The parson thought if he was lucky his bed would still have a parson-shaped bit of warmth in it. He nodded. 'The way you have put it before me, yes, Jonathan. The parallels are inescapable. But let's not cudgel our brains tonight.'

Jonathan grinned. 'I'm the one that brought you the story.'

'I won't forget that. I heard it from you first.'

Jonathan settled down happily in the kitchen chair and his eyes began to close.

The parson climbed the stairs wearily back to his room. In summer he was a different man, sprightly and alert, and people took him for a man a decade younger than his years, but in winter he sank as the skies darkened, and by December he was always tired. When he went to bed he drowned in sleep; when he was wakened from it, dragged from the bleak depths, he was somehow always unrefreshed.

He didn't know what it was, but something strange had happened tonight at the Swan at Radcot. He would go over there tomorrow. He climbed into his bed, aware that in June it would be getting light already at this time. Yet there were hours of this winter darkness ahead.

'Let the child – if there is a child – be all right,' he prayed. 'And let it soon be spring.'

And then he was asleep.

Clutching his ragged coat to him as if he believed it might afford some protection against the weather, the tramp followed the path to the river. The story he had heard had the smell of money to him – and he knew who might want to buy it. It was not a good path: rocks jutted out of the soil to trick the boots of even a sober man, and where the going was flat it was slippery. When he stumbled, as he did now and again, he flung his arms out for balance and by a miracle found it. Perhaps there were spirits in the darkness that gripped his frozen hands and held him safe. It was a ticklish thought and it made him chuckle. He stumbled on for a bit, and the going was thirsty work. His tongue was furred and stinking like a three-day-dead mouse, so he stopped for a drink from the bottle in his pocket, and then stumbled on a bit more.

When he came to the river, he turned upstream. There were no landmarks in the dark, but at about the time he thought he must surely be level with Brandy Island, he came to a spot he knew.

The name Brandy Island was a new one. In the old days it was just The Island and nobody needed another name for it because nobody ever went there and there was nothing to see. But when the new people came to Radcot Lodge – Mr Vaughan at first and later his young wife – one of the changes they made was the construction on this river-bound sliver of land of the big distillery and vitriol works, and that was what gave the island its name. Acres of fields belonging to Mr Vaughan were turned over to sugar beet, and a light railway was installed to transport the beet on to the island and bring the brandy back. There were jobs a-plenty making liquor on Brandy Island. Or there had been. Something had happened. The brandy was no good or the distillery was inefficient or Mr Vaughan lost interest . . . But the name had stuck. The buildings were still there, though the machinery lay silent, and the rail tracks still ran to the river's edge, but the crossing had been dismantled and any crates of ghostly brandy that came rattling along the rails now would end up at the bottom of the river . . .

What to do? He had thought he might stand on the bank and holler, but now he was here he realized the futility of such a thing. Then – fancy that! – he noticed a small rowing boat moored at the river's edge – a little one such as a woman might row, left there by chance at just the moment he needed it. He congratulated himself on his luck – the gods were on his side tonight.

He lowered himself into the boat, and though it rocked alarmingly beneath him, he was too drunk to panic and too much a child of the river to topple in. He settled himself and old habit rowed for him, till he felt the nudge of the island's bank. It was not the landing place, but no matter. Out he clambered, getting wet up to his knees. He climbed up the slope and made his way. The distillery loomed three storeys high in the centre of the island. To the east, the vitriol works. Behind that, the store house. He was as quiet as he could be, but not quiet enough – when his boot tangled with something and he stumbled, a hand came from nowhere and tightened on the back of his neck, keeping him down. A thumb and four fingers pressed painfully into the tendons.

'It's me,' he gasped, winded. 'It's only me!'

The fingers loosened. Not a word was uttered, but he followed the man by sound until they came to the store house.

It was a windowless space, and the air was densely fragrant. Yeast and fruit and heady sweetness with a bitter edge, so thick you could hardly inhale it but almost needed to swallow to get it down. The brazier illuminated bottles, copper vessels and barrels, all haphazardly put together. It was nothing like the modern, industrial-scale equipment that had once existed in the factory, though it had been fabricated from pieces stolen from there and with the same aim in mind: the production of liquor.

The man did not so much as glance at his visitor, but settled himself on a stool, where his slim, slight frame was darkly silhouetted against the orange light from the brazier. Without turning, he concentrated on relighting his pipe beneath the low brim of his hat. When it was done, he sucked on it. Only when he had exhaled and added a note of cheap tobacco to the odour did he speak.

'Who saw you come?'

'Nobody.'

Silence.

'No one's about. Too cold,' the tramp insisted.

The man nodded. 'Tell.'

'A girl,' the tramp told him. 'At the Swan at Radcot.'

'What about her?'

'Someone have pulled her out the river tonight. Dead, they say.'

There was a pause.

'What of it?'

'She is alive.'

At this the man's face turned, but was no more visible than before. 'Alive? Or dead? She must be one or the other.'

'She was dead. Now she is alive.'

There was a slow shaking of the head and the man spoke flatly. 'You have been dreaming. That or you've drunk one too many.'

'It is what they are saying. I only came to tell you what they are saying. Dead they took her from the river and now she lives again. At the Swan.'

The man stared back into the brazier. The messenger waited to see if there was any further response, but after a minute saw there would be none.

'A little gesture . . . For the trouble I've took. It's a cold night.'

The man grunted. He rose, casting a dark and flickering shadow on to the wall, and reached into the darkness. From it his hand extracted a small, corked bottle. He passed it to the tramp, who pocketed it, touched the brim of his hat and retreated.

Back at the Swan, the cat was asleep, curled against the chimney breast that still exhaled a gentle warmth. Its eyelids flickered with the images of cat dreams that would be even more perplexing to us than the stories our human brains concoct nocturnally. Its ear twitched and the dream faded instantly. A sound – almost nothing, the sound of grass crushed underfoot – and the cat was already on all fours. It crossed the room swiftly and silently and sprang to the window ledge. Feline vision pierced the night with ease.

Appearing by stealth from the back of the inn, a slight figure in an overlong coat, hat pulled down low, slipped along the wall, passing the window, and stopped at the door. There was a gentle rattle as he surreptitiously tested the handle. The latch was secured. Other places might be unlocked, but an inn, with its many barrels of temptation, must be locked at night. Now the man returned to the window. Unaware he was being watched, his fingers worked their way by feel around the window frame. Thwarted. Margot was no fool. Hers was the kind of mind that remembered not only to lock the door at closing time, but also to renew the putty in the windows every summer, to maintain the paintwork so the frames could not rot, to replace broken panes. A puff of exasperation emerged from beneath the low brim of the hat. The man paused and a gleam of thought passed across his eyes. But not for long. It was too cold to hang about. He turned and strode smartly away. He knew exactly where to put his feet in the dark, avoided furrows, dodged boulders, found the bridge, crossed it, and on the other side diverged from the path into the trees.

Long after the intruder had disappeared from sight, the cat followed him by ear. The drag of twigs across the woollen grain of a coat, the contact of heels on stone-cold earth, the stir of woodland creatures disturbed . . . until, eventually, nothing.

The cat dropped to the floorboards and returned to the hearth, where it pressed itself against the warm stone again and went back to sleep.

So it was that after the impossible event, and the hour of the first puzzling and wondering, came the various departures from the Swan and the first of the tellings. But finally, while the night was still dark, everybody at last was in bed and the story settled like sediment in the minds of them all, witnesses, tellers, listeners. The only sleepless one was the child herself, who, at the heart of the tale, breathed the seconds lightly in and lightly out, as she gazed into the darkness and listened to the sound of the river as it rushed by.

Tributaries

A RIVER ON a map is a simple thing. Our river starts at Trewsbury Mead, and follows a course of some two hundred and thirty-six miles to reach the sea at Shoeburyness. But anyone who takes the trouble to follow its route, whether by boat or on foot, cannot help being aware that, furlong by furlong, singleness of direction is not its most obvious feature. En route the river does not seem particularly intent on reaching its destination. Instead it winds its way in time-wasting loops and diversions. Its changes of direction are frequently teasing: on its journey it heads at different times north, south and west, as though it has forgotten its easterly destination – or put it aside for the while. At Ashton Keynes it splits into so many rivulets that every house in the village must have a bridge to its own front door; later, around Oxford, it takes a great unhurried detour around the city. It has other capricious tricks up its sleeve: in places it slows to drift lazily in wide pools before recovering its urgency and speeding on again. At Buscot it splits into twin streams to maroon a lengthy piece of territory, then regathers its water into a single channel.

If this is hard to understand from a map, the rest is harder. For one thing, the river that flows ever onwards is also seeping sideways, irrigating the fields and land to one side and the other. It finds its way into wells and is drawn up to launder petticoats and be boiled for tea. It is absorbed into root membranes, travels up cell by cell to the surface, is held in the leaves of watercress that find themselves in the soup bowls and on the cheeseboards of the county's diners. From teapot or soup dish, it passes into mouths, irrigates complex internal biological networks that are worlds in themselves, before returning eventually to the earth, via a chamber pot. Elsewhere the river water clings to the leaves of the willows that droop to touch its surface, and then when the sun comes up a droplet appears to vanish into the air, where it travels invisibly and might join a cloud, a vast floating lake, until it falls again as rain. This is the unmappable journey of the Thames.

And there is more. What we see on a map is only the half of it. A river no more begins at its source than a story begins with the first page. Take Trewsbury Mead, for instance. That photograph, do you remember? The one they were so quick to dismiss, because it wasn't picturesque? An ordinary ash in an ordinary field, they said, and so it appears, but look more closely. See this indentation in the ground, at the foot of the tree? See how it is the beginning of a furrow, shallow, narrow and unremarkable, that runs away from the tree and out of the picture altogether? See here, in the dip, where something catches the light and shows as a few ragged patches of silver in the grey shades of muddy soil? Those bright marks are water, seeing sunlight for the first time in what might be a very long time. It comes from underground, where in all the spaces beneath our feet, in the fractures and voids in the rock, in caverns and fissures and channels, there are waterways as numerous, as meandering, as circuitous as anything above ground. The beginning of the Thames is not the beginning – or rather it is only to us that it seems like a beginning.

In fact, Trewsbury Mead might not be the beginning in any case. There are those who say it's the wrong place. The not-even-the-beginning is not here but elsewhere, at a place called Seven Springs, which is the source of the Churn, a river that joins the Thames at Cricklade. And who is to say? The Thames that goes north, south, east and west to finally go east, that seeps to one side and the other as it moves forwards, that goes slow as it goes fast, that evaporates into the sky whilst meandering to the sea, is more about motion than about beginnings. If it has a beginning, it is located in a dark, inaccessible place. Better study where it goes than where it comes from.

Ah, tributaries! That's what I was meaning to come to. The Churn, the Key, the Ray, the Coln, the Leach and the Cole: in the upper reaches of the Thames, these are the streams and rivulets that come from elsewhere to add their own volume and momentum. And tributaries are about to join this story. We might, in this quiet hour before dawn, leave this river and this long night and trace the tributaries back, to see not their beginnings – mysterious, unknowable things – but, more simply, what they were doing yesterday.

What Do You Make of It?

THE DAY BEFORE the coming of the child, at half past three in the afternoon, at a farmhouse in Kelmscott, a woman stepped out of the kitchen door and in some haste crossed the yard to the barn. Her fair curls were tucked neatly into her bonnet, and her blue dress was simple, as befits a busy farmer's wife, but she endowed it with a prettiness that suggested she was still young at heart. She had a swaying gait; with every second step she stooped to the left, with every step in between she rose again. It did not slow her. Nor was she hindered by the patch that covered her right eye. It was made of the same blue fabric as her dress and a white ribbon held it in place.

She came to the barn. It smelt of blood and iron. Inside was a man who stood with his back to her. He was powerfully made, unusually tall, with a broad back and wiry black hair. As she put her hand on the door frame, he tossed a crimson-stained cloth to the ground and reached for his whetstone. She heard a ringing rise in the air as he started to sharpen the blade. Beyond him lay a row of corpses, neatly arranged snout to tail; the blood ran from them and found the shallows in the ground.

'Dearest . . .'

He turned. The darkness of his face was not the hale brown achieved by a lifetime's work out of doors under an English sun, but the kind that originated in another continent altogether. His nose was broad and his lips thick. At the sight of his wife, his brown eyes lit up and he smiled.

'Watch your hem, Bess.' A rivulet of blood was trickling towards her. 'You're in your good shoes too. I'm nearly done here, I'll be indoors in a little while.'

Then he saw the look on her face and the duet of knife and stone came to an end.

'What is it?'

For all the differences between the two faces, a single emotion animated their expressions.

'One of the children?' he asked.

She nodded. 'Robin.'

The first-born. His face fell. 'What is it this time?'

'This letter . . .'

His gaze fell to her hand. She held not a folded piece of paper, but a pile of ripped pieces.

'Susie found it. Robin brought her a jacket to mend last time he came to visit. You know how dainty she is with her needle, though she is only twelve. A very fine jacket too, I dread to think what it cost. There was a great gash in the sleeve, she says, though you wouldn't know it now. She had to unstitch the pocket seam to get some thread the right colour, and while she was about it, she found this letter, torn to pieces. I came across her in the drawing room puzzling it out like some kind of a game.'

'Show me,' he suggested, and he took a handful of her skirt to keep it out of the blood as they stepped towards the ledge that ran along one inner wall. She laid out the fragments.

'*rent*,' she read aloud, lightly touching one of the pieces. Her hand was a working one, she wore no rings except her wedding band and her nails were short and neat.

'*Love*,' he read; he did not touch the paper he read from, for there was blood under his nails and on his fingers.

'*at an end* . . . What is at an end, do you suppose, Robert?'

'I don't know . . . How did it come to be torn into pieces like this?'

'Did he tear it up? Is it a letter he received and didn't like?'

'Try putting that piece with this,' he suggested. But no, the two did not fit together. 'It is a woman's hand.'

'A good hand too. My letters are not so well formed as these.'

'You do well enough, my dear.'

'But look how straight she writes. Not a single blot. It is nearly as good a hand as yours, with all your years of schooling. What do you make of it, Robert?'

He peered silently for a while. 'There is no point trying to reconstitute the whole. What we have is only a fraction. Let's try something else . . .'

They moved the pieces round, her deft hand operating according to his instruction, and arrived at an organization of the fragments into three sections. The first was of pieces too small to be meaningful: halves of words, '*the*'s and '*of*'s and bits of margin. They put them aside.

The second set contained phrases which they read now aloud.

'*Love*'

'*entirely without*'

'*child will soon entirely*'

'*help from no quarter but you*'

'*rent*'

'*wait no longer*'

'*father of my*'

'*at an end*'

The final group was a set of fragments all containing the same word:

'*Alice*'

'*Alice*'

'*Alice*'

Robert Armstrong turned to his wife and she turned her face to him. Her blue gaze fretted anxiously and his own was grave.

'Tell me, my love,' he said, 'what do you make of it?'

'It is this *Alice*. I thought at first it was her name, the letter-writer. But a person writing a letter does not say their name so many times. They say, *I*. This Alice is someone else.'

'Yes.'

'*Child*,' she repeated wonderingly. '*Father* . . .'

'Yes.'

'I can't make it out . . . Does Robin have a child, Robert? Do we have a grandchild? Why has he not told us? Who is this woman?

What trouble is it that has made her write a letter like this? And for the letter to be torn like this. I fear . . .'

'Do not fear, Bess. What good can fear do? Suppose there is a child? Suppose there is a woman? There are worse mistakes a young man can make than falling in love, and if a child has come from it, we will be the first to welcome it. Our hearts are strong enough, aren't they?'

'But why is the letter half destroyed?'

'Supposing there is some trouble . . . There are few things that cannot be put right by love and there is no shortage of that here. Where love fails, money will usually do the trick.'

He looked steadily into her left eye. It was a good blue eye, and he waited until he saw the worry ebb from it and confidence return.

'You are right. What shall we do, then? Will you talk to him?'

'No. Not yet, anyhow.' He turned back to the pieces of paper. From the group of unreadable fragments he pointed at one. 'What do you make of this?'

She shook her head. A rip had gone horizontally right through the middle of the word, slicing top from bottom.

'I think this says, *Bampton*.'

'Bampton? Why, that's only four miles away!'

Armstrong consulted his watch. 'It's too late to go now. There is cleaning-up to do and these carcasses to be dealt with. If I don't press on it will be too dark to see what I'm doing by the time I feed the pigs. I shall get up early, and go to Bampton first thing.'

'All right, Robert.'

She turned to go.

'Watch your hem!'

In the house, Bess Armstrong went to her bureau. The key turned in the lock only awkwardly. It had been so ever since it was mended. She remembered a day when Robin was eight. She'd come home and found the bureau forced open. Papers were everywhere, money and documents missing, and Robin had taken her by the hand to say, 'I disturbed the thief, a rough-looking fellow, and look, Mother, here is the open window where I saw him make his escape.' Her husband had immediately gone out looking for the man, but she had not followed him. Instead she had put her hands to her eye patch, and slid it round so that it covered her good eye and revealed the one that looked sideways and Saw things an ordinary eye didn't. She took her son by the shoulders, and trained her Seeing eye on him. When Armstrong had come home, having found no trace of the rough-looking thief, she said, 'No, I don't suppose you did, for there was no such man. The thief was Robin.'

'No!' Armstrong protested.

'It was Robin. He was too pleased with the story he told. It was Robin.'

'I don't believe it.'

They had not been able to reach an agreement, and it was one of the things that had been buried under the weight of the days since. But every time she turned the key of the lock, she remembered.

She folded a piece of paper into the shape of an envelope. She slid all the unreadable bits of the letter into it, then gathered the set of phrases and put them in too. With the final three pieces of paper between her fingers, she hesitated, uncertain, reluctant to let them go. At last she dropped them into the envelope, with a murmur for each one, like a spell:

'Alice'

'Alice'

'Alice'

She pulled open the bureau drawer, but before she could put the pleat of paper away, an instinct halted her. Not the letter. Not the old story of the bureau and the forced lock. Something else. The sensation of a current rippling transparently through the air.

She tried to catch the tail end of the feeling and name it. Almost too late, yet she did catch it, fleetingly, for she heard the words her tongue pronounced in the empty room:

'Something is going to happen.'

Outside, Robert Armstrong finished sharpening his knife. He called his second and third sons, and together they hoisted the carcasses on to hooks to bleed them over the gulleys. They rinsed their hands in a pail of rainwater and emptied the water over the floor to wash the worst of the blood away from the slaughter area. When he had set the boys to mopping, he went out to feed the pigs. They usually worked together, but on days when he had something on his mind he preferred to feed the pigs alone.

Effortlessly, Armstrong heaved sacks and spilt the grain into the troughs. He scratched one sow behind her ear, rubbed another on her flank, according to their individual liking. Pigs are remarkable creatures and, though most men are too blind to see it, have intelligence that shows in their eyes. Armstrong was persuaded that every pig had its own character, its own talents, and when he selected a female piglet for breeding he looked not only for physical qualities but for intelligence, foresight, good sense: the qualities that make a good mother. He was in the habit of talking to his pigs as he fed them and today, as usual, he had something to say to each and every one. 'What have you got to be so grumpy about, Dora?' and 'Feeling your age, are you, Poll?' His gilts, the breeding sows, all had names. The pigs he was growing for the table he did not name, but called them all Piglet. When he chose a new gilt, it was his practice to give her a name starting with the same letter of the alphabet as her mother; it made it easy to trace the breeding line.

He came to Martha in the last sty. She was in pig, would deliver in four days' time. He filled her trough with grain and her sink with water. She lifted herself from her straw bed and waddled heavily towards the trough at the gate, where she did not immediately eat or drink, but rested her chin on the horizontal bar of the fence and scratched. Armstrong rubbed the top of her head between the ears and she snorted contentedly.

'*Alice*,' he said thoughtfully. The letter had not left his mind the entire time. 'What do you make of it, Martha?'

The sow looked at him with eyes full of thought.

'I don't know what to think, myself,' he admitted. 'A first grandchild – is that it? And Robin . . . What is going on with Robin?' He sighed heavily.

Martha pondered his boots in the mud for a moment, and when she gazed back up at him it was with a rather pointed look.

He nodded. 'Quite right. Maud would know. But Maud's not here, is she?'

Martha's mother, Maud, had been the best sow he had ever known. She had produced numerous litters of many piglets, never lost one by accident or neglect, but more than that, she had listened to him as no other sow had ever listened. Patient and gentle, she had let him speak his mind; when he shared his joys about the children her eyes lit up with pleasure, and when he told her of his worries – Robin, it was nearly always Robin – her eyes were full of wisdom and sympathy, and he never came away without feeling somehow better about things. Her quiet and kindly listening had made it possible to speak his thoughts aloud, and sometimes it was only when he spoke his thoughts that he knew he had them. It was surprising how a man's mind might remain half in shadow until the right confidante appeared, and Maud had been that confidante. Without her, he might never have known certain things about himself, about his son. On this spot, some years ago, he had shared the disagreement between himself and his wife about Robin and the theft from the bureau. As he retold the sorry tale to Maud, he saw it anew and noticed what he had registered but not paid attention to at the time. *I saw a man*, Robin had said. *I saw his boot disappearing out of the window.* It was instinctive in Armstrong to see the best in people, and his faith in the boy was spontaneous. But then, prompted by Maud's quizzical gaze, he'd remembered the watchful wait that followed the boy's story, known then in his heart what it meant: that Robin was watching to see whether he'd got away with it. It hurt Armstrong to accept it, but on this occasion Bess was right.

When they had married, Robin was already on the way, put into her womb by another man. Robert had chosen to put this fact aside. This was not difficult, for he loved the boy with all his heart. He had determined to build a family with Bess, not fragmented and splintered, but whole and entire, and he would permit no member of it to be left on the outside. There was love enough for all. Love would hold them together. But when he realized the thief who had left the bureau splintered and its contents ransacked was his own Robin, he wept. Maud had eyed him quizzically. What now? And he had found the answer. Loving the boy even more would put things right. From that day on he had defended Robin even more vigorously than before.

Maud had looked at him again. *Oh, really?* she'd seemed to say.

The thought of Maud brought tears suddenly to his eyes. One of them fell on to Martha's thick neck, clung momentarily to the ginger hair that sprouted from it, then rolled into the mud.

Armstrong brought his cuff to his face and wiped the wetness away. 'This is foolishness,' he chided himself.

Martha looked steadily at him from between her ginger lashes.

'But you miss her too, don't you?'

He thought he saw a mistiness in her eye.

'How long is it, now?' He totted up the months in his head. 'Two years and three months. A long time. Who took her, eh? You were there, Martha. Why didn't you squeal when they came and stole your mother?'

Martha gave him a long and intent look. He studied her expression, tried to decipher it, and for once failed.

He was giving Martha a final scratch when she lifted her chin from the fence and turned in the direction of the river.

'What is it?'

He looked that way himself. There was nothing to see, and he had heard nothing either. Still, there must be something . . . He and the pig exchanged a look. He had never seen that look in her eyes before, yet he had only to compare it with his own sensations to know what it meant.

'I think you're right, Martha. Something is going to happen.'

Mrs Vaughan and the River Goblins

A PEARL OF water formed in the corner of an eye. The eye belonged to a young woman who was lying in the bottom of a boat. The bead of liquid rested in the place where the pink inner of the eyelid swells into the dainty complication of a tear duct. It shivered with the rocking motion of the boat but, supported by the lashes that sprouted beneath and above it, did not break or fall.

'Mrs Vaughan?'

The young woman had rowed across the river, then drawn the blades in and allowed the little boat to drift into the reed bed which now held it. By the time the words from the bank reached her, the thick white river mist had rinsed the urgency out of them. The words drifted into her ear, washed out and waterlogged, and sounded scarcely louder than the thoughts in her own head.

Mrs Vaughan . . . that's me, Helena thought. It sounded like the name of another person altogether. She could imagine a Mrs Vaughan and it would be nothing like herself. Someone old. About thirty, probably, with a face like the portraits that hung in the hallway of her husband's house. It was odd to think that only a few years ago she had been Helena Greville. It seemed a lot longer. When she thought about that girl now, it was as if she were thinking about someone she used to know, and know quite well, but would never see again. Helena Greville was gone for good.

'It's too cold to be out, Mrs Vaughan.'

Cold, yes. Helena Vaughan counted the coldnesses. There was the cold of being coatless, hatless, gloveless. The cold of the air that dampened her dress to her skin and raised goosebumps on her chest and arms and legs. There was the cold of the air as it entered her, stinging her nostrils and making her lungs quiver. After all those came the coldness of the river. It was the slowest, taking its time to reach her through the thick planks of the boat, but when it did it burnt the points of her shoulder blades, the back of her skull, her ribcage, the base of her spine, all the places where her body lay hard against the curve of the wood. The river came nudging at the boat, draining her of warmth with its lulling, rocking motion. She closed her eyes.

'Are you there? Oh, answer me, for heaven's sake!'

Answer . . . The word dredged up a memory from a few years ago. Aunt Eliza had talked about an answer. 'Think before you answer,' she had said, 'because opportunities like this don't come every day.'

Aunt Eliza was the little sister of Helena's father. Widowed in her forties and childless, she had come to live with her brother and the child of his late marriage, to disrupt and upset them, as Helena saw it. Helena's mother had died when the child was an infant, and it was Eliza's view that her niece needed a maternal figure to take her in hand. Eliza's brother was an eccentric who had neglected to instil proper discipline and the girl was barely educated. Eliza had tried, but she had failed to have much influence. Helena had complained in the early days to her father about Aunt Eliza, and he had told her with a wink, 'She has nowhere else to go, Pirate. Just nod and say yes to whatever she says, and afterwards do just as you like. That's what I always do.' The strategy had worked. Father and daughter had continued to live together in great friendship, and neither one permitted Eliza to interfere with their days on the river and in the boatyard.

In the garden, between exhortations to slow down, Aunt Eliza had told Helena a great many things she already knew perfectly well, since they were about herself. She reminded Helena (as though she might have forgotten) that she was motherless. She alluded to her father's great age and poor health. While Helena half listened, she had drawn Aunt Eliza in a certain direction and, absorbed in what she was saying, Aunt Eliza had allowed herself to be led. They came to the river and walked along the bank. Helena breathed in the thrill of the cold, bright air, watched the ducks bobbing in the lively water. Her shoulders twitched at the thought of oars. In her stomach she felt the anticipation of that first pull out into the water, that meeting of the boat with the current . . . 'Upstream or down?' her father always said. 'If it's not the one it has to be the other – and it'll be an adventure either way!'

Aunt Eliza was reminding Helena of the state of her father's finances, which were even more precarious than his health, and then – Helena's thoughts had been drifting with the river, she might have missed something – Eliza was talking about a Mr Vaughan, his kindness and decency, and the fact that his business was thriving. 'Though if you do not wish it, your father instructs me to tell you that you have only to say so and the whole thing will be put aside and not a word more said about it,' Aunt Eliza concluded. This was initially mystifying to Helena, and then suddenly perfectly clear.

'Which one is this Mr Vaughan?' she wanted to know.

Aunt Eliza was nonplussed. 'You have met him several times . . . Why don't you pay more attention?' But to Helena, her father's friends and associates were versions of the same figure: male, old, dull. None of them were remotely as interesting as her father, and she was surprised he spent any time with them at all.

'Is Mr Vaughan with Father now?'

She darted off, ignoring Aunt Eliza's protests and running back towards the house. In the garden, she took a leap over the ferns and sidled up to the study window. By clambering on to the plinth of a large urn and clinging to the window ledge, she could just see into the room, where her father was smoking in the company of another gentleman.

Mr Vaughan was not one of the red-nosed or grizzled ones. She recognized him now as the smiling younger man with whom her father sat up late, over a cigar and a drink. When she went to bed, she could hear them laughing together. She was glad her father had somebody to cheer him up in the evenings. Mr Vaughan had brown hair, brown eyes and a brown beard. Beyond that, the one thing that set him apart was his voice. Most of the time he spoke just like any other Englishman, but once in a while something slipped out of his mouth that had an unfamiliar ring to it. She had been interested in listening out for these odd sounds and had asked him about it.

'I grew up in New Zealand,' he had told her. 'My family has mines there.'

She considered the ordinary man through the window and felt no strong objection to him.

Helena edged her heels from the urn's plinth and hung, swaying pleasantly from the window ledge, enjoying the stretch in her arms and shoulders. When she heard Aunt Eliza approach she let herself drop.

'I'll have to leave home, I suppose, if I marry Mr Vaughan?'

'You will be leaving home anyway, one day soon. Your father has been *so unwell*. Your future is *uncertain*. Naturally he is anxious to see you *settled* in life. If you were to marry Mr Vaughan, you would go to live with him at Buscot Lodge, whereas if you don't—'

'Buscot Lodge?' Helena came to a halt. She knew Buscot Lodge – a large house on a thrilling reach of the river. It had a long, broad stretch where the water was smooth and even, and a place where the river divided to flow around an island, and just before that, a spot where the water seemed to forget it was a river at all and idled, just like a little lake. There was a millwheel and St John's Bridge and a boathouse . . . She had once rowed up close to the boathouse and, standing precariously in her one-man boat, peered in. There was plenty of room in it.

'Would I be allowed to take my boat?'

'Helena, this is a serious business. Marriage has nothing to do with boats and the river. It is a binding contract, both in law and in the eyes of God—'

But Helena was off, running at full tilt over the lawn to the door of the house.

When Helena burst into the study, her father's eyes lit up at the sight of her. 'What do you think of this daft notion, eh? If it's a load of nonsense to you, just say the word. On the other hand, a load of nonsense can be just the thing if the fancy takes you . . . Upstream or down, Pirate? What do you say?'

Mr Vaughan had risen from his chair.

'Can I bring my boat?' she asked him. 'Can I go on the river every day?'

Mr Vaughan, bemused, did not answer immediately.

'That boat is at the end of its days,' her father said.

'It's not very bad,' she argued.

'Holes in it last time I looked.'

She shrugged. 'I bail.'

'Like a sieve. Surprised you get so far in it.'

'When it gets too low in the water, I come back to the bank and upturn it and then set out again,' she conceded.

They discussed the boat like two immortals for whom drowning was impossible.

Mr Vaughan turned from father to daughter during this exchange. He began to perceive the importance of boats in the matter at hand.

'I could get it mended for you,' he suggested. 'Or get you a new one, if you like.'

She thought. She nodded. 'All right.'

Aunt Eliza, who had come late to the discussion, glanced sharply at Helena. Something appeared to be concluded, but what? Mr Vaughan took pity and enlightened her.

'Miss Greville has agreed to allow me to buy her a new boat. With that business out of the way, we can now negotiate the lesser matters. Miss Greville, will you do me the honour of becoming my wife?'

Adventure either way . . .

'It's a deal.' She nodded firmly.

Aunt Eliza felt that this was all falling far short of what a marriage proposal and acceptance ought to be, and opened her mouth to address Helena, but Helena got in first.

'I know. *Marriage is an important contract in the eyes of God and of the law*,' she parroted. She had seen people conclude important contracts before. Knowing how it was done, she held out her hand for Mr Vaughan to shake.

Mr Vaughan took her hand, turned it, and bowed to plant a kiss upon it. Suddenly it was Helena's turn to be nonplussed.

Helena's fiancé was as good as his word. A new boat was ordered and the old one mended 'for the time being'. Before long she had two boats, a boathouse to put them in, a stretch of river to call her own – and a new name. A little later, her father died. Aunt Eliza went to live with her younger brother in Wallingford. And then a lot of other things happened and Helena Greville was swept clean away on the current and even Mrs Vaughan forgot about her.

Lately it was the old boat – Helena Greville's – that she chose to take out. She did not go far. Upstream or down? No. She was not in search of adventure. She merely rowed to the far side and let the boat drift into the reeds.

'Oh, this mist! Whatever will Mr Vaughan say?' came the watery voice again.

Helena opened her eyes. The air was so full of water it was opaque and she looked at it through the liquid that pooled in the corner of her own eye. She could see nothing of the world – no sky, no trees; even the reeds that surrounded the boat were invisible. She rocked and bobbed with the river, inhaled wetness with the air, watched the mist that moved sluggishly like the current of a semi-stagnant sidestream, like the rivers she knew in her dreams. The whole world was drowned, leaving only her cold self and Helena Greville's boat – and the river that shifted and pressed beneath her like a thing alive.

She blinked. The tear grew swollen, pooled and flattened, but held to itself in its invisible skin.

What a fearless girl Helena Greville had been. A pirate, her father had called her, and pirate she was. Aunt Eliza had despaired at her.

'There is another side to the river,' Eliza used to tell her. 'Once upon a time there was a naughty little girl who played too close to the bank. One day, while she wasn't looking, a goblin rose out of the water. He grasped the little girl by the hair and took her back, kicking and splashing, to his own goblin realm under the river. And if you don't believe me . . .' Had she believed her? It was hard to know, now. 'If you don't believe me, you have only to listen. Go on, listen now. Do you hear the water splashing?'

Helena had nodded. This was all wonderful to know. Goblins living under the river in their own goblin world. How marvellous!

'Listen to the sounds between the splashes. Do you hear? There are bubbles, very, very small ones that rise to the surface and pop. Those are the bubbles that carry messages from all the lost children. If your ears are sharp enough you will hear the cries of that little girl and all the other homesick children who are weeping for their mothers and fathers.'

She had listened. Had she heard? She couldn't remember now. But if the goblins had taken her away down into the water, her father would simply have come and got her back. It was so obvious that Helena Greville felt rather scornful of her aunt for not realizing it herself.

For years and years Helena Greville had forgotten the story about the goblins and their world on the other, deathly side of the river. But now Helena Vaughan remembered it. She came out in her old boat to remember it every day. The sound of the water was a semi-regular, uninsistent lapping, as the river licked and sucked at the boat. She listened to the sound and she listened to the spaces between the sound. It was not difficult to hear the lost children. She could hear them with perfect clarity.

'Mrs Vaughan! You'll catch your death! Do come in, Mrs Vaughan!'

The river lapped and the boat rose and fell, and a far-off little voice called without cease for its parents from the depths of the goblin world.

'It's all right!' she whispered, white-lipped. She tensed her cold muscles, readied her trembling limbs to rise. 'Mummy's coming!'

She leant out of the boat and, as the vessel tilted, the teardrop spilt from her eye and dropped into the greater wetness of the river. Before she could shift her weight sufficiently to follow it, something righted the boat and she felt herself fall back into it. When she looked up, an indistinct grey figure was bending over the bow of her boat, gripping the cleat. The shadow in the mist then straightened and she saw it elongate like a man standing in a punt. It raised an arm in a motion that resembled the dropping of a pole to find the riverbed, and she then felt a powerful dragging sensation. The speed of progress through the water seemed oddly disconnected from the shadow's ease of movement. The river loosened its grip and she was towed back towards the bank with a rapidity that surprised her.

A final propulsion brought the grey shape of the jetty into sight.

Mrs Clare the housekeeper was waiting and the gardener was by her side. He reached for the rope and secured the boat. Helena rose and, with Mrs Clare's hand to steady her, climbed out.

'You are frozen to the bone! Whatever possessed you, dear?'

Helena turned back towards the water. 'He's gone . . .'

'Who's gone?'

'The ferryman . . . He towed me back.'

Mrs Clare looked into Helena's dazed face in perplexity.

'Did you see anybody?' she asked the gardener in an undertone.

He shook his head. 'Unless – do you suppose it were Quietly?'

Mrs Clare frowned and shook her head at him. 'Don't go putting fancies in her head. As if things weren't bad enough already.'

Helena gave a sudden, violent shiver. Mrs Clare shrugged off her coat and wrapped it around her mistress's shoulders. 'You worry us all half to death,' she scolded. 'Come on in.'

Mrs Clare took one arm firmly, and the gardener took the other, and they made their way without stopping through the garden and back to the house.

On the threshold of the house, Helena halted confusedly and looked back over her shoulder to the garden and the river beyond. It was that time of the afternoon when the light drains rapidly from the sky and the mist was darkening.

'What is it?' she murmured, half to herself.

'What's what? Did you hear something?'

Mrs Vaughan shook her head. 'I didn't hear it. No.'

'What, then?'

Helena put her head on one side and a new focus came into her eyes as if she were extending the range of her perceptions. The housekeeper sought it too, and the gardener also cocked his head and wondered. The feeling – expectation, or something rather like it – came upon all three of them and they spoke in unison: 'Something is going to happen.'

A Well-Practised Tale

IT WAS HERE. Mr Vaughan came to a hesitant halt in the street of Oxford townhouses. He looked left and right, but the curtains in the windows of the respectable-looking houses were too thick to tell whether anybody was standing looking out. Still, wearing his hat and with the light wateriness of the air, nobody would recognize him. In any case, it wasn't as if he were going to go in. He fidgeted for a moment with the handle of his case, to give himself a plausible reason to have stopped, and looked from under his brim at Number 17.

The house shared the trim, correct air of its neighbours. That was the first surprise. He had thought there would be something to set it apart. Every house in the street was a little different from its neighbours, of course, for the builder had taken the trouble to make it so. The one he had stopped in front of had a particularly attractive light set over the front door. But that wasn't the kind of difference he meant. He had expected a gaudy colour to the front door, perhaps, or something faintly theatrical in the drape of the curtains. But there was nothing of the kind. *They are not fools, these people,* he thought. *Of course they will want to make it look respectable.*

The fellow who had mentioned the place to Vaughan was a mere acquaintance and it was something he himself had heard from a friend of a friend. From what Vaughan could remember of the third-hand tale, some man's wife had been so distraught following the death of her mother that she became a shadow of her former self, barely sleeping, unable to eat, deaf to the loving voices of her husband and children. Doctors were powerless to arrest her decline and at last, dubious yet having exhausted all other possibilities, her husband took her to see a Mrs Constantine. After a couple of meetings with this mysterious person, the wife in question had been restored to health and returned to her domestic and marital responsibilities with all her old vigour. The story as Vaughan had heard it was at so many removes it probably bore only the most tangential relation to the truth. It sounded like a lot of mumbo-jumbo to Vaughan, and he had no belief in psychics, but – so he remembered the acquaintance telling him – whatever it was this Mrs Constantine did, it worked, 'whether you believed in it or not'.

The house was impeccable in its correctness. The gate and the path and the door were neatness itself. There was no peeling paintwork, no tarnished doorknob, no dirty footprints on the step. Those who called here, he supposed, were to find nothing to encourage them in any reluctance, nothing to cause them to hesitate or draw back. All was spick and span, there was nowhere for doubt to take root. The place was neither too grand for the ordinary man, nor too humble for the wealthy. *Why, you have to admire them*, he concluded. *They have it all just so.*

He put his fingertips on the gate and leant to read the name on the brass plaque next to the door: *Professor Constantine.*

He couldn't help but smile. Fancy passing herself off as the wife of a university man!

Vaughan was about to lift his fingers from the gate, but hadn't quite done so – in fact, his intention to turn and depart was mysteriously slow to take effect – when the door to Number 17 opened. In the doorway there appeared a maid, carrying a basket. She was a neat, clean and ordinary maid, exactly the kind he would employ in his own house, and she spoke to him in a neat, clean and ordinary sort of voice.

'Good morning, Sir. Is it Mrs Constantine you are looking for?'

No, no, he said – except that the words failed to sound in his ears and he realized it was because they had not reached his lips. His efforts to explain away his appearance were confounded by his own hand that opened the latch on the gate, and his legs that stepped up the path to the front door. The maid put down her shopping basket and he watched himself hand her his case and his hat, which she placed on the hall table. He smelt beeswax, noticed the gleam of the staircase spindles, felt the warmth of the house envelope him – and all the while marvelled that he was not where he ought to be, striding away down the street, after a chance pause outside the gate to check the fastening of his case.

'Would you like to wait for Mrs Constantine in here, Sir?' the maid said, indicating a doorway. Through the doorway he saw a fire blazing, a tapestry cushion on a leather armchair, a Persian rug. He stepped into the room and was overwhelmed with the desire to stay. He sat at one end of the large sofa and felt the deep cushions mould themselves around him. The other end of the sofa was occupied by a large ginger cat that roused itself from sleep and began to purr. Mr Vaughan put out a hand to stroke it.

'Good afternoon.'

The voice was calm and musical. Decorous. He turned to see a woman in her middle years, with greying hair pulled back from a wide, even forehead. Her dress was dark blue, which made her grey eyes almost blue, and her collar was white and quite plain. Mr Vaughan was pierced by a sudden memory of his mother, which took him by surprise, for this woman was not at all like her. His mother, when she died, had been taller, slimmer, younger, of a darker complexion and never so plainly neat.

Mr Vaughan rose and began to make his apologies. 'You must think me an awful fool,' he began. 'Awfully embarrassing, and the worst of it is, I hardly know how to begin to explain it. I was outside, you see, and I had no intention of coming in – not today, at any rate, I have a train to catch . . . Well, what I'm not explaining very well is that I cannot abide a railway waiting room, and having some time to kill, it seemed I might as well just come and see where you were, for another time, that was my intention, except that your maid happened to open the door at that very moment and naturally she thought – I don't blame her in the least, bad timing, that's all, easy mistake to make . . .' On and on he went. He snatched at reasons, grasped for logic, and sentence by sentence it all evaded him; he felt that with every word he was talking himself further and further away from what he meant to say.

While he spoke, her grey eyes rested patiently on his face, and though she was not smiling, he felt gentle encouragement in the lines that surrounded her eyes so expressively. At last he ran out of words.

'I see,' she said, nodding. 'You didn't mean to disturb me today, you were just passing and wanted to check the address . . .'

'That's right!' Relieved to be so easily let off, he waited for her to initiate a farewell. Already he saw himself reclaiming his hat and case from the hall and taking his leave. He saw his feet on the chequered path to the house. He saw his hand reach for the latch on the painted gate. But then he saw the steadiness of the tranquil grey eyes.

'Yet after all that, here you are,' she said.

Here he was. Yes. He suddenly felt his hereness very acutely. In fact, the room seemed to pulse with it, and so did he.

'Why don't you sit down, Mr . . . ?'

'Vaughan,' he said, and her eyes did not give away whether or not they recognized the name, but only continued their easy watchfulness. He sat.

Mrs Constantine poured some clear liquid from an etched decanter into a glass and placed it by his side; then she too sat down, in an armchair placed at an angle to the sofa. She smiled expectantly.

'I need your help,' he admitted. 'It's my wife.'

Her face softened into sad sympathy. 'I am sorry. May I offer you my condolences?'

'No! I don't mean that!'

He sounded irritated. He *was* irritated.

'Forgive me, Mr Vaughan. But when a stranger appears at my door, it is usually because somebody has died.' Her expression did not change; it remained steady and was not unfriendly, in fact it was distinctly kind, but she waited with a firmness of purpose for him to come to the point.

He sighed. 'We have lost a child, you see.'

'Lost?'

'She was taken.'

'Forgive me, Mr Vaughan, but we use so many euphemisms in English when we speak of the dead. *Lost*, *taken* . . . These are words that have more than one meaning. I have already misunderstood you once, regarding your wife, and I should not like to do so again.'

Mr Vaughan swallowed and looked at his hand, which was resting on the arm of the green velvet sofa. He drew a nail along the fabric, raising a line in the pile. 'You will probably know the story. I expect you read the newspapers, and even if you don't, it was the talk of the county. Two years ago. At Buscot.'

Her eyes detached from him and looked into the middle distance while she consulted her memory. He ran a fingertip along the velvet, smoothing the pile flat again so that the line disappeared. He waited for her to acknowledge that she knew.

Her gaze returned to him. 'It would be better if you told me in your own words, I think.'

Vaughan's shoulders stiffened. 'I can tell you no more than is known.'

'Mmm.' The sound was neither here nor there. It did not agree with him exactly, but nor did it disagree with him. It indicated that it was still his turn.

Vaughan had expected that the story would not need retelling. After two years, he assumed that everybody knew. It was the kind of story that spread far abroad in a surprisingly short space of time. On numerous occasions he had walked into a room – a business meeting, an interview for a new groom, a social occasion with neighbouring farmers, or a grander event in Oxford or London – and seen in the glances from people he had never met that they not only knew him, but knew the story. He now expected it – though he had never grown used to it. 'Dreadful thing,' some stranger would mutter over a handshake, and he had learnt a way of acknowledging it that also indicated, 'Let no more be said about it.'

In the early days, he had had to give endless accounts of the events. The very first time, rousing the male servants, he had told them first in wild flurries of sound, fast and furious, as if the words themselves were on horseback, racing after the intruders and his missing daughter. He had told it to the neighbours who came to join the search in panting phrases, his chest contracting painfully. He told it over and over again, to every man, woman and child he met in the next hours, as he rode the country roads: 'My daughter has been taken! Have you seen strangers, anyone, making their way in haste, with a small girl of two?' The following day he told it to his banker when he went urgently to raise the ransom money, and again to the policeman who came out from Cricklade. This was where the order of events had been set down properly. They were still in the grip of things then, and this time Helena was doing the telling too. They had paced and sat down and then risen to pace again, talking one at a time or, often, at the same time, and sometimes they both lapsed into silence and stared at each other, lost for words. There was one moment that he made a particular effort to forget. Helena, describing the moment the discovery was made: 'I opened the door and went in, and she wasn't there. She wasn't there! She wasn't there!' Wonderingly, she repeated the words 'She wasn't there,' and as her head turned this way and that, her eyes sought the upper corners of the room as though their daughter might be concealed in the joint of the cornicing, or beyond it, perched in the angle of a roof joist, but the absence went on and on. It had seemed then that her daughter's absence had flooded Helena, flooded them both, and that with their words they were trying to bail themselves out. But the words were eggcups and what they were describing was an ocean of absence, too vast to be contained in such modest vessels. She bailed and she bailed, but no matter how often she repeated the effort, she could not get to the end of it. 'She wasn't there,' repeated endlessly in a voice he had not known a human being to be capable of, as she drowned in her loss, and he remained in a sort of paralysis, unable to do or say anything to save her. Thank God for the policeman. It had been he who threw her a line she could grab hold of, he who hauled her in with his next question.

'The bed had been slept in, though?'

The noise of his words reached her. Dazed, she seemed to come to herself, and nodded. In a voice that was her own again, though weak with exhaustion, she said, 'Ruby put her to bed. Our nursery maid.'

Then she had lapsed into silence and Vaughan had taken over the narrative.

'Slow down, Sir, if you don't mind,' the fellow had said, as he bent over his notebook, pencil in hand, copying it all down like a zealous schoolboy. 'Start that bit again, would you?' Every so often he stopped them, read back what he had down, and they corrected him, remembered details they had left out, discovered discrepancies in what they both knew, compared notes to get it right. Any detail might be the one to bring her back. Hours it had taken, to get down the events of a few minutes.

He had written to his father in New Zealand.

'No, don't,' Helena had protested. 'What's the point in upsetting him, when she'll be home tomorrow, or the day after?'

But he wrote the letter. He remembered the account they had given to the policeman and based his explanation on that. He wrote it out carefully. The letter contained all the facts of the disappearance. *Unknown villains came in the night*, the letter said. *They put up a ladder and entered the house by the nursery window; they left, taking the child with them.* New paragraph: *Though a ransom demand was received early the following morning and the ransom was paid, our daughter has not been returned to us. We are looking. Everyone is doing their utmost and we will not rest until she is found. The police are pursuing the river gypsies and will search their boats. I shall send further news as soon as there is some.*

There was none of the breathlessness. No painful gasps for breath. The horror of it was quite excised. At his desk, less than forty-eight hours after it had happened, he had made his account: the letters arranged themselves into words, regularly aligned, to make sentences and then paragraphs, in which the loss of his daughter was contained. In two informative pages it was done.

When Anthony Vaughan finished the letter, he read it through. Did it say everything that needed to be said? It said everything that could be said. When he was satisfied that it could say no more, he sealed it and rang for the maid, who took it for the post.

That brief and dry account, which he had reused countless times for the benefit of his business associates and other semi-strangers, was the one he brought out now. Though he had not used it for months, he found that he still had it word for word. It took less than a minute to lay the matter before the woman with the grey eyes.

He came to the end of the story and took a mouthful of water from the glass beside him. It had the unexpected and very refreshing taste of cucumber.

Mrs Constantine looked at him with her unwavering, kind look. Something seemed suddenly wrong to him. There was usually stunned shock, a clumsy attempt to console, to say the right thing, or else embarrassed silence that he filled with some remark to redirect the conversation. None of this happened.

'I see,' she said. And then – nodding, as if she really *did* see, but what was there to see? Nothing, surely – 'Yes. And what about your wife?'

'My wife?'

'When you first arrived you told me you had come to seek my help about your wife.'

'Ah. So I did.'

He felt that he needed to trace a long path back to arriving at the house, that first exchange of words with Mrs Constantine, though it could not have been much more than a quarter of an hour ago. He worked backwards through various obstacles of time and memory, rubbing his eyes, and found what it was he was here for.

'It's like this, you see. My wife is – quite naturally – inconsolable. Understandable in the circumstances. She thinks of nothing except our daughter's return. Her state of mind is lamentable. She will see no one. She permits no diversion from her distress. Her appetite is poor and in her sleep she is pursued by the most appalling nightmares, so she prefers to stay awake. Her behaviour has grown more and more strange, to the point where she is now a danger to herself. To give you just one example: she has taken to going out on the river in a rowing boat, quite alone and without any thought to her comfort and safety. She stays out for hours, in all weathers, in garments that offer her no protection. She cannot say why she does it, and it can do no good at all. It can only harm her. I have suggested taking her away, thinking that travel might restore her. I am even ready to sell up, lock, stock and barrel, and start again in some entirely new place, untainted by our sorrow.'

'And her response?'

'She says it is a very good idea and when our daughter comes home that is exactly what we will do. Do you see? If nothing changes, I foresee that she will only go from bad to worse. It is not grief that afflicts her, you must realize, but something far worse. I fear for her. I fear that with no change, her life will end in some awful accident or else in an asylum, and I would do anything – anything at all – to prevent that.'

The grey eyes remained upon him, and he was aware of all the observation going on behind the kindness. This time he made clear that he was not going to say any more and that it was her turn to speak (had he ever met a woman who said so little?), and she opened her mouth at last. 'That must be very lonely for you,' she said.

Anthony Vaughan could barely conceal his disappointment. 'That is beside the point. What I want you to do is to talk to her.'

'To what end?'

'Tell her that the child is dead. I believe it is what she needs.'

Mrs Constantine blinked twice. In another person this would be almost nothing, but in a woman of her unperturbability this counted as surprise.

'Let me explain.'

'I think you had better.'

'I want you to tell my wife that our daughter is dead. Tell her that the child is happy. Tell her she is with angels. Do messages, voices. Do the thing with the smoke and mirrors, if you are set up for it.' He glanced around the room again as he said this. It seemed unlikely that this decorous drawing room could double for service with the contraptions and curtains that he supposed were necessary for such performances, but perhaps it was another room she used for all that. 'Look, I'm not presuming to tell you your own business. You know what works. I can tell you things that will make Helena believe you. Things only she and I know. And then . . .'

'Then?'

'Then we can be sad and sorry and weep and say our prayers, and then—'

'And then, when your wife has mourned, she will find her way back to life – to you – again?'

'Exactly!' Anthony Vaughan was full of gratitude at having been so perfectly understood.

Mrs Constantine tipped her head very slightly to one side. She smiled at him. Kindly. With understanding. 'I'm afraid that won't be possible,' she said.

Anthony Vaughan started. 'Why ever not?'

She shook her head. 'For one thing, you have misunderstood – or been misled, perhaps, about what it is that happens here. It is an understandable mistake. Furthermore, what you suggest would do no good.'

'I will pay you the going rate. I will pay you double if you ask it.'

'It is not a question of money.'

'I don't understand! It is a simple enough transaction! Tell me how much you want and I will pay it!'

'I am profoundly sorry for your suffering, Mr Vaughan. To lose a child is one of the hardest burdens a human being can bear.' She frowned faintly. 'But what about you, Mr Vaughan? Do *you* believe your daughter to be dead?'

'She must be,' he said.

The grey eyes looked at him. He had the sudden impression that she could see right into his soul, that she could see aspects of his being that were in darkness even to him. He felt his heart start to beat uncomfortably.

'You didn't tell me her name.'

'Helena.'

'Not your wife's name. Your daughter's.'

Amelia. The name rose in him and he choked it down. There was a spasm in Vaughan's chest. He coughed, gasped, reached for the water again and drank half the glass of it. He took an experimental breath to see if his chest was free.

'Why?' he asked. 'Why won't you help me?'

'I would like to help you. You are in need of help. You cannot go on much longer like this. But what you have asked me today, besides being impossible, would do no good.'

He got to his feet, made an exasperated gesture with his arm. For a ridiculous moment he wondered whether he was about to raise his palms to his eyes and weep. He shook his head.

'I'll go, then.'

She rose too. 'If you ever wish to come back, please do. You will be welcome.'

'Why should I come back? You can do nothing for me. You have made that perfectly plain.'

'That's not quite what I said. Do refresh yourself, if you would like to. There is water and a clean towel on the side there.'

When she had gone, he splashed water on to his face, buried his face in the soft cotton towel, and felt marginally better for it. He took out his watch. There was a train on the half-hour and he had just time to be on it.

In the street, as he hurried, Anthony Vaughan chided himself for his foolishness. Suppose the woman had jumped at his idea? Suppose he had taken Helena there and word had got out? It might have done something for the wife of the man in the story, but Helena . . . Helena was not like other men's wives.

On the platform a number of other passengers were waiting for the train. He stood a little away from them. He did not like to be spotted. Small talk with people you were only distantly acquainted with was something he avoided whenever he could, and the curiosity of strangers, who sometimes knew his face when he did not know theirs, was even worse.

According to the station clock, the train would be approaching in a minute or two, and while he waited he congratulated himself on a narrow escape. What her game was in refusing his money he couldn't tell, but no doubt she'd intended to get a pound of flesh from him one way or another.

He was so absorbed in thoughts of his recent encounter that it took a little while for him to become aware of the sensation that tugged quietly at his mind. Then he did notice it but, still befuddled by the strangeness of the events at Number 17, it took a moment to separate this new feeling from the oddness of a little while ago. When he did, he recognized it: anticipation. He shook his head to dispel his weariness. It had been a long day. He was waiting for a train and the train was about to come. That was all.

The train arrived; he mounted, found an empty first-class carriage and sat by the window. The sense of anticipation that had begun on the platform was reluctant to fade. In fact, as the train left Oxford and he looked through the darkening mist towards the place where the river lay invisible in the gloom, the presentiment increased. The rhythm of the train on the tracks suggested words to his overtired brain and he heard them as clearly as if an unseen person had pronounced them: *Something is going to happen*.

Lily's Nightmare

ON THE OTHER side of the river from the Vaughans' grand house and half a mile downstream, there was a patch of land that was too wet even for watercress. Set back from the river, three oak trees grew there, and their roots drank thirstily from the wet soil, but any acorn that fell on the river side of its parent rotted before it could germinate. It was a godforsaken place, good only for drowning dogs, but the river must have been more biddable in the past because at one time somebody had built a cottage there, between the oaks and the water.

The little dwelling was a squat box of lichened stone containing two rooms, two windows and a door. There was no bedroom, but in the kitchen steps led up to a platform just wide enough for a straw mattress. At one end this sleeping ledge adjoined the chimney, so if the fire had been lit the sleeper's head or feet might be warm for the first hours of the night. It was an impoverished place and was empty as often as it was tenanted, for it was so cold and damp that only the desperate were willing to inhabit it. It was almost too small to have a name, so it comes as a surprise to learn that in fact it had two. Officially it was called Marsh Cottage, but it had been known for as long as anyone could remember as Basketman's Cottage. A long time ago, the basketman had been a tenant there for a dozen years or thirty, depending on whom you talked to. He collected reeds all summer long and made baskets all winter, and everybody who needed a basket bought it from him, for his goods were well made and he did not ask too much for them. He had no children to disappoint him, no wife to nag him and no other woman to break his heart. He was quiet without being morose, said good morning very pleasantly to all, and quarrelled with no one. He lived without debts. He had no sins anyone knew of or could guess at. One morning he walked into the river, his pockets full of stones. When his body knocked into one of the barges waiting to be loaded at the wharf, they went to his cottage and found potatoes in a stone jar and cheese on the side. There was cider in a flagon, and on the mantelpiece was a tobacco tin, half full. There was consternation at his demise. He had work, food and pleasure – what more could a man want? It was a mystery, and overnight Marsh Cottage became Basketman's Cottage.

Since the time of the basketman, the river had undercut the bank by washing away layers of gravel. This created dangerous overhangs that looked solid but would not hold a man's weight. When they collapsed, all that was left to contain the river was a shallow slope where the frail roots of loosestrife, meadowsweet and willowherb attempted to knit the soil together and were washed away with every high water. At equinoxes and after heavy rain, and after moderate rain that followed baking sun, and in times of snow melt, and at other times for no reason other than the random malice of nature, the river flooded on to this shallow slope. Halfway up this slope someone had driven a post into the ground. Though it was silvered by time and cracked by repeated submersion, the carved lines that marked the water level were visible still, and you could make out dates that told you when the flooding had taken place. The flood marks were numerous at the bottom of the post, and almost as numerous in the middle and in the upper section. Further up the slope a second post had sprouted, more recent. Evidently there had been floods that had entirely swallowed up the first post. This newer one had two lines in it, from eight years ago and five.

Today a woman stood next to the lower post, looking at the river. She clutched her coat to her with gloveless hands that were chapped and red with cold. Strands of hair had worked loose from her too few hairpins and hung about her face, moving with the breeze. They were so fair that the silver that had started to appear was almost invisible. If her hair was younger than her forty-odd years, the same could not be said of her face. Trouble had marked her, and permanent creases of anxiety were scored into her forehead.

The river was a good yard from the post. There would be no flood today, nor tomorrow either, yet still the woman's eyes were fearful. The water, bright and cold and fast-running, hissed as it passed. At irregular intervals it spat; when a spot of river water landed near her boot, she jumped and edged back a few inches.

As she stood there, she remembered the story of the basketman, and shuddered at his bravery, walking into the river like that with his pockets full of stones. She thought of the dead souls that are said to live in the river and wondered which ones were racing past her now, spitting at her. She thought – again – that she would ask the parson one day about the dead souls in the river. It wasn't in the Bible – at least, not so far as she knew – but that didn't mean anything. There must be a great many true things that weren't in the Bible. It was a big book, but still, it couldn't have *every* true thing in it, could it?

She turned and walked up the slope towards the cottage. The working day was no shorter in winter than in summer, and by the time she got home it was almost dark. She still had to see to the animals.

Lily had come to live in the cottage four years ago. She had introduced herself as Mrs White, a widow, and was thought at first to be slippery because she gave evasive answers to any question that touched on her past life and nervously rebuffed all friendly interest. But she appeared at church every Sunday without fail and counted out the scant coins from her purse for every modest purchase without once asking for credit, and over time suspicion faded. It wasn't long before she started work at the parsonage, first doing the laundry and then, because she was unstinting in her efforts and quick, gradually doing more and more. Since the retirement two years ago of the parson's housekeeper, Lily had taken on entire responsibility for the domestic comfort of the parsonage. There were two pleasant rooms reserved there for the use of the housekeeper, but Lily continued to live in Basketman's Cottage – because of the animals, she said. People were used to her now, but it was still held locally that there was something *not quite right* about Lily White. Was she really a widow? Why was she so nervy when anyone spoke to her unexpectedly? And what sensible woman would choose to live in damp isolation at Basketman's Cottage when she could enjoy the wallpapered comfort of the parsonage, all for the sake of a goat and a couple of pigs? Yet familiarity and her connection with the parson worked together to reduce suspicion, and she was now regarded with something closer to pity. Excellent housekeeper she might be, but still, it was whispered that Lily White was a bit soft in the head.

There was some truth in what people imagined about Lily White. In law and in the eyes of God, she was no missus at all. There had been for some years a Mr White, and she had performed for him all those duties a wife customarily performs for a husband: she had cooked his meals, scrubbed his floors, laundered his shirts, emptied his chamber pot and warmed his bed. He in return had performed the normal duties of a husband: he kept her short of money, drank her share of the ale, stayed out all night when he felt like it, and beat her. It was like a marriage in every detail in Lily's eyes and so, when he had disappeared five years ago in circumstances that she tried not to think about, she had not hesitated. With all his thieving and drinking and other bad ways, White had been a better name than he'd deserved. It was a better name than *she* deserved too, she knew that, yet out of all the names she could have had, this was the one she most wanted. So she took it. She had left that place, followed the river and come, by chance, to Buscot. 'Lily White,' she had muttered under her breath all the way. 'I am Lily White.' She tried to live up to it.

Lily gave the yellow goat some rotten potatoes, then went to feed the pigs. The pigs lived in the old woodshed. It was a stone building, halfway between the cottage and the river, with a tall, narrow opening on the cottage side for a person to go in and out, and a low opening on the other, so that the pigs might come and go between their enclosure and their mud patch. Within, a low wall separated the two ends. At Lily's end, chopped wood was stacked against the wall, next to a sack of grain and an old tin bath half full of swill. There were a couple of buckets, and on a shelf apples were slowly mouldering.

Lily lifted the buckets and carried them out and round to the pigs' outdoor mud patch. She tipped a bucketful of half-rotten cabbages and other vegetable matter too brown to identify over the fence and into the trough, then filled the old sink with water. The boar came out of the straw-lined woodshed and, without a glance at Lily, lowered his head to eat. Behind him came the sow.

The female rubbed her flank against the fence, as was her way, and when Lily scratched behind her ears, the sow blinked at her. Beneath her ginger lashes the sow's eyes were still half full of sleep. *Do pigs dream?* Lily wondered. *If they do, it is about something better than real life, by the look of things.* The sow came into full wakefulness and she fixed Lily with a peculiarly poignant gaze. Pigs were funny creatures. You could almost think they were human, the way they looked at you sometimes. Or was the pig remembering something? Yes, Lily realized, that was it. The pig looked exactly as if she were recollecting some happiness now lost, so that joy remembered was overlaid with present sorrow.

Lily had been happy once, though it was painful to recall it. Her father had died before she could remember, and until she was eleven she and her mother had lived quietly together, just the two of them. There had been little money and food was scant, but they scraped by, and after their soup in the evening they would lean close together with a blanket round them to save the fire, and at her mother's nod Lily would turn the pages of the children's Bible while her mother read aloud. Lily was no great reader. She could not tell *b* from *d* and the words quivered on the page as soon as they felt the brush of her gaze, but when her mother read aloud in her gentle voice, the words grew still and Lily found she could follow the thread after all, mouthing the words silently in time. Sometimes her mother told her about her father – how he had loved his baby daughter, watched her endlessly and, as his own health faded, said, *Here is the best of me, Rose. It lives on in this child we made together.* In time, Jesus and her father came to seem like different faces of the same man, a presence that surrounded Lily and protected her and was no less real for being invisible. That blanket, and that book, and her mother's voice and Jesus and her father who had loved her so – these happy memories only sharpened the hardship of her existence since. She could not think of those golden days without despair, came close to wishing she had never lived them. That hopeless longing for lost happiness in the eye of the pig must be how she herself looked when she remembered the past. The only God that watched over Lily now was a severe and angry one, and if her father were to look down from heaven on to his grown daughter, he would turn his face away in an agony of disappointment.

The sow continued to stare at Lily. She pushed its snout roughly away and muttered, 'Stupid sow,' as she walked up the slope to the cottage.

Inside she got the fire going and ate a bit of cheese and an apple. She eyed the candle, a short stub melded by its own wax to a scrap of broken tile, and decided to do without it for a bit longer. Next to the fire was a sagging chair, the upholstery much mended with patches of unmatching wool, and she sat wearily in it. She was tired, but nerves kept her alert. Was it one of those nights when *he* was going to come? She had seen him yesterday, so perhaps not, but you could never tell. For an hour she sat, on the alert for footsteps, and then gradually Lily's eyelids closed, her head began to nod and she fell into sleep.

The river now exhaled a complicated fragrance and blew it through the gap under the door of the little cottage. Lily's nose suddenly twitched. The odour had an earthy base with live notes of grasses, reeds and sedges. It contained the mineral quality of stone. And something darker, browner and more decomposed.

With its next breath, the river exhaled a child. She floated into the cottage, glaucous and cold.

Lily frowned in her sleep and her breathing grew troubled.

The girl's colourless hair clung slickly to her scalp and shoulders; her garment was the colour of the dirty scum that collects at the river's edge. Water ran off her; from her hair it dripped into her cloak, from the cloak it dripped to the floor. It did not drip itself out.

Fear put a choking whimper in Lily's throat.

Drip, drip, drip . . . There was no end to the water: it would drip for an eternity, it would drip until the river ran dry. The hovering child turned a malevolent gaze on the sleeper in the chair and slowly – slowly – raised a hazy hand to point at her.

Lily woke with a sudden start—

The river child evaporated.

For a few moments, Lily stared in alarm at the spot in the air where the girl had been.

'Oh!' she gasped. 'Oh! Oh!' She brought her hands to her face as if to hide the image, but also peeped between her fingers to reassure herself that the girl was gone.

All this time and it never got any easier. The girl was still furious. If only she would stay a little bit longer so that Lily could talk to her. Tell her she was sorry. Tell her she would pay any price demanded, give up anything, do anything . . . But by the time Lily got the use of her tongue, the girl had gone.

Lily leant forward, still in fear, to stare at the floorboards where the river child had hovered. There were dark marks there, she could just make them out in the fading light. She heaved herself from the chair and shuffled reluctantly across the floor. She extended her hand, placed outstretched fingers against the darkness.

The floor was wet.

Lily brought her hands together in prayer. 'Take me out of the mire, that I sink not: O let me be delivered out of the deep waters. Let not the flood drown me, neither let the deep swallow me up.' Rapidly she repeated the words until her breathing was regular, and then she got painfully to her feet and said, 'Amen.'

She felt troubled and it wasn't just the aftermath of the visitation. Was the river on the rise? She went to the window. Its dark gleam was no nearer the cottage than before.

Him, then. Was he coming? She looked for movement outdoors, strained her ears for the sound of his approach. Nothing.

It was neither of these things.

What, then?

The answer when it came was spoken in a voice so like her mother's it took her aback, till she realized it was her own: 'Something is going to happen.'

Mr Armstrong at Bampton

SOMETHING IS GOING to happen, they all thought. And soon after, at the Swan at Radcot, it did.

Now what?

On the first morning following the longest night, the clatter of hooves on cobbles announced a visitor to the village of Bampton. The few who happened to be outside at this early hour frowned and looked up. What fool was this, riding at full tilt into their narrow street? When horse and rider came into view, they grew curious. Instead of it being one of their own immature lads, the rider was an outsider, and more than that: he was a black man. His face was grave and the clouds of vapour he exhaled this cold morning lent him an air of fury. When he slowed, they took one look at him and hopped promptly into doorways, shutting their doors firmly behind them.

Robert Armstrong was used to the effect he had on strangers. His fellow humans had always been wary of him at first sight. The blackness of his skin made him the outsider, and his height and strength, which would have been an advantage to any white man, only made people more wary. In fact, as other living creatures understood very well, he was the gentlest of souls. Take Fleet, for instance. She had been called too wild to tame, and that was why he got her for a song, yet once he was in the saddle, the two of them were the best of friends within half an hour. And the cat. A skinny thing with an ear missing, which appeared in his barn one winter's morning, spitting curses and darting evil glances at all and sundry – why, now she came running up to him in the yard, tail up, mewing to be scratched under her chin. Even the ladybirds that alighted on a man's hair in summer and crawled over his face knew that Armstrong would do no more than wrinkle his nose to dislodge them if they tickled excessively. No animal of field or farmyard feared him, no; but people – ah! That was another matter entirely.

A fellow had written a book lately – Armstrong had heard tell of it – in which he proposed that man was a kind of clever monkey. A lot of laughter and indignation that had produced, but Armstrong was inclined to believe it. He had found the line that separated humans from the animal kingdom to be a porous one, and all the things that people thought unique to them – intelligence, kindness, communication – he had seen in his pigs, his horse, even the rooks that hopped and strutted amongst his cows. And then there was this: the methods he used on animals generally bore fruit when applied to people too. He could usually win them round in the end.

The sudden disappearance of the people he had glimpsed only a moment or two ago made things difficult though. He did not know Bampton. Armstrong walked along for a few yards and, coming to a crossroads, saw a boy sprawled in the grassy centre by the signpost, nose almost to the ground. He was so engrossed in studying the lie of a number of marbles that he seemed not to notice the cold – nor Armstrong's approach.

Two expressions passed across the boy's face. The first – alarm – was fleeting. It disappeared when he saw the marble that appeared as if by magic from Armstong's pocket. (Armstrong had his clothes made with large and reinforced pockets to store the items he kept habitually upon him for the taming and reassuring of creatures. As a rule he kept acorns for pigs, apples for horses, marbles for small boys and a flask of alcohol for older ones. For females of the human species he depended on good manners, the right words and immaculately polished shoes and buttons.) The marble that he showed to the boy was no ordinary one but contained flares of orange and yellow so like the flames of a fire that you would think you could warm yourself by it. The boy now looked interested.

The game that ensued was carried out with professional concentration by both parties. The boy had the advantage of knowing the terrain – which tufts of grass will bend as a marble passes and which have congested roots and will divert its path – and the game ended, as Armstrong had always intended, with the marble in the pocket of the boy.

'Fair and square,' he admitted. 'Victory to the better man.'

The boy looked discomfited. 'Was it your best marble?'

'I have others at home. Now, I ought really to introduce myself. My name is Mr Armstrong and I have a farm at Kelmscott. I wonder whether you can help me with some information? I want to know the way to a house where a little girl called Alice lives.'

'That is Mrs Eavis's house, her mother lodges there.'

'And her mother's name is . . . ?'

'Mrs Armstrong, Sir – oh! – that is just like your name, Sir!'

Armstrong was rather relieved. If the woman was Mrs Armstrong, then Robin had married her. Things were perhaps not quite so bad as he had feared.

'And where is Mrs Eavis's house? Can you direct me there?'

'I will show you, that will be best, for I know the shortcuts, it being me who delivers the meat.'

They set off on foot, Armstrong leading Fleet.

'I have told you my name, and I will tell you that this horse is called Fleet. Now you know who we are, who are you?'

'I am Ben and I am the son of the butcher.'

Armstrong noticed that Ben had a habit of taking a deep breath at the start of every answer and delivering his words in a single stream.

'Ben. I suppose you are the youngest son, for that is what Benjamin means.'

'It means the littlest and the last, and it was my father who named me, but my mother says it takes more than naming a thing to make it so, and there are three more after me and another one on the way, and that is on top of the five that came before, though all my father needs is one to help in the shop and that is my eldest brother, and all the rest of us is surplus to requirements since we do nothing but eat the profits.'

'And what does your mother say about that?'

'Mostly nothing, but when she do say something it is generally along the lines that eating the profits is better than drinking them, and then he gives her a bash and she don't say nothing at all for a few days.'

While the boy was speaking, Armstrong eyed him sideways. There were ghosts of bruises on the lad's forehead and wrists.

'It is not a good house, Sir, Mrs Eavis's house,' the boy told him.

'In what way is it not a good house?'

The boy thought hard. 'It is a bad house, Sir.'

A few minutes later, they were there.

'I'd better stand by and hold your horse for you, Sir.'

Armstrong passed Fleet's reins to Ben and passed him an apple. 'If you give this to Fleet, you'll have a friend for life,' he said, then he turned and knocked at the door of the large, plain house.

The door opened slightly and he caught a glimpse of a face almost as narrow as the crack it peered out of. The woman took one look at his black face and her sharp features twitched.

'Shoo! Off with you, dirty devil! We're not for your sort! Be on your way!' She spoke more loudly than she needed to; slowly too, as though to a half-wit or a foreigner.

She tried to close the door but the tip of Armstrong's boot blocked it, and whether it was the sight of the expensive polished leather or the desire to give him a piece of her mind more forcefully, she reopened the door. Before she could open her mouth to speak, Armstrong addressed her. He spoke softly and with great dignity of expression, as though she had never called him a dirty devil, as though his boot were not in her doorway.

'Forgive my intrusion, Madam. I realize you must be very busy and I won't detain you a minute longer than necessary.' He saw her register the expensive education that lay behind his voice, appraise his good hat, his smart coat. He saw her draw her conclusion and felt the pressure against the toe of his shoe cease.

'Yes?' she said.

'I understand you have a young woman by the name of Mrs Armstrong lodging here?'

A snidely triumphant smile pulled at the corners of her lips. 'She works here. She's new to it. You'll have to pay extra.'

So that was what Ben meant by a bad house.

'All I want is to speak with her.'

'It is the letter, I suppose? She's been expecting it for weeks. Quite given up hope.'

The sharp, narrow woman put out a sharp, narrow hand. Armstrong looked at it and shook his head.

'I should very much like to see her, if you please.'

'It is not the letter?'

'Not the letter. Take me to her, if you will.'

She led him up one, then another flight of stairs, muttering all the while. 'Why should I not think it is the letter, when all I have heard, twenty times a day this last month, is "Has my letter come, Mrs Eavis?" and "Mrs Eavis, is there any letter for me?" '

He said nothing but gave himself a mild and amenable countenance whenever she turned to glance at him. The stairwell, rather smart and grand at the entrance, grew shabbier and chillier the higher you got. On the way up, some of the doors were ajar. Armstrong caught glimpses of unmade beds, garments strewn on the floor. In one room, a half-dressed woman bent over to roll a stocking up over her knee. When she caught sight of him her mouth smiled, but her eyes didn't. His heart sank. Was this what had become of Robin's wife?

On the bare top landing where the paint was peeling, Mrs Eavis stopped and rapped sharply at a door.

There came no reply.

She rapped again. 'Mrs Armstrong? A gentleman for you.'

There was only silence.

Mrs Eavis frowned. 'I don't know . . . She has not gone out this morning, I would have heard.' Then, with sharp alarm, 'Done a runner, that's what she's done, the little trollop!' and in no time she had the key out of her pocket, opened the door and burst in.

Over Mrs Eavis's shoulder, Armstrong perceived all in a flash. The stained and rumpled sheet of the iron bed and, against it, that other, awful whiteness: an outstretched arm, the fingers splayed rigid.

'Good Lord, no!' he exclaimed, and his hand came to his eyes as though it were not too late to unsee it. So he stood, for some seconds, eyes squeezed shut while Mrs Eavis's complaints went on.

'Little minx! Two weeks rent she owes me! *When I get my letter, Mrs Eavis!* Oh, the lying vixen! What am I to do now, eh? Eating my meals, sleeping in my linen! Thought she was too good to work for money! "I'll have you out of here if you don't pay up prompt," I told her. "I don't keep girls here for nothing! If you can't pay, you'll *have* to work." I saw to it that she did. I won't have it, girls who think nothing of running up a debt and too good to pay it. She stooped in the end. They always do. What am I to do now, eh? Thieving little idiot!'

When Armstrong drew his hand away from his eyes and opened them, he looked like a different person altogether. With sorrow he looked around the small, mean room. The boards were bare and draughty, a broken pane let in knife blades of cold air. The plaster was pitted and blistered. Nowhere was there any bit of colour, of warmth, of human comfort. On the stand beside the bed there was a brown apothecary bottle. Empty. He took it and sniffed. So that was it. The girl had taken her own life. He slipped the bottle into his pocket. Why let it be known? There was little enough to be done for her, he could at least conceal the manner of her passing.

'So who are you, eh?' Mrs Eavis continued, now with a note of calculation in her voice. And although it seemed unlikely, she was hopeful enough to suggest, 'Family?'

She received no answer. The man put out a hand and drew down the lids of the dead girl, then bowed his head for a minute in prayer.

Mrs Eavis waited testily. She did not join him at 'Amen,' but as soon as his prayer was done, picked up where she had left off.

'It's just that if you *are* family, you'll be liable. For the debt.'

With a wince, Armstrong reached into the folds of his cloak and took out a leather purse. He counted the coins into her palm, then '*Three* weeks, it is!' she added as he was about to put the purse away. He gave her the additional coins with a sense of distaste and her fingers closed around them.

The visitor turned to look again at the face of the dead girl in the bed.

Her teeth looked too large for her and her cheekbones jutted in a way that suggested, whatever Mrs Eavis said, that the young woman hadn't benefited greatly from the landlady's meals.

'I suppose she must have been pretty?' he asked sadly.

The question took Mrs Eavis by surprise. The man was of an age to be the young woman's father, yet given the fairness of the girl and the blackness of the man, that was most unlikely. Something told her he was not her lover either. But if he was neither, if he had never seen her before, why pay her rent? Not that it mattered.

She shrugged. 'Pretty is as pretty does. She was fair. Too skinny.'

Mrs Eavis stepped out on to the landing. Armstrong heaved a sigh and, with a final, sorrowful glance at the cadaver on the bed, followed her out.

'Where is the child?' he asked.

'Drowned it, I expect.' She gave a callous shrug that didn't interrupt her progress down the stairs. 'You'll have only the one funeral to pay for,' she added maliciously. 'That's one blessing, anyhow.'

Drowned? Armstrong stopped dead on the top stair. He turned and reopened the door. He looked up and down, left and right, as if somewhere – in the gap between the floorboards, behind the useless wisp of curtain, in the chilly air itself – a piece of life might be concealed. He pulled back the sheet, in case a small second body – dead? alive? – might be hidden in its flimsy folds. There were only the mother's bones, too big for the flesh that contained them.

Outside, Ben was stroking the mane of his new friend Fleet. When Fleet's owner came out of the house, he was different. Greyer. Older.

'Thank you,' he said distractedly as he took the reins.

It occurred to the boy that he might not find out what all this had been in aid of – the arrival of the interesting stranger in the street, the victory that had won him the blazing marble, the mysterious visit to Mrs Armstrong in Mrs Eavis's bad house.

With one foot in the stirrup, the man halted and things took a more hopeful turn. 'Do you know the little girl from this house?'

'Alice? They don't come out much, and Alice follows behind her mother, half hiding, for she is the timid sort and pulls her mother's skirt over her face if she thinks somebody might be looking at her, but I have seen her peeking out once or twice.'

'How old would you say she was?'

'About four.'

Armstrong nodded and frowned sadly. Ben felt the presence of something complicated in the air, something beyond his understanding.

'When did you last see her?'

'Yesterday, at the end of the afternoon.'

'Where was that?'

'Up by Mr Gregory's shop. She came out with her mother and they went up the lane.'

'What kind of shop is Mr Gregory's?'

'The apothecary's.'

'Was she carrying something in her hand?'

Ben reflected. 'Something wrapped up.'

'What kind of size?'

He gestured to indicate and Armstrong understood it was something the size of the bottle he had picked up in the room and now had in his pocket.

'And the lane. Where does it go?'

'Nowhere, really.'

'It must go somewhere.'

'Nowhere 'cept the river.'

Armstrong said nothing. He pictured the poor young woman entering the apothecary's to buy the bottle of poison, then taking the lane that led to the river.

'Did you see them return?'

'No.'

'Or – perhaps Mrs Armstrong returned alone?'

'I had gone in by then to eat the profits.'

Ben was perplexed. He had the feeling that an event of significance was taking place, but he did not know what it could be. He looked at Armstrong to see whether he had been useful to him or not. Whatever it was that was happening, he felt he would like to be part of it, alongside this man who fed apples to his handsome horse and kept marbles in his pocket and looked almost frightening but had a voice full of kindness. But the dark man with the fine horse did not look at all happy and Ben felt disappointed.

'Perhaps you would show me the way to the apothecary's, Ben?'

'I will.'

As they walked, the man seemed lost in thought and Ben, though he didn't realize he was doing it, must have been thinking too, for something in the man's sombre face told him the drama they were involved in was a bleak one.

They came to a small, low building, made of brick, with a small, dingy window, above which someone had painted the word *Apothecary*, but so long ago that it was now faded. They entered and the man at the counter looked up. He was slightly built with a wispy beard. He registered the newcomer with alarm, then saw Ben and was reassured.

'How can I help you?'

'It's about this.'

The man barely glanced at the bottle. 'A refill, is it?'

'I don't want *more* of it. It would be better for everyone if there had been rather less.'

The apothecary cast a rapid and uncertain glance at Armstrong, but did not respond to his implication.

Armstrong removed the stopper and held it under the man's nose. There was something under a quarter of a bottle left. Enough to give off an aroma that rose aggressively from the back of the nostrils into the brain. You didn't need to know what it was to be wary. The smell told you to beware.

The apothecary now looked ill at ease.

'You remember selling it?'

'I sell all sorts. People want this' – he nodded at the bottle that Armstrong had placed on the table – 'for all kinds of reasons.'

'Such as?'

The man shrugged. 'Greenfly . . .'

'Greenfly? In December?'

He turned falsely innocent eyes on Armstrong. 'You didn't say December.'

'Of course I mean December. You sold this to a young woman yesterday.'

The apothecary's Adam's apple bobbed up and down. 'You are a friend of this young woman, are you? Not that I remember any young woman. Not in particular. Young women come and go. They want all kinds of things. For all kinds of reasons. You are not her father, I think . . .' He paused and, when Armstrong failed to answer, went on with sly emphasis, 'Her *protector*, then?'

Armstrong was the gentlest of men, but he knew how to seem otherwise when it served him. He turned a certain look on the apothecary and the man suddenly quailed.

'What is it you want?'

'Information.'

'Ask away.'

'Was the child with her?'

'The little girl?' He seemed surprised. 'Yes.'

'Where did they go when they left you?'

He gestured.

'Towards the river?'

The man shrugged. 'How am I to know where they were going?'

Armstrong's voice was mild, but there was no mistaking the menace in it. 'A defenceless young mother comes to you, bringing her small child with her, buys poison, and you don't think to ask yourself where she is going next? What she plans to do? Do you never consider the result of your making a miserable few pence on such a purchase?'

'Sir, if an unknown woman is in trouble, whose job is it to get her out of it? Mine? Or the one who got her into it in the first place? If she is something to you, Mr . . . Mr whoever-you-are, that's where you should address your questions. Go to the one who ruined her and abandoned her. That's where you'll find the responsibility lies for what happened next! Not that I know what happened. I'm nothing but a man who must make a living, and that's what I do.'

'Selling poison so that girls with no one in the world to help them can kill the greenfly on their December roses?'

The apothecary had the grace to look discomfited, but whether it was guilt or just the fear that Armstrong was out to make trouble for him was hard to tell.

'There is no law requiring me to know the seasons of horticultural pests.'

'Where next, Sir?' Ben asked hopefully, when they were outside again.

'I think I'm done here. For today, anyway. Let's go up to the river.'

As they went, Ben's stride grew slow and he began to waver on his feet. Coming to the river, Armstrong glanced to see where the boy had got to and saw him leaning against a tree trunk, his face green.

'What is it, Ben?'

Ben wept. 'Sir, I'm sorry, Sir, I ate some of the green apple you gave me for Fleet, Sir, and now my belly's aching and churning . . .'

'They're sour, those apples. No wonder. What have you eaten today?'

'Nothing, Sir.'

'No breakfast?'

The boy shook his head. Armstrong felt a surge of anger towards the butcher who failed to feed his children.

'It's the acid on an empty stomach.' Armstrong unscrewed his hip flask. 'Drink this.'

The boy drank and pulled a face. 'That is truly horrible, Sir, it's making me feel worse.'

'That's the idea. It's nothing more sinister than cold tea. Finish it up.'

Ben tipped the flask and with a grimace swallowed the last of the tea. Then he was violently sick in the grass.

'Good. Any more? Yes? Good. Keep it coming.'

While Ben gasped and groaned on the riverbank, watched by Fleet, Armstrong doubled back to the high street, where he bought three buns at the bakery. He returned and gave two to Ben – 'Go on, fill your stomach' – and ate the third himself.

The pair sat on the bank, and while Ben ate, Armstrong watched the river flow powerfully by. The river was quieter like this than when it dawdled. There was no idle splashing on the way, only the purposeful surge forwards, and behind the high-pitched ringing of water on shingle at the river edge was a kind of hum, of the kind you would expect to hear inside your ears after a bell has been struck by a hammer and the audible ringing has died away. It had the shape of noise but lacked the sound, a sketch without colour. Armstrong listened to it, and his mind flowed with the river.

There was a bridge, a simple one, constructed in wood. Beneath it the river was high and fast – it would sweep away anything that might fall into it. He saw the young woman here with her child, in the evening, in the dark and the cold. He spared himself the picture of her dropping her child into the water, but he imagined her distress, felt his own heart leap in horror and grief. Armstrong looked up- and down-river distractedly. He didn't know what he was expecting to see. Not a small child, he knew that – not now.

When he returned to himself, he noticed how harsh the winter felt compared to only a few hours before. His body had less resistance to the chill and inside his woollen overcoat and the layers beneath he felt the coldness of his skin. There was dankness in the undergrowth. The browns and dark golds of autumn were long gone and the softening of spring was months ahead. The branches were at their blackest. It seemed that only by some miracle could life ever return to dress the stark treetops with the haze of new foliage. Seeing it today, one would think that life was gone for good.

He tried to distract himself from his sad thoughts. Turning to Ben, he found the boy was looking more like his old self.

'Will you join your father in the butcher's shop when you are older?'

Ben shook his head. 'I shall run away.'

'Is that a good plan?'

'It is the family tradition, done first by my second-eldest brother and then by my third-eldest brother, and it will be my turn next, for Father only has need of one of us, so being as how the rest of us is not needed, I shall run away before too long – when the good weather comes, I reckon – and make my fortune.'

'Doing what?'

'I shall find that out once I am doing it, I suppose.'

'When the time is right for running away, Ben, I hope you will come to me. I have a farm at Kelmscott, and there is always a job for honest boys who are not afraid of working. Just make your way to Kelmscott and ask for Armstrong.'

Stunned by this unexpected stroke of good fortune, Ben took a deep breath and said a good many times over, 'Thank you, Sir! Thank you, Sir! Thank you!'

The new friends shook hands to seal their agreement, and then they parted.

Ben took his first steps home, his thoughts in upheaval. It was not yet ten o'clock, but it had been an adventurous day like no other. Suddenly the significance of Armstrong's sadness broke into his young mind.

'Sir?' he said, running back to Armstrong, who was already in the saddle.

'Yes?'

'Alice – is she dead, Sir?'

Armstrong looked at the river, at its directionless surface motion.

Was she dead?

He held the reins loosely in his hands and settled his feet in the stirrups.

'I don't know, Ben. I wish I did. Her mother is dead.'

Ben watched to see whether he was going to say anything else, but he didn't, so he turned and made his way home. Mr Armstrong, the farmer at Kelmscott. When the time was right he would run away – and be part of the story.

Armstrong nudged Fleet forwards. They moved at a gentle trot and Armstrong wept as they went, grieving for the loss of the grandchild he had never known.

It was always painful to him to know that a creature was suffering. He would not allow his animals to suffer, and that was why he slaughtered them himself instead of giving the job to one of his men. He made sure his knife was sharp, he soothed the pigs with calm words, distracted them with acorns, then one swift and expert twist of the knife was enough. No fear and no pain. The drowning of a child? He could not contemplate it. There were farmers who got rid of sick animals that way and it was a common thing to drown unwanted kittens and puppies in a sack, but he had never done it. Death might be a necessity in farming, but suffering – never.

Armstrong wept, and he discovered as he went that one loss brings back others. The thought of his favourite pig, the most intelligent and kindly pig he had known in thirty years of farming, suddenly afflicted him afresh as poignantly as that first morning over two years ago when he had discovered her missing. 'What happened to Maud, Fleet? I cannot reconcile myself to not knowing. Someone took her, Fleet, but who could have got her away so noiselessly? You know what she was like. She would have squealed if some stranger had tried to take her. And why steal a gilt? A pig for the table, that I can understand, people get hungry, but a breeding pig – her meat would be tough and bitter, wouldn't they know that? It makes no sense. Why steal a pig the size of Maud when there were table pigs in the very next pen?'

His heart contracted in pain at the most unbearable thought of all: anyone ignorant enough to take the biggest pig instead of a sweet-tasting small one was bound to be clumsy with the slaughterer's knife.

Armstrong was a man fully aware of his good fortune: he had health, strength and intelligence; the unorthodoxy of his birth – his father was an earl, his mother a black servant girl – had brought difficulties, but advantages too. Though his childhood had been lonely, he had received a fine education, and when he chose his path in life, he had been given a generous sum to get started. He owned fertile land; he had won the love of Bess and together they had created a large and mostly happy family. He was a man who counted his blessings and rejoiced in them, but he was also one who felt losses most keenly, and now his mind was in torment.

A child struggling in the river, Maud struggling against a dull blade, wielded by an inexpert slaughterman . . .

Dark images tore at him. Yes, one grief unleashes another, and another, and having torn open the wound left by the loss of Maud, his mind turned to the most painful loss of all and the tears ran more abundantly down his face.

'Oh, Robin. Where did I go wrong, Fleet? Oh, Robin, my son.'

A great distance now separated him from his first child, and a massive weight of sorrow sat on his heart and oppressed him. Twenty-two years of love, and now? For four years his son had not consented to live at the farm, but resided in Oxford, apart from his brothers and sisters. They didn't see him for months at a time, and then only when he wanted something. 'I tried, Fleet – but did I try hard enough? What should I have done? Is it too late?'

And thinking about Robin brought him back to the child – Robin's child – and he started the cycle all over again.

After some time of this, an elderly man came into view, leaning on a stick. Armstrong wiped his face on his sleeve and, as they came close, stopped to speak to him.

'There is a little girl gone missing from Bampton,' he said. 'Four years of age. Will you put the word out? I'm Armstrong, my farm is at Kelmscott . . .'

From his first words, he saw the man's face change.

'Then I have sorry news for you, Mr Armstrong. I heard it told last night, at the cockfighting. Fellow on his way to Lechlade for the morning train told it to all o' us. A little girl plucked out o' the river, drowned.'

So, she was gone. It was only to be expected.

'Where was this?'

'The Swan, at Radcot.'

The fellow was not without kindness. Seeing Armstrong's grief he added, 'I don't say as it's the child you are looking for. Chances are it's a different girl altogether.'

But as Armstrong geed up Fleet to gallop to Radcot, the old man shook his head and pursed his lips. He had lost a week's wages on the cockfighting last night, but still, there were others worse off than he.

Three Claims

THE LEACH AND the Churn and the Coln all have their separate journeys before they join the Thames to swell its waters, and in similar fashion the Vaughans and the Armstrongs and Lily White had their own stories in the years and days before they became part of this one. But join it they did, and we now come to the meeting of the waterways.

While the world was still smothered in darkness, someone was up and about on the riverbank: a stubby figure, clutching a coat about her, scurried in the direction of Radcot Bridge, panting steam.

At the bridge she stopped.

The usual place to pause on a bridge is the apex. It is so natural to pause there that most bridges – even youthful ones only a few hundred years old – are flattened at their upmost point by the feet that have lingered, loitered, wandered and waited there. That was a thing Lily could not understand. She stopped on the bank, at the pier stone, the massive piece of rock on which the rest of the construction was founded. Engineering was a bewilderment to Lily: stones, to her mind, did not reside naturally in the air, and how a bridge stayed up was another thing she could not fathom. It might be revealed at any moment for the illusion it surely was, and then, if she happened to be upon it, she would plummet through the air, plunge into the water and join the souls of the dead. She avoided bridges when she could, but sometimes crossing was a necessity. She balled the fabric of her skirt in her fists, took a deep breath and launched into a heavy-footed run.

It was Margot who woke first, roused by the banging at the door. The urgency of the hammering got her out of bed and she pulled her dressing gown around herself as she went downstairs to see who it was. As she descended, her memories of the previous night shook off their dream-like air and revealed themselves to her as surprising reality. She shook her head wonderingly – then opened the door.

'Where is she?' said the woman at the door. 'Is she here? I heard she was . . .'

'It's Mrs White, isn't it? From over the river?' *What's wrong here?* Margot thought. 'Come in, dear. What's the matter?'

'Where is she?'

'Asleep, I should think. There's no rush, is there? Let me light a candle.'

'There is a candle just here,' came Rita's voice. Roused by the hammering at the door, she was on her feet and in the doorway to the pilgrims' room.

'Who's that?' Lily asked nervously.

'Just me – Rita Sunday. Good morning. It's Mrs White, isn't it? I think you work for Parson Habgood?'

As the candle flickered into life, Lily looked this way and that in the room, her feet in agitated movement beneath her. 'The little girl . . .' she began again, but uncertainty entered her expression as she looked at Margot and Rita. 'I thought . . . Did I dream it? I don't . . . Perhaps I should be going.'

Light footsteps sounded behind Rita. It was the child, rubbing her eyes and tottering on her feet.

'Oh!' exclaimed Lily with an entirely altered voice. 'Oh!'

Even by candlelight they saw her blanch. Her hand flew to her mouth and she stared in shock at the girl's face.

'Ann!' she exclaimed in a voice thick with feeling. 'Forgive me, Ann! Say you forgive me, sister dear!' She got to her knees and reached a shaking hand to the child, but did not dare to touch her. 'You have come back! Thank heaven! Say you forgive me . . .' She gazed with urgent longing at the child, who seemed indifferent. 'Ann?' she asked, and with pleading eyes waited for a response.

None came.

'Ann?' she whispered again, in fearful trembling.

Still the child did not answer.

Rita and Margot exchanged a look of astonishment, then, seeing that the woman was weeping, Rita placed both hands on her shaking shoulders.

'Mrs White,' she said soothingly.

'What is that smell?' Lily cried out. 'The river, I know it is!'

'She was found in the river last night. We haven't washed her hair yet – she was too poorly.'

Lily turned her eyes back to the child and gazed at her with an expression that altered from love to horror and back again.

'Let me go,' she whispered. 'Let me get away!'

She rose shakily but with determination and made her way out, muttering apologies as she went.

'Well,' Margot exclaimed with gentle bafflement. 'I give up trying to make sense of anything. I am going to make a cup of tea. That is the best I can do.'

'And a very good thing too.'

But Margot didn't go to make the tea. At least, not straight away. She looked out of the window, to where Lily was kneeling in the cold, hands clasped at her chest. 'She is still there. Praying, it looks like. Praying and staring. What do you make of it?'

Rita considered. 'Can Mrs White have a sister so young? How old would you say she was? Forty?'

Margot nodded. 'And our little girl is – four?'

'About that.'

Margot used her fingers to count, the way she did the inn's book-keeping. 'Thirty-six years between them. Suppose Mrs White's mother had her at sixteen. Thirty-six years later she would be fifty-two.' She shook her head. 'Can't be.'

In the pilgrims' room, Rita held the wrist of the man in the bed and counted his pulse.

'Is he going to be all right?' Margot asked.

'All the signs are good.'

'And her?'

'What about her?'

'Will she . . . get better? Because she's not right, is she? She hasn't said a word.' Margot turned to the child. 'What's your name, poppet? Who are you, eh? Say hello to your Auntie Margot!'

The child gave no response.

Margot lifted her and, with maternal coaxing, murmured encouragement into her ear. 'Come on, my little one. A little smile? A look?' But the child remained indifferent. 'Can she even hear me?'

'I have wondered that myself.'

'Maybe she had her wits knocked out of her in the accident?'

'No sign of a blow to the head.'

'Simple-minded?' Margot wondered. 'Goodness knows, it's not easy having a child who's different.' She smoothed the child's hair tenderly. 'Have I ever told you about when Jonathan was born?' You couldn't live at the Swan, have it in your blood for generations and not know how to tell a story, and though she was ordinarily too busy for such things, the unusual nature of the day jolted her out of her habits and she stopped to tell one now. 'Do you remember Beattie Riddell, the midwife before you came?'

'She died before I arrived.'

'She delivered all of mine. None of the girls were any trouble, but then there was Jonathan and – I suppose I was older – it wasn't so easy. After a dozen girls, me and Joe were still hoping for a boy, so when at long last Beattie held him up to me all I saw was his little John Thomas! *Joe'll be pleased*, I thought, and so was I. I reached for him, thinking she would put him in my arms, but instead she put him down on the side and gave a sort of shudder.

'"I know what to do," she said. "Don't worry, Mrs Ockwell. It is a simple thing and cannot fail. We will get him changed back in no time, don't you fret."

'That's when I saw. Those slanting eyes of his and that funny little moon face and his ears that are so curious. He was an odd little fellow, a . . . a dainty creature . . . and I thought, *Is that really mine? Did that really come out of my belly? How did it get in there?* I had never seen a baby like it. But Beattie knew what he was.'

All the while she told, Margot was rocking the girl as though she were no weight at all, like a much smaller child.

'Let me guess,' said Rita. 'A changeling?'

Margot nodded. 'Beattie went down to the kitchen to set a fire going. I expect you know what she was going to do – put him over the fire, and when he got a bit warm and started to squeal, his fairy folk would come and fetch him back and leave my stolen baby in return. She called up the stairs, "I shall want more kindling and a big pot." I heard her go out the back to the wood store.

'I couldn't take my eyes off him, little fairy creature that he was. He gave a blink and the way his eyelid – you know what it is like, not straight like yours and mine, but set at an angle – it closed over the eye not quite like a normal baby, but nearly. I thought, *What does he make of this strange world he's come to? What does he make of me, his foster mother?* He moved his arms, not altogether like my baby girls used to, but more floppy – like he was swimming. A baby frown came into his face and I thought, *He will cry in a minute. He's cold.* Beattie hadn't wrapped him up or anything. *Fairy children can't be so very different from the ones I know*, I thought, *because I can tell he's getting cold.* I put my fingertips against his little cheek and he was all wonder, quite astonished! When I took my finger away his little mouth opened and he mewed like a kitten to have it back. I felt my milk rise at his cry.

'Beattie wasn't half cross when she came back and found him suckling. Human milk!

'"Well," she said, "it's too late now."

'And that was that.'

'Thank goodness,' said Rita, at the end of the story. 'I've heard the stories about changelings, but that's all they are. Jonathan is no fairy child. Some children are just born like that. Beattie might not have seen it before, but I have. There are other children in the world just the same as Jonathan, with the same slanting eyes and large tongues and loose limbs. Some doctors call them Mongol children, because they resemble people from that part of the world.'

Margot nodded. 'He is a human child, isn't he? I know it now. He's mine and Joe's. But the reason I was thinking about it now is because of this little one. She's not like Jonathan, is she? She's not a – what did you call it? – Mongol child? She's different in some other way. It's not easy raising a child who's different. But I've done it. I know how to do it. So even if she can't hear, and even if she don't speak . . .' Margot clutched the child closer in her arms, took a breath and suddenly remembered the man in the bed. 'But I suppose she belongs to him.'

'We'll know soon enough. It won't be long before he wakes.'

'What is that Lily doing now, anyway? I shall have to go and fetch her in if she's still there. It's too cold for a body to be praying out of doors – she'll be frozen stiff.'

She went to the window to peer out, the child still in her arms.

Margot felt it and Rita saw it: the child quickened. She lifted her head. Her sleepy stare was suddenly keen. She gazed one way and the other, scanning the view with lively interest.

'What is it?' said Rita, rising urgently and crossing the room. 'Is it Mrs White?'

'She's gone,' Margot told her. 'There's nothing there. Only the river.'

Rita came to stand at their side. She looked at the girl, whose stare continued as if she would drink the river dry with her eyes. 'There wasn't a bird? A swan? Something to catch her attention?'

Margot shook her head.

Rita sighed. 'Perhaps it was the light that attracted her,' she said. She stood for a moment in case she should see it – whatever it was, if it was anything at all. But Margot was right. There was only the river.

Margot dressed and roused her husband, noticed Jonathan was already up and out, and sighed – he had never been one to respect the conventional hours of sleep and wakefulness – then set to making tea and porridge. While she was stirring the pot, there came another knock at the door. It was early for drinkers, yet after last night there were bound to be curious souls dropping in. She unlocked, a greeting on her tongue, but when she opened the door she took half a step back. The man on the threshold had black skin. He was a head taller than most men and powerfully built. Should she be alarmed? She opened her mouth to call for her husband, but before the words were spoken the man took off his hat and nodded at her with grave good manners.

'I'm sorry to trouble you so early in the day, Madam.'

Tears trembled suddenly, unavoidably, on his lashes and he raised a hand to his face to brush them away.

'Whatever is it?' she cried, all thought of danger gone as she drew him inside. 'Here. Sit down.'

He put a thumb and forefinger into the corners of his eyes and pressed, then sniffed and swallowed. 'Forgive me,' he said, and she was struck by the way he spoke, like a gentleman – not only in the words he used, but in the way he said them. 'I understand a child was brought in last night. A child found drowned in the river.'

'That is true.'

He heaved a great breath. 'I believe it might be my granddaughter. I should like to see her, if you don't mind.'

'She is in the other room, with her father.'

'My son? My son is here?' His heart leapt at the thought and he leapt up with it.

Margot was puzzled. Surely this dark man could not be the father of the man in the bed.

'The nurse is with them,' she offered, though it was not an answer. 'They are both rather poorly.'

He followed her to the pilgrims' room.

'This is not my son,' he said. 'My son is not so tall, nor so broad. He is always clean-shaven. His hair is light brown and does not curl like this.'

'Then Mr Daunt is not your son.'

'My son is Mr Armstrong. And so am I.'

Margot said to Rita, 'It was for the little girl that the gentleman came in. He thought she might be his grandchild.'

Rita stood to one side and for the first time Armstrong set eyes on the child.

'Well!' exclaimed Armstrong uncertainly. 'What a . . .'

He hardly knew what to say. He had had in mind – and he realized his foolishness instantly – a brown-skinned child like his own. Of course, this child would be different. She would be Robin's child. At first disconcerted by the uncolour of her hair and the whiteness of her skin, he was nonetheless struck by a familiarity. He could not quite place it. Her nose was not really Robin's – unless perhaps it was, a little . . . And the curve of her temple . . . He tried to picture the face of the young woman he had seen dead so few hours earlier, but it was hard to compare that face with this. He might have been able to do it if he had seen the woman in life, but death so rapidly undoes a person and the detail of her face was hard to recall in any ordinary way. Still, he fancied there was something that linked the child to the woman, though he couldn't put his finger on it.

Armstrong became aware that the women were waiting for a response from him.

'The difficulty is that I have not met my grandchild before. My son's daughter lived at Bampton with her mother, apart from my own family. It was far from what I would have wished, but it was so.'

'Family life . . . It is not always easy,' Margot murmured charitably. After her initial trepidation she discovered she had quite come round to this large, dark man.

He gave her a half-bow in gratitude. 'I was alerted yesterday to a crisis in the household and discovered early this morning that the young woman who was her mother—'

He broke off and glanced anxiously at the child. He was used to the stares of children, but this one's eyes drifted towards him and didn't stop but kept on going, past, past, as if she hadn't seen him. Perhaps it was a form of shyness. Cats also did not like to meet an unfamiliar person's eye – they looked in your direction and then away again. He kept a length of string in his pocket to which was tied a feather; it was marvellously effective with kittens. For little girls he had a small doll made of a coat peg with a painted face and a rabbit-skin coat. He took it out now and put it in the child's lap. She felt it placed there, and looked down. Her hand closed around the doll. Rita and Margot watched her with the same attentiveness as the man and exchanged glances.

'You were saying, about the poor mite's mother . . .' Margot then prompted in a low voice, and while the child was occupied with the doll, Armstrong went on in a low murmur.

'The young woman passed away yesterday evening. Nothing was known of the whereabouts of the child. I enquired of the first man I met on the towpath and he told me to apply to you here. Though he had the story entirely upside down and I arrived believing her to be drowned.'

'She *was* drowned,' said Margot. 'Till Rita brought her in again and then she was alive.' No matter how many times her tongue repeated it, it still sounded wrong to her ears.

Armstrong frowned and turned to Rita for clarification. Her face gave little away. 'She appeared dead, but wasn't,' she said. The briefness of the formulations elided the impossibilities better than any other, and for the moment this was her version. It was laconic, but it was true. As soon as you started to put more words in, you came to unreason.

'I see,' said Armstrong, though he didn't.

The three of them looked at the girl again. The doll was lying abandoned at her side and she had returned to a state of listlessness.

'She is a droll little thing,' Margot admitted unhappily. 'Everybody finds her so. And yet, in a way that is hard to explain, you cannot help but take to her. Why, even the gravel-diggers last night – and they are not known for being soft-hearted – were won over. Weren't they, Rita? If nobody had claimed her, that Higgs would have taken her home like a lost puppy. And even with all the children and grandchildren I've got to worry about, I'd keep her, if she had nowhere else to go. And so would you, wouldn't you, Rita?'

Rita did not reply.

'We did think he was the father, the man who brought her in,' Margot said. 'But from what you say . . .'

'How is he? This Mr Daunt?'

'He will be all right. His injuries look worse than they are. His breathing does not falter and his colour improves with every hour that passes. I think it will not be long before he awakes.'

'I will go to Oxford and find my son, then. By dusk he will be here and by nightfall this matter will be settled.'

He put on his hat and took his leave.

Margot set about readying the winter room for the day ahead. Word would have got out and she expected to be busy. She might even have to open the large summer room. Rita moved between the child and the man asleep in the bed. Joe came in for a time. The little girl turned her eyes to him and watched his every move as he poured tea into Rita's cup and arranged the curtain so that the light did not disturb the sleeper in the bed. When he had done these things and came to see the child herself, she stretched out her arms to him.

'Well!' he exclaimed. 'What a funny little girl you are! Fancy being interested in old Joe.'

Rita stood to let him sit and placed the child on his lap. She stared up into his face.

'What colour would you say her eyes are?' he wondered. 'Blue? Grey?'

'Greeny-blue?' Rita suggested. 'Depends on the light.'

They were considering the matter together when there came a sudden hammering at the door for the third time that day. It made them both start.

'Whatever next!' they heard Margot exclaim, as her feet trotted hastily across the floor to the door. 'Who can it be this time?'

There came the sound of the door opening. And then—

'Oh!' exclaimed Margot. 'Oh!'

Daddy!

MR VAUGHAN WAS on Brandy Island, at the vitriol works, where he was making an inventory of every item that appertained to the factory in preparation for the auction. It was painstaking work and he could have delegated the job, but he liked the repetitive nature of the task. In any other circumstances the abandonment of his brandy business might have been a painful thing. He had invested so much in it: the purchase of Buscot House with its fields and its island, the planning, the research, the construction of the reservoir, the planting of acres of beet, the building of the railway and the bridge to bring the beet over on to the island, all that plus the work on the island itself: the distillery and the vitriol works . . . An ambitious experiment that he'd had energy for when he was single and later a newly married man and after that a new father. To tell the truth, it wasn't really that the enterprise hadn't worked; it was simply that he couldn't be bothered with it any more. Amelia had disappeared and so had his zest for the work. There was profit enough in his other enterprises – the farms were doing well and his shares in his father's mining operation made him wealthy. Why rack his brains solving one problem after another, to make a success of this, when it was so much easier to let it go? There was a peculiar satisfaction in the dismantling, auctioning off, melting down and dispersal of the world he had spent so much time and money building up. Making his meticulous lists was an opportunity to forget. He counted, measured, listed, and felt soothed in his boredom. It helped him forget Amelia.

Today he had woken grasping after the tail end of a dream, and though he could not remember it, he suspected it was the dream – too terrible to speak of – that he had suffered frequently in the first days of their loss. It left him feeling hollowed out. Later, as he crossed the yard, the wind had delivered to his ears a snatch of a child's high-pitched voice picked up some distance away. Of course, all little children's voices sound the same from afar. They just do. But the two things had unsettled him and put him in need of this dulling occupation.

Now, in the store room, his eye alighted on something that opened a chasm into the past and made him flinch. It was a jar of barley-sugar canes in a dusty corner. Suddenly she was there – fingers reaching into the mouth of the jar, delighted when two canes came out so tightly welded together that they could not be separated and she was allowed to eat them both. His heart beat painfully and the jar slipped through his fingers and smashed on the concrete floor. That had done it. He would not regain his peace of mind today, not now she had materialized here in the store room.

He called for a broom to sweep it all and when he heard running supposed it was his assistant, but to Vaughan's surprise, it was a member of his domestic staff that appeared: Newman, his gardener. Though out of breath, the man began to speak; his words were so shaken about by the great gasps of breath he was obliged to take that his meaning was not easy to make out. Vaughan caught the word *drowned*.

'Slow down, Newman, take your time.'

The gardener began again and this time something approximating the story of the girl who died and lived again emerged. 'At the Swan at Radcot,' he finished. And in a hushed voice, as though he hardly dared to say it, 'They say she is about four.'

'Christ in heaven!' Vaughan's hands rose halfway to his head, then he gathered himself. 'Try not to let my wife hear about it, will you?' he asked. But even before the gardener spoke again, he could see it was too late.

'Mrs Vaughan has gone up there already, by herself. Mrs Jellicoe who does the laundry brought the news – she heard it from one of the

Swan's regulars last night. We couldn't know what she was going to say – if we had we wouldn't have let her near, but we thought she was going to hand in her notice. The next thing we knew, Mrs Vaughan was racing down to the boathouse and there was not a thing we could do to stop her. By the time we got there, she had took the old rowing boat and was almost out of sight.'

Vaughan ran home, where the stable boy, anticipating his need, had readied his horse. 'You'll have to fly to catch her,' he warned. Vaughan mounted and took the direction of Radcot. For the first few minutes he galloped as fast as he could, then he slowed to a trot. *Fly?* he thought. *I'll never catch her.* He had rowed with her in the early days of their marriage and she was as expert a rower as any man he knew. She was slim, which made her light, and she was strong. Thanks to her father, she had been in and out of boats since before she could walk, and her blades dipped without a splash into the water, rose out of it as cleanly as a leaping fish. Where others grew scarlet and sweated with effort, her cheeks simply took on a serene rose flush, and she gleamed with contentment, feeling the pull of the water. Some women softened with grief, but in Helena it had burnt away the little softness she was starting to develop since their daughter's arrival, and honed her. She was all wire and muscle, fired with determination, and she had a half-hour head start. Fly and catch her? Not a chance. Helena was out of reach. She had been for a long time.

It was hope that had her always so far ahead of him. He had parted company with hope long ago. If Helena would only do the same, happiness might – he thought – eventually be restored to them. Instead of which she stoked her hope, fed it with any trifle she could lay her hands on, and when there was nothing to feed it, she nourished it with some stubborn faith of her own making. In vain he had tried to console her and comfort her, in vain offered images of other futures, different lives.

'We could go and live abroad,' he had suggested. They had spoken of it when they first married, it was a notion for the years ahead. 'Why not?' she had said then, before Amelia's disappearance, before Amelia had existed at all. And so he had suggested it again. They might go to New Zealand for a year – two, even. And why come back? They needn't. New Zealand was a fine place to work, to live . . .

Helena had been appalled. 'And how will Amelia find us there?'

He had talked of the other children they had always expected. But future children were immaterial, mere abstractions to his wife. Only to him did they appear incarnate, in his dreams and in his waking hours. The marital intimacies that had ceased so abruptly the night their daughter disappeared had not been resumed in the two years since. Before Helena, he had lived unmarried and more or less celibate for many years. Where other men paid for women or took up with girls they could later abandon, he went to bed alone and fell back on his own devices. He had no desire to return to this mode of life now. If his wife could not love him, then nothing. The spirit faded. He no longer expected pleasure of his own body or hers. He had given up one hope after another.

She blamed him. He blamed himself. It was a father's job to keep his children from harm, and he had failed.

Vaughan realized that he was stationary. His mount had its muzzle to the ground, exploring for something sweet among the winter bracken. 'There's nothing there for you. Nothing for me either.' He was overwhelmed with a great weariness. For a moment he wondered whether he was ill, whether he could in fact go on. He remembered somebody saying something, quite recently . . . *You can't go on like this.* Oh, it was the woman in Oxford. Mrs Constantine. What a foolish expedition that had turned out to be. But she was right about that. He couldn't go on.

He went on.

There was an unusual number of people packed into the Swan, he thought, given the time of day and the season. They looked up at him with the curiosity of those for whom something is already underway and further interest can confidently be expected. He paid them no attention and made straight for the bar, where a woman took one look at him and said, 'Follow me.'

She led him through a short panelled passageway to an old oak door. She opened it and stepped aside to let him enter first.

There were too many shocks: he could not separate one from another. Only afterwards was he able to tease out the many impressions that rushed upon him into separate strands and put words and an order to them. First there was the bewilderment of expecting to see his wife and failing to find her there. Second was the confusion of seeing a very familiar face that he had not seen for a long time. A young woman, scarcely more than a child really, whom he had once asked to marry him, and who had said *Yes*, with laughter, *yes, if I can bring my boat.* She turned a radiant face to him and smiled, her lips wide with easy happiness, her eyes brightly luminous with love.

Vaughan stopped dead in his tracks. Helena. His wife – bold, joyous and magnificent, as she had been. Before.

She laughed.

'Oh, Anthony! What's the matter with you!'

She looked down, took hold of something, speaking in a cajoling, sing-song voice that he remembered from another time. 'Look,' she said, though not to him. 'Look who it is.'

The third shock.

She turned the little person to face him.

'Daddy's here!'

The Sleeper Wakes

MEANWHILE, A MAN with black-stained fingertips and a broken face lay sleeping in the pilgrims' room of the Swan at Radcot. He lay on his back, his head on Margot's feather pillow, and but for the rise and fall of his chest, he did not stir.

There are any number of ways you might imagine sleep, none of them likely to be accurate. We cannot know what entering sleep feels like, for by the time it is complete, the ability to commit it to memory is lost. But we all know the gently plummeting feeling that precedes falling asleep and gives it its name.

When he was ten, Henry Daunt saw a picture of an ash tree whose roots plunged into an underground river in which lived strange mermaids or naiads, called the Maidens of Destiny. When he thought of the descent into sleep, it was something very like this subterranean waterway that he envisaged. He had a sense of his slumber as a lengthy swimming session, in which he navigated slowly through water that was thicker than usual, with effortless pleasant movements that propelled him in one direction or another with a kind of vivid aimlessness. Sometimes the skin of the water was only a little way above his head, and his daytime world, its troubles and pleasures, was still there, pursuing him from the other side. On those occasions he would wake feeling as though he had not slept at all. Most of the time, though, he slept easily, awoke refreshed, sometimes with the happy sense that he had met friends in his sleep, or that his mother (though dead) had communicated some loving message to him in the night. He didn't mind this at all. He did mind waking just as the last traces of some interesting nocturnal adventure were lost to the tide.

None of these things happened in the Swan at Radcot. While life was at work in him, crusting blood over gashes and doing all manner of intricate work inside the skull box that had taken such a battering at Devil's Weir, Henry Daunt sank, sank, sank to the darkest depths of his vast underwater cavern, where nothing ebbed and nothing flowed and all was as dark and still as the grave. He remained there for an unmeasurable length of time, and at the end of it, memory awoke and the still depths shivered and came to life.

A number of experiences then drifted into his mind and out again, in no particular order.

A dull sensation that was the disappointment of his marriage.

A stinging in his fingertips that was the cold he felt yesterday at Trewsbury Mead, when he had stopped the trickle that was the Thames with his forefinger and waited for the water to build up behind it till the volume became too great and it overspilt.

A whole body swooping and gliding – skating on the frozen Thames as a young man of twenty; he had met his wife that day and the gliding had continued for many weeks, all through the rest of the winter to a day at the beginning of spring that was his wedding day.

The slack-jawed astonishment, the fisticuffs in the brain, on seeing an empty space in the skyline where the roof of the old friary gatehouse used to be – he was six, it was the first time he realized the physical world could be subject to such change.

A crash of glass; his father, the glazier, cursing in the yard.

So the contents of the skull satisfied themselves that they were in place, complete, whole.

Finally came something different from all the rest. A thing that belonged in another category altogether. It was not unfamiliar – he had dreamt it before, more often than he knew. It was always out of focus, for he had never set eyes on it in the real world, only in his imagination. It was a child. Daunt's child. The one he had failed to make with Miriam, and not tried to make with anybody else. It was his future child. The image drifted past, there and gone again, and it roused a response in the sleeping man, who attempted to lift his leaden limbs to grasp it. It drifted out of reach, not without leaving behind the sense that there had been something more urgent about the dream image this time. Was it not more vivid? It was a little *girl*, wasn't it? But the moment had passed.

Now the scene in Henry Daunt's mind altered once again. A landscape, unfamiliar and unsettling, deeply personal. A blasted terrain. Jagged, rocky outcrops. Churned-up gashes in the land. Bulbous protuberances. There must have been – what? A war? An earthquake?

Consciousness cast a dim illumination and thought began to stir in Henry Daunt. This landscape was not something seen, but something else . . . These were not images, no, but pieces of information passed to his brain . . . by *his tongue* . . . The rocks translated themselves into the broken rubble of teeth. The mess of disrupted earth was the flesh of his mouth.

Awake.

He stiffened in alarm. Pain shot through his limbs, took him by surprise.

What has happened?

He opened his eyes – to darkness. Darkness? Or . . . was he *blindfolded*?

In panic his hands rose to his face – more pain – and where his face ought to be, his fingers met something foreign. Some padding, thicker than skin, unfeeling, stretched over his bones. He sought the edge of it, desperate to pull it off, but his fingers were thick and clumsy . . .

A flurry of sound. A voice – a woman:

'Mr Daunt!'

He felt his hands gripped by other hands, hands that were surprisingly strong and that prevented him from tearing off the blindfold.

'Don't scrabble! You are injured. I expect you're feeling numb. You are safe. This is the Swan at Radcot. There was an accident. Do you remember?'

A word sprang nimbly from his mind to his tongue; once there it stumbled over the rubble in his mouth and when it emerged he didn't recognize it. He had another go, more arduously:

'Eyes!'

'Your eyes are swollen. You knocked your head in the accident. You will be able to see perfectly well once the swelling has gone down.'

The hands brought his own away from his face. He heard liquid being poured, but his ears couldn't tell him what colour the liquid was or what the pitcher was made of or what size the drinking vessel was. He felt the tilt that comes when a person sits on the edge of the bed, but could not tell what manner of person it was. The world was suddenly unknowable; he was marooned in it.

'Eyes!'

The woman took hold of his hands again. 'It is only swelling. You will see again as soon as it subsides. Here, a drink. It will feel clumsy, I expect you will have lost sensation in your lips, but I will tip it for you.'

She was right. There was no warning, no touch of rim on lip, only the sudden sensation of sweet wetness in his mouth. He indicated with a grunt that he would swallow more, but 'Little sips, frequently,' she said.

'Do you remember arriving here?' she asked.

He thought. His memory seemed unfamiliar to him. There were images reflected in fragmentary style on the surface of it that couldn't really belong there. He made a noise, a gesture of uncertainty.

'The little girl you brought in – can you tell us who she is?'

A tap on wood, a door opening.

A new voice: 'I thought I heard voices. Here she is.'

The mattress returned to the level as the woman beside him stood up.

He raised his hand to his face, and this time, knowing that the insensate padding was his skin, detected a line of spikes. The tips of his eyelashes, their length half buried in the inflamed lids. He applied clumsy pressure above and below the line and pulled apart—'No!' the woman cried, but it was too late. Light pierced his eye, and he gasped. It was the pain, and something else besides: on its wave the light carried an image and it was the image he had dreamt. The drifting girl, his future child, infant of his imagination.

'Is this your little girl?' said the newcomer.

A child whose eyes were the colour of the Thames and as inexpressive.

Yes, said his leaping heart. *Yes. Yes.*

'No,' he said.

A Tragic Tale

ALL THROUGH THE hours of daylight the drinkers had been discussing events at the Swan. Everybody knew that Mr and Mrs Vaughan were in Margot and Joe's private sitting room at the back, where they had been reunited with Amelia. Word had also got about that a rich Negro, Robert Armstrong from Kelmscott, had been there at first light and that his son was expected later. The name Robin Armstrong was broadcast.

A curtain was drawn back in every man's inner theatre and their storytelling minds got to work. On the stage were the same four figures: Mr Vaughan, Mrs Vaughan, Robin Armstrong and the girl. The scenes that played out in the many heads were full of striking melodrama. There were seething looks, dark glances, calculating squints. Words were delivered in hisses, with stern decorum and in shrill alarm. The child was snatched from party to party, like a doll amongst jealous children. One farmhand of a counting disposition found his mind arranging an auction of the child, while the brawlers who had temporarily deserted the Plough indulged in fantasies in which Mr Vaughan drew a weapon from his inner pocket – revolver? dagger? – and set about Mr Armstrong with a true father's determination. One ingenious mind returned the power of speech to the child at the moment of highest tension: 'Papa!' she called, lifting her arms to Mr Armstrong and dashing for ever the hopes of the Vaughans, who fell weeping into each other's embrace. The role of Mrs Vaughan in these theatricals was confined largely to weeping, which she accomplished sometimes in a chair, frequently on the floor, and ending generally in a faint. One young cressman, in a flourish he was most proud of, imagined a role for the unconscious man in the bed: coming round from his long slumber and hearing an altercation in the next room, he would rise and enter the sitting room (stage left) and there, like Solomon, declare that the child must be sliced in two and given half to the Vaughans and half to Armstrong. That would do it.

When the last of the day had drained from the sky and it was past five o'clock and the river ran glinting in the darkness, a man rode up to the Swan and dismounted. The noise of the winter room was deafening, and before anyone noticed the door opening to let the man in, he had already closed it behind him. He stood for a little while, hearing his name in the general din, before anybody remarked on his presence, and even when they did see him, they failed to realize he was the one they were expecting. Those who had an idea what the older Mr Armstrong looked like – and the story was already being circulated that he was the bastard son of a prince and a slave girl – were waiting for a tall, strong and dark-skinned fellow; no wonder they did not recognize this young man, for he was pale and slender, with light-brown hair that fell into soft curls where it touched his collar. There was something of the boy still about him: his eyes were so palely blue they seemed nothing but reflection and his skin was soft like a girl's. Margot was the first to spot him and she was not sure whether it was her maternal or her womanly instincts that stirred at the sight of him, for whether he was youth or man, he was pleasing to the eye.

He made his way to Margot. When he told her his name in an undertone, she drew him away from the public room and into the little corridor at the back that was lit by a single candle.

'I don't know what to say, Mr Armstrong. And you having lost your poor lady too. You see, since your father was here this morning—'

He stopped her. 'It's all right. I overtook your parson on my way here. He hailed me, guessing the reason for my direction and my haste, and has . . .' He paused, and in the shadows of the corridor Margot supposed he was wiping away a tear, gathering himself to go on. 'He has explained everything. It is not Alice, after all. Another family has claimed her.' He lowered his head. 'I thought it better to come anyway, since I was so near and you were expecting me. But now I shall take my leave. Please tell Mr and Mrs Vaughan I am very . . .' – again his voice broke – '*very* pleased for them.'

'Oh, but you must not go without at least taking something. A glass of ale? Some hot punch? You have come a long way, sit and rest for a while. Mr and Mrs Vaughan are in the sitting room and hoping to offer you their condolences . . .'

She opened the door and ushered him in.

Robin Armstrong entered the room with a gauche and apologetic air. Mr Vaughan, disarmed by this, had reached out and shaken him by the hand before he realized he was going to do it.

'I'm sorry,' both men said at the same moment, and then 'Very awkward,' in chorus, so it was impossible to know which had spoken first.

Mrs Vaughan gathered herself before either of the two men seemed able to. 'We are so sorry, Mr Armstrong, to hear of your loss.'

He turned to her—

'What?' she said, after a moment. 'What is it?'

He stared at the child in her lap.

The young Mr Armstrong wavered on his feet, then sank, leaning heavily on Margot, into the chair that Vaughan had just time to place behind him before his eyes fluttered to a close and he slumped.

'Heavens above!' Margot exclaimed and she dashed to fetch Rita from the sleeping photographer's room.

'He has had a long journey,' said Helena, as she leant in kindness over the unconscious man. 'In such hope – and to find that she is not here . . . It's the shock.'

'Helena,' said Mr Vaughan, a note of warning in his voice.

'The nurse will know what to do to revive him.'

'*Helena*.'

'She is bound to have some cloves or sal volatile.'

'*Helena!*'

Helena turned to her husband. 'What is it?'

Her brow was clear, her eyes were transparent.

'Dearest,' he said, and his voice shook. 'Is it not possible that there is a different reason for the young man's collapse?'

'What reason?'

He quailed at the innocent puzzlement on her face.

'Suppose . . .' Words failed him, and he gestured in the direction of the child, who sat sleepily indifferent in the chair. 'Suppose that, after all . . .'

The door opened and Margot hurried in, followed by Rita, who with calm assurance crouched at the side of the young man and took his wrist in one hand while she held her watch in the other.

'He's coming round,' Margot announced, seeing his eyelids stir. She took one of his passive hands in hers and rubbed it.

Rita cast a sharp glance at the patient's face. 'He'll be all right,' she agreed without intonation as she put her watch back in her pocket.

The young man's eyes opened. He took a couple of light, fluttering breaths, and raised his palms to cover his dazed-looking expression. When he lowered them he was himself once more.

He looked at the child again.

'Reason says she is not Alice.' He spoke haltingly. 'She is your child. The parson says so. You say so. It is so.'

Helena nodded and she blinked away tears of sympathy for the young father.

'No doubt you are wondering why I could so easily mistake another man's child for my own. It is nearly a year since I last saw my daughter. Presumably you do not know the circumstances in which I find myself. I owe you an explanation.

'My marriage took place in secret. When my wife's family first learnt of the attachment between us and our plans for a betrothal, they placed obstacles in our path. We were young and foolish. Neither of us understood what harm we did ourselves and our families by marrying in secret, but that is what we did. My wife ran away to live with me, and our child was born less than a year later. We hoped – we trusted, even – that a grandchild would soften her parents' resistance, but that wish was in vain and they continued as unyielding as ever. Over time my wife grew fretful for the many comforts that had accompanied her life in her earlier days. She found it hard raising a child without the benefit of a household of servants to make life easy.

I did all I could to maintain her good spirits and encourage her to trust in love, but in the end she became convinced that the only way forward was for me to move to Oxford, where I had friends in positions of influence, and try my fortune there, where if things went favourably for me I might earn more and we might in a year or two be able to lead the leisured life she hankered after. So with a heavy heart I left Bampton and set up in rooms in Oxford.

'I was lucky. I found work and was soon earning more than I had before, and although I missed my wife and child a good deal, I tried to make myself believe it was all for the best. In her letters, which were not frequent, I got the impression that she was happier too. Whenever possible I came back to see them both, and so for six months we went on. Once, about a year ago, my work brought me unexpectedly upriver and I thought it would be a pleasant thing to surprise the two of them with an impromptu visit.' He swallowed, shifted in his chair. 'I made a discovery then that altered my relationship with my wife for ever. She was not alone. The person with her – the least said about him, the better. The child's way with him told me that this man was a regular in the household, an intimate of the family. Harsh words were spoken and I came away.

'A little later, and while I was still in a quandary about what to do, I received a letter from my wife in which she proposed to live with this man as his wife, and saying that she wished to have no more to do with me. I could have protested at this, of course. I could have insisted that she obey her vows. As things have turned out, I rather wish I had. It would have been better all round. But in my disarray I replied that since it was what she wished, I agreed to the arrangement, and that as soon as I had earnt what I needed to provide a proper home for her, I would come for Alice. I wrote that I expected this to be before a year was out, and from that day I threw myself into my work in order to make it so.

'I have not seen my wife since that time, but have recently taken on the lease of a house and was making arrangements to live there with the child. I expected that one of my sisters would come and be a mother to her. This morning, on the point of realizing these plans, I received a visit from my father who came with news of my wife's death. He told me at the same time that Alice was missing. From others I have learnt that my wife was abandoned by her lover some months ago, and that she and the child have been in need ever since. I can only presume that it was out of shame that she did not contact me.'

Through his entire account, Robin Armstrong's gaze was drawn persistently to the child's face. More than once he lost the thread of his tale, and had to drag his eyes away from her and concentrate to pick up where he had left off, but after a few sentences his eyes would drift back and find her again.

He sighed heavily.

'It is a story I would not willingly have told, for not only does it expose my poor wife's sad folly to the wider world, but it puts me in a bad light. Do not blame her, for she was young. It was I who encouraged her to a secret marriage, I whose weakness in crisis led to her downfall, her death and the loss of our daughter. It is a sad story unfit for the ears of good people like yourselves. I ought perhaps to have told it with greater delicacy. Had I my wits about me, my story would have been less blunt in the telling, but it takes a little while for a man to gather himself after a shock. So please forgive me if I have been improperly frank, and remember I have been driven to it by the need to give you a reasonable explanation for my reaction here today.

'It is true that on seeing your daughter I felt as if I was face to face with my own beloved Alice. But it is plain that she does not know me. And though she resembles Alice – to a very striking degree – I must remind myself that I have not seen her in nearly twelve months and children are apt to change, are they not?'

He turned to Margot.

'No doubt you have children of your own, Madam, and will be able to confirm that I am right in this?'

Margot jumped at being addressed. She wiped away the tear that Robin's story had put in her eye, and some confusion prevented her from giving an immediate answer.

'I am right, am I not?' he repeated. 'Little children are apt to change in a twelvemonth?'

'Well . . . Yes, I suppose they *do* change . . .' Margot sounded uncertain.

Robin Armstrong rose from his chair and spoke to the Vaughans.

'It was my grief that jumped ahead of my reason to recognize your child as my own. I apologize if I have alarmed you. I did not intend any harm.'

He brought his fingers to his lips, stretched out a hand and, obtaining permission from Helena with a glance, touched a gentle kiss upon the child's cheek. His eyes filled with tears, but before they could fall he had bowed his head to the ladies, bid them farewell and was gone.

In the silence that followed Robin Armstrong's exit, Vaughan turned his back to stare out of the window. The elms' branches were black against the charcoal sky and his thoughts seemed tangled in the mazy treetops.

Margot opened her mouth to speak and closed it half a dozen times, blinking in perplexity.

Helena Vaughan drew the child close and rocked her.

'Poor, poor man,' she said in a low voice. 'We must pray that he finds his Alice again – as we have found our Amelia.'

Rita did not stare and nor did she blink or speak. All the while Robin had been giving his account of himself, she had sat on the stool in the corner of the room, observing and listening. Now that he was gone she continued to sit, with the air of someone doing a mildly challenging long-division calculation in her head. What kind of a man is it, she was thinking, who appears to faint, and then comes round, though all the while *his pulse does not falter*?

After a time she evidently arrived at the end of her reflections, for she put her thinking face away and rose to her feet.

'I must go and see how Mr Daunt is doing,' she said, and she let herself quietly out of the room.

The Tale of the Ferryman

HENRY DAUNT SLEPT and woke and slept again. He emerged each time a bit less bewildered, a bit more himself. It was not like the worst hangover he had ever had, but it was more akin to that than anything else he had ever experienced. He was still blinded by his own eyelids, which pressed firmly to each other and against his eyeballs.

Till he was five years old Henry Daunt had cried persistently at night. Roused by her son's inconsolable wailing in the dark, it had taken a long time for his mother to realize it wasn't that he was afraid of the dark, but another reason. 'There's nothing to see,' he sobbed at last, heartbroken, which put an end to her misunderstanding. 'Of course there's nothing to see,' she told him. 'It's night. Night is for sleeping.' He would not be persuaded. His father had sighed. 'That boy was born with his eyes open and hasn't shut them since.' But it was he who had found the solution. 'Look at the patterns on the inside of your eyelids. Pretty floating shapes, you'll see, all different colours.' Warily, fearing a trick, Henry had closed his eyes and been entranced.

Later he'd taught himself to conjure up visions from memory with his eyes shut, and enjoy them as freely as when they were present before his daytime gaze. More freely, even. He reached an age where it was the Maidens of Destiny he conjured to entertain his night-time hours. The underground mermaids rose out of churning water, their torsos half concealed by rounded lines that might have been waves, or curling locks, but might conceivably (if you were a boy of fourteen) not have been concealment at all but the actual curves of actual breasts.

This was the image he lingered over in the dark hours. A creature with streaming hair, half-woman, half-river, cavorted with him and her caresses were so intoxicating that they had the same effect on him that a real woman might. His hand curled around himself and he was solid as an oar. A few tugs were enough, he was pulled into the current, he was the current, he dissolved into bliss.

Thinking about all this, and remembering the Maidens of Destiny, it occurred to him now to wonder what the nurse Rita Sunday looked like. He knew she was there, in the room with him. There was a chair diagonally left beyond the foot of the bed, by a window. He'd worked that much out. That was where she was now, silent, motionless – believing him to be asleep, no doubt. He tried to piece together an image of her. Her grip had been firm when she tried to draw his hands from his eyes. She was strong, then. He knew she was not short, for when she was standing her voice came from a high spot in the room. There was an assurance in her footsteps and movements that told him she was neither very young nor very old. Was she fair or dark? Pretty or plain? She must be plain, he thought. Otherwise she would be married, and if she were married she would not be here nursing a strange man alone in a bedroom. She was probably reading in the chair. Or thinking. He wondered what she was thinking about. This strange business with the girl, in all likelihood. He would think about it too, if he only knew where to start.

'What do you make of it all?' she asked.

'How did you know I was awake?' he asked when he had got over the fleeting notion that she could read his mind.

'Your breathing pattern told me. Tell me what happened last night. Start with the accident.'

How *had* it happened?

It is a good thing to be solo on the river. There is freedom. You are neither in one place nor the other, but always on the move, in between. You escape everything and belong to no one. Daunt remembered the feeling: there was pleasure in the way his body organized itself with and against the water, with and against the air, pleasure in that quivering, precarious poise, when the river challenges and muscles respond.

That was how it had been yesterday. He had been lost to himself. His eyes had seen only the river, his mind wholly engaged with predicting her caprices, his limbs a machine that responded to her every motion. There was a moment of glory, when body, boat and river combined in a ballet of withholding and giving, tension and relaxation, resistance and flow . . . It was sublime – and the sublime is not to be trusted.

It's not that he hadn't considered Devil's Weir in advance. How to manage it, whether there would be someone about to help haul the boat out and drag it round. He had been aware of the other possibility too. It being winter and there being scarcely any fall to think of . . . He knew how to do it: draw the oars in, keep them ready to steady the boat the other side, and at the same time – rapidly, in a single smooth motion – throw yourself back and lie low. Get it wrong and you'll either take a blow to the head or crack your blade, or both. But he knew. He'd done it before.

What had gone wrong? Seduced by the river, he'd fallen into that state of transcendence – that was his error. He might have got away with it, except that then – as he remembered it now – three things had come upon him at once.

The first was that, without his noticing it, time had passed and the light faded to a dim grey.

The second was that some shape – vague, hard to pin down – caught his eye and distracted him at just the moment he most needed to concentrate.

The third was Devil's Weir. Here. Now.

The current had taken possession of the canoe – he flung himself back – the river surged, a great liquid limb rising beneath him, thrusting him up – the underside of the weir, black-wet, solid as a tree trunk, hurtling in the direction of his nose – not even the time to exclaim *Oh!* before—

He tried to explain all this to the nurse. It was a lot to say when his own mouth was a foreign country and every word a new and arduous route through the alphabet. At first he was slow, his speech clumsy, and he semaphored with his hands to fill the gaps in his account.

Sometimes she chipped in, anticipating intelligently what he meant to say, and he grunted to indicate, *Yes, that's right*. Little by little, he found ways of approximating the sounds he needed and became more fluent.

'And is that where you found her? At Devil's Weir?'

'No. Here.'

He'd come round under the night sky. Too cold to feel pain, but knowing by animal instinct he was injured. Understanding that he needed warmth and shelter if he were to survive. He had clambered out of the boat carefully for fear of collapsing in the cold, cold water. It was then that the white shape had come drifting towards him. He'd known instantly that it was the body of a child. He'd stretched out his arms and the river delivered her neatly into them.

'And you thought she was dead.'

He grunted *yes*.

'Hm.' He heard her take a breath, put the thought aside for later. 'But how did you get from Devil's Weir to here? A man with your injuries in a damaged boat – you can't have done it alone.'

He shook his head. He had no idea.

'I wonder what it was that you saw? The thing that distracted you at Devil's Weir.'

Daunt was a man whose memory was made of pictures. He found one: the pale moon suspended above the river; he found another: the looming weir, massive against a darkening sky. There was something else too. It hurt his face to frown as he tried to make sense of it. Like a photographic plate, his mind usually registered clear outlines, detail, tones, perspectives. This time he found only a blur. It was like a photograph where the subject has moved, dancing through the fifteen seconds of exposure that are required to give the illusion of a single moment. He would have liked to go back and live that moment again if he could, open it up and stretch it out full length to see what it was that had left this blur on his retina.

He shook his head in uncertainty; winced at the movement.

'Was it a person? Perhaps someone saw what happened and helped you?'

Was it? Tentatively, he nodded.

'On the bank?'

'River.' That he was sure of.

'Gypsy boats? They are never far away at this time of year.'

'A single vessel.'

'Another rowing boat?'

'No.'

'A barge?'

His blur was not a barge. It was slighter, a few lines merely . . . 'A punt, perhaps?' Now that he had heard himself suggest it, the blur resolved itself a fraction. A long, low vessel navigated by a tall, lean figure . . . 'Yes, I think so.'

He heard the nurse half laugh. 'Be careful who you tell. They will have it that you have met Quietly.'

'Who?'

'Quietly. The ferryman. He sees to it that those who get into trouble on the river make it safely home again. Unless it is their time. In which case, he sees them to *the other side of the river*.' She pronounced those last words in a tone of half-comic gravity.

He laughed, felt the pull of pain at his split lip, and drew in breath sharply.

Footsteps. The firm and gentle press of cloth at his face, and the sensation of coolness.

'Enough talking for a little while,' she said.

'Your fault. You made me laugh.'

He was reluctant to let the conversation come to an end. 'Tell me about Quietly.'

Her footsteps returned to the chair and he pictured her there, plain and tall and strong, and neither young nor old.

'There are more than a dozen versions. I'll just begin and see what comes.

'Many years ago, in the days when there were fewer bridges than there are today, the Quietlys lived on the banks of the river not very far from here. They were a family with one peculiarity: the men were all mute. That is why they were called Quietly, and nobody remembers their real name. They built punts for a living and for a reasonable price would ferry you across the river from their yard and come and collect you again when you hailed them. The yard passed down from grandfather to father to son, over many generations, along with the inability to speak.

'You might think that being unable to speak would be a difficulty in the matter of romance, but the Quietlys were dependable, kindly men and there are women who like a peaceful life. It so happened that in every generation some woman was found who was content to live without conversation and bear the next generation of punt-builders, and all the little girls could speak and none of the boys.

'At the time of this story, the Quietly of the day had a daughter. She was the apple of his eye, and doted upon by her parents and grandparents alike. One day she went missing. They looked everywhere for the child, alerted neighbours, and till night fell the riverbank rang with the sound of her mother and other people calling her name. She was not found – not that day, nor the next. But after three days her poor drowned body was recovered from a spot a little way downstream, and they buried her.

'Time passed. Through the rest of the winter and the spring and summer and autumn the girl's father continued building punts as before, ferried people over the river when needed, and in the evenings sat smoking by the fireside, but his muteness altered. The silence that had once been warm, good-humoured and full of companionship grew dark and was filled with grey shadows. The year turned full circle and came to the anniversary of the day when the child had disappeared.

'On that day, Quietly's wife returned home from market to find a customer waiting. "If you need to cross the river, it is my husband you want. You will find him in the yard," she told him. But the customer, whose face she now saw was pale, said, "I have already found him. He took me halfway across the river and when we were at the deepest place he handed me the pole and stepped out of the punt."'

Rita paused to take a sip of tea.

'And he haunts the river till this day?' Daunt asked.

'The story isn't over yet. After three days, Quietly's wife was weeping by the fireside at midnight when there came a knock at the door.

She could not think of a single person likely to call on her at such a late hour. Could it be someone wishing to cross the river? She went to the door. Out of fear she did not open it, but only called, "It is too late. Wait till morning and my father-in-law will take you across."

'The answer came: "Mama! Let me in! It's cold outside."

'With trembling hands she unlocked the door and in the porch found her own little girl, the one she had buried a year ago, alive and well. Behind the child was her husband, Quietly. She clutched the girl in her arms, wept to have her back, too overjoyed at first to wonder how such a thing had come to pass. Then she thought, *It cannot be*, and she held the child at arm's length to stare at her, but it was unmistakeably the very same daughter she had lost twelve months before.

'"Where did you come from?" she asked in wonderment, and the little girl answered, "From that place on the other side of the river. Daddy came to get me."

'The woman turned her eyes to her husband. Quietly stood a little way back from the child, not in the porch, but on the path.

'"Come in, dear," she said, and opened the door wide and gestured to the hearth, where the fire was lit and his pipe was still on the mantel. But Quietly did not step forwards. She couldn't help but notice he was altered, though it was hard to say exactly how. Perhaps he was paler and thinner than he had been before, or perhaps it was his eyes that were a darker version of the colour they had been before.

'"Come in!" she repeated, and Quietly shook his head.

'She understood then that he would never be able to come inside again.

'The good woman drew her daughter inside and closed the door, and since that day any number of people have met Quietly on the river. There was a price to be paid for the return of his daughter and he paid it. For all eternity he must watch over the river, waiting for someone to get into difficulty, and then, if it is not their time, he sees them safely to the bank, and if it *is* their time, he sees them safely to that other place, the one he went to in search of his child, and there they must remain.'

They gave the story the silent pause it deserved, and when it was over, Daunt spoke again.

'So it was not my time, and Quietly towed me to Radcot.'

'If the story is to be believed.'

'Do you believe it?'

'Of course not.'

'It's a good story, nonetheless. The devoted father rescuing his child at the price of his own life.'

'It cost him more than that,' Rita said. 'It cost him his death too. There is no eternal rest for Quietly, he must exist for ever between the two states, policing its border.'

'You don't believe that either,' he said. 'Do they believe it here?'

'Beszant the boat-mender does. He reckons he saw him, when he was a youth and slipped on the jetty. The cressmen think Quietly keeps them safe when the river rises up the fields and turns them marshy. One of the gravel-diggers was a sceptic till the day he got his ankle trapped underwater. He swears blind it was Quietly that reached down and freed him.'

The conversation put Daunt in mind of the child. 'I thought she was dead,' he told her. 'She came drifting into my arms, white and cold and with her eyes closed . . . I would have sworn she was dead.'

'They all thought so too.'

'But not you.'

'I too. I was certain of it.' There was a thoughtful silence in the room. He thought of questions he might ask, but stilled his tongue. Something told him there might be more to come if he waited, and he was right.

'You are a photographer, Mr Daunt, which makes you a scientist. I am a nurse, which makes me a scientist too, but I cannot explain what I witnessed last night.' She spoke slowly and with great calm, choosing her words carefully. 'The girl was not breathing. She had no pulse. Her pupils were dilated. The body was cold. The skin was white. According to every rule in the textbook, she was dead. I had no doubt about it. After I had checked for signs of life and found none, I might easily have come away. I don't know why I stayed, except that I felt uneasy for reasons I could not explain to myself. For a short time – between two minutes and three in my estimation – I continued to stand by the body. Her hand was between my hands; my fingertips were touching her wrist. In that position I felt something flicker between her skin and mine. It felt like a pulse. But I knew it couldn't be – she was dead.

'Now, it is actually just possible to mistake your own pulse for the pulse of a patient, because there is a pulse in the fingertips. Let me show you.' He heard the rustle of her skirts behind her footsteps as she approached the bed. She took his hand, laid it palm up on her own open palm and placed her other palm over it, so that his hand was enclosed in hers and her fingertips rested lightly at the inside of his wrist. 'There. I can feel your pulse' (his blood lurched at her touch) 'and I can also feel mine. It's a very delicate pulse, but it's mine.'

He murmured a note of understanding in his throat and his senses jumped to attention to catch a flicker of her blood. It was too faint.

'So to avoid all uncertainty I did this . . .' Her hands slipped briskly away, his own was left abandoned on the counterpane; his swell of disappointment ebbed when her fingertips alighted on the tender spot beneath his ear.

'This is a good pulse point. I pressed firmly, waited for another minute. There was nothing. Nothing, and nothing, and more nothing. I told myself I was mad to be standing in the dark and the bitter cold, waiting for a pulse to beat in a dead child. Then it came again.'

'How slow can a heart beat?'

'Children's hearts are faster than adult hearts. A hundred beats a minute is quite ordinary. Sixty is dangerous. Forty is perilous. At forty, you expect the worst.'

On the inside of his eyelids he saw his own thoughts rise in blue, cloud-like shapes. Above them he saw her thoughts, deep maroon and green stripes, moving horizontally from left to right across his field of vision, like slow and intent lightning flashes.

'One beat per minute . . . I have never known the pulse rate of a child fall to less than forty per minute. Except when it falls to zero.'

Her fingertip retained its connection with his skin. In a moment or two she would come out of her distraction and remove it. He tried to keep her in this train of thought.

'Below forty and they die?'

'In my experience, yes.'

'But she wasn't dead.'

'She wasn't dead.'

'She was alive.'

'At one beat a minute? It's not possible.'

'But if it was impossible for her to be living and impossible for her to be dead, what was she?'

His blue clouds of thought dissolved. The leaf-green and plum stripes swelled with intensity and moved so far to the right that they were out of range. She exhaled a lungful of frustration, withdrew her fingers from his neck, and splinters of bronze shot up in his vision as from a falling coal in the fire.

It was he who broke the silence. 'She was like Quietly. Between the two states.'

He heard a puff of exasperation that ended in a half-laugh.

He laughed. The stretch of his skin made him cry out in pain.

'Ow,' he cried. 'Ow!'

It brought her attention back to him, brought the tips of her fingers back to his skin. As she held the cooling cloth against his face, he realized that his vision of Rita Sunday had altered in the course of their conversation. She now looked not altogether unlike the maidens of destiny.

Is It Finished?

THE WINTER ROOM was alive with voices and tightly packed with drinkers, many of them standing, for there were not enough seats. Margot stepped out from the dim corridor and nudged the nearest backs, saying, 'Step aside, please, make room.' They shuffled out of her way and she stepped into the fray. Close behind her, Mr Vaughan appeared with the child wrapped in a blanket in his arms. Behind them came Mrs Vaughan, delivering little nods of thanks to left and right.

At the sight of the child, those first drinkers hushed. Those who were a little deeper in the room caught the sudden drop of noise behind them, found Margot prodding them out of the way, and fell quiet in turn. The girl's head rested on Vaughan's shoulder, her face pressed into his neck, half concealed. Her eyes were closed. The slump of her body told them she was asleep. The silence made faster progress than the Vaughans did, and before they were halfway to the door, the peace was as resounding as the din had been a few moments before. The crowd leant and rose on tiptoes and peered hungrily to secure a better view of the girl's sleeping face, and at the back some clambered on to stools and tables to see her. Margot no longer needed to prod and nudge, for the mass of bodies parted of its own accord, and when they reached the door a bargeman stood ready to open it for them.

The Vaughans passed through the door.

Margot nodded at the bargeman to close it behind them. No one had moved. Where the crowd had parted, a curved line of floorboards was still visible. After a moment of stillness when nobody spoke, there came a shuffling of feet, the clearing of throats, and in no time the crowd remassed and the boom of voices was louder even than before.

For another hour they talked. Every detail of the day's events was gone over, the facts were weighed and combined, quantities of surmising, eavesdropping and supposition were stirred in for flavour, and a good sprinkling of rumour added like yeast to make it rise.

There came the sense that the story had now moved on. It was no longer here, at the Swan at Radcot, but out there, in the world. The drinkers remembered the rest of the world: their wives and children, their neighbours, their friends. There were people out there who did not yet know the story of the Vaughans and young Armstrong. In ones and twos, and then in a trickle that became a steady stream, the drinkers departed. Margot organized the more sober of the lingerers to escort the most drunken along the riverbank and see that they did not fall in.

When the door closed on the last of the drinkers and the winter room was empty, Joe set to sweeping the floor. He made frequent pauses to rest on the broom and catch his breath. Jonathan carried in logs. There was an uncharacteristic air of melancholy in his angled eyes as he tipped the logs into the basket by the fire.

'What's the matter, son?'

The boy sighed. 'I wanted her to stay with us.'

His father smiled and ruffled his hair. 'I know you did. But she doesn't belong here.'

Jonathan turned to fetch a second load of logs, but when he got to the door he turned back, unconsoled.

'Is it finished, Dad?'

'Finished?'

Jonathan watched his father put his head on one side and gaze up at the dark corner where the stories came from. Then his eyes came back to Jonathan and he shook his head.

'This is just the beginning, son. There's a long way still to go.'

Part 2

Things Don't Add Up

SITTING ON THE bottom step of the stairs, Lily pushed her right foot into a boot. She held on to the tongue so that it would not get trapped under the laces, but her stocking rucked half a dozen wrinkles at the back of her heel and wedged her foot forwards. She sighed. Her boots were always conspiring to thwart her. Nothing was ever right with them. They pressed on her bunions, they rubbed her raw, and no matter how much straw she packed them with overnight, they always kept a little bit of dampness back to chill her in the morning. She eased her foot out, straightened the stocking, tried again.

When both her boots were on, Lily buttoned up her coat and wound a scarf round her neck. She did not put on gloves, for she had none. Outside, the cold sliced through her coat without resistance and sharpened its blade against her skin, but she scarcely noticed. She was used to it.

Her morning routine never varied. First she went down to the river. Today the level was as she expected, neither high nor low. There was no angry rush and no menacing loitering. The water did not hiss particularly, nor roar, nor dart spiteful splashes at her hem. It flowed steadily, wholly engaged on some calm business of its own, and had not the slightest interest in Lily and her doings. She turned her back on it and went to feed the pigs.

Lily filled one bucket with grain and the other with swill. It released a warmly rotten aroma into the air. The gilt came to the dividing wall as was her habit. She liked to raise her head and scratch the underside of her chin on the top of the low wall. Lily scratched the spot behind the pig's ears at the same time. The gilt grunted in pleasure and gave her a look from beneath her ginger eyelashes. Lily heaved the two buckets out and round to the feeding place, tottering under the weight. One by one, she tipped the contents of the buckets into the trough and then pulled back the planks that barred the opening. When she had done that, she took her own breakfast out of her pocket – one of the less bruised apples from the shelf – and bit into it. She didn't mind a bit of company at breakfast time. The boar came out first – he always did, males put themselves first in everything – and lowered his snout immediately to the trough. The female came after him, her eyes still fixed on Lily, so that once more Lily wondered what the reason could be for such a stare. It was an odd look, almost human, as if the pig wanted something.

Lily finished the flesh of the apple and dropped the core into the pen, making sure it landed where the boar would not see it. The gilt gave her one last indecipherable look – regret? Disappointment? Sorrow? – then lowered her snout to the ground and the apple core disappeared.

Lily cleaned the buckets and put them back in the woodshed. A glance at the sky told her it was time to set off to work, but first, one last thing. She shifted a few logs from the pile and removed one from the third row down. From the front it looked like all the others, but at the back a hollow had been carved out of it. She tilted it and a number of coins rolled out and into her palm. She took care to replace the logs just as she had found them. Indoors she eased a loose brick from the fireplace. Though it looked no different from the others it came away easily, revealing a small cavity behind. She placed the money in the cavity and slid the brick back into place, ensuring that it was exactly level with its neighbours. She closed the door behind her and did not lock it for the simple reason that there was no lock and no key. There was nothing worth stealing at Lily White's place, everybody knew that. Then she left.

The air was knife-cold, but between the rust and black of last year's growth, green was returning to the riverbank. Lily walked briskly, grateful that the ground was hard and let no wetness through the holes in her boots. As she neared Buscot, she peered over the river, to the land that belonged to Buscot Lodge and the Vaughans. There was nobody there.

She will be indoors, then, by the fire, Lily thought. She pictured a hearth, a huge log basket, the fire itself dancing brightly. 'Don't touch, Ann,' she whispered under her breath. 'It's hot.' But they will have a fireguard, being rich people. She nodded. Yes, that's right. She has Ann in a blue velvet dress – no, wool will be warmer, let it be wool. Lily moves in spirit around the house she has never entered. Upstairs is a little bedroom where another fire burns, taking the chill off. There is a bed, and a mattress that is made not of straw but of real lambswool. The blankets are thick and – red? Yes, red, and on the pillow is a doll with plaited hair. There is a Turkey carpet so Ann's feet won't get cold in the morning. Elsewhere the pantry of this house is full of hams and apples and cheese; there is a cook who makes jam and cake; a cupboard contains jar upon jar of honey and in a drawer are half a dozen sugar canes, striped in yellow and white.

Lily explored Ann's new home in perfect contentment, and her version of the interior of Buscot Lodge faded only when she was at the door of the parsonage.

Yes, she thought, as she pushed open the kitchen door. *Ann must live with the Vaughans at Buscot Lodge. She will be safe there. She might even be happy. That is where she must stay.*

The parson was in his study. Lily knew she was rather late, but she could tell by touching the kettle with her fingertips that the parson had not yet made his own tea. She wrenched off her boots and eased her feet into the grey felt shoes she kept under the dresser in the parsonage kitchen. Her feet were always comfortable in them. She had worked for the parson for two months before daring to ask permission to keep a pair of indoor shoes under the kitchen dresser. 'Out of sight, they will be, and it will save your carpets,' she had explained, and when he had said yes, she had asked for some of the savings he kept for her, gone straight to buy them, and then brought them directly back here. Sometimes at the cottage, when she was cold and afraid of ghosts, the thought of her grey felt shoes sitting under the parson's kitchen dresser as if they belonged there was enough to make her feel better.

She boiled water, prepared the tea tray and, when all was ready, made her way to his study and knocked.

'Come!'

The parson was bent over his papers, which showed the bald patch on the top of his head; he was scribbling away at a speed that made her marvel. He came to the end of a sentence and looked up. 'Ah! Mrs White!'

This greeting was one of the pleasures of her life. Never 'Good morning!' or 'Good day!' – greetings that would do for anybody – but always 'Ah! Mrs White!' The sound of the name *White* on his lips was like a blessing.

She put down the tray. 'Shall I make some toast, Parson?'

'Yes, well, later.' He cleared his throat. 'Mrs White . . .' he began in another tone of voice.

Lily started and he adopted an expression of kindly perplexity that only increased her fear about what was coming.

'What is this I hear about you and the child at the Swan?'

Her heart lurched in her chest. What to say? Why a thing so plain to know should be so hard to explain was a puzzle, and she opened and closed her mouth more than once, but no words came out.

The parson spoke again.

'So far as I understand it, you told them at the Swan that the child was your sister?'

His voice was mild, but Lily's lungs flooded with fear. She could scarcely breathe in or out. Then she managed a gulp of air and on the exhalation words streamed out of her. 'I didn't mean any harm by it, and please don't dismiss me, Parson Habgood, and I won't cause any trouble to anyone, I promise.'

The parson contemplated her with an air no less perplexed than before. 'I suppose I can take it that the child is not your sister? We can put it down to a mistake, can we?' His mouth sketched a hesitant, experimental smile, which promised to become a steady, full one when she nodded her head.

Lily did not like lying. She had been driven to it many times, but had never got used to it, had never even grown to be any good at it, but most of all, she did not like it. To lie in her own home was one thing, but here, at the parsonage, that was not quite the house of God but was the house of the parson, which was the next best thing, lying was a much graver thing. She did not want to lose her job . . . She dithered between a lie and the truth, and in the end, unable to measure the dangers one way and the other, it was her nature that won out.

'She *is* my sister.'

She looked down. The toes of the felt shoes were showing under her skirt. Tears came to her eyes and she rubbed them away with the back of her hand. 'She is my only sister, and her name is Ann. I know it is her, Parson Habgood.' The tears she had rubbed away were replaced by others, too numerous to catch. They fell and made dark blotches on the toes of her felt shoes.

'Now then, Mrs White,' said the parson, a little flustered. 'Why don't you sit down?'

Lily shook her head. She had never sat down at the parsonage in her life. She worked here, on her feet and on her knees, fetching and carrying and scrubbing and washing, and that is what gave her the feeling of belonging. To sit down was to be just another parishioner in need of help. 'No,' she muttered. 'No, thank you.'

'Then I shall stand up along with you.'

The parson stood and came out from behind his desk and looked at her thoughtfully.

'Let us think about this together, shall we? Two minds are better than one, they say. To begin with, how old are you, Mrs White?'

Lily stared in bewilderment. 'Well, I . . . I can't say as I know. There was a time I was thirty-something. That was some years ago. I – suppose I must be forty-something now.'

'Hm. And how old would you say the little girl from the Swan is?'

'Four.'

'You sound very sure of that.'

'Because that is her age.'

The parson winced. 'Let us suppose that you are forty-four, Mrs White. We cannot be sure, but you know you are in your forties and so forty-four is likely enough. Do you agree? For the sake of the argument?'

She nodded, not seeing why it mattered.

'The gap between four and forty-four is forty years, Mrs White.'

She frowned.

'How old was your mother, when you were born?'

Lily flinched.

'Is she living, your mother?'

Lily trembled.

'Let's try another way – when did you last see your mother? Recently? Or long ago?'

'Long ago,' she whispered.

The parson, divining another dead end, decided to take another route.

'Suppose your mother had you when she was sixteen. She would have had this little girl forty years later, when she was fifty-six. A dozen years older than you are now.'

Lily blinked, trying and failing to see what all these numbers were about.

'Do you see what I am trying to explain with these calculations, Mrs White? The little girl *cannot* be your sister. The chances of your mother having two daughters so far apart in age is – well, it is so unlikely as to be impossible.'

Lily stared at her shoes.

'What about your father? How old is he?'

Lily shuddered. 'Dead. A long time ago.'

'Well, then. Let us see how things stand. Your mother cannot have brought this little girl into the world. She would have been too old. And your father died a long time ago, so he could not have given life to her either. Therefore she cannot be your sister.'

Lily looked at the splodges on her felt shoes.

'She is my sister.'

The parson sighed and looked around the room for something that would inspire him. He saw only the unfinished work on his desk.

'You know that the child has gone to Buscot Lodge to live with Mr and Mrs Vaughan?'

'I know.'

'It cannot help anyone to say the child is your sister, Mrs White. Least of all the girl herself. Think about that.'

Lily remembered the red blankets and the yellow-and-white-striped sugar canes. She lifted her head at last. 'I know that. I am glad she is there. The Vaughans can look after Ann better than I can.'

'Amelia,' he corrected her very gently. 'She is the daughter they lost two years ago.'

Lily blinked. 'I don't mind what they call her,' she said. 'And I won't make any trouble. Not for them and not for her.'

'Good,' the parson said, still frowning. 'Good.'

The conversation seemed to be at an end.

'Am I to be dismissed, Parson?'

'Dismissed? Gracious, no!'

She clasped her hands at her heart and bobbed her head, for her knees were too stiff for a curtsey. 'Thank you, Parson. I'll start the laundry then, shall I?'

He sat down at his desk and took up the page he had been writing.

'Laundry? . . . Yes, Mrs White.'

When she had done the laundry (and ironed the sheets and made the bed and mopped the floors and beaten the rugs and scrubbed the tiles and filled the log baskets and got the soot off the hearth and polished the furniture and shaken the curtains and knocked air into the cushions and gone round all the picture and mirror frames with a feather duster and put a shine on all the taps with vinegar and cooked the parson's dinner and set it ready on the table under a cloth, and washed up and cleaned the stove and left everything in the kitchen neat and tidy), Lily went and knocked again at the study door.

The parson counted her wages into her hand and she took some of the coins and returned the rest to him as usual. He opened his desk drawer and took out the tin in which he kept her savings, opened it and unfolded the piece of paper inside. On it he wrote numbers, which he had explained to her at the beginning: today's date and the amount she was giving him for safekeeping, then the new total of her savings.

'Quite a nice little sum now, Mrs White.'

She nodded and smiled a brief, nervous smile.

'Wouldn't you think of spending some? A pair of gloves? It is so bitter out of doors.'

She shook her head.

'Well then, let me find you something . . .' He left the room briefly and when he came back, held something out to her. 'These still have some use in them. No point them going unused when your hands are cold. Have them.'

She took the gloves and handled them. They were knitted in thick green wool, with only very few holes. It would not be hard to mend them. She could tell from their soft touch how warm they would be on cold mornings along the riverbank.

'Thank you, Parson. It's very kind of you. But I should only lose them.'

She placed the gloves on a corner of his desk, bid the parson farewell and left.

The walk back along the river felt longer than usual. She had to stop at so many places to collect scraps for the pigs, and her bunions complained every step of the way. Her hands were frozen. She had had gloves when she was young. Her mother had knitted them in scarlet yarn and plaited a long string to thread through her sleeves so she couldn't lose them. They had disappeared all the same. She hadn't lost them – they had been taken from her.

By the time she arrived at the cottage it was getting dark, she was cold to her bone marrow and every part of her that could ache was aching. She eyed the lower post as she went by. The river was up compared to this morning. At her feet, its edge had crept a few malevolent inches closer to the house in her absence.

She fed the pigs, and she felt the ginger pig's eye on her, but she did not return the look. She was too tired to wonder about the moods of pigs this evening. Nor did she scratch the pig behind the ears, though the creature snuffled and grunted for her attention.

The crates in the woodshed that had been empty this morning now contained a dozen bottles.

She approached the cottage nervously, opened the door and peered in, before stepping inside. There was nobody there. She checked the cavity behind the loose brick. It was empty. He had been, then. And gone.

She thought she might light a candle for company, but when she went for her candlestick, the candle was gone. So was the bit of cheese she had planned to eat, and the bread, all but the hard crust.

She sat on the steps to take her boots off. It was a struggle. She sat there in her coat and stockinged feet, looking at the damp shape on the floor where the river had dripped endlessly from the chemise of the nightmare sister, and thought.

Lily was slow at thinking; it had always been so, since she was a little thing. She was a woman who let life happen to her without troubling her mind about things more than was necessary. The events of her life, its alterations and meanders, had not been in any way the result of any decisive action on her part, but only accidents of fortune, the hand dealt by an inscrutable God, impositions by other people. She panicked at change, and submitted to it without question. Her only hope for many years had been that things would not get any worse – though generally they had. Contemplation of experience did not come naturally to her. But now that the first shock of Ann's arrival had subsided, she sat on the steps and felt a question struggling to surface.

Ann of the nightmares was a terrifying and vengeful figure, with her raised finger and her black eyes. Ann of the Swan at Radcot – Ann as Lily now saw her at the Vaughans – was a different Ann altogether. She was quiet. She did not stare, nor point, nor dart vindictive looks. She gave no appearance of being set on harming anyone, let alone Lily. This Ann who had come back was much more like Ann as she used to be.

For two hours Lily sat on the steps with the darkness of the sky pressing at the window and the rush of the river in her ears. She thought of Ann who came from the river, dripping horror on to the floorboards. She thought of Ann by the fireplace at Buscot Lodge in her blue wool dress. By the time the watermark on the floor had merged with the general gloom, she had not organized her puzzlement into a question, and she was a long way from finding any answers. All she was left with when she rose stiffly and took her coat off to go to bed was a deep and impenetrable mystery.

A Mother's Eyes

SOMETHING HAPPENS AND then something else happens and then all sorts of other things happen, expected and unexpected, unusual and ordinary. One of the ordinary things that happened as a result of the events at the Swan that night was that Rita came to be the friend of Mrs Vaughan. It began when she heard a knock at her door and found Mr Vaughan on the doorstep.

'I wanted to thank you for everything you did that night. If it weren't for you and your excellent care – well, it doesn't bear thinking about.' He placed an envelope on the table – 'A token of our thanks!' – and asked her to come to Buscot Lodge to check the child's health again. 'We took her to the doctor in Oxford – he told us she is none the worse for her ordeal, but still, a weekly examination will do no harm, eh? That's what my wife wants too – it will be good for our peace of mind, if nothing else.'

Rita fixed a day and time with him and, when he had gone, opened the envelope. It contained a generous payment, large enough to reflect the Vaughans' wealth and the significance of their daughter's life, and small enough not to be embarrassing. It was just right.

The agreed day for Rita's visit to Buscot Lodge was one of blustery rain that excited the surface of the river, turning it into an ever-changing ribbon of pattern and texture. She arrived at the house and was shown into a pleasant drawing room: the yellow wallpaper was bright, comfortable armchairs were arranged agreeably around a welcoming fire, and a large bay window overlooked the garden. On the hearthrug, Mrs Vaughan was lying on her stomach, turning the pages of a book for the child. She rolled over and sprang up in a single agile movement and took both Rita's hands in hers.

'How can we thank you? The doctor in Oxford asked all the same questions as you did and carried out all the same tests. I said to my husband, "You know what that tells us, don't you? Rita is as good as any doctor! We must have her come once a week and check that all is as it should be." And here you are!'

'It is natural after everything that has happened that you don't want to take any chances.'

Helena Vaughan had never had a female friend in her life. Her limited exposure to the company of adult women in drawing rooms had entirely failed to convince her it was a thing to be relished. Decorum and the subdued manners of a lady were lost on the girl who grew up in a boatyard, and that is why Mr Vaughan had been so taken with her – in her exuberance and robust enjoyment of outdoor life, she reminded him of the girls he had grown up with in the mining territory of New Zealand. But in Rita, Helena recognized a woman who had a purpose beyond the drawing room. There were a dozen years between them and much else to make them different, yet Helena felt inclined to like Rita, and the inclination was mutual.

The little girl, who looked rather different now in her blue dress with its white collar and her blue-and-white embroidered shoes, had looked up expectantly on hearing the door open. There was a flare of interest in her eyes that faded on seeing Rita and she returned her attention to the pages. 'You carry on looking at the book together,' Rita said, 'and I'll check her pulse while she's distracted. Not that I really need to – it's so obvious she is healthy.'

That was true. The girl's hair was now gleaming. She had a faint but distinct rosy glow to her cheeks. Her limbs were sturdy and her movements purposeful and deft. She lay on her stomach, like Mrs Vaughan, propped up on her elbows, and her feet in their embroidered indoor shoes swayed in a criss-cross motion in the air above her bent knees. Without a word, but with every air of understanding, she looked at the pages as Mrs Vaughan guided her attention to this and that in the pictures.

From the nearest armchair Rita leant to take hold of the child's wrist. The girl glanced up in surprise, then returned her attention to the book. The child's skin was warm to the touch and her pulse was firm. Rita's mind was occupied with counting the beats and eyeing the hands of her watch as they ticked around the face, but the undercurrents stirred with the memory of falling asleep in the armchair at the Swan, with the little girl on her lap.

'Everything entirely as it should be,' she said, and let the warm wrist go.

'Don't leave yet,' Helena said. 'Cook will be bringing us eggs and toast in a minute. Can't you stay?'

Over breakfast they continued to talk about the child and her health. 'Your husband told me she has not spoken?'

'Not yet.' Mrs Vaughan did not sound concerned. 'The Oxford doctor said her voice will come back. It might take six months, but she will talk again.'

Rita knew better than most that doctors can be reluctant to admit it when they do not have the answer to a question. If no good answer presents itself, some will sooner give a bad answer than no answer at all. She did not tell Mrs Vaughan this.

'Would you say Amelia's speech was normal before?'

'Oh, yes. She babbled the way two-year-olds do. Other people didn't always understand, but we did, didn't we, Amelia?'

Helena's eyes were drawn constantly to the child, and every word she spoke, whatever the subject, came out of a smiling mouth, for it seemed the mere sight of the girl was enough to make her happy. She cut the child's toast into soldiers and encouraged her to dip them into the egg yolk. The girl set about eating with grave attention. When the yolk was gone, Helena placed the spoon in the child's hand for the white and she dabbed it ham-fistedly into the eggshell. Helena watched the girl with contented absorption, and whenever she turned to Rita, the same smile played around her mouth. The happiness that had come with the girl was one she shared profligately, but when Rita felt the radiant smile alight on her, its touch filled her with misgivings. Ordinarily it would have been a joy to see a young woman so happy, especially after lengthy sorrow, but Rita could not help feeling fearful. She had no desire to puncture Helena's joy, but duty bound her to remind Helena that there was a degree of precariousness in the situation.

'What of Mr Armstrong and his missing child? Is there any news?'

'Poor Mr Armstrong.' Helena's pretty face fell into a frown. 'I feel for him. There is no news, none at all.' She sighed in a way that made plain how heartfelt her sympathy was, yet at the same time it seemed to Rita that she made no connection between Mr Armstrong's pain and her own joy. 'Do you think a father feels it as a mother does? The loss, I mean? And the not-knowing?'

'It depends on the father, I should think. And the mother.'

'I expect you're right. My father would have been devastated to lose me. And Mr Armstrong seemed a very . . .' She stopped and thought. 'A very *feeling* sort of man. Wouldn't you say?'

Rita remembered the pulse reading. 'It's hard to tell on a first meeting. Perhaps none of us were entirely ourselves. Have you seen anything of him?'

'He came for another visit. To see her again, with a more settled mind.'

There was a note of something unresolved in her voice.

'And did it work? Was he able to reach a fixed conclusion?'

'I can't say that he did,' Helena answered thoughtfully, and then she flashed a sudden look at Rita and leant to speak in an undertone: 'His wife drowned the child, you know. And then took poison. That is what they are saying.' She sighed heavily. 'They will find the body. That's what I tell Anthony – they are bound to find it and Mr Armstrong will be certain then.'

'It's been quite a while. Do you think they are likely to find her now?'

'They must. Until they do, the poor man will be in a sort of limbo. It's hardly likely she'll be found alive now, after all. How many weeks is it? Four?' She totted up the weeks on her fingers like a child. 'Nearly five. You'd think they'd have found something . . . My own idea – shall I tell you?'

Rita nodded.

'My idea is that he cannot bear the knowledge that Alice is drowned and so he clings to the notion that Amelia might be Alice to spare himself the agony. Oh, the poor man.'

'And you have seen no more of him since?'

'We have seen him *twice* more. He returned ten days later, and again ten days after that.'

Rita waited expectantly and, as she had hoped, Helena went on.

'It was unexpected, and it was just not possible to turn him away. I mean – how could we? He came in again and took a glass of port with Anthony and we talked about one thing and another, nothing much, and he didn't mention Amelia, but when she came in he couldn't take his eyes off her . . . But he didn't say that is why he came. He arrived as if he just happened to be passing, and as we were acquainted . . . what could we do but invite him in?'

'I see.'

'And so now, I suppose, we *are* acquainted, and – well, that is just how it is.'

'And he doesn't talk about Amelia? Or Alice?'

'He talks about farming and horses and the weather. It drives Anthony to distraction – he cannot bear small talk – yet what can we do? We can hardly turn him away when he is in such low spirits.'

Rita wondered. 'It seems a bit strange to me.'

'It *is* all a bit strange,' Helena agreed, and with that, her smile returned and she turned again to the girl and wiped crumbs from her mouth. 'What next?' she asked. 'A walk?'

'I ought to go home. If anybody should be ill and come for me . . .'

'Then we will walk you part of the way. It's along the river, and we like the river, don't we, Amelia?'

At the mention of the river, the child, who had sat lax in her chair since finishing her food, her eyes dreamy and far away, was filled with purpose. She gathered her attention from wherever it had wandered to and clambered down from her chair.

As they walked down the garden slope to the riverbank, the girl ran on ahead.

'She loves the river,' Helena explained. 'I was just the same. My father too. I see a lot of him in her. Every day we come down here and she is always the same, racing ahead.'

'She's not afraid, then? After the accident?'

'Not in the least. She lives for it. You'll see.'

Indeed, when they came to the river, the girl was on the very edge of the bank, perfectly balanced and rooted, but as close as it was possible to be to the racing water. Rita could not quell the instinct to reach out and place a hand on the child's collar, to hold her should she tip over. Helena laughed. 'She is born to it. She is in her element.'

Indeed, the girl was intent on the river. She looked upriver, eyebrows slightly raised, mouth open, with an air that Rita tried to read. Was it expectation? The girl swivelled her head the other way and scanned the horizon downriver. Whatever it was she was hoping for wasn't there. An expression of weary disappointment came over her, but she rapidly gathered herself and dashed ahead on her little legs towards the turn in the river.

Mrs Vaughan's eyes never left the child. Whether she spoke of her husband or her father or anything else, her eyes stayed on the girl, and her gaze never altered. It was a flood of love, tender and joyful, and on those occasions when she lifted her eyes to look at Rita, the fleeting glances still brimmed with that love, it washed over Rita and everything it saw. The experience reminded Rita of looking into the eyes of a person to whom she had given a particularly strong draught to counter pain, or a man who had taken to drinking the cheap, unlabelled alcohol that was so easily available lately.

They started walking in the direction of Rita's cottage. The child ran ahead and when she was out of earshot, Helena spoke.

'This story they are telling at the Swan . . . that she was dead and then lived again . . .'

'What of it?'

'Anthony says they are a fanciful lot at the Swan, that they'll take anything a little out of the ordinary and embroider it. He says it will all die down and be forgotten. But I don't like it. What do you make of it?'

Rita thought for a little while. What was the point of worrying a woman already anxious about her child? On the other hand, she had never been the kind to practise glib lies in the reassurance of her patients. Her way was to find a means of telling the truth in a manner that allowed the patient to take in as much or as little as he or she wanted. The person might ask further questions or they might not. It was up to them. Now she adopted the same strategy. She disguised her thinking time by pretending to pay attention to the hem of her skirt as they walked through a particularly muddy patch. When she was ready she delivered her scrupulously truthful answer in her most objective fashion.

'There were some unusual circumstances attached to her rescue from the river. They thought she was dead. She was waxen white. Her pupils were dilated – that means the black part in the centre of the iris was wide. She had no discernible pulse. There was no detectable sign of breath. When I got there, that is what I saw too. I didn't at first locate a pulse, but later I did. She was alive.'

Rita watched Helena, guessing at what she might be making of this deliberately brief account. There were gaps in it that a person might or might not notice, fill in in any number of different ways, gaps that might arouse any number of additional questions. What kind of breath is it that is not detectable? was one. What kind of pulse is undiscernible? And the word *later* that she had used, the bland little cousin of the more expressive *eventually*: I couldn't find a pulse, but *later* I did. If it implies a few seconds, the word is innocuous. But a minute? What is one to make of that?

Helena was not Rita, and she filled the gaps differently. Rita watched her forming her conclusions as she strode alongside her, her eyes on the girl a few yards ahead. The child walked sturdily, careless of the wind and the bursts of rain that stopped and started at random. Her aliveness was a fact all its own; Rita could see how it might easily overshadow all the others.

'So they thought Amelia was dead, but she wasn't. It was a mistake. And they made a story out of it.'

Helena did not seem to need confirmation. Rita did not give it.

'To think she was so close to death. To think she was found and so nearly lost again.' She drew her eyes from the girl for a brief second, spared a glance for Rita. 'Thank heavens *you* were there!'

They were nearing Rita's cottage. 'We mustn't be too late,' Helena said. 'The man is coming this afternoon to put locks on the windows.'

'On the windows?'

'I have the feeling someone is watching her. Better safe than sorry.'

'There is a lot of curiosity about her . . . That is inevitable. It will die down in time.'

'I don't mean in public places. I mean in the garden and on the river. A spy.'

'Have you seen anyone?'

'No. But I can tell someone is there.'

'There is nothing new about the kidnap, I suppose? Her return hasn't loosened tongues?'

Helena shook her head.

'Is there anything to give you an idea where she has been these last two years? There was talk about the involvement of the river gypsies, wasn't there? The police searched their boats at one time, I think?'

'They did, when they caught up with them. Nothing was found.'

'And she appeared the night the gypsies were on the river again . . .'

'To see her use a knife and fork, you might well think she'd been living with gypsies these last two years. But honestly, I cannot bear to think about it.'

The windblown waves cast a mixture of spume and droplets up into the air, from where it fell again, laying its own complicated pattern over the choppy texture of the water. While she watched the random alterations of the water, Rita puzzled over what reasons the river gypsies would have for stealing a child and returning it to the same place, apparently dead, two years later. She found no answer.

Helena had been pursuing thoughts of her own. 'If I could, I would make those years disappear altogether. Sometimes I wonder whether I have imagined her . . . Or whether it is my longing that has – somehow – brought her back from whatever dark place she has been in. In all that pain, I would have sold my soul, given my life, to have her back again. All that agony . . . And now I sometimes wonder, what if I have? What if she is not altogether *real*?'

She turned to Rita and for a fleeting moment Rita caught a horrific glimpse of what the last two years had been. The desperation was so shocking that she flinched.

'But then I only have to look!' The young mother blinked and sought the child with her eyes. Her gaze was once again love-blind. 'It's Amelia. It's *her*.' Helena took a deep, happy breath before saying, 'Time to go home. We must say goodbye, Rita, but you'll come again? Next week?'

'If you want me to. She is well, though. There is no need for you to be concerned.'

'Come anyway. We like you, don't we, Amelia?'

She smiled at Rita, who felt once again the tail end of that sweep of mother's love, enchanting and radiant and more than a little troubling.

Continuing homewards, Rita came to the spot where a mass of hawthorn growing at a curve in the path made it hard to see ahead. An unexpected smell – fruit? Yeast? – roused her from her thoughts, and by the time her mind had interpreted the dark shadow in the undergrowth as a person concealed, it was too late. She had gone past, he had leapt out, her arms were gripped behind her back and a knife was at her throat.

'I have a brooch – you can have it. The money is in my purse,' she told him quietly, not moving. The brooch was only tin and glass, but he might not know that. And if he did, the money would console him.

But that wasn't what he was after.

'Do she talk?' She could smell it more strongly now he was so close.

'Who do you mean?'

'The girl. Do she talk?'

He gave her a shake; Rita felt something jut into her back, just below the nape of her neck.

'The Vaughan child? No, she doesn't speak.'

'Is there medicine can make her speak again?'

'No.'

'So she won't ever talk no more? Is that what the doctor says?'

'She might recover her speech naturally. The doctor says it will happen in the first six months or not at all.'

She waited for more questions, but none came.

'Drop your purse on the ground.'

With shaking hands she took the cloth pouch from her pocket – it contained the money the Vaughans had given her – and dropped it, and the next moment a great blow from behind sent her flying and she landed heavily on the rough ground with gravel digging into her palms.

I'm not hurt though, she reassured herself, but by the time she'd gathered herself and got to her feet, the man and her purse were gone.

She hurried home, thinking hard.

Which Father?

ANTHONY VAUGHAN LEANT towards his looking glass, applied the blade to the soap suds on his cheek and scraped. Meeting his eye in the glass, he made one more effort to untangle his thoughts. He began where he always began: the child was not Amelia. That ought to have been the beginning and end of the question, but it wasn't. One single certainty led not to the next stepping stone but into a quagmire, no matter what direction he took. The knowledge wavered and faltered, it grew feebler and harder to maintain with every day that passed. It was Helena who undermined what he knew. Every smile on his wife's face, every burst of laughter, every joyful word she pronounced, was reason to put his knowledge aside. She had grown prettier every day in the two months the child had been with them, had regained the weight she had lost, recovered the gloss in her hair and the colour in her cheeks. Her face was alive with love, not only for the child, but for him too.

But it was not *only* Helena, was it? It was the girl too.

Incessantly Vaughan's eyes were drawn to the little girl's face. At breakfast, as he spooned marmalade into her mouth, he traced the jut of her jaw; at noon it was the dip in her hairline at the front that obsessed him; when he came home from Brandy Island after work, he was incapable of dragging his eyes away from the coiled architecture of her ear. He knew these features better than he knew his wife's or his own. He was tormented by something in them – in *her* – that seemed to mean something to him, if only he could work out what it was. Even in her absence, he saw her. In the train, watching the landscape speed by, her face was superimposed on the fields and sky. In the office, her features were like a watermark in the paper on which he set out his lists of figures. She even haunted his dreams. All sorts of characters bore the child's face. Once he had dreamt of Amelia – *his* Amelia, the real one – and even she wore the child's face. He had woken weeping.

His ceaseless tracing of her features, which began as an effort to find out who she was, gradually shifted focus and became an attempt to explain his own fascination. It seemed to him that her face was the model from which all human faces were derived, even his own. The endlessness of his staring had worn her face so smooth it was as if he saw his own reflection in it, and looking at her turned him back always to himself. This was something he could not tell Helena. She would hear only the thing he didn't mean: that he saw himself in his daughter.

Was there in fact something familiar about the child? He tried to tell himself that the sense of recognition her face aroused in him was nothing but the natural echo of that first time he had seen her. His own intensity of looking was enough, surely, to explain the sense of familiarity she aroused in him? She looked quite simply like herself and that is why he knew her. Yet honesty told him it was not at all so straightforward. The notion of memory failed to adequately capture the sensation. It was as if the child evoked in him something that had the size and shape of memory, but inversed or turned inside out. Something akin to memory – its twin, perhaps, or its opposite.

Helena knew that he did not believe the girl to be their daughter. She knew because he had told her so on the first day, as soon as they were alone after putting the child to bed. She had met the news with surprise, but was apparently untroubled by it.

'Two years is a long time in the face of any little girl,' she'd told him gently. 'You will have to be patient. Time will teach your heart to know her again.' She had put a hand on his arm, and it was the first time in two years that his wife had touched him in their drawing room and looked lovingly at him. 'Until then, put your faith in me. *I* know her.'

Now, when the issue arose, she treated his lack of faith with bemused tolerance: it was trivial, inconsequential, just her own dear, silly husband slow to catch up with events. She did little to try to persuade him. 'She still likes honey!' she noted once at the breakfast table, and 'Well, that hasn't changed!' when the girl pushed the hairbrush away. But for the most part, she just put blithe confidence in the likelihood that time would bring him to his senses. His doubts were lightweight, her manner implied, and sure to be swept away with the next strong current. He did not raise the matter himself. It wasn't that he was afraid of worrying her, but the contrary: *You see*, she would say, if he told her. *You do know her really. It is all coming back to you now.*

It was the kind of tangle that you could easily make worse in your efforts to straighten things out, and more than once Vaughan found himself considering a very simple solution. Why not decide to believe it? With her coming, the girl had broken a curse, returned them to the enchanted days of happiness. The years of pain, when they were encased in misery and comfortless to each other, were gone. The child brought straightforward joy to Helena, and to him something more complicated that he treasured, though he did not know what to call it. In a very short time it had come about that he minded when the girl ate less than usual, fretted when she cried at night, rejoiced when she reached her hand for his.

Amelia was gone, and this girl had come. His wife believed her to be Amelia. She bore some resemblance to Amelia. Life, which had been unendurable before she came, was now pleasurable again. She had returned Helena to him and, more than that, she herself had found a place in his heart. It wasn't going too far to say that he loved her. Did he want her to be Amelia? Yes. On the one side: love, comfort, happiness. On the other: every chance of a return to the way things had been . . . Well, then. What reason was there to cling so doggedly to his certainty when the current was pulling so hard in the other direction?

There was only one reason. Robin Armstrong.

'They will find the body,' Helena insisted. 'His wife drowned the child, everybody knows it, and when they find the body he will know.'

But it had been two months and no body had been found.

Vaughan had put off doing anything so far. He was a good man. Fair and decent. And he meant to be fair and decent now. There was himself, and there was Robin Armstrong, but there were also Helena and the girl. It was important that the best outcome should be found for all concerned. The situation could not go on as it was indefinitely – that did nobody any good. A solution must be found, and he was taking the first step today.

He rinsed briskly, towelled his face dry and got ready. He had a train to catch.

Although generally known as Monty and Mitch, any suspicion that this was the name of a provincial travelling circus fell away at the sight of the brass plaque attached next to the door of the sober Georgian Oxford townhouse: *Montgomery & Mitchell, Legal and Commercial.* The Thames was quite invisible from its windows, and yet its presence was felt in every room. Not only every room, but every drawer and cupboard of every room, for this was the firm of solicitors used by anyone who had business interests relating to the river, from Oxford all the way upstream for many a mile. Mr Montgomery himself was not a boating man, nor a fisherman, nor a painter of watery landscapes; in fact, he went from one year's end to the next without setting eyes on the river, yet still it could be said without a word of a lie that he lived and breathed it. The way Mr Montgomery pictured the Thames, it was not a current of water at all, but an income stream, dry and papery, and he diverted a share of its bounty every year into his own ledgers and bank accounts and was very grateful to it. He spent his days contentedly drafting bills of carriage and negotiating the wording of letters of credit, and when a rare and valuable dispute involving *force majeure* came his way, which it sometimes did, his heart swelled with delight.

On the steps, Vaughan had his hand to the bell though he did not yet pull it. He was muttering to himself.

'Amelia,' he said, a little hesitantly. Then, with perhaps too much energy, 'Amelia!'

It was a name he had constantly to practise, for it never came without having to leap over an obstacle, and the effort made it sound somewhat forced, even to his own ears.

'*Amelia*,' he said a third time and, hoping that that was good enough, he rang the bell.

Vaughan had written and was expected. The boy who answered the door and dealt with his coat was the same one who had been there on the day more than two years ago when Vaughan had come to deal with matters relating to the kidnapping of his daughter. The boy had been even younger then and quite at a loss to know how to behave faced with the wild sorrow and anguish that the visitor had displayed. Despite his strong feelings, Vaughan had wanted to reassure the boy, tell him that it was not his fault if he did not know how to look with calm deference into the eye of a madman who had lost his only child. Today the boy – for he was still a boy, if a bigger one – maintained his calm politeness as he took the coat and suspended it from a hook, but in turning back to Vaughan could no longer contain himself.

'Oh, good news, Sir! What a turn-up for the books! You must be overjoyed, you and Mrs Vaughan, Sir!'

Handshaking was not quite the done thing between a client of Monty and Mitch's and the boy who took the coats, but such was the momentousness of the day – so far as the boy was concerned anyway – that Vaughan allowed his hand to be taken and subjected to a vigorous pumping.

'Thank you,' he murmured, and if there was any shortcoming in his acceptance of these hearty congratulations, the boy was too young to perceive it and only beamed as he showed Mr Vaughan into the office of Mr Montgomery himself.

Mr Montgomery stretched out a professionally jovial hand. 'How good to see you again, Mr Vaughan. You look well, I must say.'

'Thank you. You've had my letter?'

'Indeed I have. Pull up a chair and tell me all about it. First, though, a glass of port?'

'Thank you.'

Vaughan saw the letter on Montgomery's desk. It said little, really;

the least he could get away with saying. But now, seeing it broken open and lying there, thoroughly perused, he wondered whether it was the kind of little that gave away more than it meant to. Vaughan's hand was the open, fluent kind that anyone can read upside down and, as Montgomery busied himself with the glasses, some of the phrases he had written yesterday caught his eye. '*The child having been discovered . . . girl being now in our custody . . . may be necessary to retain your services in matters relating . . .*' These were not, he now felt, the expressions of a man overjoyed at the return of his only child.

A glass was placed before him. He took a sip. The two men discussed the port, as men of business must. Montgomery would not raise the matter first, Vaughan knew, but he did create a pause, which plainly he expected Vaughan to fill.

'I realize that in my letter yesterday I set out recent events without clarifying the respects in which I may need your assistance,' he began. 'Some things are better discussed in person.'

'Quite right.'

'The fact of the matter is, there is a chance – scarcely likely, I should say, yet worth attending to – that another party might make a claim to the child.'

Montgomery nodded, as unsurprised as if he had been expecting this very eventuality. Although Mr Montgomery must have been sixty, he had the unlined face of an infant. After forty years of practising a poker face in the office, the muscles that twitch and tauten in response to doubt, worry or suspicion had atrophied to such a degree that it was now impossible to read any kind of expression in his face other than a general and permanent bonhomie.

'There is a young man living in Oxford who claims – at least, I think he *may* claim – that he is the father of the child. His estranged wife died at Bampton and his own child's whereabouts are unknown. His daughter, Alice, was just the same age, and she disappeared at more or less the same time as' – Vaughan saw the hurdle coming and was ready for it – '*Amelia* was found. An unfortunate coincidence that has permitted uncertainty to arise . . .'

'Uncertainty . . . ?'

'In his eyes.'

'In his eyes. Yes. Good.'

Montgomery listened, his face a picture of bland goodwill.

'The young man – his name is Armstrong – had not seen his wife or child in recent times. Hence his inability to be immediately certain as to the identity of this child.'

'Whereas you, on the other hand, are entirely certain of' – his level gaze was quite unaltered – 'the child's identity?'

Vaughan swallowed. 'Indeed.'

Montgomery smiled benignly. He was far too well mannered to press a client on a doubtful statement. 'The child is your daughter, then.' It sounded for all the world like a declaration, but Vaughan's uncertainty heard the question in it.

'It is . . .' (the hurdle again) 'Amelia.'

Montgomery continued smiling.

'There is no shadow of a doubt,' Vaughan added.

The smile persisted.

Vaughan felt the need to throw something in to make weight. 'A mother's instinct is a powerful thing,' he concluded.

'A mother's instinct!' exclaimed Montgomery encouragingly. 'What could be plainer than that? Of course,' – there was no fall in his face – 'it is fathers to whom the custodial right to a child belongs, but still, a mother's instinct! Nothing finer!'

Vaughan swallowed. He took the plunge. 'It is Amelia,' he said. 'I *know*.'

Montgomery looked up, round of cheek and smooth of forehead. 'Excellent.' He nodded contentedly. 'Excellent. Now, I have a good deal of experience in assessing competing claims to certain cargoes that occasionally go astray for one reason or another. Do not be offended if I use my experience – for the parallel is a useful one – to test the strength of this Armstrong's case against you.'

'It is not yet a case against us. It is not yet a case at all. For two months we have had her now, and the fellow comes every so often to see us. He comes and he watches her and he neither claims her to be his nor relinquishes his claim. Every time he turns up I am ready for him to state his mind one way or the other, but he remains silent on the issue. I am reluctant to press him on the matter – the last thing I want is to precipitate a claim, and all the while he does not say, "She is mine," it is clearly an open possibility in his own mind that she is not. I prefer not to provoke him, but in the meantime it is unsettling. My wife . . .'

'Your wife?'

'My wife believed at the outset that the situation would last only so long as his own daughter was not found. We expected every day to hear report of a child, a body perhaps, found in the river, but we waited in vain and no such news has come. We are starting to feel unsettled by the fact that the matter remains unresolved after so long, but Helena is sorry for him, knowing all too well how heartbreaking the loss of a child is. She tolerates his continuing visits to our home, even though it has gone beyond the point where he can expect to reach any sense of certainty. His own child has vanished into the blue and I fear that in the desperation of his grief it might not be beyond the machinations of his own mind to persuade him that Amelia' (the hurdle successfully jumped – he was getting better at this!) '– that Amelia is in fact his child. Grief is a powerful force, and who knows to what a man might be driven when his child is lost to him. A man is liable to imagine all manner of things rather than think his child – his only child – lost for ever.'

'You have a very acute understanding of his mind and his situation, Mr Vaughan. Then we must test the *facts* of the matter, for *facts* are what matter in law, and see what is the power of his case in principle, in case he should think to make his claim, so as to be ready when the time comes. Incidentally, what does the child herself have to say about the matter?'

'Nothing. She has not spoken.'

Mr Montgomery nodded serenely, as if nothing could have been more natural.

'And before she was taken from your care, she had the power of speech?'

Vaughan nodded.

'And Mr Armstrong's daughter – did *she* have the power of speech?'

'She did.'

'I see. Now do not be offended, remember, if I appear to treat the little Amelia as if she were a cargo gone astray and returned to sight, it is the way my experience goes. What I know is this: much weight is given to the last sighting of the cargo before it disappeared and the first sighting when it reappeared. That is what will tell us as much as can be known about the cargo while it was out of sight. Taken together with as complete a description as possible of the cargo as it was before and as it was afterwards, it will generally be enough to cast a decent enough light into the muddle to ascertain ownership within the law.'

He proceeded to ask a number of questions. He asked about Amelia before the kidnap. He asked about the circumstances in which Alice Armstrong was lost. He asked about the circumstances in which the cargo – 'Amelia,' he said, more than once, with emphasis – was found. He noted all and nodded.

'Armstrong's daughter has, to all extents and purposes, disappeared into the blue. These things happen. Yours has returned out of the blue. Which is more unusual. Where has she been? Why is it *now* that she has returned – or been returned? These are unanswered questions. It would be better to have an answer, but if there is no answer to be had, then instead we must rely on other evidence. Do you have photographs of Amelia from before?'

'We do.'

'And she resembles those photographs, now?'

Vaughan shrugged. 'I suppose so . . . In the way little girls of four resemble their own selves aged two.'

'Which is to say . . . ?'

'A mother's eye can see it is the same child.'

'But another? A more judicial eye?'

Vaughan paused, and Montgomery, as if he had not registered the pause, sailed blithely on. 'I take your point entirely about children. They change. A cargo of cheese lost on Wednesday does not transform into an equivalent weight of tobacco when it reappears on Saturday, but a child – ah! another matter entirely. I take your point. Still, to be ready, keep the photographs safe, and keep note of everything – every little detail – that tells you that this Amelia and that Amelia from two years ago are one and the same child. It is as well to be prepared.'

He took in Vaughan's glum face and smiled cheerily at him. 'Beyond that, Mr Vaughan, my counsel to you is this: worry not about young Mr Armstrong. And tell Mrs Vaughan she is not to worry either. Montgomery and Mitchell are here to do the worrying for you. We will look after everything for you – and for *Amelia*. For there is one thing, one very great thing, that stands in your favour.'

'And what is that?'

'If it comes to court, this case will be very long, and it will be very slow. Have you ever heard of the great Thames case between the Crown and the Corporation of London?'

'I can't say I have.'

'It is a dispute over which of them owns the Thames. The Crown says that the Queen travels upon it and it is essential for the defence of the nation, hence the river is in its possession. The Corporation of London argues that it exercises jurisdiction over the comings and goings of all goods upstream and down, and that therefore it must own the Thames.'

'And what was the outcome? Who owns the Thames?'

'Why, they have been arguing it for a dozen years and they have at least a dozen years of argument to go! What is a river? It is water. And what is water? Essentially it is rain. And what is rain? Why, weather! And who owns the weather? That cloud that passes overhead now, this very minute, where is it to fall? On the one bank, or on the other, or into the river itself? Clouds are blown by the wind, which is owned by nobody, and they float over borders without letters of passage. The rain in that cloud might fall in Oxfordshire or in Berkshire; it might cross the sea and fall upon the demoiselles in Paris, for all we know. And the rain that does fall into the Thames, why it might have travelled from anywhere! From Spain, or Russia, or . . . or Zanzibar! If they have clouds in Zanzibar. No, rain cannot be said to belong to anybody, whether it be the Queen of England or the Corporation of London, any more than lightning can be captured and put in a bank vault, but that won't stop them trying!'

On Montgomery's face there was the faintest hint of glee. It was the closest Vaughan had ever seen to an expression.

'The reason I tell you this is to illustrate how slow the dealings of the law can be. When this Armstrong makes up his mind to claim the girl – if he does – avoid going to court. Pay him whatever he wants to resolve the matter. It will be cheaper by far. And if he won't be paid off, then take comfort in the Crown *vs.* the Corporation of London. The case will last, if not an eternity, then at least until the child is grown. The cargo we have been speaking of, little Amelia, will be the property of her husband long before the law decides which father is her rightful owner. Take comfort!'

At Oxford station, Vaughan stood on the platform waiting for his train. As Montgomery faded from his thoughts, he was put in mind of the last occasion he had stood waiting for a train on the very same spot. He had been to town to meet a potential buyer for the narrow-gauge railway he had used for the transportation of sugar beet from field to distillery, and afterwards he had gone to locate the house of Mrs Constantine. He had found it. He had gone inside. He wondered at himself. It was such a short time ago – only two months – and so much had happened since. What was it she had said to him? *You can't go on like this.* That was it. And he had felt it too; felt in his bone marrow that she was right. Would he have gone back, as she suggested? Surely not. And yet . . . As things turned out, he hadn't needed to. Left by themselves, things had sorted themselves out, unexpectedly, miraculously even, and happily. For two years he had been miserably unhappy and now – so long as Armstrong could be managed – he did not need to be. *Take comfort!* Montgomery had said. And he would.

Just as he resolved to forget Mrs Constantine, he remembered her face suddenly. Her eyes that seemed to swim against the current of his words and enter his mind, his very thoughts . . . *I see*, she had said, and it was as if she saw not only what he said, but what he *didn't* say.

Remembering it now, he felt a touch of significance at the nape of his neck and turned, expecting to see her behind him on the platform.

There was nobody there.

'Mrs Vaughan is putting Amelia to bed,' he was told when he arrived home.

He let himself into the yellow drawing room, where the curtains were closed and the fire was burning brightly in the hearth. Lately the two photographs of Amelia had reappeared on the small desk that stood in the bay. In the first days after her disappearance, she had continued to stare from her containment behind the glass. Her ghost-like gaze, overlaid with the shimmer of the glass, had appalled him and finally, able to bear it no longer, he had lain the portraits face down in a drawer and tried to forget them. Later he became aware that the photographs were no longer there and supposed that Helena had taken them to her room. By this time he no longer visited Helena's room. Nocturnal grieving was a thing they did separately, each in their own way, and it was plain to him that nothing good would come from entering her room for any other purpose. Now that the girl had come, the photographs were back in their original place.

He had allowed his eyes to glide over them without seeing a thing.

From across the room they were mere shapes: a standard portrait of Amelia seated, and a family portrait, he standing and Helena seated with Amelia on her lap. He approached. He took the standard portrait in his hands, eyes closed, preparing himself to look at it.

The door opened. 'You're home! Darling? Is something the matter?'

He righted his face. 'What? Oh, no, nothing. I saw Montgomery today. While I was there I mentioned – in passing – the situation with Mr Armstrong.'

She looked at him blankly.

'We spoke about the possibility – the *remote* possibility – that he might make a claim in law.'

'Surely not! When they find—'

'The body? Helena, when will you give up this notion? It's been two months! If nobody has found it yet, what reason is there to think they are going to find it?'

'But a little girl has *drowned*! The body of a child doesn't just *disappear*!'

Vaughan's chest rose with a sharp intake of breath. His lungs held on to it. This wasn't how he wanted the conversation to go. He must stay calm. Slowly he exhaled.

'Yet no body has been found. We must face that fact. And it is likely – even *you* must admit the possibility – that no body will be found.' He could hear the testiness in his own voice, made further efforts to curb it. 'Look – darling – all I mean to say is that it's as well to be prepared. Just in case.'

She looked at him thoughtfully. It was unlike him to be sharp with her. 'You can't bear the thought of losing her, can you?' She crossed the room, placed her hand over his heart and smiled tenderly. 'You can't bear the thought of losing her *again*. Oh, Anthony!' Tears rose in her eyes and spilt. 'You *know*. At last you have recognized her.'

He made to put the photograph down to take her in his arms; the movement drew her attention to what he was holding and she stopped him.

She took the photograph from his hand and looked fondly at it. 'Anthony, please don't worry. All the evidence we need is here.' She smiled up at him. She was turning it in her hands so as to replace it on the table when a sudden exclamation broke from her lips.

'What is it?'

'This!'

He looked where she was pointing at the reverse of the frame. 'Good Lord! *Henry Daunt of Oxford, portraits, landscapes, city and country scenes*,' he read aloud from the label. 'It's him! The man who found her!'

'We would hardly have recognized him, bruised and swollen as he was. How strange . . . Let's get him back. He made more exposures, do you remember? We only took the two best ones, but there were two others. He might still have them.'

'If they were any good we'd have them already, surely.'

'Not necessarily.' She replaced the photograph on the table. 'The best photograph overall might not be the best of her face. Perhaps I was the one who wriggled' (she danced an exaggerated demonstration on the spot) 'or you were pulling a face' (her fingers moulded his lips into a lopsided grimace). He made an effort to respond with the kind of laugh her playfulness deserved. 'There,' she finished with satisfaction. 'You're smiling again. So, it would be better to have them all, wouldn't it? Just in case. I'm sure your Mr Montgomery would think so.'

He nodded.

She put an arm loosely around him and spread her fingers below his shoulder blade. Through his jacket he could feel each finger separately and the pad at the base of her thumb. He was not yet used to her touch; even through layers of tweed and poplin it sent a thrill through him.

'And while he is here, we can have him take new ones.'

She raised her other hand to the back of his neck; he felt a thumb stray to the inch of skin between the top of his collar and his hairline.

He kissed her and her mouth was soft and slightly open.

'I'm so glad,' she murmured as she leant into his body. 'It's the one thing I've been waiting for. Now we are really together again.'

He delivered a sound, a little moan, into her hair.

'Our little girl is fast asleep,' she whispered. 'I thought I might have an early night too.'

He buried his nose in her neck and inhaled. 'Yes,' he said. And again, 'Yes.'

The Story Flourishes

IN THE WEEKS after the mystery girl was pulled from the Thames, first dead and then alive, the Swan had done excellent business. The story had spread via marketplaces and street corners. It was recounted in family letters from mother to daughter, from cousin to cousin. It was passed freely to strangers met on station platforms, and wanderers encountered it by chance at crossroads. Everybody who heard it was sure to tell it wherever he went, until eventually there was nobody in three counties who did not know one version of it or another. A great many of these people were not satisfied until they had visited the inn where the extraordinary events had taken place and seen for themselves the riverbank where the girl was found and the long room where she was placed.

Margot made the decision to open up the summer room. She organized her daughters to come in pairs to help with the extra work, and the regulars got used to having the Little Margots present. Jonathan badgered his mother and sisters to listen to him practise his storytelling, but they were rarely able to stop and listen, for the calls on their time and attention were unending. 'I'll never get any better,' he sighed, and his lips moved as he rehearsed aloud to himself, but he got more and more muddled, putting the end at the beginning and the beginning at the end, and the middle – well, the middle hardly featured at all.

Joe lit the fire at eleven in the morning and it was kept in till midnight, when at last the crush of drinkers in the room began to thin.

The regulars scarcely bought a drink for themselves for weeks on end, as visitors stood rounds in payment for the story. They learnt in time to save their voices, for had the visitors had their way, every man who had witnessed the events that night would have been in the summer room going round the tables, talking constantly. But, as an elderly cressman pointed out very appositely, that would leave no drinking time. So they worked out a rota that saw the regulars go two by two into the summer room for an hour of telling, and then return to their stools in the winter room to quench their thirst and be replaced by two more.

Fred Heavins had crafted a good comic tale out of his side of it, which ended with the punchline, '"Nay!" said the horse.' A slantwise version like his went down well after ten o'clock, when the facts of the story had been told a dozen times over and the audience was drunk. It earnt him a great many hangovers and he was so often late for work that he was threatened with dismissal.

Newman, the Vaughans' gardener, previously a regular at the Red Lion where every Friday night he sang till he was hoarse, had now switched allegiance to the Swan and was trying his tongue at storytelling. He practised on the regulars before trying his luck with the visitors in the summer room, and made the most of that aspect of the story only he had witnessed: the departure of Mrs Vaughan from Buscot Lodge on hearing the news of the rescue of the child.

'I saw her myself, I did. She ran down to the boathouse quick as could be, and when she come out in her rowing boat – the little old one of hers – off she went, haring up the river . . . I never seen a boat move like it.'

'Haring up the river?' asked a farmhand.

'Aye, and just a little slip of a girl too! You wouldn't think a woman could row so fast.'

'But . . . *haring*, you say?'

'That's right. Quick as a hare, it means.'

'I know what it means, all right. But you can't say she was haring up the river.'

'Why ever not?'

'Have you ever seen a hare rowing a boat?'

There was a burst of laughter that bewildered the gardener and made him flustered. 'A hare in a boat? Don't be daft!'

'That's why you can't say she went haring up the river. If a *hare* can't hare up a river, how can Mrs Vaughan? Think about it.'

'I never knew that. What am I meant to say, then?'

'You have to think of some creature that *do* go swiftly up a river, and say that instead. Don't he?'

There was a round of nodding.

'What about an otter?' suggested a young bargeman. 'They don't hang about.'

Newman pulled a dubious face. 'Mrs Vaughan went *ottering* up the river . . .'

The farmhand shook his head. 'It sounds no better.'

'In fact it sounds a bit worse . . .'

'Well, what am I supposed to say, then? If I can't say *haring* and I can't say *ottering*? I've got to say something.'

'True,' said the bargeman, and a trio of gravel-diggers nodded. 'The man has to say something.'

They turned to Owen Albright, who shared his wisdom. 'I reckon you have to find another way altogether. You could say, "She rowed up the river, quick as could be . . ." '

'But he have already said that,' protested the farmhand. 'She ran down to the boathouse quick as could be. She can't run quick as can be down to the boathouse and row quick as can be upriver.'

'She did, though,' corrected Newman.

'No!'

'She did! I was there! I saw her with my own eyes!'

'Aye, so it might have happened, but you can't *tell* it thus.'

'Can't tell it how it was? How d'you make that out? I'm starting to wish I'd not told it at all, now. Telling a thing's harder than I ever knew.'

'There's an art to it,' Albright soothed. 'You'll get the hang of it.'

'I've got to the age of thirty-seven just opening my mouth and letting the words out, and never had any trouble so far. Not till I came and sat down here. I don't know as I wants the hang of it. No, I shall go on by the old way, my words shall come as they like and if I has her haring up the river, well hare she must. Else I shan't say anything at all.'

There was an exchange of anxious looks across the table, and one of the gravel-diggers spoke for them all: 'Let the man speak. He was there.'

And Newman was allowed to continue, in words of his own devising, his account of Mrs Vaughan's departure from the house.

It was not only Newman and Heavins who practised and refined their stories. All told their versions over and over, to each other and the visitors, and new details came to light. Memories were compared, adjudication made. There were splinter groups. Some remembered 'for a fact' that the feather had been placed on the lips of the child before she was taken to the long room, others were adamant that only the man's breath had been tested thus. Diverse and lengthy hypotheses were proposed to explain how Henry Daunt managed to get from Devil's Weir to Radcot whilst out cold and in a damaged boat. They refined and polished the tale, identified moments where a well-placed gesture would bring tears to the eye, introduced pauses that held the audience on the edge of their seats. But they never found an ending to the story. They came to a point – the child left the Swan with Mr and Mrs Vaughan – where the story simply tailed off. 'Is she Amelia Vaughan, or is she the other one?' someone would ask. And 'How come she was first dead and then alive again?'

There were no answers.

Regarding the first question – who was the girl? – opinion by and large was in favour of the girl belonging to the Vaughans. The return of a child missing for the past two years, a child they had all seen, was a distinctly more satisfying story than the return of a child nobody knew and who had gone missing only the day before. The more recent mystery resuscitated the first, and the kidnap was recounted as though it were only yesterday.

'Where has she been, then, this last – how long is it? – two years?'

'She will have to get her voice back and start telling, won't she?'

'And then there'll be trouble for whoever it was that took her.'

'It were that nursery maid, I'd put a week's wages on it. Remember her?'

'The girl Ruby that went out in the night?'

'That's what she says. Walking by the river at midnight. I ask you! What kind of a girl goes wandering by the river in the middle of the night? At solstice time too.'

'And solstice time is when the river gypsies are about. They cooked it up with her, that's how it was. Ruby and the gypsies, mark my words. When that little lass starts to talk, there'll be trouble for someone . . .'

The story of the kidnapped girl and the story of the found girl both had trailing ends, but if some of those trailing ends could be woven together, then that seemed to bring both stories closer to completion, which was a good thing.

As for the second question, that gave rise to longer and drunker debates.

There were some for whom the world was such a tricky thing that they marvelled at it without feeling any need to puzzle it out. Bafflement in their eyes was fundamental to existence. Higgs the gravel-digger was one such. His pay, which was enough on Friday night to last the week, was generally gone by the end of Tuesday; he always owed for more pints of ale at the Swan than he remembered consuming; the wife he only beat on Saturday night – and not always then – ran off for no reason at all to live with the cousin of the cheesemonger; the face he saw reflected in the river when he sat glumly staring into it with no bread in his belly, no ale to dull the hunger and no wife to warm him, was not his own but his father's. The whole of life was a mystery, if you delved even a little way under the surface, and causes and effects not infrequently came adrift from each other. On top of these daily bewilderments, the story of the girl who died and lived again was one he drew consolation from as he marvelled at it, for it demonstrated conclusively that life was fundamentally inexplicable, and there was no point trying to understand anything.

Certain tellers, fanciful or just unscrupulous, invented details to provide a more satisfactory answer to this question. One bargeman had a brother who'd been off with a woman the night of the great event. At first disappointed by what he'd missed, he later turned it to his advantage and developed his own version that made the most of his absence from the inn and contained the comfort of rational explanation. 'She were never dead at all! If I'd have seen her, I'd have told 'em. It's all in the eyes. You have only to look in a man's eyes to tell if he is dead or not. It is the seeing, you see, that goes out of 'em.'

Ears snapped open on hearing this and heads lifted sharply. It was the obvious way to sooth the strain of it, if you were one of those that can't stand a glaring gap in a tale, an implausibility, reality gone wrong. One or two storytellers were attracted to the security of it and their own versions began to drift in that direction. 'She was brought into the inn scarcely breathing,' someone said experimentally, but it gave rise to such disapproving glances and twists of the mouth that the teller was taken aside and given a talking-to. There were standards at the Swan; storytelling was one thing, lying quite another, and they had all been there. They *knew*.

After months of telling and retelling there was no sense of the story settling down. On the contrary, the tale of the drowned girl who lived again was puzzling, unfinished, out of kilter with what a story ought to be. At the Swan they talked about the Vaughans, they talked about the Armstrongs, they talked about death and they talked about life. They examined the strengths and weaknesses of every claim and every claimant. They turned the story this way and that, they turned it upside down and then righted it again, and at the end were no further forward than they had been at the beginning.

'It is like bone soup,' said Beszant one night. 'A smell to make your mouth water and all the flavour of the marrow, but there be nowt to chew on and though you take seven bowls of it you will be just as hungry at the end as when you sat down to the table.'

They might have let it drop. They might have given it up as one of those tales that comes from nowhere and has nowhere to go. But at the end of sentences and between words, when voices tailed off and conversations halted, in the profound lull that lies behind all storytelling, there floated the girl herself. In this room, in this inn, they had seen her dead and seen her alive. Unknowable, ungraspable, inexplicable, still one thing was plain: she was their story.

Counting

TWENTY-FIVE MILES DOWNRIVER, at Oxford's best-known boatyard, the boatbuilder himself scrawled an inky squiggle in receipt of payment of the final invoice and with a nod slid a set of shiny brass keys over the counter. Henry Daunt's hand closed over them.

On his return to the city after his eventful solstice experiences, Daunt had set things in motion. He had leased the house he'd lived in with his wife and moved into the attic room over his shop on Broad Street. There he enjoyed a spartan, bachelor existence, having a bed, a chamber pot, a table with a pitcher and basin to his name. He ate his meals at the chop house at the corner. He invested the total of the lease money and every penny of his savings into the boat. For Daunt had a plan.

In the period of unconsciousness between the shortest day and the day after, his mind had been made new, and in the bed at the Swan a new and brilliant idea had occurred to him. An idea that would combine in a single project his two great loves: photography and the river. He would make a book of photographs that would take the reader on a journey from the source of the Thames all the way to the estuary. Or perhaps just to London. Though in fact, it might have to be in several volumes and the first might go only from Trewsbury Mead to Oxford. The essence was to start. To do it, he needed two things: transport and a darkroom. The two things could be one. While his face was still shades of green and black and purple with a scarlet thread running down his lip, he'd made his first visit to the boatbuilder to explain what he needed. As it happened, there had been a boat in the yard, almost completed, whose buyer had been unable to make the final payment. It was just what Daunt wanted, and needed only finishing and fitting out to meet his requirements. Today, nearly three months later, his skin was its usual hale colour and the scar a pink line with pairs of almost invisible dots where the stitches had been – and he had the keys to his investment in his hand.

All the way upriver, Daunt and his boat met with curiosity. Her smart navy-and-white paintwork and her brass-and-cherry fittings were reason enough, but there were originalities to this boat that had never been seen before.

'*Collodion*?' asked those who could read. 'What kind of a name is that?'

He pointed to the yellow-orange of the decorative flourishes that framed his name and profession painted on the side of the boat. 'This is the colour of collodion. It's lethal. I've known it burst into flames, explode even, with no warning at all. And if you inhale too much of it, woe betide you! But apply it to glass, expose it to light and then – ah! *then* – you have magic! Collodion is the ingredient that unlocks all my art and all my science. Without it, there can be no such thing as a photograph.'

'And what's all that, then?' people called across the water, gesturing to the brackets and boxes attached so neatly to the cabin walls, and he explained that this was his photographic equipment.

'And that contraption?' they wanted to know. Secured to the cabin roof was a quadricycle, painted to match the boat.

'For getting around inland. And this box here doubles as a trailer, so that I can get my kit to wherever I want to be by road.'

The sharp-eyed noticed that there were internal shutters as well as curtains.

'It's a darkroom,' he explained, 'for a single ray of light is enough to destroy a photograph in the making.'

He stopped so often for conversations of this sort, handed out so many business cards and made so many appointments in his diary, that by the time he got upriver as far as Buscot and Radcot, he thought

Collodion was well on the way to paying for herself already. But he had debts to repay before he could start this new phase of his business: he had come to thank the people to whom he owed his life. He had come to the Swan, and before that, this place.

It was a quiet spot on the river where a small, neat cottage stood. The garden was tidy, the front door painted green, and smoke was rising from its chimney. There was suitable mooring some twenty yards on. He tied up, came back, slapping his gloved hands together to keep them warm, and knocked.

The door opened to reveal a symmetrical brow over a strong, straight nose, flanked by distinctive angles that formed a jaw, cheeks and temples.

'Miss Sunday?' He hadn't envisaged *this* . . . He shifted slightly to the side, curious to see how the light fell differently with the change of position, saw shadow flood the plain of her cheek. He felt a stir of excitement.

'Mr Daunt!'

Rita stepped forward and lifted her face to his with an intentness in her expression, almost as if she were going to embrace him, but she only trained an assessing squint on his scar. Next she placed a fingertip to his skin and traced the scar to check how raised it was. She nodded. 'Good,' she said firmly, and stepped back.

His mind was preoccupied with visual matters, but he finally found his tongue.

'I've come to say thank you.'

'You have already done that.'

It was true. He had sent money in payment, thanked her in a letter for her care, and asked for information about the girl who had died and lived again. She had written in return a letter of model clarity, thanking him for the money and telling him what she knew of the child's progress. That might have been the end of it, but his mind was unsettled by this woman who was still a visual mystery to him, for one of his assistants had come to collect him and take him home while his eyes were still swollen shut. It had occurred to him that the people at the Swan might appreciate a free photograph as a thank-you for their hospitality and that it would be entirely natural to call on the nurse at the same time.

'I thought you might like a photograph,' he said. 'A thank-you gift.'

'You've chosen a bad day to come,' she told him, in the calm voice he remembered. 'I'm busy.'

He noticed the pool of shade at the side of her nose, had to repress the urge to darken it by taking her head between his hands and turning it fractionally. 'The light is too good to waste.'

'But I've been waiting for the right temperature,' she said. 'Today's the day. I can't afford to miss it.'

'What is it you need to do?'

'An experiment.'

'How long will it take?'

'Sixty seconds.'

'I need fifteen. Surely we can find seventy-five seconds in the day if we look hard?'

'Presumably your fifteen seconds is exposure time. What about your setting-up? And the developing?'

'You help me and I'll help you. It'll go quicker with two.'

She put her head on one side and gave him an appraising look. 'You're offering to help with my experiment?'

'I am. In return for a photograph.' The photograph that had first been conceived as a gift to her had become something he now wanted for himself.

'It's *possible*. Even preferable. But whether you'd *want* to . . .'

'I do.'

She eyed him and a subtle alteration in the planes of her face told him that she was suppressing a smile. 'So you will be the subject of my experiment if I agree to be the subject of your photograph – is that right?'

'It is.'

'You're a brave and foolish man, Mr Daunt. It's a deal. We'll start with the photograph, shall we? The light will fluctuate, whereas if the temperature does it won't be by much.'

Rita's sitting room was a white-painted box with many bookshelves and a blue armchair. By the window, a simple wooden table held more piles of books and sheafs of paper densely covered with swift, fluent script. She helped carry boxes from *Collodion*, and watched with interest as Daunt set up. When all was ready, he seated Rita at this table, with a featureless piece of wall behind her.

'Lean towards me . . . Try with your chin on your fist. Yes, that's it.'

There were none of the dainty accoutrements his paying clients would have wanted: no silver brooch to catch the light, no white collar, no lace cuff. What little you saw of her dress was dark and plain. There was no embellishment of any kind and none was needed. There was only the symmetry of the line where her temples met her hairline, the strong arc of her brow, the shade that pooled in her orbit, and the depth of her thinking eyes.

'Don't move while I'm counting.'

For fifteen seconds she sat motionless and he watched her through the lens.

His best portraits – the most lifelike – were of people whose characters were by nature placid, slow to move from one state to the next. Lively souls were frequently reduced by the camera: their essence escaped the lens and all that was captured was a wax dummy, all outward resemblance with none of the quicksilver.

With Rita there was none of the goggle-eyed staring or nervous blinking that novices often displayed. Instead she opened her eyes to the camera with perfect composure. From under his cover, he saw one swell of living thought succeed another in an endless shifting movement, while all the time the muscles of her face remained unaltered. This was not one photograph, he knew by the end of the fifteen seconds. This was a thousand.

'Come,' he said, as he removed the plate, still enclosed in its case against the light. 'I want to show you how it works.'

They made their way swiftly to *Collodion*. He was holding the plate carefully, and she did not need help climbing aboard. In the cabin, the shutters already blocked out the day. He lit a candle and placed a red glass shade over it, then closed the door. A red glow illuminated the small space. They stood side by side, hemmed in by the developing table that he had extended and the bench on which he could sleep when he spent nights aboard. The planks of the ceiling were only inches above their heads, and beneath their feet was the lulling rock of the river. Daunt tried not to be aware of the size and shape of the space between their two bodies, the places where the jut of her hip narrowed it, the curve of her waist broadened it, her elbow almost closed it.

He mixed liquids from three glass bottles in a tiny vessel only an inch high and the smell of apple vinegar and old nails filled the air.

'Ferrous sulphate?' she wondered, sniffing the air.

'With acetic acid and water. It actually *is* red, it's not just the light that makes it look that way.'

He slid the plate from its case. Holding it carefully in his left hand, he tipped a minute quantity of the light-red liquid on to the plate so that the acid mix flowed across the entire surface. It was a graceful motion, fluid and economical.

'Watch. The image starts to form almost instantly – the lighter things first, but they show as dark lines . . . This line here is your cheekbone, highlighted from the window . . . Now the rest appears, blurrily at first, but then . . .'

His voice faded as they watched her face appear on the glass. They stood close in the red light, watching the shadows and lines on the glass coalesce, and Daunt felt a falling sensation in his stomach. A great dive. It resembled the feeling he'd had when, as a boy, he had let himself drop from the apex of a bridge into the river. He had met his wife while skating on the frozen Thames, one wintertime. With her he had glided into love – if it *was* love, and not some lesser cousin – unknowingly. This time he plummeted – and it was unmistakeable.

Then she was fully present on the glass. Her face delineated by light and darkness, the orbits shadowed and the pupils full of enigma. He felt that it would take very little to bring him to tears. It might be the best portrait he had ever taken.

'I must photograph you again,' he said as he rinsed the plate.

'What's wrong with this one?'

Nothing. He wanted her at every angle, in every possible light, in all moods and all positions. He wanted her with her hair loose around her face and pulled right back, concealed under a hat; he wanted her in a white chemise open at the neck and draped in folds of dark cloth; he wanted her in water and against tree trunks and on grass . . . There were a thousand photographs waiting to be taken. He had to have all of them.

'Nothing's wrong. That's why I need more.'

He slid the plate into a tray of potassium cyanide. 'This will get rid of the blue tint. See? It turns black and white and will be permanent now.'

Next to him, Rita in the red light looked with interest at the alteration, while through the clear viscosity of the liquid her eyes on glass continued to gaze thoughtfully, as they would now do for the life of the plate.

'What were you thinking about?'

She cast a quick, assessing glance in his direction – (*I want that look*) – and weighed something up rapidly (*and that one too*).

'You were there at the beginning,' she began. 'I suppose she would not be here at all if it were not for you, so . . .' and she recounted in calm detail the encounter she'd had with the man on the river path a few weeks before.

Daunt paid close attention. He discovered that he did not like the thought of Rita being accosted by a ruffian one bit, and his instinct was to offer reassurance, but Rita's account was so crisp, her manner so entirely unperturbed, that such chivalry would have been out of place. Yet he could not hear of the assault without some protective gesture.

'Did he hurt you?'

'There was bruising to my upper arm and grazing to my hands. Very minor.'

'You've made it known locally that there is a ruffian about?'

'I told them at the Swan and I let the Vaughans know of his interest in the child. They were already considering putting locks on the windows and that decided them.'

Given so little opportunity to display gallantry, he allowed Rita to lead him into analysis instead.

'Yeast and fruit . . .' she said.

'A baker-cum-thief? That's not very likely. Distilling, perhaps?'

'Yes, I wondered about that.'

'Who does distilling round here?'

She smiled. 'That's a question you won't easily get an answer to. Everybody and nobody, I should think.'

'Is there a lot of illicit liquor?'

She nodded. 'More than there used to be, according to Margot. But nobody knows where it comes from. Or nobody is willing to let on.'

'And you caught no glimpse of him.' Daunt, for whom vision was everything, frowned.

'He has unusually small hands and is a head shorter than I am.'

He eyed her quizzically.

'The bruises where his fingertips dug into my arms were smaller than expected, his voice came from a spot lower than my ear, and I felt the brim of his hat dig into me here.' She indicated where.

'That is small for a man.'

'And he's strong.'

'What do you make of his questions?'

Rita peered at the photograph of her thoughtful self. 'That is what I was considering here. If he wants to know whether the child will speak, that suggests he is concerned at what she might say. He might be frightened by what she could tell, which would imply that he has something to hide regarding the child. Perhaps he is responsible for her being in the river.'

There was a sense of something unfinished in her voice. Daunt waited. She went on, speaking slowly and carefully, as if she were still weighing it up in her own mind. 'But he was also particularly interested in knowing when she will speak again. Which might suggest his interest is less in something that has already happened and more in something to come. Perhaps he has some plan. Some notion that depends on her continuing silence.'

He waited while she organized her train of thought.

'Which is it? Past or future? It may be the first, but I incline towards the latter. We must wait till the summer solstice – perhaps then we will know more.'

'Why the summer solstice?'

'Because he believes it will be plain by then whether the child will speak or not. According to the Oxford doctor, that is when her muteness will either be gone or be permanent. It's nonsense, of course, but my assailant didn't ask for my opinion and I didn't give him the benefit of it. I only told him what the doctor had said. Six months from the drowning – if we can call it that – takes us to the summer solstice. Whether or not she speaks by then might be the factor that will determine his actions.'

His eyes met hers in the flickering red light.

'I would not want anything bad to happen to her,' he said. 'When I first saw her, I thought . . . I wanted . . .'

'You wanted to keep her.'

'How did you know that?'

'It's the same for everybody. The Vaughans want her, the Armstrongs want her, Lily White wants her. Jonathan wept when she left the Swan, and Margot was more than ready to have her. Why, even the cressmen would have taken her home and raised her if there'd been nobody else. Even I . . .' Something flickered in her eyes, there and gone again. *I particularly want that*, he thought. 'So of course you wanted her,' she continued smoothly. 'Everyone did.'

'Let me photograph you again. There will be light enough for another one.'

He lifted the red shade and snuffed out the candle and Rita leant to open the shutters. The day outside was dank and cold and grey, and the river was iron cold.

'You agreed to help me with my experiment.'

'What is it you want me to do?'

'You might change your mind once you know.'

She told him her intentions and he stared.

'Why on earth would you want me to do that?'

'Can't you guess?'

Of course he could. 'It's her, isn't it? Her heart slowed. You want to know how it happened.'

'Will you help?'

The first part was easy. At her kitchen table, while water was heating over the fire, she took his wrist in one hand and held her pocket watch in the other. For sixty seconds they sat in silence and she counted his pulse. At the end of a minute she made a note with a pencil that she wore on a string around her neck.

'Eighty beats a minute. A little high. It might be the anticipation.'

She tipped the water into a tin bath by the fire.

'It's not all that hot,' he said, testing it with his finger.

'Tepid is better. Now – are you ready? I'll turn my back.'

He undressed to his shirt and long johns while she looked out of the window, then put his coat on. 'Ready.'

Outside, the ground was unyielding and the cold penetrated Daunt's bare feet. The river ahead appeared smooth, but occasional shivers gave away the presence of deeper turbulence. Rita got into her little rowing boat and pushed off a couple of yards into the water. When she had lodged the nose of the craft in the reeds to secure it, she held her thermometer in the water for a few moments to test the temperature and noted it.

'Perfect!' she called. 'Ready when you are.'

'How long will it take?'

'Only a minute, I should think.'

On the bank, Daunt took off his coat, then his shirt. He stood in his long johns, and reflected that when in the early days of his widowhood he had contemplated the possibility of finding himself undressed in the company of a woman, this was not what he had imagined.

'All set,' she said, with her unaltered calm voice, her gaze fixed firmly away from him and on the pocket watch.

He entered the river.

The first touch of the water made his bones contract. He set his jaw, went three steps deeper. The freezing line rose up his limbs. He found he could not bear it to creep up to his genitals, instead he bent his knees and took the shock of immersion in a single motion. He lowered himself to the neck and gasped, surprised that his chest could expand in the water's grip. A few strokes took him to the side of the boat.

'Wrist,' she instructed.

He raised his wrist. She took it in her right hand, held the watch in her left and said nothing.

He endured it for what must have been a minute. She was still looking at the watch, her eyes blinking calmly every so often. He endured it for what felt like another minute.

'God! How much longer?'

'If I lose count we have to start again,' she murmured, the concentration on her face unchanging.

He endured an eternity.

He endured another.

He endured a thousand eternities – and then she let go of his wrist, took up the pencil and noted something neatly on the pad of paper, while he gasped and rose, scattering water from the river. He made for the bank, ran to the cottage, to the tin bath of tepid water they had prepared in advance, and when he was in it, she was right – the heat bloomed all over him.

When she entered the kitchen he was entirely submerged.

'Feel all right?' she asked.

He nodded, teeth chattering, and then his body took over from his mind for a time as it put all its vigour into recovering from the shock of the cold. When he was himself again, he looked over to the table. Rita was frowning out of the window as the light faded. The pencil was no longer round her neck, but stuck over her ear, the cord dangling on to her shoulder. *I want that*, he thought.

'Well?'

'Eighty-four.' She lifted the paper on which she had noted the figures. 'Your heartbeat rises in response to submersion in cold water.'

'*Rises?*'

'Yes.'

'But the girl's pulse fell . . . We found the opposite of what was meant to happen.'

'Yes.'

'It was for nothing, then.'

She shook her head slowly. 'Not nothing. I've ruled out a hypothesis. That's progress.'

'What's hypothesis two?'

She bent her head back to look at the ceiling, arm raised, elbow crooked around her head, and puffed out a long sigh of frustration. 'I don't know.'

Lily's Visitor

LILY WHITE WAS not asleep and she was not awake. She was in that border territory where shadows move like waves, and illumination – faint and perplexing – comes and goes, like feeble sunshine through deep water. Then she emerged abruptly into wakefulness in her bed in Basketman's Cottage.

What was it?

He was stealthy as a cat, opening the door without making a noise, stepping so lightly on the flags he was soundless. But she knew him by the odour of woodsmoke, sweetness and yeast that he always brought with him and that alarmed her senses so. It held its own, even against the dank riverine smell of the cottage. Then she heard him too: the grating of stone on stone. He was retrieving the money from the hiding place.

The sudden burst of a match strike. From her bed on the high ledge she saw the flare of light and the hand, with its bruises and scars, that tilted the candle wick into it. The wick caught and the circle of light grew steady.

'What you got for me?' he said.

'There's cheese there and a bit of that ham you like. There's bread in the basket.'

'Today's?'

'Yesterday's.'

The light moved over to the side and there was the sound of rummaging.

'Going mouldy, isn't it. Should've got me some today.'

'I didn't know you was coming.'

The circle of light floated back to the table, where it was set down, and for a little while the only sound was of ravenous eating, mouthfuls barely chewed, famished gulps. Lily lay in the dark, silent and unmoving, her heart trembling.

'What else is there?'

'Apples, if you want.'

'Apples! What do I want with apples?'

The glow of light rose again and hovered along one bare shelf and then the other. It crossed to the cupboard, examined the emptiness within, it reached into the back corners of a drawer and still found nothing.

'What do he pay you, that parson of yours?'

'Not enough. You told me that before.'

She tried not to think of her savings, safe in the parson's desk drawer, for fear the hovering light would reveal them to him.

A click of exasperation came out of the darkness.

'Why haven't you got me a bit of something sweet? What do you do for him, up at that parsonage? Apple pie? Bread pudding with damson jam? All sorts, I bet.'

'I will, next time.'

'Don't you forget.'

'I won't.'

Now that her eyes had adjusted, she could make out his shape in the dark. He sat at the table, his back to her, the shoulders of his coat sticking out wider than the frame beneath them; he was still in his wide-brimmed hat. By the sound of it, he was counting the money. She held her breath.

When the money wasn't right, it was she who got the blame for it. *What had she taken? Where had she hidden it? What selfish plan was she brewing with it? What kind of loyalty did she call that?* There were no answers to these questions that would satisfy him. Whatever she said, her answers were always met with his fists. The truth was, she had never once taken his money – she might be stupid, but she wasn't *that* stupid. The money did puzzle her though. She had questions of her own she'd have liked to ask, but didn't dare. She had pieced together where it came from well enough. Overnight and coinciding with his visits, those bottles and barrels full of a potent and illegal brew appeared in her woodshed. There they remained through daylight hours, and with the next darkness they disappeared, taken by his distributors and replaced by money for the next delivery. But what happened to the money after he'd got it? In a single night he took more money from the hiding place here than she earnt in a month at the parsonage, and she was sure he had other places that worked the same way too. He was hiding out in some place where there was no rent to pay, didn't gamble and never paid for a woman. He didn't touch drink either – never had, only encouraged others to ruin and emptied their purses in exchange. She'd tried to add it up, the money he had from here in a year, doubled or trebled, or multiplied sevenfold, but the numbers set her head spinning. Even without coming to the end of her sums she knew it was enough to make him rich, yet he turned up here, once a week or twice, in his ancient coat smelling of the distillery, all skin and bone, and famished. He ate her food and helped himself to her candles. She didn't dare keep a single nice thing in the cottage, because whatever it was he would take it, sell it, and the money would disappear. Even a pair of green woollen gloves with holes in the fingers would disappear into his pockets. There was a mystery in Vic's life that sucked all his money into it, and all hers too. Except what she had the parson keep back for her. It didn't make sense.

He gave a grunt of satisfaction and she breathed again. The money was right. With that done, he now leant back in the chair and took a breath. He always relaxed once he'd counted the money. She didn't.

'I always done all right by you, didn't I, Lil?'

'Always,' she responded, and before she answered she made a silent apology to God for lying. God understood that there were times a person just couldn't tell the truth.

'Looked after you better than your old ma ever did, eh?'

'You did, yes.'

He made a sound of contentment in the back of his throat.

'So what do you want to go calling yourself Lily White for?'

Lily's throat tightened. 'You said not to use your name when I come here. Nothing to connect us, you said, so . . .'

'Didn't have to be White, though, did it? Could've chose any name under the sun. That Whitey, he was no husband to you anyway. Not in the eyes of the Lord. Do he know that, your parson?'

'No.'

'No,' he repeated with satisfaction. 'I didn't think so.' He let the implied threat hang in the air before going on, 'I'm no fool, Lil. I knows why you chose that name. Shall I tell you?'

'Tell me.'

'You cling to that name like you never clung to the man himself. Lily White. Innocent and blameless, like the lilies of the field. That's what you like, isn't it?'

She swallowed.

'Speak up, Lil! Can't hardly hear you. But naming a thing don't make it so. You cling to that name like it'll wash you clean, same way as you scour this table, same way as you clean for that parson. Like it'll *redeem* you . . . Aren't I right, Lil?'

He took her agreement for granted.

'See, I *know* you, Lily. But what's done is done. There's no getting round it, some things can't never be scrubbed away.'

It was all she could do to keep her tears silent, but then even that was too much: her throat quivered and the next spasm of tears sounded loud in the room.

'Don't go upsetting yourself,' he said calmly. 'Things could be worse. You got me, haven't you?'

She nodded.

'Eh?'

'Yes, Vic.'

'I wonders whether you deserves me, sometimes. You've let me down at times, Lil.'

'I'm sorry, Vic.'

'So you say. More than once I've been disappointed in you.

Running off with Whitey. Years it took me to find you then. Any other man would've given up on you, but I didn't.'

'Thank you, Vic.'

'But are you grateful, Lil?'

''Course I am!'

'Really?'

'Truly!'

'So why'd you go letting me down again? That girl at the Swan . . .'

'They wouldn't let me take her, Vic. I tried, I tried my best, but there were two of them and—'

He wasn't listening. 'Could've made a fortune round the fairs with that. The Dead Girl That Lived Again. Imagine the queues. You could've given up skivvying for the parson, and with your honest face the queue to see her would've been a mile long. 'Stead of that she's gone up to the Vaughans' place, I hear.'

She nodded. He brooded, and she thought, *Perhaps that will be it. Perhaps he's gone to that dreaming place he goes to when he's had something to eat and got some money in his pocket, the place where he makes his secret plans.* But then he spoke again.

'We stick together, you and me, don't we?'

'Yes, Vic.'

'It's like there's a thread that joins us together. No matter how far you go or how long you're gone, that thread is always there. You know it is, 'cause sometimes there's a tug on it . . . You know that feeling, don't you, Lil? Except it's more than a tug, it's more like a boxer's fist in your chest that gives your heart a great wallop.'

She knew the feeling. She'd felt it many a time. 'Yes, Vic.'

'And we know what it is, don't we?'

'Yes, Vic.'

'Family!' He let out a profound sigh of satisfaction.

Now he stood and brought the circle of light across the floor and up the steps to her bed. The candle came close to her face. She squinted. Behind the glow was Victor, but, dazzled, she could not make out his expression. She felt the blanket being tugged away, and the light played for a little while on the folds of her nightgown over her breasts.

'I gets it in mind you're still that girl you used to be. You've let yourself go. All skin and bone. Used to be a pretty thing, you did. Back then. Before you run off.' He stretched out on the mattress; she inched away, he inched into the space and put an arm around her. The arm was slim in the coat sleeve, but she knew the strength in it.

His breathing deepened and he began to snore. She was reprieved – for now, at least – but still she could not stop the racing in her chest.

Lily did not move. She lay awake in the dark, breathing as gently as she could for fear of waking him.

After a scant hour, the candle had burnt out and a faint light seeped into the room. He didn't shift and stretch like most people did when they woke up. He didn't move an inch, just opened his eyes and asked, 'What money you got from that parson?'

'Not a lot.' She made her voice as meek as she could.

He reached for the purse she kept under her pillow and, standing, tipped the contents into his palm.

'I had to get the cheese for you. And the ham,' she explained. 'Leave me something, will you? Just a bit?'

He grunted. 'Don't know what you do with your money. What is it – don't you trust me?'

''Course I do.'

'Good. This is for your own good, you know that.'

She nodded meekly.

'All this,' he gestured expansively, and she didn't know whether he meant the cottage or the liquor in the woodshed or some other thing, bigger and less visible, behind it all and including it. 'All this, it's not for me, Lil.'

She watched him. You had to. You couldn't afford to miss a thing, with Vic.

'It's for *us*. For the *family*. You wait. One day you won't have to go skivvying for that old parson no more. You'll live in a great, white house ten times finer than that. You and me and—'

He broke off sharply, but his thoughts didn't. They carried him on, and she saw how his gaze softened as he gloated over the future he kept hugged to himself so privately.

'Now this' – and he waved his closed fist so she could hear the pennies rattling – 'is an investment. You've heard me talk about my scheme, haven't you?'

'This last five years, yes.' It'd been a recurring theme. Whether he was in a good mood or bad, whether the money was right or wrong, the scheme always lulled him. It made him quiet and it took the edge off the sharp look in his eyes. Sometimes when he mentioned it, his thin mouth twitched in a way that, if it were some other mouth, might have resulted in a smile. But he was as secretive about this scheme as about everything he did, and she was as ignorant of what it was as she had been when she first heard of it.

'It's a lot longer than five years.' The nostalgia in his voice was almost musical. 'That's just when I told you about it. Twenty years ago, I reckon I started plotting it out. Longer than that, even, if you look at it one way!' He twitched in self-congratulation. 'And soon the time'll be ripe. So don't you worry about your pennies, Lil, they're safe with me. It's all' – his mouth twisted – 'all in the family!'

He slid a couple of coins back into her purse and dropped it on the bed, rose and descended the steps to the kitchen.

'I've put a crate in the woodshed,' he told her in a new tone of voice. 'Someone'll come and take it away. Same as always. And there's a couple of barrels in the usual place. You didn't see 'em come and you won't see 'em go.'

'Yes, Vic.'

Then, helping himself to her three new candles on the way, he opened the door and was gone.

She lay in bed, thinking about his scheme. Not work at the parsonage any more? Live in a great, white house with Vic? She frowned. This cottage was cold and damp, but at least she had her days at the parsonage and was often alone at night. And – who else would be there? The words sounded again in her head. *You and me and—*

And who?

Did he mean Ann? *For the family*, he'd said. He must mean Ann. After all, he was the one who had come to her in the night with instructions to cross the river to the Swan at first light to fetch back the child who'd died and lived again.

She thought of her sister with Mr and Mrs Vaughan, in her bedroom with red blankets and the log basket piled high, and pictures on the wall.

No, she decided. *He must not have her.*

Gone! Or, Mr Armstrong Goes to Bampton

'WHAT CAN I do?' Armstrong asked for the hundredth time, as he paced in front of the fireplace in his own drawing room. Bess sat knitting by the fire. For the hundredth time, she shook her head and admitted that she didn't know.

'I'll go to Oxford. I'll have it out with him.'

She sighed. 'He won't thank you for it. It'll only make things worse.'

'But I have to do something. There are the Vaughans, living with the girl and getting more attached to her with every day that passes, and Robin does nothing! Why doesn't he make his mind up? What's the cause of the delay?'

Bess looked up doubtfully from her work. 'He won't tell you anything until he's ready. And even then, perhaps not.'

'This is different. This is a *child*.'

She sighed. 'Alice. Our first granddaughter.' She looked wistful, but then shook her head. 'If she is. It will end badly if you have it out with him. You know what he's like.'

'Then I shall go back to Bampton.'

She looked up. Her husband's face was set, determined.

'What will you do there?'

'Find someone who knew Alice. Bring them to Buscot. Put them in front of the child, and find out once and for all who she is.'

Bess frowned. 'And you think the Vaughans will allow that?'

Armstrong opened his mouth and closed it again. 'You're right,' he admitted, with a gesture of helplessness. Yet he could not let the matter drop. 'Still, at least if I go, I can find someone who *would* know, and once I've done that I can talk to Robin and see whether he wants to speak to the Vaughans, and – oh! I don't know. The thing is, Bess, what else is there? I can't do *nothing*.'

She looked at him fondly. 'No. You were never any good at that.'

The lodging house in Bampton was no more respectable-looking than before, but it had a merrier air than the last time he had seen it. Through an open upper window he heard the tune of a fiddle and the arhythmic wooden tapping that you hear when inebriated people dance on bare floorboards, having rolled the carpets back. Bursts of female laughter were interspersed with clapping, and the noise was so boisterous that he had to ring twice before he was heard.

'Come in, my duck!' exclaimed the woman who answered the door, shoeless and red-faced with exertion or liquor, and without waiting she withdrew upstairs, beckoning him to follow. He climbed the stairs, and he remembered climbing them the last time, when the poor dead woman in the room at the top was still just a letter-writer to him, and Alice a mere name. The woman led him to the first floor, where a number of men and women were hopping about in country style while the fiddler tried to catch them out by playing faster and faster. She pressed a glass of crystal-clear liquor into his hand, and when he demurred, invited him to dance.

'No, thank you all the same! In fact, I'm here to see Mrs Eavis.'

'She's not 'ere, thank the Lord. You'll have a lot more fun without 'er, lovey!' and she took his hands and tried again to get him to dance, though her efforts were compromised by her intermittent difficulties in remaining upright.

'I won't keep you from your friends any longer then, Miss, but perhaps you could tell me where to find her?'

'She's gone away.'

'But where?'

She pulled a face indicative of great mystification. 'Nobody knows.' Then, clapping her hands for attention, she shouted over the music, 'The gentleman wants Mrs Eavis!'

'Gone away!' cried two or three dancers in unison, with much laughter, and they seemed to dance all the merrier for her absence.

'When did this happen?' He took his purse and clasped it so that she could see it clearly as he asked the question. The sight of it sobered her and she answered as fully as she possibly could. 'Six or seven weeks ago, I should say. A fellow came to see her – so I hear – and she let him into her drawing room and they was there all evening long, and when he went away she went about all puffed up with a secret for a few days, and soon after a trap come to the door and took her cases and off she went.'

'Were you here before Christmas? I wonder. There was a Mrs Armstrong lived here with her little girl, Alice?'

'The one that died?' She shook her head. 'We're all new since then. Nobody stayed long when Mrs Eavis was here, 'cause nobody liked her, and when she went, them that owed her money scarpered.'

'What do you know of Mrs Armstrong?'

'She was not the right sort for this place. That's what I heard. Did the cooking and the cleaning here. She was pretty in a skinny sort of way – and there's some that likes that, takes all sorts – and once the customers had seen her, there was some that wanted a bit. But she wouldn't. That set old Eavis against her. Said she wasn't having no silly girl giving herself airs, and gave the key to her room to one of the gentlemen to teach her a lesson. The day after that, she did what she did.'

'She had a lover, I think? Who abandoned her?'

'Husband, is what I heard. Mind you, lovers, husbands, it's all the same, isn't it? A girl's better off on her own. Give them what they want, then take the money and bye-bye. Not her, though. She was the wrong sort for this life.'

Armstrong frowned. 'When will Mrs Eavis be back?'

'Nobody knows, and I hope it'll be a good long time. I'll be off as soon as she comes back, that's for sure.'

'So where has she gone?'

The woman shook her head. 'She'd come into some money, and she was going away. That's all I heard.'

Armstrong gave the woman some coins, and again she offered him a drink, or a dance, or 'anything you like, my duck'. He refused politely and took his leave.

Come into some money? It wasn't impossible, he supposed on his way down the stairs, but after the bad taste left by his first visit to the house, he felt inclined to doubt everything about Mrs Eavis.

Back in the street he regretted the journey, for it had wasted his time and his horse, but since he was there, another idea resurfaced that he had already thought of and discounted. Now that he considered it again, it seemed to him that it was a better idea than Mrs Eavis, in any case. He would find Ben, the butcher's boy. He remembered Alice, and would know at a glance whether the child at the Vaughans' was her or not. The word of a child would weigh very little in deciding the matter in law, but that hardly mattered – it was not the law he was thinking of. It seemed to him that his own certainty one way or the other would be a very valuable thing in its own right. If Ben recognized the child as Alice, Armstrong would have solid reason to pursue things further with his son. And if the boy did not, he would share that information with the Vaughans, and so give them the certainty they craved and that Robin was unable to offer of his own accord.

Armstrong walked up the high street, half expecting to see Ben by just bumping into him as he had before. But Ben was not on the grassy mound where they had played marbles and he was not visible in his father's shop and he was not loitering in the street. When he had peered into every side alley and shop window without result, he stopped a passing grocer's boy of about Ben's age to ask his whereabouts.

'He's run away,' the boy told him.

Armstrong was perplexed. 'When was this?'

'Few weeks ago. His dad give him a right beating till he were black and blue. Next thing, he were gone.'

'Do you know where he went?'

The boy shook his head.

'Was there anywhere he talked of going?'

'Some farm over Kelmscott way. A grand fellow over there was going to give him a job, he said. There'd be bread and honey and a mattress to sleep on and paid on the dot every Friday.' The boy sounded wistful for such a place. 'I never believed in it, though.'

Armstrong gave him a coin and went to the butcher's shop. A young man was at the block, with a weighty knife, dark with blood. He was chopping a loin into chops. At the sound of the bell, he looked up. His features were strikingly like Ben's, though the sullen expression was entirely his own.

'What do you want?'

Armstrong was used to hostility and could assess with accuracy how deep it went in a person. As often as not, people reserved their curtness for those who were, like him, unfamiliar. Difference was upsetting, and people armed themselves with aggression when they met it. With kindness in his voice, he could usually disarm them. Though their eyes told them to fear him, their ears were reassured. But some men went about in their armour every day and showed the blades of their swords to all. The whole world was the enemy. That kind of antipathy he could do nothing about, and that was what he met here. He made no attempt to please, just said, 'I'm looking for your brother Ben. Where is he?'

'Why? What's he done?'

'Nothing that I know of. I've got a job for him.'

From an archway at the back of the shop, an older voice emerged. 'No good for anything but eating the profits, that lad.' The words sounded as though they came from a mouth stuffed with food.

Armstrong leant to look through the archway into the room beyond. A man of about his own age sat in a stained armchair. On a table at his side was a loaf of bread and a large ham, with several slices cut from it. The butcher's cheeks were as pink and fatly gleaming as the meat. A pipe rested in the ashtray. A glass was half full of something and the bottle it came from rested in the man's lap, against his round belly, unstoppered.

'Any idea where he might have gone?' Armstrong asked.

The man shook his head. 'Don't care. Lazy blighter.' He speared another slice of ham with his fork and crammed it whole into his mouth.

Armstrong turned away, but before he could leave, a small, shrunken woman shuffled into the back room carrying a broom. He stood back to let her through into the shop, where she started to sweep the sawdust. She hung her head so that he could not see her face.

'Excuse me, Ma'am . . .'

She turned. She was younger than he had expected from the slowness of her movements, and her eyes were nervous.

'I'm looking for Ben. Your son?'

There was no light in her eyes.

'Do you have any idea where he might be?'

She gave a listless shake of the head, unable, it seemed, to rouse the energy for speech.

Armstrong sighed. 'Well . . . thank you.'

He was glad to be outdoors again.

Armstrong found water for Fleet and then he and the horse made for the river. This stretch was broad and straight and at times the water appeared so still you might take it for a solid mass, till you threw something in – a twig or an apple core – and saw with what powerful rapidity it was carried away. On a felled trunk not far from the bridge, he unwrapped his own lunch and took a mouthful. The meat was good, and so was the bread, but the sight of the butcher's greed had cut his appetite. He broke the bread into small crumbs and strewed them around for the little birds that came pecking, then he sat very still, looking into the water. Surrounded by robins and thrushes, he reflected on the disappointments of his day.

The failure of his visit to Mrs Eavis was bad enough, but the discovery that Ben was missing had lowered his spirits still further. He remembered the boy's care in looking after Fleet. He pictured the way he had eaten so ravenously when Armstrong offered him buns. He reflected on the boy's cheerful spirit. He thought of the dismal air in the butcher's shop, the monstrous father, the browbeaten mother and the first son, dead at heart, and marvelled at Ben's optimism. Where was the boy now? If, as the grocer's boy had said, he was making for Kelmscott – for Armstrong and the farm – why had he not arrived? It was no more than six miles – why, a boy ought to cover that distance in only a couple of hours. What had become of him?

And there was the girl. What could he do to further matters there? His heart sank at the thought of a child caught between two families, the impossibility of making sure she was in the right place. And from the child, his thoughts turned to Robin, and then his heart almost broke. He remembered the first time he had held him. The infant had been so small and light, yet the whole of life was present in the tentative movement of his arms and legs. During Bess's pregnancy, Armstrong had looked forward to loving and caring for this child, had awaited the day with excitement and impatience, yet still when the moment came he was overwhelmed by the strength of the feeling that swept over him. The infant in his arms obliterated all else, and he had vowed that this baby would never feel hungry or lonely or be placed in danger. He would love and protect this child, who would grow up a stranger to sorrow and loneliness. The same feeling rose in his chest now.

Armstrong wiped his eyes. The sudden movement made the robins and thrushes fly up and away. He got to his feet and answered Fleet's greeting with a rub and a pat.

'Come on. We're too old to ride to Oxford together, and in any case I haven't the time. But let's go to Lechlade. I'll leave you near the station and take the train. The boys will feed the pigs when they see I'm not back.'

Fleet harrumphed softly.

'Foolish?' he answered. He hesitated, one foot in the stirrup. 'Quite possibly. But what else is there? I can't do nothing.' He swung into the saddle and they turned upstream.

Armstrong asked for his son's lodgings. He made his way to a part of town where the streets were broader, the houses larger and well maintained. When he came to the street to which he had been sending letters these last two years, he slowed, uneasy, and when he came to Number 8 – large and grand and painted white – he halted at the gate and frowned. This was all too expensive by a long way. His own home, the farmhouse, was not overly modest, he did not hesitate to spend on the comfort and well-being of his family, but this grandeur was on another level altogether. Armstrong was not a stranger to fine villas – the accident of his birth meant that several grand households had opened their doors to him in his early years – and he was unintimidated by this display of wealth, yet he was troubled at the thought of his son residing in such a place. Where would he get the money for it? But might it be that he lodged in a single room in the attic? Or – was it possible? – perhaps there was another street in another part of town that bore the same name?

Armstrong entered by the second, smaller gate that lead by a narrow path to the back of the house and knocked at the kitchen door. It was answered by a girl of eleven or twelve with a lank plait and a downtrodden air, who shook her head at his suggestion of there being two streets with the same name.

'In that case, is there a Mr Robin Armstrong here?'

The girl hesitated. She seemed at once to shrink into herself and to scrutinize him more intently. The name was plainly known to her, and Armstrong was about to encourage her to speak when a woman of about thirty appeared behind her.

'What do you want?' Her voice was hard-edged. She stood rigidly upright, arms folded across her chest, her face the kind that didn't know how to smile. Then something in her altered. A subtle alteration in the set of her shoulders, something brazen in her eyes. Her lips remained set but gave the impression that if he played his cards right they had it in them to soften. Most people when they saw Mr Armstrong were so surprised at the colour of his skin that they saw nothing else, but some – women mostly – noticed that his face was very handsomely put together.

Armstrong did not smile and he put no note of coaxing cajolery in his voice. He carried apples for horses and marbles for small boys, but for women such as this one, he was careful to offer nothing at all.

'Are you the lady of the house?'

'Hardly.'

'The housekeeper?'

A brief nod.

'I'm looking for a Mr Armstrong,' he said neutrally.

She gave him a challenging look, waiting to see whether the good-looking stranger was going to make any effort to please her, and when he met her gaze with a steadily indifferent look of his own, shrugged.

'There is no Mr Armstrong here.'

She shut the door.

It was not an easy matter to linger in a smart Oxford street for any length of time, so, unwilling to draw attention to himself, Armstrong paced the streets that ran parallel. At every intersection of the path, he looked left and right, knowing he ran the risk of missing his object altogether, but when the hands of his watch had gone all the way round one hour and were halfway round the next one, he caught a glimpse of a slight figure with a long plait down her back. He pressed his pace to catch up with her.

'Miss! Excuse me, Miss!'

The girl stopped and swung round. 'Oh! It's you.'

She seemed smaller and even more miserable in the open air than she had in the doorway.

'Don't let me hold you up,' he said, seeing her shiver. 'Come along. I'll walk with you.'

'I don't know why she didn't tell you,' the girl offered before he had even asked the question. 'Is it you that writes the letters?'

'Yes, I write to him here.'

'But he don't live here.'

'Doesn't he?'

Now Armstrong was really puzzled. He had received answers to his correspondence. Brief and short – requests for money, mostly – but containing references to his own letters. He must be receiving them. Armstrong frowned.

The girl sniffed in the cold and turned a corner. She walked at a fast pace for such a small person.

'Mr Fisher says "Never mind the letters" and puts them in his pocket,' she adds.

'Ah.' That was something, anyway. Did he dare go back and ring that gleaming bell at the front step and ask for Mr Fisher?

As if she could read his thoughts, the girl told him, 'Mr Fisher won't be in for hours. Don't hardly get out of bed till midday, he keeps such late hours at the Green Dragon.'

He nodded. 'And who is this Mr Fisher?'

'A rotten man. He hasn't paid me for seven weeks. What do you want with him, anyway? Does he owe you money? You won't get it.'

'I have never met Mr Fisher. I am the father of Mr Armstrong. Presumably the two of them are associates.'

The look she gave him then told him everything he needed to know about Mr Fisher and his associates. Then he saw something start to dawn in the eyes of the child. If she had no liking for Mr Fisher and his associates, what was she to make of the father of one of those men?

'The thing is,' he reassured her, 'I fear that my boy might have fallen in with Mr Fisher. I'd like to get him out of harm's way, if I can. Have you seen a friend of Mr Fisher who is a young man of twenty-four, with light-brown hair that curls where it meets his collar, and sometimes wears a blue jacket?'

The girl stopped. Armstrong came to a halt a pace or two later, turned back and saw her face. If it were possible, she was whiter than before.

'You said you was Mr Armstrong's father!' she hissed.

'And so I am. He does not resemble me, it is true.'

'But that man . . . you just described him . . .'

'Yes?'

'*It is Mr Fisher!*' She spat the words at him, with a childish fury at being fooled. Then her face altered suddenly from outrage to fear. 'Don't tell him I told you! I never said a word! I never said nothing!' There was a plea in her voice, and tears in her eyes.

Seeing she was about to flee, Armstrong put his hand in his pocket and drew out coins. She suppressed the instinct to run and eyed the money. 'How much does he owe you?' he asked gently. 'Does this cover it?'

Several times her gaze shifted between the coins and him. She was wary, as though he were some kind of monster and the money most likely a trick. When it came, the snatch of her fingers was unexpected. In a flash the money was gone and she with it, apron strings and plait flying behind her as far as the first side street, where she turned and disappeared.

Armstrong got himself away from the moneyed part of town, and when he came to a busy street of shops and workplaces, entered the first public house he came to. He bought himself a drink, and one for the blind man who sat by the fireside. It was easy enough to lead the conversation from this public house to drinking places in general, and then to the Green Dragon in particular.

'It's decent enough between May and September,' the man told him. 'They put wooden tables outside and get some girls to serve the drinks. They water the beer and they overcharge, but folk put up with it for the roses they has clambering all over everywhere.'

'And in winter?'

'It's a bad sort of place. Damp in the timbers. Thatch wanted renewing when I could see, and that was twenty year ago. They say the windows are so cracked it's only the dirt what holds them together.'

'And the people?'

'Bad 'uns. You can buy and sell anything you wants at the Green Dragon – rubies, women, souls. If you have a difficulty in your life, go to the Green Dragon between the beginning of September and the middle of April and you'll find someone to remove it for you. For the right money. That's what they say, and it's true enough.'

'What do you do if you have a difficulty in spring or summer?'

'You 'ave to wait. Or do it yourself.'

'And where is it, this place?' Armstrong asked as he reached the bottom of his glass.

'You don't want to be going there. You're not the kind. I might not see very much, but I can hear your voice. It's not a place for a gentleman such as yourself.'

'I must. There is someone there and I must find him.'

'Do he want to be found?'

'Not by me.'

'Does he owe you money? It's not worth it.'

'It's not money. It's – family.'

'Family?' The man looked wistful.

'My son. I fear he's got in with the wrong sort.'

The blind man reached out a hand, and when Armstrong took it, he felt the man's other hand grip his forearm, measuring the size and power of it.

'I'd say you're a man that can look after yourself.'

'If I have to.'

'Then I'll tell you where to find the Dragon. For your son's sake.'

The directions Armstrong received took him right across town once more and out the other side. As he walked, it began to rain. He came to a meadow as the sky was turning shades of pink and apricot. On the other side of it was the river. He crossed a bridge and turned upstream. The path was edged with brambles and willows that dripped rainwater on to his hat, and the knuckles of ancient tree roots protruded from the ground beneath his feet. The light grew dimmer, as did his thoughts, and then he perceived through thickets of yew and holly and elder the outline of a building, and squares of dull light that were its windows. He knew he was in the right place, for it had the unmistakeable air of having been adopted by people who like to keep their doings out of sight and in the dark. Armstrong paused at the window and peered through the thick glass.

Inside was a low room, made lower still where the ceiling bulged in the middle. A pillar of oak, thick as three men standing together, had been placed as a support to hold it up. Gas lamps struggled to make an impact on the shadows, and were scarcely aided by the candles on the tables. It was only the end of the afternoon, but the place had the feeling of night. A few solitary drinkers sat in the shadows along the walls, but the best illumination came from the fire that was blazing in the hearth, and near it was a table, around which five men were seated. Four of the five men had their heads bent over a card game, but one sat up, his chair tilted on its back legs and leaning against the wall. His eyes were almost shut, but Armstrong guessed from the angle of his head that the appearance was a ruse. Between the narrow slits of his eyes, his son – for it was Robin – was casting about for a glance of the other men's cards.

Armstrong passed the window and opened the door. As he stepped inside, all five players turned in his direction, but the air was thick with smoke and he was half concealed behind the pillar – he was not yet recognized. Robin lowered his chair to the floor and signalled to someone in a dark corner, as he squinted blindly through the fug to where Armstrong stood.

A second later, Armstrong felt his arms gripped by an unseen person from behind. His assailant was smaller than he was by a head and a half, and his arms were slim, yet they gripped him like wire rope. The sensation of being held against his will was unfamiliar to Armstrong. He was not certain of being able to free himself, for all that the man was so small that the brim of his hat jutted between Armstrong's shoulder blades. A second fellow, with a single black brow that sat low over his eyes, came close and scrutinized him.

'Peculiar-looking fellow. Don't know 'im,' he announced.

'Get rid of him, then,' Robin said.

The men tried to turn him back to the door, but he resisted.

'Good evening, gentlemen,' he said, knowing that his voice alone would be enough to perturb things. He felt surprise in the hold of the wire-rope man, but the grip did not loosen. The monobrow peered at him again and, uncertain, turned back to the table, too late to see what Armstrong had seen: the flash of surprise on Robin's face, instantly suppressed.

'I think you'll find your Mr Fisher will see me,' Armstrong said.

Robin rose. He nodded to his guards, and Armstrong felt his arms released.

The two men returned to the shadows and Robin approached. He wore the same expression that Armstrong had seen a thousand times before, from early childhood to dawning manhood. It was the petulant fury of a child whose parent stood in his way. Armstrong was surprised to see how intimidating it looked on the face of a grown man. Had he not been Robin's father, had he been a less powerfully built man, he might well have been afraid.

'Outside,' Robin muttered. They stepped out of the inn and stood a yard apart, in semi-darkness, on a bank of gravel between the river and the inn.

'Is this where your money goes? Gambling? Or is it the house you're always in need of funds for? You are living beyond your means.'

A puff of disdain emerged from Robin's nostrils. 'How did you find me?' he asked dully.

Armstrong couldn't help being surprised by his son. Always he expected something better.

'Have you no better greeting than that for your father?'

'What do you want?'

'And your mother – you don't ask after her?'

'You'd tell me, I suppose, if anything was wrong.'

'Something *is* wrong. But it is not your mother.'

'It's raining. Say what you have come to say, so I can go back inside.'

'What are your intentions regarding the child?'

'Ha! Is that all?'

'*All?* Robin, this is a child we are talking about. The happiness of two families is at stake here. These are not things to make light of. Why the delay?'

In the fast-dying light, he thought he saw his son's lip give a cynical twist.

'*Is* she yours? If she is, what do you mean to do about it? And if not—'

'It's none of your business.'

Armstrong sighed. He shook his head and took another direction. 'I went to Bampton.'

Robin looked at his father more intently, but said nothing.

'I went back to the house where your wife lodged. Where she died.'

Robin still said nothing, and the intensity of his hostility did not waver.

'This lover your wife took – they know nothing of such a man.'

Still nothing.

'Who have you told this to?' There was menace in Robin's voice.

'I meant to bring the landlady to Buscot to see the child, but she—'

'How dare you? This is my business – mine alone. I'm warning you – keep out of my affairs.'

It took Armstrong a moment to recover. '*Your* business? Robin, there is a child's future at stake here. If she is your child, then she is my grandchild. If she is not your child, she is the Vaughans' child. In neither instance can it be said that it is your business. One way or the other, it is family business.'

'*Family!*' Robin spat out the word like a curse.

'Who is her father, Robin? A child needs a father.'

'I've done all right without one.'

Robin swivelled, scattering the gravel under his heels, and was starting back to the Green Dragon when Armstrong gripped his shoulder. Armstrong was only half surprised when his son swung round violently and a fist came towards him. Instinct brought his arm up to protect himself, but before the wildly thrown fist could make contact, his own fist met flesh and teeth, and Robin cursed.

'Forgive me,' Armstrong said. 'Robin – I'm sorry. Are you hurt?'

But Robin continued directing kicks and punches towards his father in an awkward scuffle, while Armstrong gripped his shoulders to hold him at a distance, so that fists and feet landed their blows at the far extent of their reach, when most of the power was gone out of them. He had held Robin off like this numerous times when he was a child and a juvenile; then his only concern had been to stop Robin hurting himself in his fury. Now his son's blows were more expert, and there was greater strength behind them, but they were still no match for his own greater height and power. Gravel flew, and curses, and Armstrong was aware that the noise would almost certainly bring observers to the windows.

What ended the affray was the sound of the inn door opening.

'All right?' came a voice through the rain.

Abruptly Robin abandoned the fight. 'All right,' he answered.

The inn door remained open; presumably someone continued to watch from the doorway.

His son turned to go without a handshake.

'*Robin!*' Armstrong called in a low voice after him. And lower still: '*Son!*'

A few yards away, Robin turned. He spoke low too, barely audible above the rain, but his words reached their target and hurt as his fists could never have done: 'You are *not* my father, and I am *not* your son!'

He reached the door, exchanged a word with his companion there, and they went inside, closing the door without looking back.

Armstrong walked back along the river. He blundered into willow, half tripped on one of the gnarled roots that lurked in the dark, and rainwater ran down his neck. His knuckle was stinging. The damage he'd barely felt at the time was now intensely painful. He had caught Robin's lip and teeth. Raising his hand to his mouth, he tasted blood. His own or his son's?

The river ran past, agitated by the rain and its own rush, and Armstrong stood silent and still in the rain, lost in his own reflections. *You are not my father, and I am not your son*. He would give anything to take that moment back. What could he have done differently? What could he have said to make it better? He had blundered, and perhaps that blundering had severed ties that might otherwise – in a few weeks or months or years – have been stimulated to warmth and affection again. What had just happened felt like the end of everything. He had lost his son and, with him, the world.

The rainwater ran with his tears, and the words sounded again and again in his thoughts. *You are not my father, and I am not your son*.

At last, wet and cold, he shook his head. 'Robin,' he answered, in words only the river heard, 'you may not want to be my son, but I cannot help but be your father.'

He turned downstream and began the long journey home.

Some Stories Are Not for Telling

THERE ARE STORIES that may be told aloud, and stories that must be told in whispers, and there are stories that are never told at all. The story of the marriage of Mr and Mrs Armstrong was one of these latter ones, known only to the two parties to whom it belonged and the river. But as secret visitors to this world, as border-crossers between one world and another, there is nothing to prevent us sitting by the river and opening our ears; then we will know it too.

When Robert Armstrong turned twenty-one, his father offered to buy him a farm. A land agent suggested a number of properties and Robert went to visit them all. The one that matched his hopes and expectations the best was that belonging to a man called Frederick May. Mr May had been a good farmer, but he had had only daughters and those daughters had married men with land enough of their own, all except one who was crippled and unmarried and stayed at home. Now that Mr May was old, he and his wife had decided to sell up all but the patch of land around the small cottage that they also owned, not far from the farmhouse. They would live in the cottage and grow vegetables and flowers and let someone else have the trouble of the land and the big house. With the proceeds of the farm they would be well off, and if the prospect of a good dowry was not enough to marry off their youngest child, well, at least the money would be a safeguard for her when they had passed away.

Robert Armstrong looked over the land and saw that it was irrigated by the river. He saw that the banks were firm and the waterway free from weeds and rubbish. He noticed how well maintained were the hedgerows, and that the cattle were gleaming and the fields ploughed straight. 'Yes,' he said. 'I'll have it.'

'You can't sell it to him, not that foreign fellow,' people said. But all the other potential buyers tried to beat Mr May down on price, and played one trick after another to get some advantage, and the black fellow offered the asking price and stuck to it, and what is more, Mr May had been with him as he walked round the farm, had seen that he appreciated the straightness of his plough lines, had seen how he was with the sheep and the cows, and before long he had forgotten the colour of Mr Armstrong's skin and understood that if he was to do the best thing for his land and his livestock, then Mr Armstrong was the man.

'What about the men who have worked for me so long?' asked Mr May.

'Those that want to stay shall stay, and if they work well over time they shall see their wages go up, and if they do not work well, then they must go after the first harvest,' said Armstrong, and so it was agreed.

A handful of labourers refused to work for a Negro, but the rest stayed, though they muttered at first. Over time, as they got to know the new boss, they discovered that his blackness was only superficial and that underneath it all he was a man like any other, and even a bit better. A handful of the men – young like himself – clung on to their contempt, sniggered to his face and made gestures behind his back. They used their scorn for him as a reason to be slack in their work – why should they labour for a man such as he? – but they still took their pay on a Friday, and when they spent it in the inns around Kelmscott they spoke ill of him. He appeared not to notice, but in reality he was keeping a close eye on them while he waited to see whether or not they would settle.

In the meantime, Robert Armstrong had to make friends. The man he knew best was the man he had bought the farm from, and he took to calling once a week on Mr May in the cottage not very far from the farmhouse. There he would sit for an hour, discussing farming with this man who was happy to talk about the work that had been his life and that he had grown too frail to do. Mrs May would sit knitting in the corner, and the more she heard their visitor's voice, which was better educated than most, and the more she heard his laughter, which was generous and rolling and made her husband laugh in turn, the more she liked him. From time to time their daughter came in, bringing tea or cakes.

Bessie May had fallen ill as a small child and the lasting result was that she swayed from side to side in her gait. As she walked, there was a distinct sinking as she stepped on to the left foot. It drew stares from strangers, and even people who knew her and knew the family said that she ought to be kept in instead of going about 'like that'. If it had only been the gait they might have frowned less than they did, but there was also the eye. She wore a patch over her right eye – not the same one all the time, but a different one depending on the colour of her dress. She had, it seemed, as many patches as dresses, sometimes made from offcuts of the same fabric, with ribbon ties that went around her head and disappeared into her pretty fair hair. She had an air of neatness about her, a care for her appearance that people found troubling. It was as if she thought she was the same as any other girl, as if she expected the same prospects. She ought, according to public opinion, to have retreated into the family home, to have made plain that she knew what everybody else knew: that she was unmarriageable, that she was destined for spinsterhood. Instead she hobbled into the heart of the church to take her place in the middle pews when she might have slipped in at the back and sat quite unnoticed. In good weather she limped to the bench on the green and sat with a book or a piece of embroidery; in winter she wore gloves and walked wherever the ground was level enough; when it was freezing she cast envious glances at those whose legs permitted them to risk the ice. Behind her back, malicious boys – the same ones, in fact, who made jeering gestures behind Robert Armstrong's back – imitated her swaying, drooping way of walking. People who knew her from childhood, before she wore the patch, remembered the way her eye showed too much white, while the pupil veered up and away. You couldn't tell where she was looking or what she was seeing, they said. There had been a time when Bessie May had friends. A little coterie of girls, who walked to and from school together, called at each other's houses, took each other's arms when they walked. But as the girls became little women, these friendships fell away. The other girls were afraid, perhaps, that Bessie's deformities might be contagious, or that the men would keep their distance from any girl with Bessie at her side. By the time Robert Armstrong bought the farm, Bessie was lonely. She walked with her head high, smiling, and outwardly there was no alteration in her manner to the world, but she knew that the world had altered in its manner to her.

One of the alterations was in the way that the young men of the village behaved. At sixteen, with her fair curls and her pretty smile and her neat waist, Bessie was not without attraction. If you saw her seated, when the patch was away from you, you would think her one of the loveliest girls in the village. This was not lost on the young men, who began to eye her in a vulgar way. When lust and scorn live alongside one another in the same heart, they make devilry. If they came upon her in an empty lane, the young men leered at Bessie, rushed at her, knowing she could not easily hop sideways to avoid their outstretched hands. More than once, Bessie arrived home from an errand with a muddied skirt and grazed hands, having 'tripped'.

Robert Armstrong knew what the gang of young men on the farm thought of him. In his discreet scrutiny of them, he had also understood what they thought of Bessie May. One evening when he arrived for one of his regular visits to the May household, Mr May shook his head. 'Not tonight, Armstrong.' His friend's trembling hands and tearful eyes told him of some crisis. Watching the young men on the farm, hearing a snatch of laughing conversation in which Bessie's name was mentioned boastfully by one of the lads, accompanied by a vulgar gesture, he feared he knew what the crisis was.

In the next few days, he did not see Bessie. She was not at church and she was not on the bench by the green. She did not run errands to the village and she did not tend the garden. When she reappeared, something had changed in her. She was neat and active as before, but the simplicity and naturalness of her interest in the world had been exchanged for something grimmer. A determination not to be beaten.

Overnight, he thought about it. He made his decision and then he slept, and when he woke the decision still seemed to be a good one. He intercepted Bessie on her way to take her father's lunch to him, on the riverbank where the hawthorn gave way to the hazel. He saw her start and take fright when she realized there was nobody else in sight. He put his hands behind his back and looked at his feet as he spoke her name. 'Miss May. We have spoken little before, but you know who I am. You know I am a friend of your father's and the owner of this farm. You know I pay my debts on time. I have few friends, but I am nobody's enemy. If you should ever need anyone on your side, I beg that you would come to me. There is nothing I should like more than to ease your life. Whether that be as a friend or as a husband is a decision that is yours to make. Please know that I am at your service.' He raised his head to meet her astonished eye, gave her a brief bow and departed.

The following day, he came to the same place at the same time and she was already there. 'Mr Armstrong,' she began, 'I don't know how to talk the way you talk. You have finer words than me. Before I can say anything to you about what you said yesterday, there is something I must do. I will do it now, and when I have done it you might feel different about it all.'

He nodded.

She lowered her head, raised her fingers to her patch, and tugged it over the bridge of her nose until it covered her good eye and her other eye was revealed. Then she turned her right eye on him.

Armstrong examined Bessie's eye. It seemed to quiver with a life of its own. The iris, off-centre, was the same blue as its twin on the surface, but contained undercurrents of darker shades beneath. The pupil, a familiar thing that one saw in every face, every day, was made strange in Bess's face by its skew. Suddenly he was distracted from his staring by the realization that *he* was the one being examined. He felt himself dissected, naked under her gaze. Exposed to her focus, he suddenly remembered incidents of boyish shame. Moments came back to him when he had behaved less honourably than he would have wished. He remembered instances of ingratitude. He felt a pang of remorse and resolved not to do the same again. He also felt relief that these small acts of neglect were all he had to regret in his life.

The moment did not last long. When she was done, Bessie lowered her head and readjusted the patch. She turned her everyday face back to him, and it was altered. There was surprise in it, and something else that warmed him and made his heart thrill. Her good eye softened, contained dawning affection, admiration even. It was the kind of sentiment that one day – could he bring himself to believe it? – might lead to love.

'You are a good man, Mr Armstrong. I can tell. There is something you should know about me though.' She spoke low and her voice was unsteady.

'I know it.'

'I don't mean this.' She indicated her patch.

'Nor do I. Nor your limp either.'

She stared at him. 'How do you know?'

'The man works on my farm. I guessed.'

'And you still wish to marry me?'

'I do.'

'But what if . . . ?'

'If there is a baby?'

She nodded, reddened and looked down in embarrassment.

'Do not blush, Bess. No shame attaches to you in this. The shame lies on another's shoulders. And if there is a child, then you and I will raise it and love it just as we will raise and love our own children.'

She lifted her face and met his steady gaze. 'Then yes, Mr Armstrong. Yes, I will be your wife.'

They did not kiss and they did not touch. He simply asked her to let her father know that he would call on him later that day.

'I will tell him.'

Armstrong visited Mr May and the marriage was agreed.

When the young man who had been troublesome at the farm and worse than troublesome to Bessie arrived at work the next morning with his usual swagger, Armstrong was waiting. He gave him the wages he was owed, and dismissed him. 'If I ever hear of you within twelve miles of this place, it will be the worse for you,' he told him, and his tone was so restrained that the young man looked up with astonishment to see whether he had heard right. But the look in Armstrong's eye told him that every word was meant, and instead of the insolent answer he had in his mind to deliver, he was silent as he left, and his curses were under his breath.

The engagement was announced and the wedding followed soon after. People talked. They always do. The church was filled with the curious on the wedding day of the swarthy farmer and his deformed, pale bride. There was money there – oh, she had done well, in that respect – and with her blue eyes and blonde hair and trim figure he had, in that at least, done better than he could ever have expected. Yet the congratulations were tinged with the colour of pity and nobody envied the couple. There was a general feeling that it made sense for the two unmarriageables to have found each other, and every unmarried guest present felt a pang of relief: thank goodness they would not be obliged to make such devastating compromises in their own choices. Better a poor labourer than a landowner with a Negro mother; rather a rough laundry maid than a farmer's daughter with a boss eye and a limp.

When Bessie's stomach began to swell a few months after the marriage, it was a scandal. What kind of an infant would it be? A monster, surely. After children started calling out cruel names to Bessie in the street, she stopped going out beyond the extent of the farm. She waited her time nervously, but Armstrong talked soothingly to her. The sound of his voice comforted her, and when he placed his hands on her growing belly and said, 'All will be well,' she could not help but think it would.

The midwife who delivered the child went directly to her friends on leaving, and they passed the news rapidly to all others. What monster was it that had emerged from between the legs of boss-eyed Bessie, put there by her dark husband? Those who expected three eyes, woolly hair and shrivelled limbs were disappointed. The baby was normal. And not only that. 'Beautiful!' she rhapsodized. 'Who'd have thought it? The loveliest baby I ever did see.' And before long, the rest saw it too. Armstrong went on horseback here and there, and on his knee they all saw the child: light curls, a bonny complexion and a smile so charming you could not help but smile back.

'Let us call him Robert,' Armstrong said, 'like me.' And so he was christened, but because he was little they called him Robin, and as he grew they continued with Robin, for it was a way of telling father and son apart. And in time there were other children too, girls and boys, and all of them hale and happy. Some were dark and some less dark and some were almost fair, though none so fair as Robin.

Armstrong and Bessie were happy. They had made a happy family.

Photographing Amelia

TOWARDS THE BEGINNING of the last week of March came the day of the spring equinox. Light equalled dark; day and night were perfectly poised; even human affairs enjoyed a moment of balance. The river was high – it is the way of the river to be high at the equinoxes.

Vaughan woke first. It was late – they had slept through the birdsong, through the fading of the darkness – and light was waiting behind the curtains.

Next to him, Helena was still asleep, one arm flung above her head on the pillow. He kissed the tender flesh on the inside of her arm. Without opening her eyes, she smiled and shifted closer to his warmth. She was still naked from last night. These days they slipped from pleasure into sleep and from sleep into pleasure again. Under the bedclothes his hand found her ribcage, travelled the smooth curve to her waist, her hip. Her toes came to nudge his.

Afterwards, he said, 'You go back to sleep for another hour if you want. I'll give her breakfast.' She nodded, smiling, and closed her eyes again. They were both capable now of sleeping lengthily, nine or ten hours at a stretch sometimes, making up for the years of insomnia. It was the child's doing. She had mended their nights. She had mended their marriage too.

In the breakfast room, he and the child sat in companionable silence. When Helena was present she chatted constantly to the girl, but he did not attempt to talk to her or to gain her attention by any deliberate means. Instead he buttered her toast, spread the marmalade and sliced it into soldiers, while she watched, absorbed. She ate with concentration, in a self-contained reverie, until an over-generous blob of marmalade fell from the edge of the toast on to the tablecloth, and she glanced up to see whether he had seen it. Her eyes – which Helena called green and he called blue and that were gravely fathomless – met his, and he smiled at her, a small, kindly, undemanding smile. There came a slight, fleeting twitch of her mouth in return, and though it had happened a dozen times before, he still felt his heart lurch at it.

He felt the same leap in the chest when she turned to him for reassurance. Though she was fearless on the river, she was nervous of all sorts of other things: the approach of horses on cobblestones, doors that slammed, over-familiar strangers who reached down to tweak her nose, the beating of rugs with brooms, and it was him she looked to when she was startled. In unfamiliar situations, it was his hand she reached for, he to whom she raised her arms to be lifted out of some perceived danger. He was touched by her selection of him as her protector. Two years ago, he had failed to protect Amelia; this felt like a second chance. With every danger averted, he felt his faith in himself returning.

The child still did not speak, she was often absent, sometimes indifferent, yet her presence gladdened him. A hundred times a day, his mind made the journey from Amelia to this child and from this child back to Amelia. The path between the two of them was now so well travelled that it was impossible to think of one without the other. They had become aspects of the same thought.

The maid came to clear the breakfast things.

'The photographer is coming at half past ten,' he reminded her. 'I expect we'll have coffee first.'

'It's the day the nurse comes – will she have coffee too?'

'Yes, coffee for everyone.'

The maid looked anxiously at the child's hair that was still tangled from sleep.

'Should I try and brush Miss Amelia's hair for the photographs?' she offered, eyeing the tangle with a doubtful expression.

'Let Mrs Vaughan do it when she's up.'

The maid looked relieved.

There was something Vaughan needed to do to prepare himself before Daunt arrived.

'Come on, little one,' he said.

He lifted the child and carried her into the drawing room. He sat at the desk and placed the girl sideways on his lap so she could see into the garden.

He reached for the photograph of Amelia with himself and Helena.

With the coming of the girl, his fear of memory, so powerful that he had sought to bury his daughter's face entirely, had lessened. He had had the sense – irrational, he knew – that Amelia herself was looking for him, and that he owed it to her to meet her gaze. Across that awful divide. Now that the moment had come, with the girl on his lap, he found that the task did not seem so difficult as he had feared.

He turned the image to face him and looked at it through the haze of the child's unbrushed hair.

It was a traditional family pose. Helena was seated with Amelia on her knees. Behind them stood Vaughan himself. Knowing that the slightest quiver of emotion might end in a disastrous waste of time, money and effort, he had stared too fiercely and as a result looked intimidating to those who didn't know him and comic to those who did. Helena had been entirely unable to suppress her smile, but delivered it so steadily to the camera that her beauty was crisp in every detail. On her knees: Amelia.

On a photograph three inches by five, his daughter's face was small – smaller even than the thumbnail of the child on his lap. At two, she retained that undefined quality in her face that lingered from her baby years. Moreover, she had been unable to keep entirely still. The indistinct features had something universal about them; they lent themselves as easily to the face of the little girl on his lap as to the daughter he had tried so hard to lock away out of sight and out of mind. Her feet must have moved too, for they were a blur, spectral, boneless, the kind a ghost might hover on. Around her small body was a froth of petticoat and skirt that dissolved into transparency at its edges. The hands were lost in its spume.

The child shifted in his lap and he looked down. A bead of water had appeared on her hand. She raised it to her mouth and licked it, then looked up at him with casual curiosity.

He was weeping.

'Silly Dada,' he said, and bent to kiss her head, but she squirmed free. She crossed the room to the door, where she stopped and turned and extended a hand towards him. He followed, put his hand in hers and allowed himself to be led out of the house, into the garden and down the shallow gravel slope to the river.

'What's this in aid of?' he wondered aloud. 'Is this supposed to make me feel better?'

She stared up the river and down, and when there was nothing to see, looked around for a good stick to prod and poke with at the water's edge. When she had done with that, she passed the stick to Vaughan to continue, while she selected some large stones from the slope to take and wash in the water. The washing seemed without purpose, and out of nowhere Vaughan was struck by the notion that he had stood here once before and watched Amelia wash stones. Did he not remember a time, some years ago, when the two of them had been at the river's edge, just like this, rinsing stones for no reason and prodding at the soft mud in the shallows? He raised his head to work out whether the memory was genuine or whether it was some curious reverse echo, by which the present seems to duplicate itself in the past.

The girl had stopped her labour with the stones. On all fours, she bent close to the water's surface as if it were a mirror. Looking back at her was another girl – one he knew.

'Amelia!'

He grasped for her, but at his touch she was gone and his fingers were wet.

The girl sat up and turned her ever-changing eyes on him in an attitude of mild concern.

'Who are you? I *know* you're not her – but if you are . . . *if* you are – am I going mad?'

She handed him the stick and indicated with a vigorous motion that he should dig a channel with it. She lined it with her stones. She was exacting in her expectations and it took some time before she was satisfied. Then, he understood, they were to watch it. They saw how the water trickled in, and how it silted up, and how rapidly the work of the river undid the work of a man and a child.

In the end, they carried the coffee outdoors and down to the boathouse. It was generally agreed that a riverside setting would be more interesting than an indoor photograph, so they must make the most of the dry weather while it lasted.

Once they'd got the camera in position, Daunt went to prepare the first plate. 'While I'm gone, here are the other exposures. From last time.'

Helena unfastened the hinged lid of the wooden box. The interior was lined with felt. It contained, each in its slot, two glass plates.

'Oh!' Helena said, when she was holding the first up to the light. 'How strange!'

'It takes you aback, doesn't it?' Rita said. 'Light and shade are reversed.' She peered at the same plate. 'I fear Mr Daunt was right and you already have the best ones. This one is rather blurred.'

'What do you think, darling?' Helena asked, passing the plate to Vaughan.

He glanced at the plate, saw a smudge of a child, and looked away again.

'Are you all right?' Rita asked.

He nodded. 'Too much coffee.'

Helena removed the second plate from the box and studied it. 'They are blurred, it's true, but not so much that you can't see the thing that matters. It is Amelia. That's perfectly plain.' Her voice contained no unsettling intensity, no rising note of hysteria. It was measured, mild even. 'This question in Mr Armstrong's mind will never come to anything, but the lawyer thinks we should be ready, just in case.'

'Mr Armstrong's visits continue?'

Helena's nod was unperturbed. 'They do.'

Rita caught Vaughan's face as it flinched at the sound of the other man's name.

But then Daunt was there. Helena slid the plates back into the box and swung the child into her arms with a wide smile. 'Where do you want us for the new photographs?'

Daunt looked to the sky to gauge the sun, then pointed. 'Just there.'

The girl fidgeted and struggled, turned her head and shuffled her feet, and one expensive plate after another had to be abandoned that was not worth developing.

Just as they were on the point of becoming dispirited, Rita made a suggestion.

'Put her in a boat. She'll settle on the water, and the river is steady.'

Daunt eyed the river to see how much motion there was in it. The current was untroubled. He shrugged and nodded. It was worth a try.

They carried the camera to the bank. Helena brought the little rowing boat from the days of her girlhood out to the jetty and secured it.

The river pulled at the boat with even energy, tautening the mooring rope. The girl stepped into it. There was no rocking, no need to get her balance. She stood, poised on the shifting water.

Daunt opened his mouth to ask her to sit down, but there then came one of those moments that mean everything to a photographer and he thought better of it. The wind chased the heavy cloud from the sun and put in its place a scant white veil that softened the light and blurred shadows. In response the water lightened to a pearlized finish at the very moment that the girl turned to gaze upriver in just the direction the camera needed. Perfection.

Daunt whipped away the lens cover and all fell silent, willing the sun, the wind and the river to hold. One. Two. Three. Four. Five. Six. Seven. Eight. Nine. Ten. Eleven. Twelve. Thirteen. Fourteen. Fifteen.

Success!

'Ever seen developing in process?' Daunt asked Vaughan as he light-proofed the plate and extracted it from the camera. 'No? Come and watch. You'll see the darkroom, and how I've kitted it out.'

*

'That cloud is heading back,' Helena said, craning her neck to look skywards as the men disappeared into the darkroom. 'What do you reckon?'

'We'll be all right for a bit.'

They returned the little old rowing boat to the boathouse and took out the larger one, suitable for two rowers and a child. Rita set it rocking as she got in and had to find her balance again. Helena stepped in deftly, barely altering the equilibrium of the boat in the water, and before she could turn to lift the child, there she was, by her side, having stepped from land to water as though it were the most natural thing in the world.

They seated themselves, the child on the passenger seat, then Helena, Rita behind. From the minute the boat drew out into the current, Rita felt the power of the other woman's stroke.

'Amelia! Sit down!' Helena cried, with a laugh. 'She does insist on standing. We shall have to get her a punt or a gondola if she keeps on!'

The little girl's back stiffened as she raised her head to look intently ahead, but the river was empty, theirs was the only vessel out in the bad weather, and when she slumped, Rita felt the poignancy of her disappointment. 'What is it she looks for?' she wondered aloud.

Helena shrugged. 'She is always interested in the river. She'd spend all day here if she could. I was just the same at her age. It's in the blood.'

It was not an answer to her question, but nor was it a deliberate evasion. For all the intensity and constancy of Helena's gazing at the child, Rita had the impression that in certain ways she failed to actually see her. She saw Amelia, her Amelia, for that was what she needed to see. But there was more to this child than that. She, Rita, could not see the child without the urge to lift her into her arms and comfort her. It was an instinct that perplexed her and she tried to bury it in questions.

'Still no notion about where she was before?'

'She's back. That's all that matters now.'

Rita tried another tack. 'No news about the kidnappers?'

'Not a thing.'

'And the window locks – do you feel secure now?'

'I still get the feeling that someone is watching.'

'You remember the man I told you about? The one who asked me whether she was speaking and what the doctor had said?'

'You haven't seen him again?'

'No. But his interest in the six months it might take for her voice to return does make me wonder whether that is the time to look out for him.'

'The summer solstice.'

'That's right. Tell me about the nursery maid Amelia had in the old days . . . What became of her?'

'It is good news for Ruby that Amelia is back. She struggled to find work afterwards. There was so much malicious gossip.'

'People thought that Ruby had something to do with it at the time, didn't they? Because she was absent from the house?'

'Yes, but—' Helena stopped rowing. Rita was getting out of breath from the exertion, so they allowed the river to carry them along, Helena doing just enough to keep them straight. 'Ruby was the best of girls. She came to us at sixteen. Had lots of little brothers and sisters, so she was experienced with little ones. And she loved Amelia. You only had to see them together.'

'So why wasn't she at home the night it happened?'

'She couldn't explain. That's why people thought she had something to do with it, but more fool them. I know she wouldn't have harmed Amelia.'

'Did she have an admirer?'

'Not yet. She had the same dreams as most girls that age. Meeting a nice young man, courtship, marriage, a family of her own. But that was all still in the future. She wanted it, was putting money aside for the future, like a sensible girl, but it hadn't happened yet.'

'Might there have been a secret admirer? Some charming rogue she wouldn't have wanted you to know about?'

'She wasn't the type.'

'Tell me how it happened.'

Rita listened to Helena recount the night of the kidnap. Her voice grew taut as she remembered the events; every so often she paused – to look at the child, Rita guessed – and when her voice took up again it was softer, reassured by the presence of the child who had returned so unexpectedly from nowhere.

When she got to the part where Ruby returned, Rita interrupted.

'So she arrived back from the garden? And what did she say to explain herself?'

'That she had gone for a walk. The policemen took her into Anthony's study and questioned her for hours. Why go for a walk in the cold? Why go at night? Why go when the river gypsies were about? They badgered and bullied her. She wept and they shouted, but still she gave no other answer. She'd been for a walk. That's all she would say. She went for a walk for no reason.'

'And you believed her?'

'Don't we all do unexpected things from time to time? Don't we all break habits and entertain the thought of something novel? At sixteen we are too young to know what we are – and if a girl suddenly wants to go for a walk though it is dark, why should she not? I was out on the river at all hours at that age, winter and summer alike. There was nothing ill in it. It might be different if Ruby was a sly or devilish girl, but there is no malice in her. If I am Amelia's mother and I say so, why will others not believe it?'

Because it needs an explanation, thought Rita.

'Once the police got it into their heads that it was the river gypsies, they forgot all about Ruby and her nocturne. I wish everybody else had too. Poor girl.'

A spattering of raindrops broke the surface of the river, and both women looked up. The rainclouds were regrouping.

'Had we better turn back?'

They hesitated, but another heavier burst of rain pocked the water around them and they turned the boat.

It was hard going against the current. Before long the rain was falling not in experimental squalls but with steady purpose, and Rita felt her shoulders become soaked. The rain dripped from her hair and into her eyes. Her wet hands felt sore and she concentrated hard to match the pace that she knew was less than Helena would produce with a stronger mate.

At last a cry from Helena told her they had arrived. They drew close to the jetty and Rita at last had a hand free to wipe the rain out of her eyes. Able to see again, she caught a glimpse of movement in the bushes on the opposite bank.

'We are being watched,' Rita told Helena. 'Don't look now, but there is someone hiding in that scrub. Listen, this is what we'll do . . .'

At the boathouse Helena lifted the child out of the boat and on to the bank, and in the pouring rain the two of them made their way in a half-run to the shelter of *Collodion*. Rita stepped back into the boat with the rope, took up her oars and was away again, steering a course directly across the current. She was tired, and not fast, but if anyone tried to run they would have to break cover and be seen.

There was no mooring point on the other side, only the reeds to stop the boat. Rita scrambled out and up the bank. She paid no heed to the muddying of her hem, or the fact that she was wet up to her knees and her shoulders were drenched with rain, but made directly for the cluster of shrubs. As she approached, the branches shivered – whoever was there was trying to bury deeper into concealment. She looked through the maze of branches to where a sodden figure crouched with its back to her.

'Come out,' she said.

The figure didn't move, but the hunched back shook as if the person were weeping.

'Lily, come out. It's only me, Rita.'

Lily began to edge backwards, branches and thorns catching at her clothes and her hair. Once she had crawled out a little way, leaving some of her own hair behind in the shrubbery, Rita was able to help her by reaching in to detach the clinging spines, one after another, from the wet cloth of Lily's dress.

'Dear, oh dear . . .' Rita murmured as she smoothed Lily's hair. Her hands were criss-crossed with scratches. A bramble had caught her face; beads of blood sat along the red line like berries until they fell in crimson tears down her cheeks.

Rita took out a fresh handkerchief and pressed it very gently to Lily's cheek. Lily's eyes flickered nervously between Rita, the river and the far bank, where Daunt, Vaughan and Helena were on deck, oblivious to the rain, looking across. Beside them the girl leant out over the water with her fathoms-deep stare, while her father held the back of her dress.

'Come across,' Rita soothed. 'I'll wash that scratch for you.'

Lily started in fear. 'I can't!'

'They won't be cross,' she told her in her kindest voice. 'They thought it was someone who wanted to hurt the little girl.'

'I won't hurt her! I never wanted to hurt her! I never did!' Abruptly she gathered herself and turned to hurry away.

Rita reached after her – 'Lily!' – but Lily would not be held back. She reached the path, and before she had quite scurried out of earshot called back over her shoulder to Rita on the bank: 'Tell them I meant no harm!' And then she was gone.

By the time Rita had cleaned her dress and given her boots a chance to dry out, it was getting dark. Henry Daunt offered to take her home in *Collodion* to save another drenching. They made their way down the garden to the jetty. Daunt offered his hand to help her where the path was uneven underfoot, but she did not take it, so he confined himself to pushing low branches out of the way. Once the two of them were on board, he navigated his way by moonlight to her cottage. It had rained on and off all afternoon, and now that they had reached her home it suddenly drummed heavily on the roof of the boat.

'It will ease in a bit,' he said, over the noise. 'No point going straight in, you'll be soaked to the skin before you reach the door.'

Daunt lit a pipe. The cabin was snug when two people were in it, because of all the photographic kit, and her proximity together with the lateness of the hour made him conscious of her wrists and hands, the hollow of her throat that glowed palely in the candlelight. Rita tugged at her sleeves as if aware of her naked hands and, fearing she was about to decide to go in anyway, Daunt found a question for her.

'Does Lily still believe the child is her sister?'

'I believe so. The parson spoke to her about it and she was unshakeable.'

'It can't be so.'

'It's most improbable, yes. I wish I had been able to persuade her to come across. I'd have liked to speak to her.'

'About the girl?'

'And about herself.'

The rain seemed to ease. Before she could notice it, he asked another question.

'What of that man who troubled you before? Have you seen any more of him?'

'Nothing.'

Rita tucked her muffler firmly into her lapels, concealing her throat. She was preparing to leave, but the percussion redoubled on the roof. She sighed in a way that was also an embarrassed smile and her arms fell to her side again.

'Do you mind this smoke? I'll put it out if you like.'

'No, it's all right.'

He put his pipe out anyway.

In the next silence, he became acutely aware that the bench behind them, which neither had made a move to sit on, was also his bed. It seemed suddenly to take up a huge amount of space. He lit a candle and cleared his throat.

'It's a miracle, the light we had for the exposure,' he said in order to dispel the silence.

'A miracle?' Her eyes were teasing.

'Well, not exactly a miracle. Not by your exacting standards.'

'It's a good photograph,' she offered.

He unstrapped the box in which he had the plate and held it not too close to the flame. The candlelight flickered it into life. Rita took half a step so that she was standing as close to him as she could without touching him, and she leant to peer at the glass.

'Where is the one from two years ago?' she asked.

He took it out of the box and held it for her to see. He could see raindrops in her hair as she bent to look.

It was too dark to compare the images in detail, but the idea of making the comparison put the question in his mind and he was certain it was in hers.

'Two years ago I photographed a child of two, and today I photographed a child of four, and I do not know whether it is the same child or a different one. Is it her, Rita? Is it Amelia?'

'Helena believes so.'

'And Vaughan?'

'He is not so sure. I once thought he was convinced it was another child altogether; now he is wavering.'

'What do *you* think?'

'The child of two years ago and the child of today are like enough that it is possible, but not so alike that it is certain.'

She placed her hands on the edge of the developing table and leant against it. 'Look at it from another perspective. Today's photograph.'

'Yes?'

'How do you think she looked? I don't mean clarity and composition, your usual judgements on your work, but the girl herself. How was she?'

He peered at the image, but the candlelight made it hard to read the expression on the little girl's face. 'Expectation? Not really, is it. Nor hope.'

He turned to Rita for elucidation.

'She's sad, Daunt.'

'Sad?' He looked again at the photograph while she continued speaking.

'She stares up- and downriver, in search of something. Something she longs for. Something she has been expecting every day, and every day it doesn't come, and still she waits and still she looks and still she yearns, but the hope dwindles with every day that passes. Now she waits hopelessly.'

He looked. What she said was true. 'What is it she's waiting for?'

Suddenly he knew the answer to his own question. 'Her father,' he said at the same time as Rita opened her mouth and said, 'Her mother.'

'Does she belong to Robin Armstrong, after all?'

Rita frowned. 'According to Helena, she's indifferent to him, but if she hasn't seen him for a long time – and he admitted as much at the Swan – she wouldn't remember.'

'So she might be his.'

Rita paused, frowning.

'Robin Armstrong is a man who's not what he seems, Daunt.' He saw her weighing up how much to tell him. She came to a conclusion. 'His faint at the Swan was faked. His pulse was far too steady. The entire thing was play-acting.'

'Why?'

Her face had the grim and hungry look it always had when her knowledge of a thing was thwarted. 'I don't know. But that young man is not what he seems.'

The rain had slowed. She picked up a glove, put it on, and when she reached for the other found that Daunt had it in his hands.

'When can I photograph you again?'

'Have you nothing better to do than take photographs of a country nurse? Surely you must have enough by now.'

'I have nowhere near enough.'

'My glove?' She would not be coaxed into coquettishness, not even over a glove. Flirting got you nowhere. She refused to play with undercurrents and scorned gallantry. Directness was the only approach she recognized.

He relinquished the glove and she turned, ready to leave.

'When I see you with the girl . . .'

She paused, and he saw her back stiffen.

'What I wonder is, haven't *you* ever wanted . . .'

'A child?' Something in her voice opened the door to hope.

She turned and looked him full in the face. 'I'm thirty-five. Far too old for all that.'

It was a clear rebuff.

In the silence that followed, it became obvious that at some point the rain must have stopped, because they heard it start up again, a gentle patter.

Rita exclaimed and refolded her muffler. He shuffled round her elaborately to open the door; it was a dance in which they both leant exaggeratedly away from each other.

'Shall I see you to your door?'

'It's only a few yards. Stay in the dry.'

And she was gone.

Thirty-five, he was thinking. It was young enough. Had there been something unresolved in her voice? His memory played the exchange again, trying to catch every inflexion, but his auditory memory was no match for his visual one and he did not want to expose himself to false hope and wishful thinking.

He closed the door behind her and leant against it. It was natural for women to want children, wasn't it? His sisters had them and Marion, his wife, had been disappointed not to become a mother.

He picked up the cases for the glass plates, and before sliding them in, took another look at today's exposure. The child gazed out of the glass, upriver, longingly. Looking for her father? Yes, he could believe that. For a long moment he gazed longingly back, then he closed the glass into its box, and pressed his knuckles into his closed eyes to rub the yearning away.

The Genie in the Teapot

THE WATER LEVEL was nearing the top of the first post, as Lily expected after all the rain. Every year it was like this, for a day or a few days or a week. It made her wary. Still, there was no angry rush and no menacing loitering either. The water did not hiss or roar or dart spiteful splashes at her hem. It flowed steadily, wholly engaged on some calm business of its own, and had not the slightest interest in Lily and her doings.

What would the parson say? Lily emptied the feed into the trough, and when she put the bucket on the ground, thought she might as well sink down with it. It wasn't so very long ago she had feared he might dismiss her because she missed a day's work when Ann came back. Then there'd been the awful day when he wanted to know how old she was and when she last saw her mother. After that she had gone round the skirtings behind the heavy furniture, beaten the dust out of the curtains in the spare bedroom that was never used, washed down the walls of the privy, cleaned the underside of the kitchen table where spiders liked to nest in the corners, but nothing settled her nerves, and for several Thursdays in a row it was a relief not to be given her notice at the same time as her wages. Now it was worse. Would word of her concealment in the shrubs opposite the Vaughans' boathouse have reached the parson?

'What to do?' she sighed aloud as she put the bucket down and the boar started to root around for the best bits. 'I don't know.'

The sow tautened her ears. Even in her worried state, Lily half smiled.

'Droll creature – you look for all the world as if you are listening to me!'

A quiver ran through the pig. It began with the trembling of her nostrils, and then every ginger hair of her body shivered as in response to a breeze, rippling down her spine and twitching the curl of her tail. When the wave had completed its journey, the sow stood to attention, poised in readiness for something.

Lily stared. She noticed that the dullness that had clouded the sow's eye for so long had lifted. The small eyes with their large pupils were now filled with light.

Then something happened to Lily too. She felt her gaze shift from looking at the sow's eye to looking *into* it. And there she saw—

'*Oh!*' she cried, and her heart burst into a flurry of beating, for it is a startling sensation to look at something and find that inside it is *another living soul looking back*. Lily would have been no less astonished to be addressed by a genie from inside her teapot, or have the lampshade bow its head to her.

'Well I never!' she exclaimed, and she took a few gasping breaths.

The sow shifted her trotters restlessly and made a breathing noise that also signified agitation.

'Whatever is it? What do you want?'

The sow became still and did not shift her gaze from Lily's, but stared with an air of divine delight.

'Do you want me to talk to you? Is that what it is?'

She scratched the sow's ear, and the sow grunted softly in a way that Lily understood to be satisfaction.

'You've been lonely, have you? Is it sadness made your eyes so dull? I don't suppose he's much company for you. Nasty brute. They're no good, men. Not Mr White, and certainly not Victor who brought you here, and not his father before him. None of 'em. Well, the parson's all right . . .'

She chatted to the pig about the parson, about his kindness and his goodness, and as she did, her own problems returned to her thoughts.

'I don't know what to do,' she admitted softly. 'One of them's bound to have told him. Not that photographer fellow, I haven't never seen him in church, but the Vaughans or the nurse. I wasn't doing anything bad, yet it *looks* bad . . . And if they haven't said anything yet, it'll come before long. What am I to do? If I have to leave the parsonage . . .'

A tear dropped from her eye and she left off scratching the sow to wipe it away.

The sow blinked sympathetically.

'Tell him myself? Well, perhaps . . . I suppose it would be better if he heard it from me first. I could explain. Tell him I meant no harm by it. Yes, I'll do that.'

Was it foolish, talking to a pig? Of course it was – but nobody was there to hear, and besides, it was a good idea of the pig's, that she should tell the parson herself. Lily rubbed her face dry on her sleeve.

She stood scratching the sow's ear a little longer, then told her, 'Go on, eat something. He'll leave none for you, otherwise.'

She waited to see that the sow had her snout in the trough, then put the bucket away, transferred Victor's money from the log to its hiding place in the cottage, and set off for work.

She walked upstream and, in her new confidence born of the idea that had come to her thanks to the sow, took her eyes off the water and noticed the brightness of the day. She did not linger when she passed the Vaughans' garden, merely glanced briefly over the river and saw that nobody was there. Seeing the clump of elders and bramble where she had hidden caused her spirits to flag, but she rallied them by visiting Ann in her mind. Over there, in the safety of the Vaughans' house, her sister lived a life that Lily had never known. It was one of comfort and wealth, things Lily could only guess at. She saw a fire burning in a large hearth, a well-stocked basket of logs, a table with several dishes of hot food, enough for everyone and something left over. In another room there was a bed, a real one, with a soft mattress and two warm blankets. For months she had been embellishing her notion of Ann's life at Buscot Lodge, but now, with the spring freshness starting to show, a new idea occurred to her. Had the Vaughans thought to give Ann a puppy?

A beagle would be patient and gentle with her. But spaniels had beautiful silky ears. Ann would like stroking the ears of a spaniel, she was sure. Or a terrier? A little terrier puppy would be full of fun. She lined up the puppies, and in the end it was the tail that swayed her: surely a terrier had the very best tail for wagging. A terrier it was. She added the puppy to Ann's blankets and log basket and fur-lined boots and rejoiced at the new detail. A cheerful little companion, yapping with pleasure as he chased and returned the red ball Ann threw, and later fell asleep on her lap. And Lily herself haunted these fantasies, an invisible figure who diverted wasps from the flowers that Ann bent to smell, who removed thorny brambles from the bushes where the red ball landed, damped the sparks that leapt from the fire on to the hearthrug. She averted all dangers, managed all risks, protected from all harm. Nothing could hurt Ann while she lived in the Vaughans' house and while Lily watched over her from afar: the child's life was nothing but comfort, safety and delight.

'Come! Ah! Mrs White!'

Her name was like a blessing in his voice, and it gave her courage. She placed the tea tray on his desk. 'Shall I pour a cup for you?'

'No,' he murmured distractedly, without lifting his head. 'I'll do it.'

'Parson . . .'

He touched the paper with his pen and added another few words in the margin, and she marvelled again at his quickness with ink.

'Yes, what is it?'

He looked up. She felt her throat tighten.

'Yesterday, when I was walking home along the river . . . I happened to stop. It was just opposite where the garden of Buscot Lodge comes down to the bank. Mrs Vaughan was out on the river with Ann.'

The parson frowned. 'Mrs White—'

'I never meant to do no harm,' she went on, in a rush, 'but they saw I was looking – the nurse rowed over to where I was, after Ann and Mrs Vaughan had got out—'

'Have you been injured, Mrs White?'

'No! That's to say, it's just a scratch, it was the brambles on the riverbank, that's all . . .'

She fidgeted with her hair as if she might still veil the evidence.

'I never meant to go,' she said again. 'I happened to be passing that way because it's the way home, I didn't go particular or anything – and it don't seem wrong to look. I never touched her, I never went near, I was on the other bank altogether, she never even saw me.'

'If anyone has come to harm, Mrs White, it seems to be you. I will tell the Vaughans that you meant no harm when you were looking at Amelia yesterday. Her name is Amelia, Mrs White. You know that, don't you? You said Ann just then.'

Lily gave no answer.

The parson went on with great kindness in his voice and in his expression, 'I'm sure nobody is afraid that you mean to hurt her. But think of the Vaughans. Think of what they have been through. They have lost her once already. It might be distressing for them to have the child watched so closely by someone outside the family. Even if she does – perhaps – resemble a sister of yours whose name is Ann.'

Again she did not answer.

'Well, Mrs White. Perhaps we have finished with that topic for today.'

The interview was over for now. She crept towards the door. On the threshold she turned, timidly.

The parson had returned to his papers, his teacup halfway to his lips.

'Parson?' Her voice was little more than a whisper, like a child who thinks by speaking quietly she can avoid interrupting an adult engaged on some important task.

'Yes?'

'Do she have a puppy?'

He looked bewildered.

'The little girl at the Vaughan's – the one they call Amelia. Do she have a little dog to play with?'

'I don't know. I have no idea.'

'Only, I think she would like one. A little terrier. When you see Mr Vaughan, when you tell him that I won't stare across the river no more, perhaps you could ask him?'

The parson was lost for words.

Part 3

The Longest Day

IN SUMMERTIME, THE Swan at Radcot was as sweet a spot as you could imagine. The grassy banks sloped down from the inn, and the river lent itself contentedly to the leisure and delight of mankind. There were skiffs and sculling boats for hire, punts for fishing and pleasure too. Margot carried the tables outdoors in the morning sun, and if it should get too hot in the middle of the day, picnic blankets could be spread in the generous shade of the trees. She called on her daughters, three at a time, and the Swan proliferated with Little Margots working in the kitchen, pouring drinks, and running in and out with trays of food, lemonade and cider. With smiles for all, they never tired. You could say, with truth, that there were few spots more idyllic than the Swan in summer.

This year was different. It was the weather. The spring rain had been regular and moderate in quantity, pleasing the farmers, who looked forward to a good harvest. As the weeks drew on to summer and hopes grew for sunshine, the rain continued, increasing in frequency and duration. The leisure boaters set off optimistically in light drizzle, counting on it clearing up later in the day, but when the rain set in in earnest, as it always did, they packed up early and went home. Four or five times, Margot had looked at the sky and put the tables out, but rare was the day she didn't have to go out and bring them in again, and the summer room stood empty. 'It's a good thing we had such a good winter,' she concluded, recalling the crowds that packed the room to hear the story of the drowned girl who came to life again.

'We'd be struggling if it wasn't for that.' Two of the Little Margots were sent back to their husbands and children, and she and a single daughter managed the workload with Jonathan to help.

Joe was poorly, his chest not improved by the summer mists that hung with clammy warmth over the riverbank. This was the time of year when he'd usually been able to count on his lungs drying out, but the change of season helped him little this time and he'd continued to sink into his spells as frequently as in wintertime, and he sat quiet and pale by the hearth while the regulars drank and talked around him.

'Don't worry about me,' he said in response to any enquiry. 'I'm all right. I'm working up a story.'

'It will get better at solstice time, I expect,' Margot said.

The summer solstice was traditionally the day of the summer fair, and this year it was also to be the wedding day of Owen Albright and his housekeeper, Bertha. What with the wedding breakfast in the morning, and the fair-goers who would doubtless want to quench their thirst in the afternoon, Margot was expecting it to be a busy day. For a while her optimism seemed like wishful thinking, but then, in the third week of June, things did in fact pick up. First people wondered whether the rain showers were sparser, and then they actually were. Patches of blue appeared in the grey and lingered, and twice in a row the afternoons were dry. There came to be a sense of expectation as the longest day drew near.

Solstice day dawned – and the sun shone.

'In fact,' thought Henry Daunt as he set up his camera outside the church for the wedding photograph, 'it's *too* bright. I'll have to take it here, sheltered from the glare.'

The celebrants came out of the church. The parson was his summer self: this morning he had opened his window and stood naked to the waist, feeling the sun on his white chest and his pale face, saying, 'Glory, glory, glory!' Only he knew this, but everyone saw his lively smile and enjoyed his vigorous shake of the hand as they came down the steps.

Daunt positioned Owen and his new wife at the spot that was just right and arranged Mrs Albright's hand through Mr Albright's arm. Owen, who was struggling to remember to call his wife Bertha and not Mrs O'Connor, knew what it was to have his portrait taken; he had done it once before, some years ago. Bertha had seen a great number of photographs, so she too knew what to do. The pair held themselves stiffly upright and turned grave, proud faces towards the camera. Even the teasing from Owen's drinking pals at the Swan could not crack their solemn faces, and their newly married dignity was transferred by sunlight on to glass, where it would outlive them for a long, long time.

When it was done, the wedding party gathered itself for the walk along the riverbank. 'What a day!' they said as they went, looking up to the clear blue sky. 'What a splendid day!' And they came, a joyful procession, to the Swan at Radcot, where Margot had put flowers on the tables on the riverbank and the Little Margots were waiting with pitchers of cool drinks covered with beaded cloths.

The events of six months ago seemed very distant now, for on a summer's day winter always feels like something you have dreamt or heard spoken of, and not a thing you have lived. The unexpected sun made their skin tingle, they felt sweat at the backs of their necks, and a goosebump was suddenly a thing impossible to imagine. Yet the longest day of summer is the reversed twin of winter's long night, and, this being so, one solstice inevitably recalls the other; and if there were some who did not connect the two days, Owen himself reminded them.

'Six months ago,' he told the wedding party, 'I decided to make Bertha my wife. Inspired by the miracle that happened here at the Swan that you all know of – the rescue of little Amelia Vaughan, who was found dead and came to life again – I felt like a new man, and requested the hand in marriage of my housekeeper, and Bertha did me the honour of accepting . . .'

After the speeches, talk of the girl was renewed. Events that had taken place on this very riverbank, in the dark and in the cold, were retold under an azure sky, and perhaps it was an effect of the sunshine, but the darker elements of the tale were swept away and a simpler, happier narrative came to the fore. A little girl who had been kidnapped was returned to her parents, making her and the Vaughans and the whole community very happy. A wrong was righted, a family restored. The great-aunt of one of the gravel-diggers tried to say that she had seen the child on the riverbank and that the girl had no reflection, but she was hushed; no one wanted a ghostly tale today. The cider cups were refilled, the Little Margots came one after the other and indistinguishably with plates of ham and cheese and radishes, and the wedding party had enough joy to drown out all doubt, all darkness. Six months ago, a miraculous story had burst wildly and messily into the Swan; today it was neatened, pressed, and put away without a crease in it.

Mr Albright kissed Mrs Albright, who blushed red as the radishes, and at noon precisely the party rose as one to continue their celebrations by joining the fair.

Between Radcot's neatly hedged fields was an awkwardly shaped piece of land that had fallen to common use. Today it contained stalls of all kinds and all sizes. Some of them were professional-looking affairs with awnings to protect the goods from the sun; others were no more than a tarpaulin spread upon the ground with wares set out upon it. There was stuff that a person might actually need – pitchers and bowls and beakers; cloth; knives and tools; skins – but there was just as much frippery designed to incite cravings. There were ribbons, sweet delicacies, kittens, trinkets of all sorts. Some of the traders carried goods in baskets. These wandered here and there, and each and every one declaimed the authenticity of his own wares and warned against the other crooks whose goods were counterfeit, expensive, and would break the minute the charlatan had packed up and gone. There were pipers and drummers and a one-man band, and as the fair-goers walked, they wandered into and out of the range of love songs, drinking songs and sentimental songs of loss and hardship. Sometimes they could hear two at once and the notes bumped into and fell over each other in their ear.

Mr and Mrs Vaughan walked along the river from Buscot Lodge

to the field where the day's festivities were to take place. They held one hand each of the child who swung between them. Helena was faintly irritable – she was disappointed, Vaughan thought, that the doctor's prediction about the return of the girl's speech had not turned out as she hoped – yet it was less her mood than his own that was casting a shadow over the day.

'Are you sure about this?' Anthony Vaughan asked his wife.

'Why ever not?'

'Will she be safe?'

'Now we know it was only Lily White watching us – a poor, harmless creature – what is there to worry about?'

Vaughan frowned. 'But that fellow who accosted Rita . . .'

'That was months ago. Whoever he was, he can hardly try anything when we are surrounded by so many people who know us. Our own farmers and servants are here. Everyone from the Swan. They wouldn't let anyone harm so much as a hair on her head.'

'Do you really want to expose her to the pointing and the gossip?'

'Dearest, we can't keep her from the world for ever. There is so much to amuse a child here. She will adore the boat races. It would be cruelty to keep her away.'

Life had been so much better since the arrival of the child. Helena's happiness had come as such a relief to him that it had brought a surge of joy to his own heart. Their renewed love was so like the first years of their marriage that it was possible to forget that the long chill of despair had ever been. They had buried the past to live in pleasure and delight. Yet now that the novelty of their new-found marital happiness had worn off, he was unable to pretend to himself that it rested on secure foundations. The child swinging between them, with her mute inscrutability, her colourless hair and her ever-changing eyes, was at once the cause of their happiness and a threat to it.

During the day, Vaughan was occupied and better able to distract himself from his endless and circular preoccupations, but at night his insomnia had returned. He suffered repeatedly from variations on the same dream. In it, he walked in a landscape – a wood, a beach, a field, a cave, the terrain was different every time – searching for something.

Then, coming to a clearing, or rounding a tree, or arriving at an archway, there she was, his daughter, waiting for him, as if she had been there all along, just waiting for her papa to come and find her. She raised her arms to him, crying *Daddy!*, and he ran to grasp her and lift her into his arms, his heart overflowing with gratitude and love – and woke to the leaden realization that it was not Amelia. It had been the girl. The changeling had reached into his dreams and attached her face to the memory of his own lost daughter.

Helena herself was ignorant of the fragility of their bliss; the strain of worry fell on him alone. This created a distance between himself and his wife, which she was as yet unaware of. In her belief that the child was Amelia and that he too was persuaded of it, she had constructed a sense of security as impressive as a moated castle. He alone knew how flimsy it really was.

When his own dreams showed him how easy it was to place this child's face on Amelia's shoulders, he was tempted to join Helena in her certainty. Sometimes it seemed so obvious, so simple a thing to do, that he felt guilty at his own stubbornness in resisting. Already he called the girl Amelia in front of his wife. He was more than halfway there. But then, always, the other thing. The knowledge. Underneath it all, a little girl whose face he could not even remember, but whom he could not – would not – forget.

There was something else besides. When he lay in his bed at night, whether awake or asleep, searching endlessly for his daughter in imaginary landscapes and finding, time after time, the little interloper, sometimes another face altogether swam into view and oppressed his heart. Robin Armstrong. For it was all very well to toy with the idea of succumbing to happiness and allowing the girl to replace his daughter in his heart and his mind, as she had replaced her in his home, but to do so was to deprive another man of his child. Vaughan wanted Helena to be happy, but what if her happiness came at the price of condemning another man to the agony of loss they had only just left behind? As much as the girl, as much as Amelia, it was Robin Armstrong who haunted Vaughan's nights and turned him to stone in his bed.

As they arrived at the edge of the fair, they met the crowds. He noticed several people glance at them, look again, whisper and point. Farmers' wives pressed flowers into the child's hand, she was patted on the head, little children ran up and kissed her.

'I'm not convinced this is for the best,' Vaughan said mildly, when a burly gravel-digger knelt at her feet and played her a short air on his fiddle before placing a forefinger gravely on her cheek.

Helena let out a short, exasperated breath, quite unlike her usual equable self. 'It's that silly story. They think she can work miracles – give them protection or something. It's just silly superstition and it'll pass, given time. Anyway, the boat races start at two o'clock. There is no need for you to stay if you don't want to. We are going to watch,' she told him firmly. Then, to the child, 'Come on.'

He felt the little hand detach from his. When Helena turned away, his own legs did not instantly follow, and in that moment of hesitation one of his farmers stopped to speak to him. By the time he was free again, his wife and the girl were out of sight.

Vaughan turned off the wide central axis where the going was slow. He made his way between the awnings and covered stalls, searching. Everywhere he went, he ignored the calls of the tradespeople. He did not want ruby rings for his sweetheart. He waved away macaroons, remedies for gout and digestive ailments, pocket knives (stolen most likely), charms to give a man irresistible appeal, and pencils. The pencils looked decent enough, and he might have bought some another day, but his head was starting to ache and he felt thirsty. He could stop at one of the places that sold drinks, but there were queues, and he'd sooner find his wife and the girl first. He pressed on through the crowd, making slow progress. Why should the sun come out so hot on this of all days, when so many were congregated together? The throng thickened to stagnation and he was obliged to stop altogether, then he found a sluggish current and inched forward again. He felt the sweat on his brow. His eyes began to sting with salt. Where the hell were they?

With the sun in his eyes, he felt dizzy. It only lasted a moment, but before he could gather his senses, a hand fell on his arm.

'Fortune, Sir? This way.'

He attempted to shake the hand away, but his movements had the effortful and vague feeling of swimming underwater. 'No,' he said, but perhaps he only meant to say it, for he never heard it spoken. Instead a drape was pulled invisibly aside and the hand that he felt but scarcely saw tugged him inside. He stumbled heavy-footed into darkness.

'Sit you down.' The fabric of the fortune-teller's dress was so like the gaudy interior of the tent that it receded into it, and her face was veiled.

A chair was placed behind him, knocking the backs of his knees so that he had no option but to sit. He turned to see who had put it there. There was no one, but a bulge distorting the drape of one length of tawdry silk was the size and shape of a shoulder. Someone was concealed there, ready to prevent the customers from making a quick getaway without paying for their handsome strangers and journeys overseas.

All he wanted was a glass of something cold.

'Look here,' he said, rising. But he bumped his head on the low cross-brace of the tent, and as he saw stars, he felt the woman grasp his wrist with more power than you would think possible of such a small hand, and from behind, pressure on both his shoulders forced him firmly back into his seat.

'Let me read your hand,' said the woman. Her voice, reedy and ill-educated, had an odd note to it that he registered but did not immediately pay attention to.

He gave in. It was probably quicker to go through with it than to negotiate his way out.

'You have had a lucky start in life,' she began. 'Good luck and talent were your godparents. And you have done well since. I see a woman.' She peered into his palm. 'A woman . . .'

Mrs Constantine came to mind. How much better she'd have done this! He remembered her jasmine-scented room, her calm, still face, her sombre dress and pristine collar, her purring cat. He longed for that room. But he was here.

'Fair or dark?' he asked, with false joviality.

The fortune-teller ignored his comment. 'A happy woman. Who was lately unhappy. And also a child.'

He exclaimed in exasperation. 'I suppose it shouldn't surprise me that you know who I am,' he told her testily. 'This is in very bad taste. Look, I'll give you something for your time and let's bring this to an end.' He tried to free his hand from hers to reach for his purse.

The fortune-teller only tightened her grip and he marvelled that a woman could be so strong. 'I see a child,' she said, '*who is not your child*.'

Vaughan froze.

'There. You're not going anywhere now, are you?' She released her hold and dropped the pretence of reading his palm. Her voice had a triumphant note in it, and the significance of the oddness of her voice and the strength of her grip suddenly occurred to him. It wasn't a woman at all.

'Got your attention now, haven't I? The child in your house – the one that has made your lady wife so happy – is not your child.'

'How do you know that?'

'That's my business. The thing is, I could ask you the very same question: how do *you* know it? But notice that I don't ask you. And *why* don't I ask you? For the very simple reason that I don't need to. Because *I know the answer already*.'

Vaughan felt himself come adrift, knew there was nothing to hold on to and gave in to the tug of a cold undercurrent.

'What do you want?' His voice was feeble and he heard it from a great distance.

'For the fortune-telling? Nothing. I'm too honest to charge for telling a man what he already knows. But what about your wife? Would she like her fortune told?'

'No!' Vaughan burst out.

'I thought not.'

'What do you want? How much?'

'My, you *are* in a rush. Do you do all your business at this speed? No, let's take our time to consider. Understand what are the things that really matter. Events later this afternoon, for instance . . .'

'What events?'

'Suppose there was to be an event . . . My advice to you – I offer it freely, Mr Vaughan – would be to stay well out of things. Not involve yourself.'

'What are you going to do?'

'Me?' The voice was one of injured innocence. '*I* shan't do a thing, Mr Vaughan. And nor will you, if you want your wife kept out of our little secret.'

The tent was suddenly airless.

'There'll be time later to work out the terms of our arrangement,' the man in the veil said, with an air of finality. 'I'll be in touch.'

Vaughan rose, desperate for air, and this time met with no obstacles as he made his way outside.

Back in the open air, Vaughan walked in agitation, without knowing where he was going. Such was the churn of his thoughts that he was incapable of putting two ideas in a row, let alone coming to any kind of conclusion. He perceived the crowds around him only dimly. But then the musicians and the hawkers fell silent. Conversations fell away. Even Vaughan in his disturbed state became aware that something was happening. Reopening his eyes to the outer world, he realized that everybody had stopped their aimless milling and come to a standstill. All were looking in the same direction.

A woman's voice screamed in panic. 'Get away! Away with you!'

It was Helena.

Vaughan sprinted.

Meanwhile, the Armstrong family had also decided to come to the fair. Robert Armstrong was looking unusually ebullient, as he walked with Bess at his side and six of his seven children around them. He had a letter from Robin in his pocket. The letter was contrite. In it, Robin begged forgiveness. He apologized a dozen times for attempting to strike his father. He promised to make amends. He expressed every desire to live a better life, to give up the gambling and the drink and his ne'er-do-well friends at the Dragon. He would come and meet them at the fair, and show his father how sincere was his remorse.

'He does not mention Alice,' Bess had said, reading over his shoulder and frowning.

'With everything else he intends to put right, the question of the child must surely be resolved too,' her husband had replied.

From his great height, Armstrong scanned the crowd for his eldest son. They had not found him yet, but he was probably here, looking for them in the crowd; they would be bound to come across him sooner or later.

Armstrong bought knives for his middle boys, hair ribbons and brooches for the bigger girls, and for the little ones, figurines of animals carved in oak: a cow, a sheep and a pig. They ate hot pork patties, and although the meat wasn't anywhere near as good as Armstrong's own, it still had a good flavour from being cooked in the open air.

Armstrong left his wife and children clapping their hands in time to the music played by the one-man band, and wandered on to the photographer's stand, where he found Rita. She always attended the solstice fair. There would be insect bites, heatstroke and alcohol-induced stupors to deal with, but while waiting to be needed, she generally helped out at one of the most popular stands to allow as many people as possible to see her and know where to find her in need. She was helping organize the queue of customers for booth portraits today and taking appointments in Daunt's diary for future sittings.

'That is Mr Henry Daunt, I think?' he asked her. 'He looks better than the last time I saw him.'

'He has healed, but there's still a scar underneath his beard. It's Mr Armstrong, isn't it?'

'That's right.'

Armstrong studied the prints for sale: river scenes, boating teams, local churches and picturesque places. He expressed an interest in having a family photograph taken.

'You could have your photograph taken today, if you would like. I'll add you to the list and tell you what time to come back for it.'

He gave a regretful shake of the head. 'My eldest isn't here yet, and I would like a photograph of us all at home, at the farm.'

'Then Mr Daunt can visit you, and then he would have the time to take a series of photographs, indoors and out. Let me look at his diary and see what day would suit you.'

As she spoke, Armstrong ran his eye over the panel of prints showing scenes from previous fairs. Morris dancers, teams of rowers, hawkers of goods, tug-o'-war giants . . .

They began to talk about dates, but Armstrong abruptly cut himself off with an '*Oh!*' that made Rita look up sharply.

He was staring at one photograph in particular with an air of great shock.

'Are you all right, Mr Armstrong?'

He was deaf to her words.

'Mr Armstrong?'

She sat him down in her seat, and pressed a glass of water into his hand.

'I'm all right! I'm all right! Where was that photograph taken? How long ago?'

Rita checked the index number and looked it up in Daunt's log.

'It's the fair at Lechlade, three years ago.'

'Who took this photograph? Was it Mr Daunt himself?'

'It was.'

'I must consult him.'

'He is in the darkroom on his boat at the moment. He cannot be disturbed – the light would destroy the photograph he is developing.'

'Then let me buy this photograph and I will come back and speak to him later.'

He pressed the coins into Rita's hand, did not wait to have his purchase wrapped, and hurried away, clutching it in both hands.

Armstrong was unable to take his eyes from the photograph, but after nearly tripping on the guy rope to one of the tents, he realized he must put it away and make a concerted effort to find his wife and children. He put the frame away, took a deep breath and set to looking about him. Then came the second surprise of the day.

Turning out of a tent where he had hoped to spot Bess, it was not his wife but Mrs Eavis, the landlady from the 'bad house' where Robin's wife had ended her days, who surged into view. He saw her first in profile: her blade of a nose was unmistakeable. She was back from her holiday! He could have sworn she'd seen him too, for her face turned in his direction and he thought he detected a flicker of her eye. But apparently not, for though he called her name, she turned and walked purposefully away.

Armstrong dodged the wandering fair-goers who were in his way, and stepped swiftly after her. For a little while he made steady gains through the crowd. He was almost near enough to put his hand on her shoulder at one point, but a concertina expanded with a wheeze and when he had successfully got around it she had disappeared from view. He looked left and right at every opportunity, between the stalls and tables, and was surprised how quickly he found her again. Coming to a crossroads in the fair, he saw her standing still, looking around her as if waiting for someone. He raised an arm to hail her, but the minute her eyes turned in his direction off she went again.

He was on the point of giving up when suddenly ahead of him a great stillness fell. Nobody moved. Then a cry rent the air – a woman's voice, in panic: 'Get away! Away with you!'

Armstrong ran.

Vaughan arrived at the place where the crowd thickened and had to shove his way through. When he reached the heart of it, he found Helena on her knees on the ground, her skirt stained with the mud of so many tramping feet. She was weeping wildly. Over her stood a tall, dark-haired woman with a long, sharp nose and wide pale lips, who had contrived to be standing between Helena and the child, while Helena made frantic attempts in the slippery mud to reach around her wide skirts and lay her hands on the little girl.

'I don't know,' the woman was explaining, to nobody in particular. 'I was only being friendly. Whatever's wrong with that? Awful fuss to make when all I did was say, "Hello, Alice." ' Her voice was loud – a fraction louder perhaps than was necessary. She noted the arrival of

Vaughan, then, turning to the crowd, addressed them as one. 'You heard me, didn't you? You saw?' There were a few nods. 'Saying hello to the daughter of my former lodger I haven't seen in a long while – what could be more natural than that?'

The tall woman placed her hands on the girl's shoulders.

Murmurs arose from the crowd. They were reluctant, indistinct, confused, but they confirmed that yes, it was as she said. Satisfied, the woman nodded to herself.

Vaughan crouched to put an arm protectively around his wife, while she stared in mute, wide-eyed shock, gesturing for him to take hold of the girl.

The crowd parted with a murmur and out of it emerged someone else they recognized.

Robin Armstrong.

Seeing him, a light of satisfaction, as at some scheme brought successfully to fruition, animated the tall woman's face and was instantly suppressed, then with a violent swiftness that took everyone by surprise, she gripped the child and raised her up. 'Look, Alice!' she pronounced. 'It's Daddy!'

Helena's cry of pain was accompanied by the gasp that came as a single sound from the crowd, and then silence fell, shocked and confused, as the woman delivered the child into Robin Armstrong's arms.

Before anyone could gather themselves to react, she had turned and launched herself into the throng. In the face of her sharp-nosed velocity the crowd parted, then closed behind her and she was lost to sight.

Vaughan stood and looked at Armstrong.

Armstrong looked at the child and in a broken voice spoke words into her hair.

'What did he say?' the crowd asked, and word was passed from mouth to ear in a Chinese whisper. 'He said, "*Oh my darling! Oh my child! Alice, my love!*"'

The onlookers waited, as at the theatre, for the scene to continue. Mrs Vaughan had fainted, it seemed, and Mr Vaughan was turned to stone, while Robin Armstrong had eyes only for the child, and his father, Mr Armstrong, stared as if he couldn't believe his eyes.

Something had to happen next, but there was uncertainty in the air. The actors had forgotten their lines and each one waited for the other to pick up the story. The moment seemed destined to be without end, and murmurs were rising from the audience when a voice rose above the confusion.

'May I help?'

It was Rita. She stepped into the circle and knelt beside Helena.

'We have to get her home,' she said, but she looked quizzically at Vaughan as she said it. Vaughan, his eyes locked on the girl in Robin Armstrong's arms, seemed incapable of action.

'What are you going to do?' Rita said in an urgent mutter.

Now Newman, the Vaughans' gardener, appeared, with another of the manservants from the household. Between them, they lifted Helena from the ground.

'Well?' Rita said, and she took hold of Vaughan's arm to rouse him out of his inertia, but all he was capable of was a minimal shake of the head before he turned his back and, with a nod, instructed the servants to begin the task of carrying Helena's senseless body back to Buscot Lodge.

All eyes were on the Vaughans' departure, and then, as one, the crowd looked back to the remaining players. The little one opened her mouth, and everybody waited for the wail that was certain to come. But she only yawned, closed her eyes and rested her head heavily on Robin Armstrong's shoulder. The slackness of her small body said she had fallen instantly asleep. The young man gazed with an expression of infinite tenderness at the face of the sleeping child.

There was a shifting in the crowd and voices were heard.

'What's happening, Mother?'

And: 'Why is everybody so quiet?'

Bess, with her swaying gait and a ribboned eye patch, emerged, leading a procession of children, all come too late to witness the events.

'Look, there's Papa!' one cried, spotting Armstrong.

'And Robin!' came another little voice.

'Who is that little girl?' the smallest of the family asked.

'Yes,' echoed Armstrong's deep voice, and it was grave, though it spoke quietly so as not to be heard by the crowd. 'Who is that little girl, Robin?'

Robin put his finger to his lip. 'Hush!' he said to his brothers and sisters. 'Your niece is sleeping.'

The children crowded around their half-brother, their bright young faces turned to the child, who was now invisible to the crowd.

'It's raining!' someone said.

Suddenly, from being a few drops of water it became a downpour. Faces ran with water, skirts were flattened against legs, hair was slicked to the scalp. With the rain came the realization that they had been staring not at a piece of theatre but at other people's misfortunes. Embarrassed, they remembered themselves, and ran for cover. Some made for the trees, some for the refreshment tent – and a good number ran to the Swan.

Philosophy at the Swan

THE STORY THAT had been told with an air of conclusiveness at the wedding breakfast was now taken up again, and all agreed it had taken a distinctly new turn. They repeated the events of the afternoon over and over, recalling every detail: the sharp-nosed woman, Helena Vaughan's dramatic faint, Mr Vaughan's frozen stare and Robin Armstrong's tenderness. When they had remembered everything there was to remember, the alcohol encouraged them to recall things they only half remembered and even to invent things they did not remember at all. They fell to questions: What would the Vaughans do now? How would Mrs Vaughan bear it? Might Vaughan yet persuade Robin Armstrong to give the child up? Why had they not come to blows? Might they yet, tomorrow or the day after?

The drinkers fell into factions, some insisting that the girl was Amelia Vaughan, pointing to Mrs Vaughan's certainty, others shaking their heads and pointing out that the child's fine hair was more like the soft waves they remembered on Robin Armstrong's head. They went back, reconsidered every element of the story in the light of these recent revelations, weighed the evidence this way and that. The night of the kidnap suddenly came to the surface, for if this child was indeed Alice Armstrong, then what on earth had happened to Amelia Vaughan? They had put the story of her disappearance away following her reappearance, but now they revisited it and plumbed its depths again.

Henry Daunt, taking a break at the end of a long day's photography, was sitting in the corner of the winter room eating a plate of ham and potato with watercress.

'It was that nursemaid,' the cressman leaning at the window insisted. 'I always said she had something to do with it. What keeps a girl out at that time of night if it isn't mischief?'

'Ah, but there's mischief and mischief . . . It might not be kidnap mischief she were out for, but the other kind,' his fellow drinker suggested.

The cressman shook his head. 'I'd have got into mischief with her if she'd have had me, but she wouldn't. She wasn't the type. Did you ever hear of her getting into mischief with anybody?' They kept a very accurate record of which girls were liable to get into mischief and which were not, so the information was close to hand. No. She was not the type.

'What happened to her afterwards?' Daunt asked them.

They consulted with each other. 'Couldn't get another job. Nobody wanted her looking after their children. She went to Cricklade, where her grandmother lives.'

'Cricklade? Dragon country.' Cricklade was a quaint town a few miles away, renowned for its intermittent infestations of dragons. He had thought of taking some photographs there for his book.

Daunt tucked into his meal, listening as the events of two years ago were disinterred, rediscussed, loose threads were picked out of the old story and today's events, and efforts made to knit it all together and make of the two things a single tale. But the threads left gaps too wide to be darned.

One of the Little Margots brought Daunt a dish of apple pie and poured thick cream over it. Jonathan lit a new candle at his table and lingered.

'Can I tell you a story?'

'I'm all ears. Tell me a tale.'

Jonathan looked into the dark corner where the stories came from, and his eyes betrayed a very great act of concentration. When he was ready, he opened his mouth and the words came out in a great flood:

'Once upon a time, there was a man drove his horse and cart into the river – and he weren't never seen again! – Oh, no!' His face twisted and he flapped his hand in frustration. 'That's not right!' he cried with good-natured annoyance at himself. 'I missed the middle bit!'

Jonathan went to practise on someone else and Daunt ate Margot's pastry and listened to one conversation and then another. Robin Armstrong's tragic tale, the likeness of his hair to that of the child, the river gypsies, the instincts of a mother . . .

Beszant the boat-mender sat while others picked the story apart and put it back together again in a hundred different ways. Whether the child looked like the Vaughans or the Armstrongs, how she had been first dead then alive, these were mysteries he shook his head at, comfortable in his own ignorance. But where he did have knowledge, he applied it. 'She ain't Alice Armstrong,' he said firmly.

They pressed him for an explanation.

'Mother were last seen at Bampton, heading to the river, the little mite with her. 'Tis so, I believe?'

They nodded.

'Well now, in all my life, and I'm seventy-seven, I ain't never seen a body – or a barrel or as much as a lost cap – float upstream. Have you? Anyone?'

They shook their heads, every one.

'Ah, then.' He delivered his words with an air of finality, and for a fleeting, fragile moment, it seemed that one thing at least was securely tethered in this story that slipped through your fingers like water. But then one of the cressmen opened his mouth.

'But before last solstice night, did you ever expect to see a girl what's drowned come to life again?'

'No,' said Beszant, 'I can't say as I did.'

'Well then,' the cressman concluded sagely, 'just 'cause a thing's impossible, don't mean it can't happen.'

The philosophers of the Swan fell to thinking and very quickly to disputing. Does the occurrence of one impossible thing increase the likelihood of a second? It was a greater conundrum than they had ever known and they went at it with great thoroughness, leaving no stone unturned. Many bottles of ale were consumed and many headaches borne out of their efforts to elucidate the matter. They drank and they pondered and they drank and they discussed and they drank and they argued. Their thoughts eddied round, discovered currents within currents, met countercurrents, and at times they felt tantalizingly close to a breakthrough, yet for all the intensity of their debate, at the end of it they were none the wiser.

Partway through, Daunt, who had remained sober, rose and slipped unnoticed out of the inn and back to *Collodion*, moored a few yards upstream by the old willow. He still had work to do.

The Shortest Night

AT BUSCOT LODGE, the servants had carried their mistress upstairs to her bedroom and left her to the care of Rita and the housekeeper. Helena seemed unaware of the hands that undressed her and pulled a nightdress over her incessantly shaking body. Her skin was bloodless, her eyes stared at nothing, and though her lips twitched she neither spoke nor responded to speech. They lay her in her bed, but she did not sleep; instead she reared up at frequent intervals, reaching out as she had for the girl, as though the scene at the fair were being repeated here in her own house, over and over. Then there came great spasms of tears that racked her body and she cried out, wordless howls of horror and pain that reverberated through the house.

At last Rita managed to get her to take a sleeping draught, but it was mild and slow to take effect.

'Can't you give her something stronger? Distressed as she is . . .'

'No,' said Rita, with a frown. 'I can't.'

At last the concoction won out against Helena's overstimulated mind, and she began to quieten. Even then, in the final moments before sleep overtook her, she made a motion as if to rise from her bed. 'Where . . . ?' she mumbled as she blinked dazedly, and another word, 'Amelia . . .' But eventually her head was on the pillow and her eyes closed and the devastation of the day was erased from her features.

'I'll go and tell Mr Vaughan she is sleeping,' Mrs Clare the housekeeper said, but Rita detained her for a few minutes first with some questions about Helena's health in recent times.

When Helena woke, it was to painful remembrance of what had gone before, with no lessening of the pain or the agitation.

'Where is she?' she wept, in anguish. 'Where is she? Has Anthony gone to fetch her home? I must go myself. Who has her? Where is she?' But the body was too exhausted to put her desperate desires into action, she had not the strength to push away the blankets and stand unsupported; to have taken a boat and rowed to Kelmscott or taken the train to Oxford was utterly beyond her.

The enormity of her grief was so great it wore her out, and when weariness took over, she lay wordless on the pillow, her limbs unmoving, her eyes unseeing.

During one of these interludes, Rita took her hand and said, 'Helena, are you aware that you are expecting a baby?'

Helena's eyes slowly turned to hers, uncomprehendingly.

'When we brought you home and put you in your nightdress, I couldn't help noticing you are putting on weight again. And Mrs Clare tells me you have been eating so many radishes it has made you feel sick and she has been making you ginger tea. But it is not the radishes that are making you feel unwell. It is your pregnancy.'

'It is impossible,' said Helena, shaking her head. 'My monthly signs came to an end when we lost Amelia. They have never restarted. So it cannot be as you say.'

'It is not with the first bleeding that your readiness to conceive commences, but in the few weeks before. If in that time a baby starts, the signs will not have a chance to begin again. This is what has happened in your case. In about half a year you will be a mother again.'

Helena blinked. It took time for the information to sink in to a mind made turbulent with grief, but it finally happened, and then she exclaimed, 'Oh!' very gently and brought her hand to her belly and placed it there. A small smile pulled feebly at her lips, and the tear she shed was not the same kind of tear that had wetted her pillow before.

A faint frown crossed her face, and she said, 'Oh!' a second time, in puzzlement, as though, following her initial surprise, enlightenment had been shed on some dark and distant aspect of her mind.

With that she closed her eyes and fell into a deep and natural sleep.

Downstairs, Vaughan was standing in the dimness of his study, looking out of the window. He had not lit the lamps. He had not taken his jacket off. He had not moved, it seemed, for hours.

When Rita knocked and came in, she found Vaughan glazed, more than half absent, a man too enmeshed in his previous thoughts to attend to the present. 'Yes,' he told her in a hollow voice, when she said Helena was sleeping, and 'No,' when she asked whether he himself needed a draught to help him sleep. 'Yes,' he said, when she stressed that Helena must be preserved from any further shocks.

'It's particularly important,' she emphasized, 'now that there is a new baby on the way.'

'Right,' he said dully, leaving her uncertain whether he had actually taken the news in. Plainly he believed the conversation to be at an end, for he turned back to the window and returned to whatever it was that held his mind hostage.

Rita let herself out into the garden, by the doors whose new locks were now redundant, and went down to the river. The summer rain burst slackly on her shoulders in fat, warm drops, which seemed to contain double their weight of water. Though it was evening it was not yet dark, and the light fell on wet leaves and puddled paths, casting everything in glinting silver. The river's gleam was lent a hammered finish by the incessant raindrops.

Rita felt a swell in her own throat. For hours she had been preoccupied with medical matters, had taken refuge in the demands and challenges of her work. Now that she was alone, sorrow welled up in her, and she allowed tears to join the raindrops on her face.

She had never once visited Buscot Lodge without seeing the girl. At every visit she had taken the child on her knee, or thrown pebbles with her into the river, or watched ducks and swans sail by, reflected in the water. When that little hand had reached for hers, she had pretended to herself that her pleasure in this gesture of trust was a small and unimportant thing. But when she had seen the tall woman with the spike for a nose swing the child away from the Vaughans and into the arms of Robin Armstrong, the instinct that had caused Helena to reach out imploringly to the girl had found an echo in her own breast.

Sobbing in a way that she scarcely recognized, Rita attempted to gather herself. 'You are being very foolish,' she addressed herself. 'This is not like you.' The stern words had no impact. 'It's not as if she were your child,' she continued, but at these words her tears only redoubled.

Leaning against a tree trunk, Rita gave way to her feelings, but after ten minutes of bitter weeping there was no end in sight to her sorrow. She remembered the solace God had once brought her in the days when she had faith. 'You see why I don't believe in You?' she addressed him. 'Because at times like this I'm on my own. I *know* I am.'

Her self-pity did not last long. 'This is no good,' she exhorted herself. 'Whatever's the matter with you?' She rubbed her eyes with violent energy, cursing the rain in language that would have scandalized the nuns, and picked up her pace, throwing herself into a headlong dash along the path, till the breathlessness of exertion replaced the heaving of emotion in her chest.

As she neared the Swan, the din of voices filled the air. The farmhands and the cressmen and the gravel-diggers were exhilarated by the day of festivity in a long season of hard work, and intoxicated too. The endlessness of the daylight gave rise to all sorts of excess, and regulars and visitors alike were making the most of it. Despite the rain, some were outside on the riverbank. Soaked to the skin, they imbibed, not minding – not even noticing – the rain that diluted the liquor, as they told each other rambling versions of the afternoon's events.

Rita had no wish to be drawn into the throng. People had seen her leave the fair with the Vaughans, and if they saw her now, they would inevitably stop her and want the story. She had no intention of telling anyone what was the Vaughans' private business, but getting that across to a crowd of curious drunks would be no easy matter. She turned up the collar of her cape, trying not to mind the rivulets of water it sent down her neck, and dipped her head so that her face was hidden. For the rest she would have to count on speed and the drunkenness of the crowd to get past unnoticed.

Because her head was down, she failed to spot one of the farmhands, relieving himself into the river. He turned, buttoning up rather haphazardly, and she almost ran into him. He was drunk, but not too drunk to apologize, 'Pardon me, Miss Sunday,' before he staggered off to his fellow drinkers. He was bound to talk, and her chances of getting beyond the inn unaccosted were slight.

'Rita!' she heard, and sighed, bowing to the inevitable. 'Rita!' the voice came again, low and urgent, and now she realized it did not come from the tables on the bank. It was from the river. There was *Collodion*, moored half concealed under the willow. And there was Daunt, beckoning her aboard. She reached the ladder, climbed the first rungs. His hand reached down, she put hers into it, felt herself hauled up and was aboard.

Below deck all the last boxes, bottles and photographic plates had been stowed away. The only sign of the business of the day was the paperwork on the table, where Daunt had been logging the day's plates and takings. There was a glass of hock beside it; he took down a second glass, filled it and placed it in front of Rita.

They had last seen each other in the crowd that gathered to witness the scene between the Vaughans and Robin Armstrong. They had parted there when Daunt, seeing the tall woman divide the mass of spectators to depart, had taken off in pursuit.

'Did you catch up with her?'

'The pace she was moving, I couldn't close the distance. I was weighed down.' He gestured to the heavy box in which he carried extra plates. 'She spoke to nobody. Stopped to look at nothing. Made directly for the far field, and when she got to the gate someone was waiting for her with a pony and trap. She climbed up and away they went.'

'Back to her brothel at Bampton?'

'Presumably. Most polite people call it a lodging house. For an unmarried woman raised in a convent, you have a remarkable frankness about such a place.'

'Daunt, I spend a large part of my working life dealing with the consequences of those activities that take place between men and women and which polite language skirts around. If you knew half of what that job involves, you would understand why a mere word has no power to shock me. Bringing a child into the world is too bloody a thing to be photographed and you will never see it, but I – I see it *all the time*.'

Rita had not touched her wine, but she took the glass now and drank the contents in a single draught. As she did this, lids lowered, Daunt noticed the swelling and pinkness around her eyes.

'You would make a good father, Henry Daunt. You *will* make a good father one day. They won't tell you about the blood. You'll be sent away, out of sight, out of hearing. By the time you are allowed back they'll have cleared it all away. Your wife will look pale and you'll think it's because she's tired. You won't know her blood is being wrung out of the sheets and into your drains. The housekeeper will scrub away at the stains in the bedsheets till they look as innocuous as if someone spilt a cup of breakfast tea in bed about five years ago. There'll be cloves and orange peel in the room so you won't notice the smell of iron. If there is a doctor, he might advise you man to man not to attempt marital intimacy for a time, but he won't go into detail, so you won't know about the tears and the stitches. You won't know about the blood. Your wife will know. If she survives. But she won't tell you.'

He refilled her glass. She drank it.

Daunt said nothing.

He drained his own glass.

'I know now,' he said carefully. 'Now that you've told me.'

'Give me another, would you?' she asked.

Instead of refilling the glass that she held out to him, he placed it on the table and took her hand in his. 'This is why you don't have children? Why you don't *want* to have children? Darling—'

'Don't!' She took a handkerchief from her pocket and blew her nose. 'When your wife has her baby, send for me. I'm named after Saint Margaret, the patron saint of childbirth, remember. I'll do my best for her. For the baby. And for you.'

She refilled her glass herself, and this time she did not drink it in a single gulp but took a little sip, and when she looked at him again the fury had gone out of her and she had gathered herself.

'Helena Vaughan is pregnant,' she told him.

'Ah,' he said nervously. And, 'Ah,' again.

'That's more or less what she said. "Oh," and "Oh." '

'Are they . . . pleased?'

'Pleased? I don't know.' She frowned at the table. 'What's going on, Daunt? What really happened this afternoon?'

She looked at him for an answer.

'It didn't seem real,' he said.

She nodded. 'The way Mrs Eavis delivered her lines. It sounded – rehearsed.'

'And she made sure everyone heard.'

'Robin Armstrong turning up at exactly the moment he did . . . Not a second earlier or later, just in time for her to grab the girl and pass her to him.'

'Did you see the look she gave him, when he first arrived?'

'Yes – as if she was expecting to see him—'

'– but was relieved he was there—'

'– a just-in-the-nick-of-time look—'

'– but gone again before anyone could really pay attention to it.'

'It was like something at the theatre.'

'Orchestrated.'

'Planned. Right up to Mrs Eavis's departure, with her transport waiting for her in the lane.'

'After you left in pursuit of Mrs Eavis, Robin Armstrong made a great show of emotion. Overwhelmed by tender feelings – "Alice, oh Alice," too quietly to be heard by anyone other than the nearest onlookers.'

Daunt pondered. 'You think it wasn't genuine? Yet if it was said quietly, and not declaimed like Mrs Eavis's speeches . . . ?'

'It made him more plausible, and he could count on it being overheard and broadcast. He's a much more talented actor than Mrs Eavis.'

'I heard what everyone else was saying about him. They were all convinced.'

'They weren't there when he pretended to faint when he first saw the girl.'

'You read his pulse . . .'

'It was as steady and unflustered as any pulse I've ever taken.'

'But why pretend then?'

'Buying himself thinking time?'

Daunt puzzled over it, but came to no conclusion. 'What about Vaughan? Why didn't he do something?'

Rita frowned and shook her head. 'He's in a peculiar state. It's as if he's absent from himself. I told him Helena is pregnant and he barely replied. He seemed unable to take it in. I wonder whether we're wrong about it, Daunt. Perhaps he does believe the girl is Amelia, after all. He seems defeated.'

They sat in silence, and the river rocked beneath them, and the noise from the Swan carried raucous and unruly in the air.

'We might as well finish this, eh?' said Daunt.

Rita nodded, yawning. It was dark now. The day had stretched her thin, to the point where she felt the boundary of herself, her skin, dissolving into the atmosphere. Another glass and she might lose herself altogether. How she longed for the girl. She felt bereft. Daunt's couch was there; she suddenly pictured herself stretched out upon it. Where would Daunt be in this fantasy? Before her imagination could answer the question, as Daunt uncorked the bottle for a last refill and was about to pour, *Collodion* dipped and tilted.

Rita and Daunt stared at each other in surprise. Someone had come aboard.

A knock at the cabin door. A woman's voice, 'Hello?'

It was one of the Little Margots.

Daunt opened the door.

'I need to speak to Miss Sunday,' she said. 'I spotted you coming here, and then when Dad was took bad I thought . . . Sorry, Mr Daunt.'

Daunt turned back into the cabin, while behind him Little Margot ostentatiously looked in the other direction. Rita rose.

On her way out, she gave him a weary smile. "I'm sorry. About what I told you. It's women's business.'

He took her hand, might have raised it to his lips, but instead gave it a comradely squeeze and she was gone.

All knew that Joe was unwell, and nobody tried to delay Rita as she followed Little Margot up the bank and through the public rooms to Joe and Margot's private quarters. The innkeeper lay on the hastily improvised bed in the room that was furthest from the river. His chest rose and fell in an unmusical struggle, but his gaze was calm, so calm that the noisy effort of his lungs might have belonged to another person altogether. His limbs lay in patient stillness. With a twitch of the eyebrow he communicated that his daughter could rejoin her mother at work, then, when they were alone, smiled his mild smile at Rita.

'How many – more times – can I – do this?' he asked between gasps for breath.

She didn't answer straight away. It wasn't a real question anyway. She put her ear to his chest and listened. She measured his pulse, assessed his pallor.

Then she sat down. She didn't say, *There's nothing I can do*, because this was Joe. He'd been keeping one step ahead of death for half a century. There was nothing about dying he didn't know.

'I reckon – a few – more months,' he wheezed. He paused to concentrate on the job of siphoning oxygen out of the swampy air. 'Half a year – maybe.'

'Something like that.'

Rita did not look away. Part of her job was to help people face what was coming. Dying could be lonely. A nurse was often an easier person to talk to than family. She held his gaze with hers.

'I'd have liked,' – another inadequate breath – 'a better summer.'

'I know.'

'I shall miss – Margot. The family. This world has – marvellous things – I shall miss –'

'The river?'

'There will – always be – the river.'

He closed his eyes, and she watched the arduous heaving of his frail chest, planning the draughts she could make and bring to Margot tomorrow to aid his suffering without weakening him further. He fell into a slumber animated by presences visible only to him. Once or twice he uttered words, mostly indecipherable, but she thought she heard *river . . . Quietly . . . story.*

After a time he opened his eyes, blinking as he surfaced.

'Have you spoken to Margot?' she asked.

His eyebrows told her no.

'Wouldn't it be better? Give her a bit of warning?'

The eyebrows indicated yes.

He closed his eyes, slipped back into sleep. She thought he might sleep longer this time, but as she was about to get up and slip out of the room, he opened his eyes again. He had the look he had when he was sinking.

'There are stories you have never heard on the other side of the river . . . I can only half remember them when I am this side . . . Such stories . . .'

'He's very poorly,' she told Margot. 'I'll bring you something tomorrow that will make him more comfortable.'

'It's this rain. He won't pick up till the weather improves.'

A customer called for cider and she didn't need to answer. When Margot came back, she said to Rita, 'You look worn out yourself. The night is almost over and I bet you haven't had a bite to eat since lunchtime. Sit here, where nobody can see you, and have a plate of something. You won't be bothered and you can slip out the back afterwards.'

Gratefully Rita sat down to bread and cheese. The door was ajar. There was a great din of conversation and in it she heard Vaughan and Armstrong mentioned many times. She couldn't think about it any more. Thank goodness for the gravel-diggers.

'There is this fellow,' she heard one say, 'and he reckons – he reckons, I'm telling you – that humans, like you and me, are a kind of monkey!' He explained Darwin as best he could, to the hilarity of his mates.

'And I have heard another thing like that!' cried another. 'That men once had tails and fins and lived beneath the water!'

'What? Under the river? I never heard such a thing!'

They disputed the matter back and forth, and the one who said it insisted that he had heard it in an inn ten miles upstream, and the other insisted he had made it up.

'It can't be,' said another. 'You'd ask Margot to fill your glass and all that'd come out'd be . . .' he completed his sentence with an impression of underwater speech that tickled the others so much they all tried it. Very ingeniously, they then found the trick of blowing bubbles through the liquor left in their glasses. There was great laughter, much spluttering, and finally the sound of someone enjoying himself so much he fell off his chair, and floundered like a landed fish on the stone flags.

Rita passed her plate to the Little Margot in the kitchen, let herself out the back door and crept away. It was nearly morning. She might sleep for an hour.

Great Lakes Underground

LILY HAD SEEN the events of the afternoon from the back of the crowd, her view so obscured by the broad shoulders of working men and the summer hats of their companions that she had been able to make it out only with the help of her neighbours. The taller spectators broadcast what they had heard and the sharp-eared echoed what they had heard, but poor Lily, once she had struggled against the departing throng to the place where the encounter had taken place, found rain falling on an empty arena.

She went to the parsonage and burst into the parson's office in a great flurry of words and tears.

'Take your time, Mrs White,' he counselled, but she would not, and eventually he made out the gist of the story, and eventually she fell silent and breathed again.

'So the child has been recognized by the deceased Mrs Armstrong's landlady, is that it? And she is with young Mr Armstrong now?' He shook his head, frowning. 'If what you say is true . . . I don't know how poor Mrs Vaughan will take it. Are you quite certain of this, Mrs White?'

'As sure as day is day! I saw it. I heard it. Or as good as. But tell me, Parson, how can a young man like that have the care of a little girl? He won't know. Suppose he don't know how to sing her a lullaby when she wakes in the night? And does he have a guard on the fireplace? A lot of young men don't, you know. What about her doll? Did she take that with her?'

The parson did his best, but it was an anxiety no mortal could soothe, and Lily was still distressed as she left the parsonage. Walking back along the riverbank she was prey to the very worst thoughts and memories. All the while Ann had been with the Vaughans, Lily had been able to take refuge in thinking of the child's well-being whenever she felt afraid, for the child was with Mrs Vaughan, but that comfort was lost to her now. Ann had been placed into the arms of a young man – a widower, without a wife – so who would take care of her now? Mothers could be trusted, but . . . The past came back to her with all the more force for having been held at bay for six months. She remembered the very beginning of it all.

'Do you find it lonely living without a father?' her mother had asked one day. 'Do you think it would be nice to have a father again?' Sometimes when adults asked questions they already knew the answer they wanted you to give, and Lily liked to give the answer that made her mother smile. Her mother was smiling on the front of her face as she asked the question, but Lily could see the worry behind. Lily felt her mother's scrutiny as she thought about her answer.

'I don't know,' she'd said. 'It's nice, isn't it, just us?'

Her mother had seemed relieved. But some time later the question had returned, so Lily thought she must have got it wrong the first time. She watched her mother's face, wanting only to please her, and tried again. 'Yes, I would like a daddy.'

The look on her mother's face then was one that was kept mostly on the inside, and Lily was no closer to knowing if it was the right answer.

Soon after that a man came to their rooms. 'So, you are little Lily,' he'd said, looming over her. His teeth seemed to slope backwards into his mouth, and after the first glance she knew she did not like looking at his eyes.

'This is Mr Nash,' her mother explained nervously. In response to a glance from the man, she rushed on, 'He is going to be your new father.' She looked to him for approval and he nodded, without smiling.

The new father stood aside.

'This,' he said, 'is Victor.'

Revealed behind him was a boy, shorter than Lily but older. His nose was stunted, his lips so meagre they were all but invisible. His eyebrows were as pale as his skin and his eyes were slits.

A hole opened in the boy's face. *He is going to eat me*, was Lily's first thought.

'Smile at your new brother,' her mother's voice prompted.

Hearing a note of fear, she glanced up, caught a complicated to-and-fro of glances between her mother and the new father. It seemed to enmesh her mother in a tangle she was unable to escape from. *Is it my fault?* Lily wondered. *What did I do wrong?* She didn't want to get things wrong. She wanted to make her mother happy.

Lily turned to Victor and smiled.

When Lily arrived back at Basketman's Cottage, she knew before she even opened the door. The river smell was never so strong it could cover the fruity, yeasty odour, nor could the rain wash it away.

'I had to go to the parsonage,' she began, but before she could get her excuse out, the first blow landed on her upper arm. The next found the softness of her belly, and as she turned away from his fists, it was her back and shoulders that took the attack. Mr White had battered her too, but he was a drinker, and though he was big he had not had the expertise of Victor nor half his strength. His blows had been weighty, but in comparison to this, lax, flabby. She'd been able to dodge Old Whitey's poorly launched punches, deflect his knuckles, and when he did land a blow home, the bruises had faded in a week. Victor, though, had been beating her for nearly thirty years. He knew every one of her tiny repertoire of feints and ruses, teased her into moving one way so he could land a blow the other; he went about it with cold concentration, unmoved by pleas or tears. All she could do was let him.

He never touched her face.

When it was over, she lay on the floor until she heard him pull up a chair and sit down.

She got to her feet, straightened her dress.

'Are you hungry?' She tried to make her voice as ordinary as possible. He didn't like a fuss afterwards.

'I've eaten.'

That meant he'd have left nothing for her.

At the kitchen table, he exhaled with an air of satisfaction she recognized.

'Have you had a good day, Victor?' she asked timidly.

'A good day? A good day? I should say so.' He nodded with a secret air. 'Things are coming on nicely.' She hovered on her feet. She would not sit down unless he told her to, but there being no food she could not occupy herself with preparing a meal.

He glanced towards the window.

Will he go now? she hoped.

But it was summer solstice night. Even in this rain, people would be about at all hours. Would he want to stay there all night?

'River's up. Scaring you silly, I expect. Giving you nightmares, is it?'

In fact, the nightmares had ceased since Ann had arrived at the Swan. Her sister couldn't be in two places at once, she supposed. But she needn't tell Victor that. It would give him satisfaction to think she was still suffering from the visitations that had tormented her for so long. She nodded.

'Fancy being afraid of water. It's everywhere. Places you can see it. Places you can't. Places you know about it and places you don't. Funny thing, water.'

Victor was a man who liked knowing. One of the best ways of avoiding his torments was to be ignorant about something and let him put you straight. Now he was enjoying his expertise and wanted to explain at length.

'There's as much water hidden underground as there is above,' he told her. 'Enormous caverns of it, deep underground, vast as cathedrals. Think of that, Lily. Think of that church you like so much, full right up of water, deep and dark and still. Imagine that amount of water but underground, like a lake. All kinds of water down there, there is.'

She stared. It couldn't be true! Water underground? Whoever heard of such a thing?

'Fountains and springs and wells,' he went on, watching her sharply through his narrow eyes. She felt her heart pounding. Her throat was dry. 'Ponds too. Brooks and rivers and marshes.' She felt her knees weaken. 'And lagoons. Bet you never even heard of lagoons, have you, Lily?' She shook her head, pictured awful creatures, made of water, like dragons that spewed water instead of fire.

'It's a marvellous fact of nature, Lily. There we go about our business on the surface of the earth, but beneath our feet, down there,' – with a gesture to his feet – 'there are great lakes underground.'

'Where, exactly?' Her voice was full of fear and she was trembling.

'Why, anywhere. Here, maybe. Right under your cottage.'

She quivered in horror.

His eye travelled up and down her body.

It might not be over yet, she thought. *He might want the other thing too.*

He did.

Two Strange Things

AND HOW DID the night end over in Kelmscott, at the Armstrong farm? They sat up late, later than the children had ever stayed up before. There were candles on the table and all were in their nightgowns except Armstrong, but no one had any thought of going to bed. The girl sat on the lap of the eldest daughter, and the other children gathered round smiling to pet her and offer their favourite toys as Armstrong and Bess looked on. The boys and girls were enchanted, exclaiming at her every movement, every blink of her tired eyes. The youngest, only a couple of years older than the girl herself, offered his new wooden toy bought that day at the fair, and when she grasped it in her little fingers, exclaimed joyfully, 'She likes it!' The older girls had brushed her hair and plaited it, washed her face and hands, and dressed her in one of their outgrown nightdresses.

'Is she staying?' they asked a dozen times. 'Is she going to live with us now?'

'Is Robin coming home to be her daddy?' another little voice piped up, but with a note of worry about such a thing.

'We'll see,' said Armstrong, and his wife cast a sidelong glance at him.

Coming away from the fair, as soon as they had put some distance between themselves and the crowds, Robin had put the child into his mother's arms and gone his own way back to Oxford, giving no clear account of his intentions or when they might expect to see him at the farm again. There had not yet been a chance for Armstrong and Bess to consult each other about the events of the day out of the hearing of the children.

The child's eyes began to close and the children hushed around her. On the brink of sleep, her fingers loosened their grip on the little toy and it fell to the floor with a bump that woke her again. Looking dazedly around her, her face pulled into a weary frown, and before she could open her mouth to cry, Bess lifted her away and said, 'Come on. Bed, all of you!'

There was some arguing over the child, all wanting to have her sleep in their room, but Bess was firm: 'She'll sleep with me tonight. If you have her with you, nobody will close their eyes.'

She set the older girls to making sure the little ones got to bed, and took the child to her own bedroom. Bess sang softly to her as she laid her down and tucked her in, and in moments the girl's eyes fluttered and she inched into the shallows of sleep.

Bess lingered over the bed, searching for a hint of her own features in the child's. She sought Robin in the sleeping face. She looked for echoes of her other children there. She would not think of *him*, the one who had fathered Robin before Armstrong had married her. She had buried his face years ago, and would not disinter it now.

She remembered the letter that had started it all, the torn fragments in Robin's pocket that she and Armstrong had pieced so unsuccessfully together. 'Alice, Alice, Alice,' she had repeated then. The name was on the tip of her tongue tonight, but she hesitated to pronounce it.

When the child's light breathing told her she was deeply asleep, Bess crept away.

Armstrong was in the armchair by the unlit hearth. There was an air of unreality about the scene, she in her nightclothes, he in his outdoor jacket, candles in the dark but no fire, and the muggy softness of the day still lingering. Her husband looked grave as he turned the little wooden figurine in his hands abstractedly.

She waited, but he did not speak, lost in his own thoughts.

'Is it her?' she asked, after a time. '*Is* she Alice?'

'I thought you might know. A woman's instinct, or your Seeing eye.'

She shrugged, touched the patch over her eye. 'I'd like it to be her. She's a dear little thing. They have taken to her.'

'They have. But what about Robin? Is he up to something?'

'If I know Robin, yes, more than likely. But you are usually his champion – what makes you think so?'

'That woman. Mrs Eavis. She led me there, to that spot, Bess. I'm as sure as it is possible to be. She deliberately let me see her, then she led me on a mad chase all around the fair, till she came upon the Vaughans, and so timed it that I arrived just right to have the whole scene played out before me.'

He fell to pondering, and Bess waited, knowing he would share his thoughts with her when he had them ordered.

'What did she have to gain by acting as she did? It is nothing to her whose child it is. Money is what governs that woman, so somebody, somewhere is paying her. Somebody paid for her to go away on her mysterious travels, so she was unavailable to identify the child one way or the other, and somebody has produced her now.'

'And you think that person is Robin? But . . . I thought you said he didn't care about the child?'

He shook his head in confusion. 'I did say so. It is what I thought.'

'And now?'

'Now I don't know what to think.'

He brooded for a long minute and Bess was about to say it was late and they should get at least a few hours' sleep, when he spoke again. 'There was another strange thing happened today.'

He was staring at Freddy's wooden toy, a carved figurine of a pig.

'I went to see that photography stand at the fair. I thought we might have a photograph taken, all of us together, here at the farm. I was looking at the photographs for sale there – some were of fairs in recent times – and look what I found.'

He reached into his capacious farmer's pocket, took out the small photograph in the frame and handed it to Bess.

'A pig! Well, I never. And it can tell the time!' She squinted to make out the lettering on the placard beside the animal. 'And it knows what age you are! Fancy that.'

'Look closer. Look at the pig.'

'A Tamworth. Like ours.'

'Don't you recognize her?'

She looked again. Bess was familiar with the pigs, but still, to her one pig was very like another. She knew her husband though.

'It's not . . . ? Can it be . . . ?'

'It is,' he said. 'It's Maud.'

Part 4

What Happened Next

TWO DAYS AFTER the summer fair Daunt returned to Oxford, where he found himself distracted from his regular work by the oddity of the dramatic change in circumstances of the child. He was uneasy about it for several reasons, and one, he realized, was that he missed her. It was ludicrous – all the while she had been at the Vaughans' he had seen her only once, for the photographs. Yet there had been a connection between them: Daunt's role in saving the girl had forged a link between himself and the family, created a door that he could knock at and count on being opened at any time. He had photographed the girl with the Vaughans and found himself more than halfway to friendship with the family. For a short time he had enjoyed the expectation of seeing the child he had rescued grow up, had imagined he would see her change from a little girl to a bigger one and then to adulthood. Now all that was gone and he felt bereft. He was reminded in his sorrow of that moment of violent recognition at the Swan when he had so unwisely and painfully pulled his swollen eyelids apart to see her. He remembered how powerful had been the urge to claim her. His rational mind had since got the better of him, but reason was no balm for this loss.

When he was not thinking about the girl, he thought about Rita, and that was no better. If the girl had done one thing, it was to bring home to him how much he wanted a child. His wife had been the disappointed one when their marriage had not resulted in children; his own longing had been late in coming, but he felt it now.

On the wall of his room over the shop he kept a collection of his favourite photographs. They were not framed, but simply tacked up. He gazed at them now in painful perplexity. Were there ways of avoiding pregnancy? He had a notion that there were, but that they might not be altogether reliable. And in any case, since he wanted children . . . Rita couldn't have made her feelings about the matter plainer, and though he had been surprised – he had seen her tenderness towards the girl, assumed too much – he knew he would be doing her an injustice to try to make her change her mind. Her knowledge of her own mind was what he admired about her. To expect her to bend to his wishes would be to expect her to be other than herself. No, she would not change, so he must.

One by one he took the photographs down, indexed them according to his system and filed them in the drawers in the shop. He would not forget her easily – he had exposed his gaze to her face for too long, and time had fixed it. It would not even be possible to avoid her in person – he could not disentangle himself from the story of the girl, in which Rita was also involved. But he could at least refrain from seeking to spend time alone with her. He resolved that there would be no more photographs. He would have to teach himself not to love her.

The consequence of this wise resolution was that the very next morning he left his assistant in charge, went upriver in *Collodion* with his camera and knocked at her door.

She met him with a weak smile. 'Do you have news of her?'

'No. Have you heard anything?'

'No.'

She was pale and there were shadows under her eyes. He set up a standard three-quarter-profile seated portrait, then went to prepare the plate. When he returned, a quick assessment of the light told him it would want twelve seconds. Rita settled herself in position and offered her face to the camera. In her usual direct fashion, she hid nothing. Her gaze brimmed with grief. It would be a magnificent portrait, a portrait of her feelings that would be at the same time a portrait of his own feelings, but he felt none of his usual pleasurable anticipation.

'I can't bear seeing you so unhappy,' he said, as he inserted the plate holder.

'You are feeling no better than I am,' she said.

He arranged the drape over himself, exposed the glass and whipped the lens cap away, having never felt more miserable behind a camera in his life.

One – Swiftly and without allowing light into the camera he ducked down . . .

Two – and out of the black cloth . . .

Three – and ran around the camera . . .

Four – where he took Rita in his arms . . .

Five – and said, 'Don't cry, darling . . .'

Six – though his own cheeks were wet too . . .

Seven – and she lifted her face to him . . .

Eight – and their lips found each other, until . . .

Nine – remembering the photograph, he ran . . .

Ten – back to the camera . . .

Eleven – under the black cloth, being careful of the light, and . . .

Twelve – replaced the cover over the plate.

They took the plate to *Collodion* and in the darkroom developed an ectoplasmic scene. They both stared sombrely at the faded figure of Rita overlaid with a blur of light and shadow, a sense of transparent action and silken flurry, motion without substance.

'Is that the worst photograph you have ever taken?' she asked.

'It is.'

Somehow, in the red light they found themselves in each other's arms. They did not so much kiss as press lips hard to skin and mouth and hair; they did not caress, but grasped. Then, as if it were the act of a single mind, they drew apart.

'I can't bear this,' she said.

'Nor can I.'

'Would it make it easier if we didn't see each other?'

He tried to match her for honesty. 'I think it would. In the end.'

'Well, then. I suppose . . .'

'. . . that's what we must do.'

Then there was nothing more to say.

She turned to go and he opened the door. In the doorway she stopped.

'What about the Armstrong visit?'

'What Armstrong visit?'

'The photographic session at their farmhouse. It's in your diary. I booked it on the day of the fair.'

'The girl is there.'

She nodded. 'Take me with you, Daunt. Please. I've got to see her.'

'What about your work?'

'I'll put a note on the door. If anybody needs me, they'll have to come and find me there.'

The girl. He'd thought he wasn't going to see her again, and yet there was an appointment in his diary . . . The world seemed suddenly less unbearable.

'All right. Come with me.'

Thruppence

'THERE'LL BE TIME later to work out the terms of our arrangement,' the fortune-teller had said. 'I'll be in touch.' For six weeks there was no sign, but Vaughan knew better than to think he might be reprieved. The blow had to fall, and when at last a letter in an unfamiliar hand appeared on a tray at his place at the breakfast table, he was almost relieved. The letter summoned him to an isolated spot on the river, early one morning. When he arrived, he thought he was the first there, but as soon as he had dismounted to stand on the muddy path, a figure emerged from the undergrowth, a slight man in a long coat that was too wide for him. He wore a hat low over his face.

'Good morning, Mr Vaughan.'

His voice gave him away: it was the fortune-teller.

'State what it is that you want,' Vaughan said.

'It's more about what *you* want. You do want her, don't you? You and Mrs Vaughan?'

Helena was very quiet these days. She seemed pleased about the baby, talked from time to time about plans for their lives to come, but her liveliness had gone. Future life and past losses coexisted in her, two halves of a single experience, and she bore her grief and her hope in a subdued manner.

It wasn't only Helena who was grieving. He missed the girl too.

'Are you suggesting I can get her back? Robin Armstrong has a witness,' Vaughan pointed out. 'Not the best of witnesses, it's true, given her profession, but if I were to go against him in a court of law, I dare say *you* would knock me down again pretty fast.'

'He could be amenable.'

'What are you implying? That the man might be induced to sell his own child?'

'His own child . . . Well, she might be. Or she might not. He don't care one way or the other.'

Vaughan did not answer. He was more and more disconcerted by this encounter.

'Let me spell it out for you,' the man began. 'When a man's got something he don't give tuppence about and another man wants it enough, thruppence will usually do it.'

'So that's it. If I give Mr Armstrong thruppence, along the lines of your suggestion, he will relinquish his claim. Is that what you have come to tell me?'

'The thruppence was just by way of illustration.'

'I see. Something rather more than thruppence, then. What's your master's price?'

The man's voice instantly altered. 'Master? Ha! He's not my master.' Beneath the brim of the hat the meagre mouth twitched as if he found something privately comic in the turn the conversation had taken.

'But you are doing him a service in carrying this message for him.'

The man gave the smallest possible indication of a shrug. 'You might see it as a service to yourself.'

'Hmm. You'll be taking a percentage, I presume?'

'I stand to benefit from the arrangement – as is only natural.'

'Tell him I'll give him fifty pounds if he gives up his claim.' Vaughan was fed up with the whole business and turned to walk away.

The hand that came down on his shoulder was like a vice. It gripped him and spun him round. Again he stumbled and this time, rising, caught a glimpse of the man's face: an unfinished-looking nose and lips, his eyes two slits that narrowed as soon as they knew they'd been seen.

'I hardly think that's going to do it,' the man said. 'If you want my advice, I would say something in the region of a *thousand* pounds might be more in order. Think it over. Think of the little girl that Mrs Vaughan misses so much! Think of new life to come – you have no secrets, Mr Vaughan, not from me! Information swims to my ears like fish to the net – and let us pray that Mrs Vaughan keeps well and suffers no sad shocks. Think of your family! For there's some things you can't put a price on, Mr Vaughan, and the most important is family. Think on that.'

The man turned sharply and headed away. When Vaughan peered to see beyond the curve in the path, the way ahead was empty. He had turned in somewhere across the field.

A thousand pounds. Exactly what he had paid in ransom money. He ran through the value of the house and land and the other property and figured out how it could be achieved. To purchase a lie. A lie that was still a lie and might be uncovered at any time. A lie that might be purchased by instalments, with this only the down payment.

His thoughts eddied, too fast to grab hold of, conclusions always out of reach.

Vaughan took the other direction to walk home. When he came to his own jetty he walked out on it, and sat down with his feet dangling over the edge. He put his head in his hands.

Once he might have been able to see his way through all this, taken action to arrive at a clean solution, when he was himself, when he was a better man, when he was a father. But now, he was no more able to direct the current of his life than a piece of debris can control the stream that carries it.

Vaughan stared into the water and the old yarns about Quietly came to mind. The ferryman who takes you to the other side of the river, when it is your time to go, and when it is not, returns you safely to the bank. How long, he wondered, did it take to drown?

He looked at his feet, so close to the jetty edge. Beyond and below, the water surged, black and endless, without thought and without feeling. He sought his own reflection in the water, but it gave him no mirror in the darkness and his own mind saw a face in the water. Not his own, but his lost daughter's. He remembered the formless face that had come to precision in Daunt's darkroom, liquid running over it, and in the black mirror of the water he saw Amelia.

Vaughan crouched over the edge of the jetty, rocking forwards and back on his feet as he wept.

'*Amelia.*'

'*Amelia.*'

'*Amelia.*'

With every repetition of her name he rocked more violently. *Is this how it ends?* he wondered. Calibrating the forward and backward motion of his body, he knew he was always in control. With every forward motion he could be certain the return was coming. But there was momentum. It was building. If he did nothing, the degree of oscillation would be reached where the return would be outside his control. *Why not?* he thought. *I don't have to do anything except allow it.* Forward and back. Forward and back. Forward and back. Edging nearer to where it would be forward and – down – to the point where the laws of physics would take over and the body surrender to gravity. But not yet. A few more to go. Forward and back. Forward – nearly there now, a fraction of an inch away – and back. Forward—

The void took him, and as he tipped into it, in his head a voice said, *You can't go on like this.*

Hearing it, his arm shot out. His body was claimed by gravity, but his hand shot out for something – anything! – and closed on the rope tied to the jetty post. He fell, with a jolt to the heart and a wrench to the shoulder. Swinging one-handed, feeling the rope flay his palm as he slipped, his free hand swooped to grasp it while his legs flailed wildly in search of a toehold. Agonizingly, hand over hand, he heaved the weight of his body – his desperate, living body – on to the jetty, and when he arrived, collapsed on to it and lay there, gasping for breath while pain radiated from his shoulder.

You can't go on like this, Mrs Constantine had said. She was right.

Retelling the Story

HE TURNED INTO the road with a kind of relief. The turbulence in his head that had plagued him for so long narrowed to a single objective. It was not a plan, nor a thought that brought him here. It was scarcely his own volition, for he had given up decision-making and abandoned will, too exhausted to do anything but succumb to the inevitable. He was here because of something more fundamental than that. Vaughan was not a man to bandy about words like *fate* and *destiny*, but he would not have denied that it was something of that kind that drew him to the gate, the front path and the pristinely painted front door of Mrs Constantine.

'You said I could come back. You said you could help.'

'Yes,' she said, glancing at his bandaged hand.

A vase of roses now scented the room where the jasmine had been, but the cat was in the same place. When they were seated, Vaughan began.

'They found a drowned child in the river,' he began. 'At winter solstice time. She lived with us for half a year. You might have heard of it.'

Mrs Constantine made a non-committal face. 'Tell me,' she said.

He told. Riding to the Swan after his wife, finding her there with the child, Helena's certainty, his own equal but opposing certainty. The other claimants. Taking the child home. The passage of time, and with it the gradual erosion of his certainty.

'So you started to believe she was your child, after all?'

He frowned. 'Almost . . . Yes . . . I'm not sure. When I came to see you before, I mentioned that I couldn't remember Amelia's face.'

'You did, yes.'

'When I tried to remember her, it was this child that I saw. She doesn't live with us any more. She lives with another family. A woman turned up at the summer fair who said she was not Amelia. She said she was Alice Armstrong. That is what people seem to believe now.'

She waited in a way that invited him to say more.

His eyes held on to hers. 'They are right. I know they are.'

He was here now. He had come at last to the place he had avoided for so long. But Mrs Constantine was there.

His words came in a smooth stream. The story slipped evenly from his lips. It began much as it had the first time, with drowsy slumber shattered by his wife's cry in the night, but his words were no longer the dusty containers of desiccated meaning they had been before. They were freshly forged things, alive with significance, and they carried him back in time to the night it began, to the night of the kidnap. The haste to reach his daughter's room, the shock of the open window and the empty bed. Rousing the household, the search through the night. He told of the message that came at dawn. He told of the slow hours till the appointed time.

He took another sip of water and it barely stopped the flow of words.

'I rode to the place alone. It was not an easy journey – there was not a star in the sky to light my way and the road was rough and pitted. At times I got off and walked alongside my horse. I was not always sure where I was, for the landmarks I was familiar with in daylight were lost in the night. I had to judge by my sense of the time that had elapsed and by the feel of the terrain beneath my feet – and by the river, of course. The river has its own light, even at night. I was familiar with its contours and every so often I recognized a certain bend or angle that told me where I was. When I saw that the night shimmer of the water was crossed by a darker band, I knew I was at the bridge.

'I dismounted. I could see nothing and no one – though there might have been a dozen men standing motionless a few yards away and I would not have known it.

'I called out, "Hoy there!"

'There was no answer.

'Then I called, "Amelia!" I thought it would reassure her, to know I was near. I hoped they had told her I was coming, that she was going home.

'I listened hard for an answer or, if not an answer, a sound: a step or a shifting or breathing. There was only the lapping of the river, and underneath it that other sound of the river, that low, deep noise that you don't usually notice.

'I stepped on to the bridge. I crossed. At the other side, I placed the ransom money in its bag by the pier stone, according to the note's instructions. As I rose, I thought I heard something. Not voices, and not steps, something less distinct than that. My horse heard it too, for he gave a whinny. I stood for a moment, wondering what was to happen next, and realized that I should move away from the pier stone to give them a chance to take the money. Presumably they would want to have it in their hands, feel the weight of it, before releasing Amelia. I stepped back on to the bridge. I picked up speed, ran over – and the next thing I knew, I was flat on my face in the dark.'

The account that emerged from Vaughan's mouth came all by itself. He called on no stock phrases, no rehearsed words. His telling had its own energy and speed, and with them it brought the past into the room, its dark and its chill. He shivered, and his eyes took on the glazed look of those who are seeing the vision of memory.

'The aftershock of the fall left me dazed. It was a moment before I got my breath back. I shifted to see whether I was injured, wondered whether someone had been lying in wait to cosh me. I got to my knees, expecting another blow to dash me down again, but none came and I knew then I had merely fallen. I tried to collect myself. Waited for the world to settle. It was only a little while later that I gathered myself to stand, and as I did so my leg brushed against something. I realized straight away that this soft but solid bundle was the thing that had tripped me up. I groped to get some sense of what it was, but in my gloves I could not tell. I took off my gloves and felt again. Something wet. Cold. Dense.

'I was afraid. Even then, before I struck the match, I feared what it could be.

'When I had a bit of light, I found that she was not looking at me. That was a relief. Her face was angled away, and she was staring fixedly towards the river. It was the strangest thing, for her eyes had the shape of Amelia's eyes. She was dressed in Amelia's clothes and her feet were in Amelia's shoes. Her features were like Amelia's too. Amazingly like. And yet it seemed to me, quite plainly, both then and for some time afterwards, that she was *not* Amelia. *Not* my child. How could she be? I knew my child. I knew how her eyes alighted on me, how her feet danced and shuffled, how her hands reached and fidgeted and grasped. I took this child's hand in mine and it did not tighten around my fingers the way Amelia's would have. Something glinted. Amelia's necklace with the silver anchor was round her neck.

'I picked her up, this child who could not – *must not* – be Amelia. I found a place where the bank was not too steep and scrambled down to the water's edge. I carried her into the water and when I was waist deep I laid her down. I felt the river take her from me.'

Vaughan paused.

'It was a nightmare, and that was the only way I could think of to end it. *My* daughter, *my* Amelia, was alive. You do see, don't you?'

'I do.' Mrs Constantine's eyes, sad and unfaltering, held his.

'But what I know now – what I have known for a long time – is that it *was* Amelia. My poor child was dead.'

'Yes,' said Mrs Constantine.

Now the banks of the river burst and Vaughan felt the water stream from his eyes. His shoulders shook and he rocked forward and back and his weeping seemed endless. The tears slipped from his eyes on to his cheeks, they ran down his face, they trickled from his jaw to his neck and seeped into his collar, they dripped from his chin and dampened his knees. He raised his hands to his face and the tears wetted his fingers, then his wrists and cuffs. He wept and wept until he was drained.

Mrs Constantine was there with her vast and kind gaze that had accompanied him all the while.

'When the girl from the river came home with us, I had strange thoughts. Sometimes I wondered . . .' he shook his head in embarrassment, but a man could tell Mrs Constantine anything without fear of being found ridiculous. 'Sometimes I wondered, what if she wasn't dead? What if I put her in the river and she floated away and came to her senses? What if she drifted somewhere – to someone – and they kept her for two years and then – I don't know how – or why – was found floating in the river again, and so came back to us? It's quite impossible, of course, but thoughts like that . . . When one wants an explanation . . .'

'Tell me about Amelia,' she said, after a pause. 'What was she like in life?'

'What kind of thing do you want to know?'

'Anything.'

He thought. 'She was never still. Even before she was born she was a wriggler, that's what the midwife said, and when she arrived and was put in her cot, her arms and legs made waving motions – as if she would swim into the air and was surprised she couldn't. She used to clench and stretch her little hand and when she saw her fist turn into a palm with fingers there would be a look of sheer amazement on her face. She was quick to crawl, my wife said, and it made her legs strong. She liked to cling to my fingers and I raised her up, feet on the floor so that she could feel the ground supporting her. We couldn't always be holding her hand while she tottered about. One day I had some papers to go through in the drawing room and she came patting my ankles for attention, wanting to be lifted to her feet, and I was too busy. And then, suddenly, a little hand pulled at my sleeve and there she was, upright at my side. All by herself she had pulled herself up using the chair leg and her face was all pleasure and surprise! Oh, you should have seen her! A thousand times she toppled over, but never cried, just upped and tried again. And once she'd found her feet she was never satisfied to sit again.'

He felt himself smiling at the memory.

'Can you *see* her now?' Mrs Constantine's voice was so low and soft that it barely rippled the air.

Vaughan saw Amelia. He saw the strand of hair that went the wrong way, the indistinct colour of her lashes and their perfect curl, the speck of sleep dust in the corner of her eye, the precise curve of her cheek and the flush of the skin over it, the padded swell of her lower lip, the stubby fingers and their fine nails. He saw her not here in this room and not now in this hour, but in the infinity of memory. She was lost to life, but in his memory she existed, was present, and he looked at her and her eyes met his and she smiled. He met her eyes again, felt the meeting of their gaze, father and daughter. He knew that she was dead, knew that she was gone, but here, now, he saw her, and knew that this far – and this far only – she was restored to him.

'I see her,' he said, nodding, smiling through tears.

His lungs were his own again; the weight of his head no longer made his shoulders ache. The beat of his heart in his chest was steady. He did not know what the future held, but he knew it existed. He felt a stirring of interest in it.

'There is to be a new baby,' he told Mrs Constantine. 'At the end of the year.'

'Congratulations! That is good news.' He felt the pleasure of it all over again in her response.

He took a great, deliberate lungful of air, and when he had expelled it, put his hands on his knees and made ready to rise.

'Oh,' exclaimed Mrs Constantine mildly. 'Have we finished?'

Vaughan arrested the movement and wondered. Was there something else? It all came back to him. How could he have forgotten?

He told her about the fortune-teller at the fair, the opportunity to buy Robin Armstrong's interest in the child, the implied threat that his knowledge of Amelia's death might be shared with his wife.

She listened closely. When he came to an end, she nodded. 'That isn't what I was expecting when I asked whether we were finished. I was remembering that when you first came to me there was a particular difficulty you wanted to resolve . . .'

He thought back to their first meeting. It was such a long time ago. What had prompted him to come then?

'Relating to your wife . . .' she went on.

'I asked you to tell Helena that Amelia was dead.'

'That's right. You invited me to name my price, I seem to remember. And now you are considering paying a stranger a very large sum of money indeed to *stop* him telling Helena the very same thing.'

Oh. He sat back in his chair. He hadn't thought of it in that light.

'What I am wondering, Mr Vaughan, is how much it would cost if *you* were to tell your wife what happened that night?'

Later, when he had drunk the clear liquid that tasted of cucumber and rinsed his face in the water that was neither too hot nor too cold, and dried it again, he said farewell to Mrs Constantine. 'This is what you do, isn't it? I understand now. I thought it was smoke-and-mirrors stuff. Trickery. You do bring back the dead, but not in that way.'

She shrugged. 'Death and memory are meant to work together. Sometimes something gets stuck and then people need a guide or a companion in grief. My husband and I studied together in America. There is a new science over there: it can be explained in complicated ways, but you won't go far wrong in thinking of it as the science of human emotion. He got a job here in Oxford, at the university, and I apply my learning in the field. I help where I can.'

He left her remittance on the hall table.

On leaving the house, Vaughan felt an unexpected coolness about his knees and collar. It was apparent too at his wrists. His clothing was damp still where his tears had trickled into his cuffs and on to his collar and dripped on to his knees. *It's amazing*, he thought. *Whoever would think a human body could have so much water in it?*

Photographing Alice

COLLODION CARRIED RITA and Daunt downriver to the farmhouse at Kelmscott, and on the way their conversation – about the Vaughans, the Armstrongs, but mostly about the child herself – effectively masked their constraint in dealing with one another. But when each one knew the other was looking elsewhere, when they were sure of not being seen, they cast quick glances of love and sorrow, bailing out the excess feeling that threatened otherwise to capsize them.

At Kelmscott, the younger children were waiting for them on the bank. They waved as soon as they saw the smart navy-and-white houseboat decorated with its vivid yellow-orange flourishes. Rita looking out avidly, was quick to spot the girl. She was with them, waving; then another child, a boy, the youngest one and closest to her in age, took her hand and they ran together back to the farmhouse.

'Where has she gone to?' Daunt asked, distracted by her absence as he tried to concentrate on mooring.

'Back to the house,' Rita said anxiously, but then, 'Here she is! They just went to fetch the older ones.'

All the Armstrong children made themselves useful in sensible ways, from the big boys who listened carefully to Daunt before lifting the heavy equipment, to the little ones who were all given something light and unbreakable by Rita, which they then carried with a great sense of self-importance over the field and to the house. The unloading was completed in record time.

Rita was always conscious of the girl. Whatever she was doing she had one eye on her, noticing how the other children treated her affectionately, how the older ones were patient with her and the smaller ones went slowly in order not to leave her behind. It occurred to her to wonder whether the little girl had lacked the companionship of other children at the Vaughans', and couldn't help feeling that the kindness of these children must be good for her.

Bess showed them into the dining room, and there was more busyness as Armstrong and his big sons moved the table and arranged chairs according to Daunt's instructions.

'We don't want a photograph of me,' Bess said. 'Why, I'm here all the time, if anybody needs to know what I look like!'

But Armstrong insisted and the children backed him up, and soon the photographs were all set up: the first was to be of Armstrong and Bess; they would take the whole family portrait later.

'Where is Robin?' fretted Armstrong. 'Half an hour ago he should have been here.'

'You know what young men are. I told you not to count on him,' murmured his wife.

Robin's contrition, which had so affected her husband, had not removed her own doubts about her son. 'He was always better in words than in acts,' she reminded him, but when Armstrong chose to forgive – as he always did – she did not press the matter. Then, seeing her eldest son with the child in his arms at the fair, she discovered to her own surprise that hope had rooted faintly in her heart. She kept an eye on it, with the painful curiosity of a gardener who watches the frail progress of a plant that cannot possibly thrive. The absence of her son's visits to the child did not pass unnoticed. Armstrong had written to let Robin know the day and time of the photography session, as though his presence were a thing he could now take for granted, but there had been no answer, and she for one was not unsurprised at his absence.

'We'll take you and Mrs Armstrong first,' said Daunt. 'That will give him plenty of time, if something has held him up.'

He seated Bess on the chair and placed Armstrong behind her, then slid the plate into position while he explained again the need to keep still. When all was ready, he ducked under the dark cloth and removed the cover as Rita stood behind the camera and encouraged the pair of sitters to look consistently in the one direction. In ten seconds the Armstrongs had time to feel all the things that people felt when they were having their photograph taken for the first time: abashed, stiff, nervous, significant, and rather foolish. But half an hour later, when they were looking at the finished article, developed and washed and dried and framed, they saw themselves as they had never seen themselves before: eternal.

'Well . . .' said Bess wonderingly, and it seemed that she was going to complete the sentence, but she fell into silence instead, while her eyes flickered all over the photograph of a neat middle-aged woman wearing an eye patch and a dark, stern man behind her with one hand on her shoulder.

Meanwhile Armstrong looked over her shoulder at the photograph and told her how beautiful she looked in it, but his eyes returned time and time again to his own grave face. His mood seemed to turn sombre as he looked at himself.

The interest in the photograph had distracted them all, but eventually it was time to prepare for the second group and Robin had still not come. No horse had been heard on the cobbles, no door opening in the hall. Armstrong went to find the maid anyway, to see whether he might have come in quietly at the back, but no. He was not there.

'Come now,' Bess said firmly. 'If he's not here, he's not here, and there's nothing we can do about it. Living in Oxford as he does, he can go to Mr Daunt's studio any time and have his photograph taken. It will be a hundred times easier for him.'

'But it would have been such a thing to have all the children together! And there is Alice!'

Indeed, there was Alice.

Bess sighed and took her husband's arm encouragingly. 'Robin is a man now, and not a child to do as his parents tell him. Come, let us make the best of it. Here are the others, all six of them, eager and happy to take their place alongside us and Alice. Come.'

She coaxed Armstrong into taking his place in the grouping. All the children shuffled a little to the left or right to fill the space left for their missing brother.

'All set?' Daunt asked, and Mr Armstrong gave one last glance in the direction of the window, just in case.

'All set,' he answered with a sigh.

For ten seconds Armstrong, his wife and their six younger children stared into the eye of the camera, of time, of the future, and cast themselves into immortality. Rita, watching from the corner of the room, noticed that the one they called Alice fixed her gaze on a point still further off, beyond the camera, beyond the walls, beyond Kelmscott, somewhere so far-flung it might be beyond eternity.

While Daunt was developing the photograph, Mrs Armstrong and her daughters prepared the table for tea, and the boys changed into their work clothes to feed the animals. Rita found herself alone with Armstrong just as the sun came out and the rain stopped.

'Would you like to see the farm?' he invited.

'I would.'

He picked up the little girl and hardly seemed to feel her weight on his arm as they went outside.

'How is she?' Rita asked. 'Do you find her well?'

'I'm not sure I can tell you. Ordinarily I am pretty good at knowing living creatures, whether they be human or animal. It's a matter of observation. With chickens you can see restlessness in their feathers. A cat can tell you a lot by the way it breathes. Horses – well, they're a bit of everything. Pigs look their meaning at you. This little one is hard to know. A mystery, aren't you, piglet?' He gave her hair a fond stroke as he looked tenderly at her.

The girl glanced at him, then at Rita, not with any particular sign of recognition, but as though she had never seen her before. Rita reminded herself that this had always been the case, even at the Vaughans' where she had been a regular visitor.

As they walked, Armstrong pointed out things that might interest Rita or the child, and the girl looked where she was bid and in between times rested her head on the man's broad shoulder and drew in her gaze, to contain herself in her own inner world again. Rita sensed that behind the farmer's talk of the farm, his mind was turning over some private unhappiness, and took it to be the absence of his son. She did not make idle conversation, but walked along beside him until her quiet presence encouraged him to unburden himself.

'A man like me gets used to recognizing himself from the inside. The inside is what I am familiar with. Nor am I much given to studying my outward appearance in the looking glass. It is a curious thing, to see oneself in a photograph. It is a meeting with the outer man.'

'True enough.'

When Armstrong spoke again, it was to ask a question: 'You do not have children, I think?'

'I'm not married.'

'May it come to you. I have known no happiness to compare with my wife and my children. Nothing means so much to me as my family. You will have guessed something, I suppose, of my story?'

'I don't like guessing. But I know what they say at the Swan, that your parents were a prince and a slave girl.'

'That is fanciful, but there is a little truth in it. My father was a rich man, my mother a black servant. They lived in the same household when they were very young, not much more than children, and I was conceived out of love and ignorance. I suppose you could say I was lucky, my mother too. Most families would have thrown her out, but my father owned his part in it. He wanted, I believe, to marry her. Such a thing was impossible, of course. But the family was a compassionate one, and they did their best. My mother was cared for until I was born and weaned, then she was moved to another town and suitable work was found so that she could meet her needs respectably until she married – which a few years later she did, to a man of her kind. I was placed in a home for children who, for one reason or another, could not live with their families but had some money behind them, and later sent to school. A rather good one. Thus I was raised on the edge of two families, one rich and one poor, one black and one white, and was never at the heart of either. I grew up largely outside of family life. Most of my early memories are of school, but I knew both my parents. Twice a year my father would come and take me out of school for a day. Once I remember climbing up into the carriage where he was waiting for me and being very surprised to find another boy, rather smaller than me, already there. 'What do you make of this little chap, then, Robert?' my father said to me. 'Shake hands with your brother!' What a day that was! I remember a place – I have no idea where it was, to be honest – with grass lawns. I threw a ball endlessly to my brother and eventually he managed to catch it once or twice and how he danced for joy at that. I shall never forget it. Later on, while my father stood below to catch us if we should chance to fall, I showed him where to put his feet to get up into a tree. It was not a very big tree, but then he was not a very big boy. We were both of us too young to know what difference lay between us, but I started to realize it when we returned to school and I climbed down from the carriage and the two of them went off – together – to a place called home. I don't know what happened after that. I never saw that boy again, though I know his name and that there were other brothers and sisters who followed him. Perhaps my father was not supposed to encourage us to know one another and was found out. Perhaps he just thought better of it. Whatever the reason, I never saw my brother again. I don't suppose he even remembers me. I cannot even be sure he knows of my existence. So much for my father's family.

'I was not altogether a stranger in my mother's house. I was allowed sometimes to make brief visits in the holidays. I have good memories of those times. Her home was full of talk and movement, laughter and love. She was as good a mother to me as she dared to be; more than once she put her arms around me and told me she loved me, though I was so unused to such treatment that my tongue tied in knots and I scarcely knew how to embrace her in return. Her husband was not an unkind man, either, though he was always telling my brothers and sisters to mind what they said in my presence. "Robert's not used to your scallywaggery," he used to say whenever the chatter grew too boisterous. I never wanted to come away from that house. I always thought that the next time I went would be the time I would be allowed to stay, and every departure was a disappointment. Eventually I noticed that with every visit I was less and less like my brothers and sisters, not more. There came a time when these holiday visits – already infrequent – stopped altogether. It was not a sudden end. There was no word to say it would not happen again. Just several holidays in a row when the visit didn't happen and the dawning knowledge that it was over. The borderline between myself and my brothers and sisters had become a solid wall.

'When I was seventeen my mother sent a message asking for me. She was dying. I went back to the house. It was much smaller than I remembered. I entered her bedchamber and the room was full of people. My brothers and sisters were already there, of course, sitting at the bedside, kneeling on the floor to be close to her. I could have asked to stand beside her and hold her hand for a moment, and if she had been in possession of her senses and known my presence I'm sure I would have, but it was too late for that. I stood just inside the door, while my siblings sat and knelt at the bedside, and when she had breathed her last one of my sisters remembered me and said that perhaps Robert would read – "for he do read so beautiful," she said – so I read some verses from the Bible in my white man's voice, and once that was done there seemed to be no reason to remain. I asked my stepfather on my way out whether I could help in any way and he said, "I can look after my children, thank you, Mr Armstrong." He had always called me Robert before, but I suppose I was a man now, and he gave me that name instead, the name that came from nowhere, plucked from the blue, belonging to neither of my parents, but mine alone.

'I attended her funeral. My own father came with me. He arranged that we would slip in quietly at the back and be gone before the other mourners turned to leave.'

Here Armstrong paused. A cat had emerged from the barn, and on seeing the farmer it trotted over, paused a yard and a half from the man to crouch on its haunches, and then leapt like a jack-out-of-the-box to land on his shoulder.

'What a spectacle,' said Rita, as the cat settled and rubbed its cheek against his jaw.

'She is a quaint and affectionate creature,' Armstrong said with a smile as they walked on, the cat balanced like a pirate's parrot on her owner's shoulder.

'I did not belong, you see, Miss Sunday. In neither place. In neither heart. There we have it. I know what it is like to be on the outside. Don't misunderstand me, this is not a complaint but an explanation, though I have been very prolix before getting to the point. Forgive me, these are things a man speaks of very infrequently and there is a certain – I don't know quite what to call it . . . pleasure? Relief, at any rate, in unburdening oneself.'

Rita met his look and nodded.

'My parents were good people, in their hearts, Miss Sunday. Both of them, I feel sure, loved me so far as they were permitted to. The fact is, they were not free to love me as they would have wished. My wealth separated me from my maternal siblings and my skin separated me from my brothers and sisters on the other side. I was no doubt a difficulty and an embarrassment to my stepmother and stepfather alike. Nonetheless, I am and have always been extraordinarily aware of my good fortune. Why, even before Bess I knew I was lucky.

'You see, I know what it is not to belong, and when Robin was born, I saw myself in him. More in him, if truth be told, than in any of the others, strange as it may seem. The others are mine in the sense that the world understands. They are my flesh and blood and I love them. I love my boys and girls more than life itself. Seeing them together, I see my mother's children, the pleasure they take in each other and in their parents. It gives me joy to know I have been able to make this life for them. But when I see Robin – who is not my own, not in the same way, and that is my good Bess's misfortune and not her fault – well, I see a child on the edge of things. I see a child who could so easily have fallen between the cracks in families. Who could have been lost. And I determined – not on the day he was born; no, long before that – to hold him dear in my heart. To cherish him as a child needs to be cherished. To love him as every child deserves to be loved. My wish was always to ensure that he would always know he belonged in my heart. For if there is one thing I cannot bear, it is the suffering of a child.'

Armstrong fell silent, and when Rita glanced at his face, she saw that the man's cheeks were glazed with tears.

'Such feelings do you credit,' she said. 'You are the best of fathers. What I have seen of your family today tells me that.'

Armstrong looked into the distance. 'A hundred times that boy has broken my heart. And he will do it a hundred times more before my days are done.'

They had come to the pig pens. Armstrong fished into a pocket and took out a few acorns. The young pigs came to him with friendly grunts and snuffles and he dealt out acorns and patted flanks and scratched behind ears.

Now Daunt hailed them. He was returning from *Collodion* with the finished and framed photograph of the Armstrong family. He showed it to Armstrong, who nodded and thanked him.

'But Mr Daunt, there is another of your photographs I must speak to you about.'

From his pocket he drew out a small frame and turned it to show Rita and Daunt.

'The fortune-telling pig! You brought it on the day of the fair.'

'So I did, Miss Sunday.' Armstrong looked grave. 'You will remember too that on seeing this pig I was overcome with emotion. Mr Daunt, I know that pig. Her name is Maud. She was my pig. This pig here' – he indicated the sow daintily eating acorns – 'is her daughter Mabel, and that little one there, her granddaughter Matilda. Three years or so ago, without a sound, she was taken from this very pen, and from that day I never saw her again until your photograph came to my attention.'

'She was stolen?'

'Stolen . . . Kidnapped . . . Whatever word you will.'

'Is it an easy thing, to steal a pig? I wouldn't want to try and move one.'

'I don't know why she didn't complain. A pig can squeal to wake the whole house if she wants to. There were red stains between here and the road – at first I feared it was blood, but in fact it was raspberry stains. She had a great fondness for raspberries. I suppose that is how they enticed her away.'

He sighed heavily, pointed to a corner of the picture.

'Now, what do you see here? I believe I see a shadow. I have looked and looked, and it seems to me that it is possible that this shadow belongs to a person, and that this person was standing to the side, out of the way, while the photograph was being exposed.'

Daunt nodded.

'This photograph is nearly three years old, and I understand that it might not be possible after such a long time to remember who that person was. And perhaps it was not even the person who had charge of Maud at all, but some other person. But I have been thinking that *if* you were a remembering sort of man, you might be able to tell me something about the owner of this shadow.'

As he spoke, Armstrong looked at Daunt with an expression that had more expectation of disappointment in it than hope.

Daunt closed his eyes. He consulted the images he had stored in his mind. The photograph had primed his memory.

'A small man. Shorter than Miss Sunday here by eight inches. Slim build. The most striking thing about him was his coat. It was oversized, both too long for him and too broad across the shoulders. I wondered at the time why he wore it on a bright summer day when everyone else was in shirtsleeves. I fancied he might be ashamed of his stature and had hopes the largeness of his garment might convince the eye that there was a matching man inside it.'

'But what did he look like? Was he old or young? Fair or dark? Bearded or clean-shaven?'

'Clean-shaven, and his chin was narrow. More than that I cannot say, for he wore his hat so low over his face that he was close to being invisible.'

Armstrong peered at the photograph, as if by dint of staring he could see beyond the edges of the frame and find the short-statured stranger.

'And he was accompanying the pig?'

'He was. There is only one other thing I can tell you about him that might be at all significant. I asked him whether he would stand by the pig for the photograph, and he would not. I asked him again, and still he said no. In light of what you have told us today about the theft of your pig, it is telling, is it not, that the man was so adamant he would not be photographed?'

The littlest of the Armstrong girls now came running behind them and called out that tea was ready. She asked for her niece to be put down, and Armstrong put the girl on to her two feet on the ground. Hand in hand, niece and diminutive aunt ran ahead indoors, the older child moderating her speed for the little one.

'Excuse the informality,' said Armstrong, 'but we have tea in the kitchen. It saves time and we can all eat in our work clothes.'

Indoors a large table was set with bread and meat and there were different kinds of cake, and a wonderful smell of baking in the air. The big children put butter on bread for the little ones, and the littlest of all was sat on the knee of her biggest uncle-brother and allowed to have the best of everything. Armstrong himself was intent on making sure that everybody, child and guest, had everything they needed, and in passing plates here and there across the table, was in the end the only one with an empty plate.

'Serve yourself, my dear,' prompted Mrs Armstrong.

'I will in a minute, only there is Pip, who cannot reach the plums . . .'

'He would sooner starve than see his children go without,' she told Rita as she pushed the plums nearer to her son and with the other hand placed bread and cheese on her husband's plate, though he was now outside the kitchen door pouring milk into a saucer for the cat.

One of the Armstrong girls interrogated Rita on the topic of medicine and ailments and was so quick to follow and understand that Rita turned to the girl's mother and said, 'You have a nurse in the making here.' At the other end of the table, the children were full of questions for Daunt about photography and boating and the quadricycle.

When only crumbs were left, Daunt noticed a lightening in the room and put his head out of the door.

'Is the darkroom still set up?'

Rita nodded.

'Could we make the most of the light, do you think? Mr Armstrong, a photograph of the farmer at work, perhaps? Will your horse stand still for ten seconds?'

'She will if I am with her.'

Fleet was brought into the courtyard and saddled up. Daunt kept a close eye on the sky. Armstrong mounted.

'What about that little cat?' Rita wondered aloud. 'Where has she got to?'

The cat was found and brought and lifted to sit purring on her master's shoulder.

At this Armstrong's children, understanding the nature of the photograph, went to fetch the dog. The elderly dog amiably allowed herself to be led to a spot beside Fleet's forelegs, where she sat upright and looked directly at the camera like the most obedient subject. And then, when all was in place, Armstrong started.

'Matilda!' he exclaimed. 'We cannot leave Matilda out!'

His middle son swivelled and set off at great speed.

The cloud that had hovered immobile in the sky began to drift slowly. Daunt watched its gradual movement and looked anxiously over to the corner where the boy had disappeared. As the cloud picked up speed in its passage across the sky, he opened his mouth to speak: 'I think we'll have to—'

Back the boy came, at a run, with something under his arm.

The cloud drifted faster.

The boy passed a wriggling bundle of pink flesh up to his father.

Daunt pulled a face. 'We can't have movement.'

'She'll not move,' said Armstrong. 'Not if I tell her.' He lifted the piglet and murmured something into her ear while the cat eavesdropped, her head on one side. He tucked the piglet into the crook of his arm with her rear tucked under his elbow, and the entire tableau – man, steed, dog, cat and piglet – fell into an attitude of perfect stillness for fifteen perfect seconds.

Rita waited with Bess in the kitchen while the Armstrong boys helped Daunt carry the kit back to *Collodion*. Bess's eye kept returning to the photographs, and Rita looked over her shoulder. The child sat on the lap of one of the older Armstrong girls. Around them the other five children had been unable to repress their smiles and beamed steadily at the camera. The newcomer to the family stared at the lens. Her eyes, which in life were so perplexing with their indefinable and ever-shifting green-blue-muddy-greyness, were simplified here by the absence of colour, and Rita was troubled, as she had been troubled by the photograph of Amelia in the boat. The child had a resigned, withdrawn air in the photograph that was less visible in person.

'Is she happy, Bess?' she asked doubtfully. 'You're a mother. What do you think?'

'Well, she plays all right, and runs about. She has a healthy appetite. She likes going down to the river and the big ones take her for a walk every day so she can look around and splash about.' Bess's words said one thing, her tone implied another. 'But later in the day she gets so tired. Much more tired than she ought to be, as if everything is twice as tiring for her as for another child. The light goes out of her, she gets so weary, the little dear, and instead of sleeping, all she can do is cry. There's nothing I can do to console her.'

Bess fidgeted with her eye patch.

'What is your eye condition? Is it something I could help with? I'm a nurse – I'd be happy to take a look.'

'Thank you, Rita, but no. I put my eye away a long time ago. It doesn't trouble me so long as I don't look at people with it.'

'Why ever not?'

'Sometimes I don't like what I see with it.'

'What do you see?'

'What people are really like. When I was a girl I thought that everybody could see into the heart of other people. I didn't realize that what I could see was hidden to everybody else. People don't like it, having their true selves known, and it got me into trouble more than once. I learnt to keep what I saw to myself. I only understood what a person of my age could understand, mind, and that was some protection, I suppose, but as I grew I liked it less and less. Too much knowledge is a burden. When I was fifteen I sewed my first patch and I've worn one ever since. Of course, everybody thinks I'm ashamed of my eye. They think I am concealing my ugliness from them, when in truth it is their ugliness I am hiding.'

'What an extraordinary ability,' said Rita. 'I am intrigued. Have you ever taken your patch off and tried it since those days?'

'Twice. But I have thought of it often since we had this addition to the family. I have thought of taking off my patch to See her.'

'To find out who she is?'

'It won't tell me that. It will only tell me what it feels like to be her.'

'It would tell you whether she is happy?'

'It would.' Bess looked at Rita in uncertainty. 'Shall I?'

They looked out of the window where the girls were playing with the cat. The Armstrong girls were laughing and smiling as they pulled a piece of twine for the cat to leap at. The child eyed their antics listlessly. Every so often she tried a smile, but it seemed to wear her out, and she rubbed her eyes.

'Yes,' said Rita.

Bess stepped into the yard, and returned with the child. Rita took the girl on her lap and Bess sat down opposite her. She slid her eye patch over so that it covered her good eye, keeping her face fully averted from the girl until she was ready. Then she tilted her head and fixed the girl in the line of sight of her far-seeing eye.

Bess's hand flew to her mouth and she gasped in dismay.

'No! The poor little girl is so lost! She wants to go home to her daddy. Oh, the poor child!' Bess seized the little girl and rocked her, pouring out all the comfort she was capable of. Over her head, she spoke to Rita. 'She does not belong with us. You must take her back to the Vaughans. Take her home today!'

Truth, Lies and the River

'WHAT DOES YOUR medical science make of Mrs Armstrong's Seeing eye?' Daunt asked from the helm.

'You are the optical scientist. What do *you* say?'

'There is no eye, human or mechanical, that sees the souls of children.'

'Yet here we are, taking this little girl back to the Vaughans on the basis of Bess's reaction. Because we trust her.'

'Why do we trust a thing neither of us believes?'

'I didn't say I don't believe it.'

'Rita!'

'Perhaps it is this way: Bess was ill as a child; her limp and her eye set her apart from the other children. She had more opportunities to observe – and more time to consider what she observed. She became an outstandingly good judge of character, and learnt what it is to live alongside other human beings and to know more about them than they do themselves. But understanding other people's sorrows and wishes and feelings and intentions as closely as she does must be wearing. She found her gift uncomfortable, persuaded herself that it was her eye that had the talent and drew a veil over it.

'She was already more than half aware that the child wasn't happy. I suspected as much myself. So did you, I think?'

He nodded.

'She is very experienced with children. When she took her patch off, she allowed herself to see what she already knew.'

'And we trust her judgement, which is why we are taking the child back to Buscot Lodge.'

The girl was on the deck, holding the hand rail and watching the water. At every bend in the river she looked ahead. When she had scanned every vessel in sight, her eyes returned to the water. She seemed to look not so much at the surface, rendered opaque by the motion of the water displaced by *Collodion*'s passage, but through it and beyond.

They came to the boathouse at Buscot and moored. Daunt lifted the child down; without hurry and without surprise, she recognized the way back to the house and led them there.

The maid gasped with surprise and rushed them straight to the drawing room.

When they entered, the Vaughans were sitting close together on the sofa, his hand on her belly. At the intrusion, they looked up. The aftermath of powerful feeling was still present in Vaughan's tear-stained face, Helena's wide-eyed pallor. Rita and Daunt had felt themselves to be at the heart of a great event as they brought the child back to Buscot Lodge in *Collodion*, and to come into the house and know that something momentous had been happening here too was disconcerting. But it was true: something vast had come and gone in this room, so grave that the very air vibrated with the knowledge that nothing would ever be the same again.

But now, seeing the child, Vaughan rose to his feet. He took a step, and another, and then ran to the door to sweep the girl into his arms. He held her at arm's length as though he could scarcely believe she was there, then placed her on his wife's lap. Helena placed a hundred kisses on the little girl's head, called her 'darling' a thousand times, and the pair, man and wife, laughed and cried at once.

Daunt answered the question that the Vaughans were too overcome to ask. 'We've been photographing the Armstrongs this afternoon. They are certain she's not Alice. She belongs here, after all.'

Vaughan and Helena exchanged a glance in which they agreed something silently together. When they turned back to Daunt and Rita, they spoke as one:

'She is not Amelia.'

*

They sat on the bank. It was better to tell such stories close to the river than in a drawing room. Words accumulate indoors, trapped by walls and ceilings. The weight of what has been said can lie heavily on what might yet be said and suffocate it. By the river, the air carries the story on a journey, one sentence drifts away and makes room for the next.

The child pulled her shoes off and stood in the shallows, carrying on her usual business with sticks and stones, pausing every once in a while to glance up- and downriver, while Vaughan told Daunt and Rita what he had told Helena, and before her, Mrs Constantine.

When he fell silent, having told all, Helena said, 'I knew she was dead. The night he came home without her, I knew. It was on his face. But I could not bear to know it, and he did not say it, and between us we pretended it was not so. We colluded. We made a falsehood together. And it almost destroyed us. Without the truth, we could not grieve. Without the truth, we could not console each other. In the end, I was so tormented by the deceitful hope I clung to, I was ready to drown myself. Then the girl came, and *I recognized her.*'

'We were happy,' said Vaughan. 'Or rather, Helena was happy, and I was happy that she was happy.'

'Poor Anthony's lie was the greater, but it was not so enduring as my own. I feasted on the sight of the girl. I buried all the painful truth and saw only her.'

'And then Mrs Eavis said, "Hello, Alice!" '

'It was not Mrs Eavis who changed things. It was you, Rita.'

'Me?'

'You told me there was going to be another baby.'

Rita remembered the moment. 'You said, "Oh," and then you said, "Oh," again.'

'One "oh" for the new baby. The other for the knowledge that came with it, that this little girl had never stirred in my womb. I knew then that she was not Amelia. Though I missed her quite as much as if she had been. She brought me back to life, and brought me back to Anthony, and I can't help but love her, our little mystery child, whoever she is.

'She changed us. We have wept for Amelia and we will weep again. There are rivers of tears waiting to be shed. But we will love this little girl like a daughter, and she will be a sister to the baby that is to come.'

They walked back to the house, the Vaughans ahead with the child who was neither Amelia nor Alice between them. She seemed to have accepted her return to Buscot Lodge, as she had accepted her departure from it.

Rita and Daunt fell behind as they followed.

'She can't be Lily's sister,' Daunt said in a low voice. 'That still doesn't make sense.'

'Then whose is she?'

'She's no one's child. So why shouldn't the Vaughans have her? They love her. She can have a good life with them.' There was a note in his voice that Rita recognized, for the same regret and longing rested in her own breast. She remembered the night she had fallen asleep in a chair at the Swan with the sound of Daunt's breathing in the room and the child sleeping on her lap, her ribcage rising and falling in harmony with her own. *I could keep her*, had been the thought that had drifted into her then and never left. But it was no good. She was an unmarried woman with a job. The Vaughans were much better placed to care for the child. She must content herself with loving her from a distance.

Rita took a short breath, expelled it, and with determination turned her mind to other things. She considered the implications of what Vaughan had just told them and shared her thoughts with Daunt in a murmur. 'Whoever it was that kidnapped Amelia . . .' she started.

'. . . also killed her,' finished Daunt in the same undertone.

'They can't be allowed to get away with it. Someone must know something.'

'Someone always knows something. But who? And what do they know? And do they even know the significance of what they know?'

Struck by an idea, Daunt stopped. 'There might be a way . . .' He scratched his head doubtfully.

They caught up with the Vaughans and Daunt set out his idea.

'But will it work?' Helena asked.

'There's no way of knowing.'

'Unless we try it,' Vaughan said.

The four of them stood in front of the house. Mrs Clare the housekeeper, who had heard them coming, opened the door, then, when nobody moved, closed it again.

'Shall we?' Rita asked.

'I can't think of any other way,' Helena said.

'Well, then,' Vaughan said, turning to Daunt. 'How would you begin?'

'With the dragons of Cricklade.'

'Dragons?' Vaughan looked confused, but Helena knew what Daunt was referring to.

'Ruby's grandmother!' she exclaimed. 'And Ruby.'

The Dragons of Cricklade

CRICKLADE IS A town stuffed full of stories. As they passed the church on the quadricycle, Daunt explained some of them to Rita.

'According to legend,' he said as they made their way through the town, laden with all the photographic equipment, 'if a person is unlucky enough to fall from the tower, his friends and family will be diverted from their grief by the spectacle of a stone effigy of their loved one springing naturally from the ground where he fell. I rather regret I have so slim a chance of photographing that.'

They did not stop at the church but headed north, and on the road leading out of the village towards Down Ampney kept a lookout for a thatched cottage with beehives.

'You must go, please,' Helena had begged Rita. 'Daunt will never get anything out of Ruby by himself. She'll trust you. Everybody does.'

So here she was, sitting behind Daunt among the boxes as they bumped and jolted along the country roads, keeping her eyes peeled. 'There,' she pointed, spotting the distinctive tops of beehives behind a hedge.

A white-haired woman was in the garden, making her way on tottering legs towards the hives. At the sound of Rita's greeting she turned transparent eyes in their direction. 'Who's that? Do I know you?'

'My name is Rita Sunday and I've come to buy honey. You must be Mrs Wheeler. I have Mr Daunt here, a photographer. He would like to talk to you about dragons for his book.'

'A book? I don't know about that . . . But I don't mind telling you about the dragons. I might be ninety but I can remember it as if it was yesterday. Come and sit here, and we'll have bread and honey while you ask your questions.'

They sat on a bench in a sheltered corner and the woman went to the door and spoke briefly to someone inside. When she returned, she told them about the dragons. She was a child of three or four when the dragons had come to this very cottage. It was the first time they'd been seen in Cricklade for nearly a hundred years, and nobody had seen them again since. She was the only living person in Cricklade today who had seen them. She had woken with a cough, heat in her throat, and seen flames in the hole in the ceiling where there ought to have been only thatch. 'I got out of bed and went to the door, but I could hear the dragons roaring outside on the landing so I didn't dare open it. I went to the window instead, and there was my father looking in – he had climbed up into the branches of the tree outside, despite them smouldering and being ready to burst into flame at any minute, and he smashed the glass with his foot and reached in and lifted me out. It was a scramble getting down to the ground, and when we got there, the neighbours took me out of his arms and laid me on the ground and rolled me over and over. I couldn't think what they were doing! But my nightdress was on fire, you see, though I didn't know it at the time, and they rolled me to smother the flames.'

The woman delivered her story tranquilly, as though it had happened so long ago it belonged to another person altogether. From time to time, when they asked a question, her pale, candid eyes turned benevolently in the direction of whoever spoke to her, though it was plain she could not see. A thin girl with a pinched look brought a tray to the table and set out slices of bread, a dish of butter and a jar of honey with a spoon. She gave an unsmiling nod to the visitors and went back to the house without raising her eyes.

'Shall I butter the bread?' Rita offered, and Granny Wheeler said, 'Thank you, dear.'

'My grandmother kept her honey in there,' she nodded at the stone outbuilding, 'in a great big canister as big as a bath, and she took the top off and dropped me in it, stark naked, and that's where I stayed for the rest of the night. There was no honey to sell that year, for nobody wanted to eat it after I had sat in it up to my neck.'

'And did you see the dragons? The ones you heard behind the door? What I would give to have a photograph of a dragon – a rich man I'd be!'

She laughed. 'You'd have better things to do than stand about taking photographs if you saw them! Yes, I saw them. I was sitting in the honey when I saw them fly away. Hundreds of them, there were.' She looked up as if she could still see them now. 'Great flying eels, picture that and you will have it about right in your mind's eye. No ears and no eyes, that I could see. No scales, nor even any wings to speak of. Not a bit like any dragon I ever saw in a picture. Just long and dark and sleek and quick. They were twisting and writhing and the sky was so full of them that to look up at them all was like staring into a pan of boiling ink. Now how do you like my honey?'

They finished eating and the old woman reminisced some more about the night of the dragons.

'Look up there!' She pointed to the roof. 'I can't see it no more, my eyes aren't good enough, but you can see it. The dark marks over the window.'

It was true, there were scorch marks just beneath the level of the thatch.

'That would make a fine detail in the photograph,' Daunt suggested. 'Yourself just here, next to the hives, and the place where the fire was in the background. There will be sky in the picture too – where the dragons were.'

With very little reluctance Granny Wheeler was cajoled into appearing in the photograph, and while Daunt set up, Rita continued talking to her.

'You must have been badly burnt?'

Granny Wheeler rolled up her sleeve and showed her arm. 'That's what I'm like all down my back, from my neck to my waist.' A large area of skin was discoloured, taut and unlined.

'This is most unusual,' Rita said. 'Such a large area to be burnt. You haven't had any trouble with it since?'

'Oh, no.'

'Because of the honey? I use honey when my patients are burnt too.'

'Are you a nurse?'

'Yes, and a midwife. I work a few miles downstream. At Buscot.'

The woman started. 'Buscot?'

There was a pause. Rita swallowed a piece of bread and honey and waited until, tentatively, the old woman went on.

'You might know something about the child that went missing there two years ago . . .'

'Amelia Vaughan?'

'That's the one. They said she came back – but now I've heard it might not be her after all. What do they say about it now? Is it Amelia or not?'

'A woman did come forward who appeared to recognize the child as another little girl, but the other family came to think she was not theirs, so she is back with the Vaughans again. Nobody knows who she is really, but she is not Amelia.'

'Not Amelia! I did so hope . . . For the sake of the Vaughans, but also for the good of my own family. My granddaughter was nursemaid to the Vaughans. She has had no end of trouble since that little child was took. All manner of things have been said about her. Nobody who knows her believes a word of it, but there are so many who hear the story first and see her in the light of it. All she wanted in life was a nice young man and a family of her own, but there aren't many men prepared to take on a wife mixed up in something like that! She fretted herself sick with it all. Couldn't sleep and hardly ate a thing. Wouldn't go out in case anybody spoke harshly to her, wouldn't hardly come out of her room, some days. I didn't hear her laugh for months on end . . . And then word came that the girl was back! Returned by the river, they said. Them that had gossiped about Ruby had to bite their tongues then. The tide started to turn. Ruby came out of her shell a bit. She even got work, helping out at the school she used to go to. She got a bit of her colour back, started to take an interest in life again. Sometimes in the evenings she went with the other young ladies from the school for a turn around the streets, and who was I to say no, after all the hardship she'd suffered? Why shouldn't she have a bit of fun like the other young ones do? She met Ernest. They got engaged. They was going to get married in July. But just after solstice time a jealous girl took her aside and whispered that the child they found at Buscot was not Amelia after all, that the lost girl was still lost. The talk started up again. Ruby was still under suspicion. She called off the wedding the very next day. "How can I marry and have children with everybody whispering these things about me? I will not be trusted with my own babies! It's not fair on Ernest. He deserves better than me." That was the gist of it. Ernest did his best to talk her out of it. He won't listen to the gossips. He says the wedding is only postponed and the engagement stands, but she won't see him, though he comes asking after her every day. The school said she had better leave and she never goes beyond the garden walls now.'

The blind woman sighed. 'I was hoping for better news, but you have only confirmed what I knew already.' She made to stand up slowly on her ancient bones. 'I may as well fetch you that honey while we're waiting.'

'Sit down a little longer,' said Rita. 'I know the Vaughans. They trust Ruby. They know she did no harm.'

'That is something,' the woman acknowledged, settling back into her seat. 'They were good people. They never said anything harsh about her.'

'Mr and Mrs Vaughan would like nothing better than to get to the bottom of this business of the kidnap. Because if your granddaughter had nothing to do with it, somebody else did – and that person must be caught and brought to justice. If that could be brought about it would be a great help to Ruby, in her position.'

The dragon-seer shook her head. 'They looked into it at the time and found nothing. I suppose it were the river gypsies, and they won't never be caught now.'

'But supposing something new were to be tried?'

The old woman looked up and her transparent eyes peered at Rita in perplexity.

'I believe everything you have told me about Ruby and how good she is, because I have heard it all before, from the Vaughans themselves. It is not fair that she should not marry. It is not fair that she should not have the children she wants and would be such a good mother to. Tell me now, if there was a way of bringing the truth to the surface, of exposing the true culprits and clearing Ruby's name, would she help? Would she play a part in it?'

The woman's eyes wavered.

The door to the house opened and the scrawny young woman who had served the bread and honey stepped out.

'What would I have to do?'

While Daunt positioned Granny Wheeler alongside her hives and beneath the lintel stained by dragon flames, Rita sat with Ruby, their two heads together, explaining the plan.

When she had finished, the girl stared at her. 'But that's magic!'

'It isn't, but it will seem so.'

'And it will make people tell the truth?'

'It might. If somebody knows something they haven't told yet. Something they didn't know was important, perhaps. If that person is there, and if we are lucky, yes.'

Ruby lowered her eyes again, to the white-knuckled hands with bitten nails that she clasped tightly in her lap. Rita said no more to persuade her, but left her to her thoughts. The hands fidgeted and twisted and at last came to stillness.

'What do you need me to do, though? I can't do magic like that.'

'You won't have to do magic. All you need to do is tell me who persuaded you to leave Buscot Lodge that night.'

A feeble light of hope had come into Ruby's eyes. Now her lip trembled and the hope died. She dropped her head into her hands.

'Nobody! I've said it over and over again and they don't believe me! Nobody!'

Rita took the girl's hands and drew them gently away. She kept them clasped in her own and turned to look fully into her tearful face.

'Then why did you go out?'

'You wouldn't believe me! No one would. They would call me a silly liar.'

'Ruby, I know you are an honest girl. If there is something unbelievable at the bottom of all this, I am the person to tell. Perhaps with two minds we will be able to work it out.'

The years since the kidnap had worn Ruby down to the bone. She was wan-faced and dark circles were carved under her eyes. It was hard to believe she was not yet twenty. The future that had appeared possible when Amelia seemed to be found and she got engaged had been dashed again. She gave no sign that she had faith in Rita's ability to help her. Unconvinced that the revelation could do her any good, she had nevertheless reached a point where she was simply too exhausted to maintain her position any longer. So, shoulders slumped, her voice flat and at the end of her strength, Ruby told.

The Wishing Well

THERE WAS A wishing well at Kelmscott. The well was reputed to have a great many magic powers, including the ability to cure physical ills of all the well-known kinds, in addition to aiding in the resolution of all sorts of marital and familial dilemmas. Faith in the powers of the well was strengthened by one verifiable and unique feature: whatever the weather, and whatever the season, water from the well at Kelmscott was always ice cold.

With its simple stonework and wooden canopy the well was picturesque and Daunt had photographed it more than once. In spring the froth of hawthorn flower made a good backdrop. Climbing roses scrambled up the posts in summer. He had taken a third picture of it looking starkly beautiful in a wintry cap of snow. He lacked an autumn photograph to complete the quartet.

'Let's stop,' he suggested, pointing at the well, which was wreathed with evergreen foliage into which the villagers had tied ribbons and straw decorations. 'We have the light.'

He set up the camera and returned to *Collodion* to prepare the plate, while Rita lingered by the well, drawing up a pail of water and testing its temperature. It was as the legend said: the water was biting cold.

When Daunt returned, he inserted the plate in the camera.

Daunt had not photographed Rita for some time, and she knew the reason. Their photographic sessions had been intimate. To find the pose he would take her head in his hands and tilt it one way and the other, while she observed his face as he watched the light pool and flood according to the contours of her bones. When he found the right position their eyes would meet wordlessly, before he let go of her to return to the camera. And when the plate was exposed, and he was hidden beneath the black curtain, when all was silence and stillness, she nevertheless felt an intensity of communication, as everything she did not say to him in words overspilt into her gaze. Of course he had stopped taking her photograph. It was necessary.

Today's photograph was a sudden shift, which was puzzling. Perhaps it meant that he had succeeded in freeing his heart, and could now behave with her in an ordinary way. She could not help being dismayed that he might have achieved this so easily, when the current of her own feelings still ran high.

'Where shall I stand?' she asked uncertainly.

'Right behind the camera,' he said, pointing to the dark curtain.

'You want me to *take* the photograph?'

'You've seen me lift the cover of the plate and take off the lens cap. Don't let the light in under the curtain. Count to fifteen seconds and put the cover back. Don't start counting till I've raised the water and gone under.'

'What do you mean?'

'You plunge your face into the water and it's supposed to show you the fulfilment of your wish.'

From under the black cloth, through the glass, Rita watched Daunt dip his fingertips in, then shake off the icy drops with a shudder. It put her in mind of the day at the river when he had stripped almost naked to plunge in up to the neck and help her in the experiment that had demonstrated the very opposite of what she had hoped. His blanched face had been rigid with cold that day, but he had not complained and had remained submerged to his Adam's apple while she counted to sixty.

'What are you going to wish for?' she called.

'Doesn't it break the magic if you tell?'

'Quite likely.'

'Well then, I'm not telling.'

She had so many wishes she wouldn't know where to start. To see Amelia's kidnappers punished for their crime. To care for the girl and keep her from harm always. To find a way out of this eternal to-ing and fro-ing between loving Daunt and fearing pregnancy. To understand what happened to the girl's heartbeat on winter solstice night.

'I'm ready.' Daunt took a breath, and plunged his face into the ice-cold water.

At one, Rita raised the cover of the plate and removed the lens cap.

At two, she became aware of a thought rising from the depths of her mind.

At three, the thought surfaced and she knew instantly and beyond all doubt that it was significant.

At four, her brain working faster than she could keep up with, she had abandoned the camera, not caring what light got in under the hastily thrown-up curtain, and was running to the well, taking her watch from her pocket at the same time.

At five, she was at the well and had taken Daunt's wrist between her thumb and fingertips to take his pulse, while opening the cover of her watch.

Six was completely forgotten – she was counting other numbers now.

Daunt's pulse throbbed under Rita's fingertips. The second hand of her watch turned around the clock face. Her brain was empty of everything except the two beats, clockwork and human. They ran alongside each other, each one according to its own rhythm, then – the shock. In the moment it happened, her mind did not falter. Instead it narrowed its attention even further so that she could read the action of Daunt's heart and what it meant as clearly as if she held it in her hands. The universe was nothing but the life of this heart and her own mind counting and knowing.

After eighteen seconds, Daunt reared up from the water, frozen-faced and colourless. His features locked in a rigid mask, he looked more like a corpse than a living man, except that he gasped for breath, staggered and sat down.

Rita kept hold of his wrist, did not even glance up, maintained her count.

After a minute, she put her watch away. She took paper and a pencil from her pocket, dashed down the figures with trembling fingers and laughed a brief, startled laugh before turning to him, wide-eyed and shaking her head at the extraordinariness of it all.

'What is it?' he said. 'Are you all right?'

'Am *I* all right? Daunt – are *you* all right?'

'My face is cold. I think I'm going to—'

To her alarm he leant away, as if nauseous, but after a moment turned back to her. 'No. It's settled.'

She took his hands in hers and scrutinized him intently. 'Yes, but – *Daunt* – how do you *feel*?'

He returned her intensely puzzled stare with a mild version of the same thing.

'I feel a bit peculiar, actually. Must be the chill. But I'm all right.'

She raised the piece of paper.

'Your heart stopped.'

'What?'

She looked down at her notes. 'I got here at – let's call it six seconds after immersion. It was about that. Your heartbeat was at its normal rate then – eighty beats per minute. At eleven seconds it stopped altogether for three whole seconds. When it restarted, it was at a rate of thirty beats per minute. Once you were out of the water it remained at that rate for seven seconds. Thereafter it rose rapidly.'

She took his hand and felt for his pulse again. Counted. 'It's back to normal. Eighty beats a minute.'

'Stopped?'

'Yes. For three seconds.'

Daunt paid attention to the beating of his heart. He realized he had never done that before. He slid a hand inside his jacket and felt the power of the pump in his chest against his hand.

'I'm fine,' he said. 'Are you sure?' It was a ridiculous question. This was Rita. She didn't make mistakes about things like that. 'What made you think of it?'

'The cold water made me remember the first experiment at the river. And I was suddenly struck by the fact that that day you weren't completely submerged, only up to the neck, and so today the part of you in icy water was the only part that wasn't before. And I suppose I must have connected that with the head injuries I've treated in the past, and the knowledge that so much of what makes us human is contained there . . . Everything came together and I just left the camera and ran . . .'

It was a discovery. Joy surged through her. Instinct made her reach for Daunt's hand, but she did not take it, for it was plain her jubilation was not shared. He rose from the grass, looking tired and drawn. 'I'd better retrieve this over-exposed plate,' he said flatly as he made for the camera.

They dismantled and packed up in strained silence, and when everything was stowed away he was still.

'I didn't wish for anything,' he told her abruptly. 'I don't believe in wishing wells. Though you seem to have been granted your wish. If I had been the wishing type I might have wished for you and a child. Both things. Together. But I don't know if I could bring myself to wish for a thing you don't want. I have imagined it, Rita. The two of us allowing our feelings to run away with us, nature taking its course, realizing a child is on the way . . . What's the value of happiness that can only come at the price of another person's despair?'

Collodion took them upriver to Rita's cottage, slicing the water, creating a churn of noise and splash and leaving a long trail of turbulence in its wake. They went in silence. When they came to Rita's cottage they murmured a stiff goodnight, and he went on to the Swan.

Letting herself into the cottage, Rita put her notebook on the table she used as a desk and turned to the page of the day's annotations. A secondary exhilaration caused a little leap of the heart. What a discovery! It was followed by a sinking. What kind of a wishing well was it that gave you the thing you most wanted, without even wishing for it, and made you at the same time so painfully conscious of everything else you could not have?

The Magic Lantern Show

AT THE SWAN, summer turned to autumn and the rain did not cease. There were no more frowning conversations about the danger of a poor harvest, for it was now a certainty. No amount of sunshine could change anything. The crops sat stunted and blackening in the fields, and how could you harvest them anyway, with the ground so waterlogged? The laid-off farmhands tried to get jobs at the gravel works and elsewhere, and although all went to the Swan for respite from their worries, a mood of anxiety hung over the winter room.

In this atmosphere word got round that the child had come back from the Armstrongs and was living with the Vaughans again. What to make of it? They supposed she was not Alice after all. They supposed she was Amelia again. This deviation of the story was not met with enthusiasm. A story ought to go clearly in one direction, then, after a distinct moment of crisis, change to go in another. This slipping back on the quiet to the original lacked the requisite drama. Later it was said that the Vaughans had been heard calling the child Milly. Whether this was an abbreviation of Amelia or another name altogether was the source of some debate, but it didn't match up to the early arguments over the colour of her eyes, and when measured against the passionate debate about whether or not the fact of being impossible means a thing can't happen, it was distinctly lacklustre. The relentlessness of the rain dampened their enthusiasm too. In fact, stories began to grow as weak as the crops in the field. Sometimes the tellers even found themselves drinking in silence. When Jonathan tried to tell his tale about the farmer who drove his horse and cart into the lake and then something or other that he couldn't altogether remember, and ended 'and he was never seen again!', he was met with little encouragement.

Joe ailed too. More and more often he lay sinking in the room at the back; when he appeared infrequently in the winter room he was frailer and paler than ever. Though he struggled for breath he told a story or two – strange ones, brief in the telling and stirring to hear; in their endings they seemed to open on to infinity, and nobody could explain or retell them afterwards.

Against this background, and nourished by the continuing uncertainty about the child's identity, a seed that had been sown some months ago and given rise to nothing at the time saw a belated germination. The great-aunt of one of the gravel-diggers reckoned she'd seen the child had no reflection when she looked in the river. Now the second cousin of a cressman said that was all wrong. He'd seen the child staring in the river and had witnessed this mystifying thing: the child had *two* reflections, each one resembling the other in every detail. Spurred by this, other stories began to circulate. That the girl had no shadow, that her shadow had the form of an old crone, that if you looked too long into those peculiar eyes of hers she would benefit from your distracted state to slice your shadow from the soles of your feet and eat it.

'It's happened to me!' an elderly widow with ailments both real and imaginary told Rita, staring at her feet and pointing. 'The witch's child has eaten my shadow!'

'Look up, instead,' Rita encouraged her. 'Where is the sun?'

The widow searched the sky. 'Drowned. Quite drowned.'

'Yes. There is no sun today, and that is why you have no shadow. There is nothing more to it than that.'

The widow seemed reassured, but it didn't last. The next thing Rita heard from a patient was that the girl had eaten the sun and brought the rain to wreck the harvest.

In the Swan, they heard this and shrugged. Did it make sense? They recalled that she was dead and then alive again, which no ordinary human could do, but a witch's child? They pondered, but refrained from endorsing the theory.

Then, in early September, all of this was pushed aside by a novelty. A poster appeared, pinned to one of the beams in the wall of the Swan; it announced that on the night of the autumn equinox there would be a magic lantern show. It was to be provided free by Mr Daunt of Oxford as a gesture of thanks to the people whose quick action and presence of mind had done so much to aid him when he was injured nine months ago.

'It is a story told in pictures,' Margot explained to Jonathan. 'With pictures on glass, I believe, and light passed through them. I don't know how it works, you'll have to ask Mr Daunt.'

'What kind of a story is it?'

But that was a secret.

On the day of the equinox the inn was closed to drinkers – even regulars – until seven o'clock in the evening. Some of the regulars had not been able to believe that this applied to them; they turned up anyway and were outraged at being denied entry. They heard constant noise from inside and saw that the door was forever being opened and closed to allow in strong young men carrying great boxes and crates. They went away, to tell others that they had not been allowed in and that there was something extraordinary going on.

Daunt had begun his preparations early. A hundred times he ran between *Collodion* and the inn, organizing his own assistants and Armstrong's boys. Which containers, in which order, to which room . . . At one point, six men were needed to carry in a large heavy rectangle, concealed under packaging. They lifted it with grave attention and as they inched up the slope, sweating and with strained faces, Daunt did not so much as blink, so intent was his gaze. When it had been carried into the inn successfully, there was a communal sigh of relief and refreshments for all, before they got back to the more ordinary lifting and carrying. Only when Daunt and the Ockwells were alone were the blanket and packing case taken off and the mysterious shape revealed to be a great pane of glass.

'I'll set it up here. Nobody must come behind the curtain. The glass will be invisible in the dark. We don't want any injuries. Now, how's that paint drying in the main room, for the magic lantern?'

In the afternoon Rita arrived, accompanying a woman who was so draped under a shawl that it was impossible to see her face. Most of the Little Margots came to help, and one of them brought her youngest daughter with her, a little girl of three, who had her own very important role to play.

At half past six, Jonathan was given the honour of unlocking the door and holding it open to let the curious inside. They were all directed to the right, into the large summer room. The Swan was transformed. A velvet drape covered one wall, concealing the arch into the winter room, and another wall – in front of the chairs – had been repainted in fresh white. The tables had gone and instead rows of chairs were serried together, facing the white wall. Behind the seating, raised on a small platform, stood Henry Daunt, with a curious mechanical device and a box of glass plates.

A great many people came in and there was the din of many conversations at once: the farm labourers and the gravel-diggers and all the regulars and their wives and children, and countless people from the neighbouring villages who had got to hear of the show. Armstrong was there with Bess and his older children. He sat with an air of grave restlessness. He had an inkling about part of the content of the show, had indeed helped with the preparation of it. Robin had been invited but was nowhere to be seen, which surprised nobody. The Vaughans were staying away. Knowing in advance what the story was to be, both agreed it would be better not to attend. After all, there was no certainty it would come to anything. They had contributed what was necessary and their presence would in any case be felt in other ways. The Little Margots served cider to all and at precisely seven o'clock Daunt made a short speech of thanks to Joe and Margot. Joe was about to close the door when Lily White arrived, panting, holding a covered basket.

Lily had to sit on a stool at the back, for all the seats were taken. On her knees she held the basket with the red cloth cover, beneath which something was wriggling. She placed a hand to quieten the puppy she had bought that afternoon as a gift for Ann, and it settled. Where *was* Ann? She peered over the heads of the audience, looking for a small child's head between two adult ones, but before she had scanned more than a few rows, the lanterns were dimmed and the room was plunged into darkness.

There was an expectant stir, the scuffing of feet on the floor, the arranging of skirts, some throat-clearing; then through all that, a crisp mechanical click was heard and—

Ooh!

Buscot Lodge materialized spectrally on the white wall. The home of the Vaughans: its pale stone facade pierced with seventeen windows arranged in such orderly fashion that nobody could imagine anything but harmony under its quiet grey roof. A few looked to see how the image had flown on to the wall from Daunt's machine at the back, but most were too entranced to think of that.

Click. Buscot Lodge disappears and Mr and Mrs Vaughan are suddenly in their place. Between them, the wriggling blur of a child – Amelia, aged two. There is a murmur of feeling from the women in the audience.

Click. Giggles – this is not what anyone was expecting: an advertisement, writ large in the stream of light. Daunt reads aloud for the benefit of those who are not quick with their letters, and while he reads, others comment in whispers:

STELLA
The
Sapient Pig
THIS MOST EXTRAORDINARY CREATURE
Will Spell and Read, Cast Accounts,
PLAY AT CARDS,
Tell any Person what o'clock it is to a Minute
BY THEIR OWN WATCH
Also
TELL THE AGE OF ANY ONE IN COMPANY;
And what is more Astonishing, she will
Discover A Person's Thoughts
A Thing never heard of before
Moreover
In Private Audience she will
REVEAL THE FUTURE
Including
SUCCESSES FINANCIAL AND MATRIMONIAL

'It is the pig from the fair!'

'Sapient? Whatever is that?'

''Tis a clever word meaning wise. Which is a thing you would know if you was sapient yourself.'

'Spells better than I do myself, that pig do!'

'I wish it didn't play so well at cards. I lost thruppence to it.'

'Seventy-three, that pig said I was! I was that cross!'

'I left before she started discovering the thoughts. I couldn't bear to have a pig rummaging in my thoughts, never, never, never!'

'Shilling a time, they was wanting for a private audience. Daft! Who's got a shilling round 'ere to spend on an audience with a pig?'

The mechanical noise comes again, the advertisement makes way for the pig herself. In fact it is not Maud, but her daughter Mabel, who looks exactly the same to everyone but Armstrong. Seated opposite the pig is a young woman they all recognize.

'Ruby!'

The hum of conversation fades abruptly.

In the image, Ruby proffers a shilling, and a dark-sleeved arm reaches down to take it from her. At the same time, she gazes into the eyes of the pig.

Now a voice breaks into the darkness – and it is the voice of Ruby herself.

'Tell me my fortune, Stella. Who will I marry? Where will I meet the one who is to win my hand?'

The audience gasps and there is shifting in seats as people turn their heads to look in the direction of the voice, but nobody can see anything in the dark, and in any case, from another side of the room, voiced by one of the Little Margots, the pig replies, 'Go to St John's Lock at midnight on winter solstice night, and look in the water. There you will see the face of he who is to win your hand.'

Click. A clock face gleams in the darkness: it *is* midnight!

Click. St John's Lock: everybody knows it. And here is Ruby again, on hands and knees, staring intently into the river.

'Well I'm blowed,' somebody says, and 'Shhhh!' says everybody else.

A *click*, St John's Lock again. Ruby is standing, hands on hips in an attitude of vexation.

'Nothing!' comes the voice of Ruby again. 'Nothing at all! It's a mean trick!'

This time nobody stares at the source of the sound. They are all too absorbed in the story that is unfolding before their eyes in the magical darkness.

Click. Buscot Lodge again.

Click. The interior of a child's room. A small child's form under the blanket.

Click. The same room, but a dark-clad figure leans over the bed with his back to the audience.

Not a foot shuffles, not a hand fidgets. The Swan holds its breath.

Click. The same room, where the bed is now empty. The window is open to the sky.

The Swan flinches.

Click. An exterior view of the house from the side. A ladder reaches to the open window.

The Swan shakes its many heads in disapproval.

Click. Two people from behind. His arm is around her shoulders. Their heads are bowed towards each other in grief. There is no doubt who they are. It is Mr and Mrs Vaughan.

Click. A piece of paper, once crumpled but smoothed out:

Mr Vaughan,
£1,000 ensures the safe return of your daughter.

The Swan lets out a gasp of outrage.

'Hush!'

Click. A desk on which lies a money bag, bursting at the seams.

Click. The same money bag, this time positioned at the far side of Radcot Bridge, only a very little way from where they are all seated now.

Murmurs of consternation.

Click. Mr and Mrs Vaughan wait by the fireside. The clock visible between them says six o'clock.

Click. The same photograph, except that it is now eight o'clock.

Click. Eleven o'clock. Mrs Vaughan's head is on her husband's shoulder in an attitude of despair.

The Swan swoons and sobs in sympathy.

Click. A gasp! The foot of Radcot Bridge again – but the money is gone!

Click. From behind, Mr and Mrs Vaughan are seen collapsed in each other's arms.

The Swan is roused. There is open weeping, a good many exclamations of outrage and horror, threats are made against the perpetrators: one would wring their necks, another would hang them, a third wants to tie them in sacks and drop them off the bridge.

Click. ***WHO KIDNAPPED LITTLE AMELIA?***

The Swan falls silent.

Click. The image of the pig reappears. Daunt takes a stick and uses it in the current of light to delineate what the Swan failed to notice before. There is a shadow.

There is a hushed 'Oh!'

Click. It seems to be the same scene, though in fact it is Mabel again, standing in for her mother. This time the picture is cropped so that only the pig's tail is visible – and at the centre of the image is the bottom of a long coat, a few inches of trouser leg and a pair of boot toecaps.

There are gasps of shock. 'It was not the pig that tricked Ruby! It was him!'

Someone stands, pointing, and shouts, 'So it were *him* that took Amelia!'

Understanding floods the Swan, which now speaks in a hundred voices:

'He were a short fellow!'

'Skinny as a broomstick!'

'There weren't nothing to him!'

'That coat – too wide across the shoulders.'

'And long on him.'

'Always in that hat, he were.'

'Never took it off!'

They remember him, all right. Everybody remembers him. But nobody is capable of giving any description beyond the coat and the hat and the size of the man.

And when did anyone last see him?

'Two year ago.'

'Two year? Close to three if it's a day!'

'Aye, getting on for three.'

Consensus is reached. The man with the pig was an undersized man in an oversized coat with a low hat and nobody has seen him for nearly three years.

Daunt and Rita confer. They have been all ears, but there is nothing to indicate that anybody here is about to divulge information beyond what is already known.

He leans and murmurs in her ear, 'I think I've wasted everyone's time.'

'It's not over yet. Come on. Part two.'

While outrage fills the room, Daunt and Rita slip behind a curtain. Rita goes over the instructions again with the Little Margot and her child, while Daunt checks devices concealed elsewhere whose purpose is not evident from their appearance but would be familiar to any theatrical-effects manager or spiritualist. 'I'll nod when I'm ready for you to draw back that curtain, all right?'

At the back of the room in her dark corner, Lily has never seen anything like these huge images on the wall, so lifelike and so impossible. When they said it was going to be a story told in pictures she'd had in mind the illustrated children's Bible whose pages she used to turn while her mother read. She didn't know it would be reality in black and white, flattened like pressed flowers and laid tall and broad on the wall. She didn't know it would touch on her own life. Her hand clutches at her throat, and she stares, all pulse and sweat and tremble, and there is nowhere in her terrified brain for thought to find a foothold. She has fallen into a waking nightmare.

A fork chiming on glass makes her jump. It sets the air ringing and quietens the audience. They settle in their seats: there is more to come.

Instead of a *click* comes the swooshing sound of a curtain being drawn to one side. Those closest to the velvet drape are aware of movement. The arch into the winter room is now exposed and there is sudden light.

Heads turn, disconcerted.

There is a tense, shocked silence.

In the winter room there is a child. But it is no ordinary child. And it is no photograph. The girl's hair moves as if lifted by a wave, her white chemise floats gauzily, and – strangest of all – her feet do not touch the floor. Her form shifts and shimmers, is at once there and absent. Her face bears the faintest trace of features: the hint of a nose, eyes that stare in faded fashion, a mouth too washed out to speak from. The white folds of her gown float around her as if the air were water, and she drifts insubstantially.

'Child,' comes Ruby's voice, 'do you know me?'

The girl nods.

'You know me to be Ruby, your old nurse who loved you and took good care of you?'

Another nod.

Nobody moves. It is either fear or the fear of missing something that keeps them in their seats.

'Was it me who took you from your bed?'

The child shakes her head.

'It was another, then?'

The child nods, slowly, as though the questions are arriving only distantly into the other realm where she is now.

'Who was it? Who took you to the river and drowned you?'

'Yes, tell us!' someone calls from the audience. 'Tell us who!'

And the girl, whose face is transparent enough to be any child's, raises a hand, and her finger points . . . not at the screen but into the room, at the audience themselves.

Pandemonium. There are shrieks and confused cries. In their shock, people rise to their feet and chairs are knocked over. In the reflected light they turn and stare, here and there, anywhere the shifting, shimmering finger might be pointing, and everywhere are faces like their own: appalled, stunned, tear-stained. Someone faints; someone wails; someone moans.

'I didn't mean to do it!' whispers Lily, her words unheard in all the commotion. With shaking hands and streaming eyes she opens the door and flees, as if the optical illusion is at her heels.

When everybody had gone, the Little Margots and the Armstrong children set about restoring the inn to order. The little ghost, robust in her everyday appearance as Margot's youngest granddaughter, yawned as they pulled the flimsy white garment over her head and she stomped around the room in her clogs. The great mirror was packed into its huge rectangular case and heaved away with care and much grunting. The velvet curtain was taken down and folded, and the gauze voile rippled and shivered as it was dropped into a bag. The gas light was dismantled. Element by element, the illusion of the ghost was dismantled, packed away and removed, and when it was gone and they all looked at each other in the interior of the Swan as it appeared on a normal evening, they saw that their hope was gone too.

Robert Armstrong's shoulders slumped, and Margot was unusually quiet. Daunt came and went between the inn and *Collodion* with boxes, so low in spirits that nobody dared speak to him. Rita went to see Joe, who was in bed. He raised his eyes to her in expectation, and when she shook her head, he blinked sorrowfully.

Only Jonathan was his usual merry self, untouched by the general mood. 'I *nearly* thought it was real,' he repeated. 'Even though I knew about the mirror and the gauze and the gas light. Even though I knew it was Polly. I *nearly* believed it!'

With the others, he was replacing the chairs in their original places. Then as he made for the final few stools at the back, he exclaimed, 'Well I never! Who left you behind?'

A puppy cowered in the corner of the room, under the last stool.

Robert Armstrong came to see. He bent down and lifted the animal in his large hand. 'You are too small to be out in the world by yourself,' he told the puppy, and it sniffed his skin and scrambled to be held closer.

'It belongs to the woman who came in at the end,' said Daunt. He consulted his memory and listed every detail of her appearance.

'Lily White,' said Margot. 'She lives at Basketman's Cottage. I didn't even know she was here.'

Armstrong nodded. 'I'll take this little fellow home. It's not far, and my boys are not ready yet in any case.'

Margot turned to her granddaughter. 'Now, little Miss, I reckon we've had enough haunting for one day, eh? Time for bed!' and the little girl was whisked away.

'Just an illusion,' said Daunt. 'And it hasn't achieved much.' He turned to Ruby, who was sitting on a box in the corner, trying not to cry. 'I'm sorry. I hoped for more. I've let you down.'

'You tried,' she told him, but the tears spilt all the same. 'It's the Vaughans who will feel it hardest.'

Of Pigs and Puppies

ARMSTRONG TUCKED THE puppy inside his coat to keep it warm, leaving a button undone so it could put its nose out and sniff the night air. It squirmed comfortably against him and settled.

'I had better come with you,' Rita said. 'Mrs White might be alarmed at the arrival of a stranger so late and after such an unsettling end to the evening.'

They headed up to the bridge in silence, each considering their disappointment in an evening that had cost so much in time and effort and come to nothing. They crossed over a river full of stars and on the other side came before too long to the place where the bank had collapsed and the river expanded into new breadths. They had to concentrate to get over the gnarled roots and ropes of ivy in the dark. Through the ringing of the river, they heard a voice.

'She knows it was me! I never meant to do ill! I swear! I wouldn't have hurt a hair on her head! She is so cross that I took her and I drowned her – she raised her finger! She pointed me out! She knows it was me that did it.'

The pair of eavesdroppers stared into the darkness as though they might hear the better for it, waiting for the reply of the person she was speaking to, but no voice came. Rita made to step forward, but Armstrong put out a hand to halt her. Another sound had reached his ears. A muffled snuffling. It was an animal sound. It was a pig sound.

His brain began to stir.

When the sound of the pig fell still, Lily's voice sounded again. 'She will never forgive me. What am I to do? Wickedness like mine is so terrible I can never be forgiven. God Himself has sent her to punish me. I must do as the basket-maker did, though I am so afraid. Oh! But I must do it and suffer the eternal torments, for I do not deserve to live a day longer in this world . . .'

The voice disintegrated into choked tears.

Armstrong strained his ears to listen to the animal snuffling that replied to Lily's words. Was it . . . ? Surely not. And yet . . .

The puppy yapped. Their presence revealed, they stepped from the concealment of the poplars and started to walk up the slope.

'Just friends, Mrs White,' Rita called ahead. 'Returning the puppy to you. You left him behind after the magic lantern show.' Lily's distress was visible now. 'He's come to no harm. We've taken care of him.'

But as Rita was approaching Lily, speaking soothingly all the while, Armstrong ran in a powerful dash up the slope. He ran straight past Lily and all the way to the pigsty, where he fell to his knees in the mud, put his hands through the bars of the fence, and cried, 'Maud!'

Armstrong gazed with love and disbelief at the face he had thought never to see again. Though she was older and thinner, weary and with an air of sadness, though her skin had lost its rosy gleam and her hair its bright copper shine, he knew her. Nor did the pig take her eyes off him. And if there had been any shadow of a doubt, her own welcome would have dispersed it, for she got up instantly, agitated her trotters in an excited dance and put her snout to the fence so that he could caress her ear and rub her bristly cheek. She pressed at the fence as though she would knock it down to reach her old, dear friend. As Maud's eyes softened with the emotion of the reunion, Armstrong felt his throat ache with tears.

'Whatever has happened to you, my love? How did you come to be here?'

He took acorns from his pocket, and Maud kissed them gently from the palm of his hand, as so few pigs ever learnt how to do, and his heart filled with joy.

Lily, meanwhile, continued to rub her eyes and to repeat, 'I didn't mean it. I didn't know!'

Rita looked from Lily to Armstrong and the pig and back to Lily again.

Where to begin?

'Lily, what were you saying when we arrived? What was it you didn't mean to do?'

As if she hadn't heard, Lily repeated, 'I didn't know! I didn't know!'

At last, after several more efforts from Rita, she seemed to hear the question.

'I have told it all to the pig,' she sniffed. 'She says now I must confess to the parson.'

Of Sisters and Piglets

THE PARSON IN his nightshirt and dressing gown invited his nocturnal visitors to sit. Armstrong took a chair against the wall, and Rita sat on the sofa.

'I have never once sat down at the parsonage,' Lily said. 'But I have come to confess and after today I will never come here again, so I suppose I will sit.' She sat nervously next to Rita.

'Now, what's this about confession?' the parson asked, with a glance at Rita.

'I did it,' Lily said. She had sobbed all the way along the riverbank, but now she was in the parsonage her voice was drained. 'It was me. She comes out of the river and points her finger at me. She *knows* it was me.'

'Who points her finger?'

Rita explained to the parson about the illusion at the Swan, and what they had meant to achieve by it, then turned to Lily. 'It was not real, Lily. It wasn't meant to frighten you.'

'She used to come to Basketman's Cottage. She came out of the river and pointed her finger at me – she was real, I know she was, she dripped on to the floorboards and left them damp. When I didn't confess but kept my wickedness secret, she came to the Swan, and now she points her finger at me there. She knows it was me.'

'What is it that you did, Lily?' Rita crouched in front of Lily, holding her two hands in hers. 'Tell us plainly.'

'I drowned her!'

'You drowned Amelia Vaughan?'

'She is *not* Amelia Vaughan! She is *Ann*!'

'You drowned your sister?'

Lily nodded. 'I drowned her! And she will not let me rest till I have confessed.'

'I see,' said the parson. 'Then you must confess. Tell me what happened.'

Now that it had actually come to it, Lily was calm. Her tears dried, her muddled notions cleared. With her hair come adrift from her hairpins, and her eyes wide and blue in her thin face, she looked younger than her years as she told the story by candlelight in the parsonage.

'I was twelve, I think. I might have been thirteen. I lived with my mother in Oxford and with us my stepfather and stepbrother. I had a little sister, Ann. We had piglets in the back yard that we were to fatten to sell, but my stepfather did not look after them properly and they ailed. My sister was not strong. She was small, and though she was loved by me and by my mother, my stepfather was disappointed in her. He had wanted another boy. Sons were what mattered, in his eyes. He resented the food that I ate and the food my sister ate, and we were in fear of him – my mother too – and I tried to eat less so my sister, who was so frail, could have more. But she didn't thrive. One day, when my sister was sick in bed, my mother put me in charge while she went out to buy some medicine for her. I was to get the meal prepared, and listen out in case my sister had a coughing fit. My stepfather would have been angry at her buying medicine, for it was very expensive and girls were really not worth it. I was very nervous and so was Mother. While Mother was out, my stepbrother came into the kitchen with a bundle. It was a sack, tied tight with string. One of the piglets had died, he told me. I was under orders from my stepfather to take it to the river and drop it in, to save the trouble of digging a hole and burying it. I told my brother I had to prepare the dinner and he should take the piglet to the river, but he told me my stepfather would beat the living daylights out of me if I didn't do as I was told. So I went. The bundle was heavy. When I got to the river, I put the bundle down on the bank where the drop was steep and pushed it in. Then I went home. When I came to our street, all the neighbours were out of doors and there was a great hubbub. My mother came running up to me. "Where is Ann?" she said. "Where's your sister?"

'"In our bedroom," I replied, and she cried out and wept, and asked again, "Where is Ann? Why weren't you here and where has she gone?"

'One of the neighbours had seen me go by before, with the heavy burden in my arms, and she said, "What was in that sack?"

'"A piglet that died," I said. But when they started to question me about where I had taken it and what I had done, I could not answer but was tongue-tied in confusion.

'Some of the neighbours ran down to the river then. I wanted to stay close by my mother, but she was so angry with me for not watching over my sister that she was no comfort and in the end I went to hide.

'My stepbrother was a watchful one. He knew the places I used to hide in when my stepfather was in a temper. He found me out. "You know what was in that sack, don't you?"

'"It was a piglet," I said, for I believed it was.

'And then he told me what I had really done. "It was Ann in that sack. You have drowned her."

'I ran away, and I have never told anybody the truth about my sister from that day to this.'

Later, Rita suggested and the parson agreed that Lily should stay the night in the guest room at the parsonage. Like a small child, Lily acquiesced.

When the bed was made and Lily was about to go upstairs to get into it, and Rita was making her farewells to the parson, Armstrong cleared his voice and spoke for the first time.

'I wonder – before we depart . . .'

They all looked at him.

'It has been a long night and for Mrs White a very exhausting one, but if I could ask just one question before we go?'

The parson nodded.

'Lily, how did my pig Maud come to be at Basketman's Cottage?'

Having confessed her one great crime, Lily's other secrets were no longer anchored down. 'Victor brought her.'

'Victor?'

'My stepbrother.'

'What is his surname, your stepbrother?'

'His name is Victor Nash.'

At that name, Armstrong started as though he had sliced through his own finger with his slaughtering knife.

The Other Side of the River

'HE CAN'T BE in the factory,' Vaughan said. 'I've been selling off the contents and people have been coming and going for months. If anyone was hiding out in there, he'd have been spotted. And the vitriol works have high windows – the light would be visible for miles. No, the only place big enough for a distillery and hideout that's concealed and undisturbed is the old store house.'

His forefinger jabbed at the place on the plan of Brandy Island.

'Where's the landing spot?' asked Daunt.

'Here's where he'll be expecting anyone to come in. If he keeps an eye out, this is where he'll be watching. But it's possible to land on the island from the far side. Away from the factory and the other buildings. Take him by surprise.'

'How many men will we be?' Armstrong asked.

'I can provide eight men from the household and farms. I could raise more, but we'd need more row boats and that might rouse suspicion.'

'I could take a greater number on *Collodion*, but it would be noisy and too visible. Fewer of us in row boats is the only way.'

'Eight men, plus we three . . .' They looked at each other and nodded. Eleven. It would be enough.

'When?' said Vaughan.

At dead of night, a small flotilla of row boats left the jetty at Buscot Lodge. Nobody spoke. Blades barely disturbed the ink-blank water as they dipped in and out of it. Oars creaked and water lapped against the sides of the vessels, but these sounds were lost in the low grumble of the river. Invisibly the rowers slipped from land over water to land again.

At the far side of Brandy Island, they hauled their boats out of the river and up the steep slope to conceal them under the hanging branches of the willow. They knew each other by silhouette, nods were all that were needed for communication, for every man had his instructions.

They separated into pairs and spread out along the bank, to make diverse routes through the vegetation towards the factory. Daunt and Armstrong were the only ones unfamiliar with the island. Daunt was with Vaughan, Armstrong with Newman, one of Vaughan's men. They pushed branches out of their way, stumbled over roots, moved blind in the darkness. When the vegetation thinned and gave way to paths, they knew they were nearing the factory. They skirted walls, hastened across open areas with barely a sound.

Daunt and Vaughan came to the store house. Hemmed in by the factory on one side and dense trees on the other, the glow from its windows would have been invisible from both banks. In the darkness, the two men exchanged a look. Daunt pointed to the other side. A hint of movement stirred in the trees, illuminated by the faint light from the building. Others had arrived.

Armstrong made the first move. He rushed at the door, and kicked at it with his full bodyweight. It left the door swinging, half off its hinges. Vaughan pushed it fully open, and Daunt was right behind him as they surveyed the room. Vats and bottles and barrels. Air thick with yeast and sugar. A small brazier, recently tended. A chair, empty. Daunt pressed his hand to the cushion. It was warm.

He had been there, but he was gone.

Vaughan allowed a curse to escape his lips.

A sound. Outside. From the trees.

'That way!' came a cry. Daunt, Vaughan and Armstrong joined the others. There was a great scramble through the undergrowth as men rushed to give chase, following the direction of the sound. They crashed through branches, broke twigs underfoot, exclaimed when they stumbled, until they did not know whether the sounds they were following were those of the quarry or the hunters themselves.

They regrouped. Though they were dispirited, they had not given up. They quartered the terrain, covered every yard of the island. They delved into every bush, peered up into the branches of every tree, searched every room and every corridor of every building. Two of Vaughans' men approached a tangle of thorny branches and began to beat it methodically with heavy sticks. On the far side, movement: a figure, bent low, suddenly leapt and with a splash disappeared.

'Hoy!' they shouted to alert the others. 'He's gone in!'

Before long the others had joined them.

'He's out there somewhere. We flushed him out of hiding and heard the splash.'

The hunters peered out across the dark river. The water shimmered and glinted, but there was no sign of their quarry.

When he first entered the water he thought the cold would kill him outright. But when he surfaced and found himself not dead, nowhere near, he discovered it wasn't so deadly after all. He'd emerged from his great dive in a place that had advantages. The river, it seemed, was his ally. Where a great branch bent low over the river, he could cling on, half out of the water, while he worked out what to do. Returning to the island was out of the question. He'd have to get across. Once in the central flow, the river would carry him downstream, and if he edged towards the bank all the time, he was bound to find a place to haul himself out. After that . . .

After that he'd work things out as best he could.

He unlocked his arms from the branch, let himself fully into the water and kicked away.

There came a shout from the island – he'd been spotted – and he ducked under the surface. There, he was distracted by a festival of movement and light above his head. A fleet of stars went sailing by. A thousand tiny moons shimmered past him, elongated like baby fish in a shoal. He was a giant among fairies.

It occurred to him suddenly that there was no great urgency. *I'm not even shivering*, he thought. *It's almost warm.*

His arms were heavy. He wasn't sure whether he was kicking or not.

When the cold river doesn't feel cold, that's when you know you're in trouble. He'd overheard that somewhere. When? Long ago. It troubled him and a sense of foreboding pressed down on him. In a panic he scrabbled, but his limbs would not obey him.

He had woken the river now; its current took hold of him. Water in his mouth. Moonfish in his head. Knowledge: a mistake. He groped for the surface; his hands met trailing, floating plants. He grasped to haul himself up, but his fingers closed on gravel and mud. Flailing – twisting – the surface! – gone again. He took in more water than air, and when he cried for help – though who had ever helped him, was he not the most betrayed of men? – when he cried for help, there were only the lips of the river pressed to his, and her fingers pinched his nostrils shut.

All this for ever . . .

Until, when there was no resistance left in him, he felt himself grasped, lifted up and out of the water as if he weighed no more than a willow leaf, and lain down, down to rest, in the bottom of a punt.

Quietly? He knew the stories. The ferryman who took those whose time had come to the other side, and who took those whose time had not come to safety. He'd never believed the tale, but here he was.

The tall, lean figure thrust the pole up to the heavens and let it fall through his fingers till it bit the riverbed, and then, with what grace, with what remarkable power, the punt sped through the dark water. Victor felt the drag of it as he smiled. Safety . . .

Half of the men stayed on the island, positioned at points where they would see if he tried to land. The others returned to the boats and went out on the water, searching.

'It's damn cold,' Daunt muttered.

Armstrong put a hand in the water and pulled it out quickly.

'Are we looking for a living man or a corpse?' he asked.

'He can't survive long,' Vaughan said grimly.

They rowed around the island, once, twice, three times.

'He's had it,' pronounced one of Vaughan's men.

The others nodded.

The hunt was over.

The row boats made their way back to the jetty and to Buscot Lodge.

The parson wrote to the vicar of the parish in which Lily had lived with her mother and stepfather. He received a prompt reply. One of the members of that congregation had a keen memory of the events from thirty years ago. There had been a great hue and cry when Ann was first found to be missing. A rumour started that the older girl had drowned her sister in the river out of jealousy. Neighbours had rushed to the river, but the sack had not immediately been found. While her mother joined the search party, her first-born ran away.

Some hours later, the child was found, alive and well. At some distance from the house, and further than she could have walked unaided. She had a raging fever. No medicine could save her and a few days later she died.

The sack was also found. It contained a dead piglet.

Lily was never found. Her heartbroken mother died a few years later. The stepfather was hanged for crimes unrelated to this one that finally caught up with him, and the stepbrother was a bad lot who couldn't hold down a job for long, and who had not been heard of for years.

'You are not to blame,' the parson told Lily.

Rita put an arm around the confused woman. 'Your stepbrother was the one who tricked you, out of jealousy and because he has a destructive soul. He knew you were innocent, but has encouraged you to believe you are guilty ever since. You did not drown your sister.'

'So when Ann came out of the river to the Swan, what did she want?'

'It wasn't Ann. Ann is dead. She is not angry with you and she is at peace.'

Rita told her, 'What you saw at Basketman's Cottage were nightmares, and then, in the Swan, an illusion. Smoke and mirrors.'

'And now that your stepbrother is drowned,' the parson told Lily, 'he can't frighten you any more. You can keep your own money, and give up Basketman's Cottage and come and live in the warmth here, at the parsonage.'

But Lily knew more about rivers than anyone, knew that drowning was a more complicated thing than other people suspected. Victor drowned was no less terrible to her mind than Victor alive – in fact, it was more terrible. He would be angry at her for having given him away; she dare not make him angrier by leaving the place where he knew he could find her. She had only to remember what had happened when she'd run away with Mr White. He had been found dead, and the beating she'd got from Victor – she was surprised she hadn't been found dead too. No, she didn't dare anger him.

'I think I will carry on at Basketman's Cottage,' she said. The parson tried to persuade her, and Rita tried to persuade her, but with the insistence of the meek she got her way.

When Armstrong went to collect Maud from Basketman's Cottage, he found that she was in pig.

He did not like to move her in her delicate state. She was being well looked after, he could see that.

'Would you take care of her, Mrs White, till her litter arrives?'

'I don't mind. What about Maud? Does she mind staying?'

Maud did not mind, and so it was agreed.

'And when I take her home with me, I will give you a piglet in exchange.'

Part 5

The Knife

THE CHICKENS WERE flustered, the cat evaded his stroking hand to slink away unhappily along the wall, and the pigs stared with a gaze that told of something ominous. Armstrong frowned. What was it? He had only been away two hours, seeing some cows for sale.

His middle daughter came flying from the house and as she flung her arms around him he could be in no doubt that something bad had happened. She was too breathless to speak.

'Robin?' he asked.

She nodded.

'Where's your mother?'

She pointed towards the kitchen door.

All was in upheaval. Soup bubbled unwatched on the stove; pastry was abandoned on the marble. Bess stood behind the rocking chair, gripping its rail, a fierce, protective air about her. In the rocking chair sat his eldest daughter, Susan, hunched and pale-faced. Her arms were crossed oddly over her chest, her hands up by her neck. Around her were clustered the three littlest ones, who plucked at her skirt in concern.

Bess's fingers released their grip on the chair with relief as he came in, and she turned a troubled eye upon him. With a gesture she warned him not to say anything.

'Here,' she said to the little ones who were clinging to their sister, 'take this to the pigs.' She swept the peelings into a bowl and handed them to the biggest child; after a final consoling pat on their sister's knee, they did as they were told.

'What did he want?' he asked, as soon as the door had closed.

'The usual.'

'How much this time?'

She told him the sum and Robert stiffened. It went far beyond the amounts Robin had had from them before.

'What sort of trouble is he in to want that kind of money?'

She made a dismissive gesture. 'You know what he is. One lie after another. A good investment, a once-in-a-lifetime opportunity, a loan till next week . . . I'm not beguiled, he knows that. His smooth ways haven't worked on me for a long, long while.' She frowned. 'But nobody would have been taken in, not today. He was out of breath. Couldn't keep still; desperate for money and to get away again. He kept going to the window, all on edge. Wanted to send his brother to the gate to keep a lookout, but I wouldn't let him go. Before long he gave up lying and started shouting, "Just give me the money, I'm telling you! Or it'll be the death of me!" He was banging his fists on the table, saying it's all our fault and if we hadn't given the girl back to the Vaughans he wouldn't be in such a corner. There was a quiver in his voice. Something's frightened him.

' "What on earth is it has put you in this state?" I asked him and he said somebody was after him. Somebody who would stop at nothing to get what he wanted.'

'His life was in danger, he said,' added Susan from the rocking chair. ' "If you don't give me the money, I'm a dead man." '

Armstrong rubbed his forehead. 'Susan, this isn't a conversation for you. Go and sit in the drawing room while I talk about this with your mother.'

His daughter turned her eyes to her mother. 'Tell him, Mother,' she said.

'I refused him the money. He spoke angrily to me.'

'He said she had always been against him. He called her unnatural. He said things about her from before she married you—'

'Susan overheard it all. She came in.'

'I was going to tell him not to be so angry with Mother. I was going to—'

His daughter's eyes filled with tears.

Bess put her hand on her daughter's shoulder.

'He turned so quickly. In a flash he had your knife from its sheath on the back of the door. He took hold of Susan . . .'

Armstrong stiffened. The knife on the back of the door was his slaughtering knife that he never put away in its sheath without having honed it to a lethal sharpness. With fresh understanding he took in his daughter's hunched position, her stricken face.

'I would have got away from him,' Susan said. 'I could have, except . . .'

Robert crossed the floor, took his daughter's hand and removed it from her neck. She was clutching a bloodstained cloth. In a curve across the tender skin was a vivid line of red. It went deep enough to break the skin, was a fraction of an inch away from severing the main vessels of life. All the breath in his body left him.

'Mother cried out and the boys came in. Robin hesitated when he saw them – they are almost as big as he is now, and strong, and there were two of them. His grip wavered and I twisted away . . .'

'Where is he now?'

'He has gone to the old oak, downstream, near Brandy Island. He said to tell you to find him there. You are to take the money or his life is over. That was the message.'

Armstrong left the kitchen and went further into the house. They heard the door to his study open and close. He was in there for mere moments and when he returned he was buttoning his coat.

'Please don't go, Father!'

He placed a hand on his daughter's head, kissed his wife's temple and then, without a word, he left. Scarcely had the door shut on him than it opened again. He felt for his knife behind the door. The sheath was there, but it was empty.

'He has it still,' said Bess.

Her words met the closing door.

The torrential downpours of the day had given way now to even, persistent rainfall. Each drop of water, whether it landed on river, field or rooftop, on leaf or man, made its sound, and each sound was indistinguishable from the rest; together they made a blanket of wet noise that wrapped around Armstrong and Fleet and isolated them.

'I know,' the rider told his mount with a pat. 'I'd sooner be indoors myself. But needs must.'

The path was pitted and stony and Fleet walked along attentively, picking her way between the holes and avoiding the obstacles. From time to time she raised her head to sniff the air, and her ears were alert.

Armstrong was deep in thought.

'What can he want with so much money?' he wondered aloud. 'And why now?'

Where the path dipped, they splashed through sitting water.

'His sister! His own sister!' Armstrong exclaimed, shaking his head, and Fleet whinnied in sympathy. 'Sometimes I think there is nothing more a man could do. A child is not an empty vessel, Fleet, to be formed in whatever way the parent thinks fit. They are born with their own hearts and they cannot be made otherwise, no matter what love a man lavishes on them.'

On they went.

'What more could I have done? What did I miss? Eh?'

Fleet shook her head and sent drops of water flying from the reins.

'We loved him. We did, didn't we? I took him about with me and showed him the world. I taught him what I knew . . . He knew wrong from right. He had that from me, Fleet. He cannot say he did not know.'

Fleet moved forward in the dark, and Armstrong sighed.

'You never took to him, did you? I tried not to see it. The way you put your ears back and shied when he came close. What had he done to you? I didn't want to think ill of him, and I don't want to now, but even a father cannot turn a blind eye for ever.'

Armstrong raised a hand and rubbed away the wetness from his eye.

'Nothing but a bit of rain,' he told himself, though the ache in his throat told him otherwise. 'And then there is the girl. I should like to know what to make of that, Fleet. What has he got himself mixed up in there? No father would dally the way he did. What kind of father is it that does not recognize his own child? She was not his child, and he knew it from the start. So what was that all about? Will he tell me what the trouble is, do you think? How can I make things right if I do not know what they are? He ties my hands behind my back and then complains that I do not help him enough.'

He felt the weight in his pocket. He had filled a purse with money from the safe and it was heavy.

Fleet stopped. She trotted nervously on the spot, twitching and fretting in the harness.

Armstrong lifted his head and sought an explanation. His eyes found only darkness. The rain had washed all scent from the air, and muffled sound. His human senses told him nothing.

He leant forward in the saddle. 'What is it, Fleet?'

She skittered again, and this time he caught the splash of water at her feet. He dismounted and the water came over the top of his boots.

'The flood. It has come.'

It Begins and Ends at the Swan

IT HAD BEEN raining for weeks. There was enough to do securing against the flood, without reminders that they must make ready too for the river gypsies. For it was their time to come up the river and a bit of flood water wouldn't stop them. In fact, it would only help them come closer to the properties: the houses and cottages, the outbuildings and barns and stables. Every bit of equipment and machinery must be put indoors, every door must be locked. The river gypsies would help themselves to anything that was unsecured, no matter how unlikely. A flower pot on a windowsill was not safe and woe betide the gardener who left a hoe or a rake leaning by the back door. Moreover it was the night of the winter solstice, a year to the day since the child had come. Most importantly of all, there was Helena, whose lively quickness had almost deserted her in these last days of waiting for the birth of their child. But Vaughan's men had now done everything that was possible. He thanked them and went to find his wife.

'I'm so tired,' she said, 'but come down the garden with us before you take your coat off. We want to see the river.'

'The water is already twenty yards up the garden. It's hardly safe for a child, in the dark.'

'I've told her the river might come into the garden and she is so excited. She's longing to see it.'

'All right. Where is she?'

'I fell asleep on the sofa – she's probably wandered down to the kitchen to see Cook.'

They went to the kitchen, but she wasn't there.

'I thought she was with you,' Cook said.

Vaughan's eyes met Helena's in sudden alarm.

'She will have gone to look at the river – we'll find her there, ahead of us.' Although the words she spoke were certain, there was a quiver in Helena's voice that revealed her doubt.

'You stay here – I'll be quicker alone,' her husband said, and went running out of the room, but Helena followed.

She made slow going. The lawns were mud, the gravel paths washed away by the torrential rain of the last weeks. Her mackintosh did not fasten over her belly now, and as the cold rain soaked her dress she wondered whether she had overestimated her strength. After a pause to rest she went on again. She pictured what she was going to see: the child, standing spellbound at the water's edge, fascinated by the rising river.

Coming to the gap in the hedge where the river was visible, she stopped. There was her husband, shaking his head, speaking urgently and gesticulating with the gardener and two of the other men, who nodded, serious-faced, and ran hastily away to do his bidding.

Heat broke out all over her body and her heart pounded. She broke into an ungainly run, calling Vaughan's name as she went. He turned to see her eyes widen as she lost her footing in the mud, and though he got there in time to break her fall, she gave a great cry of pain.

'It's all right, I've put word out – they are looking for her. We'll find her.'

Breathless, she nodded. Her face was white.

'What is it? Your ankle?'

She shook her head. 'It's the baby.'

Anthony cast his eye up the garden, cursing himself for having sent all the men out to search for the child. He calculated the distance to the house, the slippery paths, the darkness, and set all that against the dark pain in his wife's eyes. Could he do it? There was no other way. He felt her full weight in his arms and readied himself to start.

'Hoy!' he heard. And again, louder: 'Hoy there!'

Collodion came floating tranquilly over the vast water.

When they had got Helena on board and were moving again, Daunt told him, 'Rita is at the Swan. I'll take Helena there, then we can go back out in *Collodion* and look for the girl.'

'Is Rita's cottage flooded?'

'Yes, but it's more than that . . . It's Joe.'

There were few drinkers in the Swan. Winter solstice it might be, but a flood was a flood and all the young men were needed elsewhere, boarding up doors, moving furniture upstairs, herding cattle to higher ground . . . The only men in the inn were those unfit to limit the river's damage: the old and the infirm, and the ones already drunk when the flood came. They did not tell stories. Joe the storyteller was dying.

In his bed, in the little room that was as far from the river as it was possible to get and still be in the Swan, Joe was drowning. Between spells of gasping for breath, he muttered sounds. His lips moved ceaselessly, but the underwater noises did not resolve themselves into words anyone could understand. His face grimaced and his eyebrows twitched expressively. It was a gripping story, but one that no one but he could hear.

Joe's daughters came and went between the sickbed and the winter room. The Little Margots had today put aside their blithe smiles and wore the same grave sorrow as their mother, who sat beside the bed, Joe's hand in hers.

There was a moment when Joe seemed to surface momentarily. He half opened his eyes and delivered a few syllables before sinking again.

'What did he say?' Jonathan asked, bewildered.

'He called for Quietly,' his mother replied calmly, and her daughters nodded. They had heard it too.

'Shall I go and fetch him?'

'No, Jonathan, it's not necessary,' Margot said. 'He's on his way.'

All this was heard by Rita as she stood by the window, looking out at the great lake that lay all around the Swan like a blank page, that came within a few feet of its walls, isolating the inn and making an island of it.

She saw *Collodion* come into view. In deep water she saw Daunt launch the row boat. He helped Helena into it – she was a dark silhouette – and rowed towards the entrance of the Swan. By his solicitude, Rita understood the significance of Helena's sudden arrival.

'Margot – Mrs Vaughan is here. It looks as if it is her time.'

'It's a good thing there are plenty of us here, then. My girls will be able to help.'

In the busyness of Helena's arrival, Daunt drew Rita aside for a moment.

'The girl is missing.'

'No!' She clutched her belly, felt a shrinking there.

'Rita – are you all right?'

She made an effort, gathered herself. A man was dying. A baby was about to be born.

'How long? Where was she last seen?'

Daunt told her what little he knew.

One of the Little Margots called to Rita, wanting instructions.

Rita's face was white. It held a look so full of dread that for once Daunt had no desire to photograph it.

'I have to go. Joe and Helena need me. But Daunt—' He turned back into the room to catch her last, ferocious words: *'Find her!'*

Thereafter the hours were very long, and very short. While the water lay unperturbed and indifferent all around, the women at the Swan were engaged with the human pursuits of dying and being born. On one side of the wall, Helena struggled to deliver her baby into this world. On the other side, Joe struggled to depart it. The Little Margots got on with everything that needed to be done so that life could begin and end. They carried water and clean cloths, filled log baskets and stoked fires, lit candles, made plates of food that nobody had an appetite for but ate anyway out of good sense, and all the while they also wept and soothed and calmed and comforted.

Rita went to and fro between the two rooms, doing whatever was needed. Between the two rooms, in the corridor, was Jonathan, unsettled and fretful.

'Have they found her, Rita? Where is she?' he wanted to know every time she left Helena.

'We won't know anything till they come back and tell us,' she told him, letting herself back into Joe's room.

They gave themselves over to time. There were hours that might have been minutes, and then Rita heard Margot say, 'Quietly is coming, Joe. Goodbye, my love.'

Rita remembered what she had heard in the Swan a year ago: *You have only to look in a man's eyes to tell if he is dead or not. It's the seeing that goes out of them.* She saw the seeing go out of Joe.

'Pray for us, Rita, would you?' Margot asked.

Rita prayed, and when she had finished, Margot loosened her hand from Joe's. She joined his hands together, then placed her own hands in her lap. She allowed two tears to escape, one from each eye.

'Never mind me,' she said to Rita. 'You get on.'

On the other side of the wall, there were minutes that might have been hours, then a contraction at last delivered a baby. In a slick rush it dropped into Rita's hands.

'Ah!' whispered the Little Margots in shocked delight. 'What *is* it?'

Rita blinked in surprise.

'I've heard of this. I've never seen it. The sac usually bursts before the baby emerges. That's the water breaking. This one didn't break.'

The perfect infant was in an underwater world. Eyes fast shut, with liquid movements, little fists dreamily opening and closing, it was sleep-swimming inside a transparent, water-filled membrane.

Rita touched the pearly sac with the tip of a knife, and a great split ran around it.

Water splashed.

The baby boy, opening his eyes and mouth at the same time, discovered to his great astonishment air and the world.

Fathers and Sons

FLEET'S HOOVES SPLASHED through the water. In the dimness of the night, there was a flat sheen like pewter all around, disturbed only by their own movements. Armstrong thought of all the small land creatures, mice and voles and weasels, and hoped that they had found safety. He thought of the birds, the night hunters, thrown from their normal feeding ground. He thought of the fish that strayed without knowing it from the main current and now found themselves swimming through grass a few inches above the ground, sharing territory with him and with his horse. He hoped Fleet would not tread on any creature lost in this landscape that no longer belonged clearly to earth or water. He hoped they would all be well.

They came to the oak, near Brandy Island.

He heard a sound. As he turned, a silhouette separated itself from the darkness of the tree trunk.

'Robin!'

'You took your time!'

Armstrong dismounted. In the semi-darkness his son hunched against the cold and shivered in his thin jacket. His words had been spoken abruptly with a man's swagger, but a quiver cut into his voice and left the boldness in tatters.

Compassion flared instinctively in Armstrong, but he remembered the curved line of red on his daughter's neck. 'Your own sister,' he said in a dark voice, and shook his head. 'It is beyond belief . . .'

'It's Mother's fault,' Robin said. 'If she'd only done what I said, it need never have happened.'

'You blame your mother?'

'I blame her for many things, and yes, that is one.'

'How can you try to make this her fault? Your mother is the best woman in the world. Whose hand held the knife to Susan's throat? Whose hand has the knife still?'

There was silence. Then:

'Have you brought the money?'

'There will be time to talk of money later. There are other things we must speak of first.'

'There is no time. Give me the money now and let me go. There is not a minute to lose.'

'Why the rush, Robin? Who is after you? What have you done?'

'Debts.'

'Work your way out of debt. Come home to the farm and work like your brothers.'

'The farm? It's one thing for *you* to get up at five every morning to feed the pigs in the cold and the dark. *I* am made for a better life.'

'You'll have to come to some arrangement with whoever made you the loan. I can't pay it all. It's too much.'

'This isn't some gentlemanly loan I'm talking about. This is not a banker, ready to renegotiate terms.' There came a sound that was a sob or a laugh. 'Give me the money – or you send me to the gallows. *Hush!*'

Their ears strained in the darkness. Nothing.

'The money! If I do not get away tonight—'

'To go where?'

'Away. Anywhere. Where nobody knows me.'

'And leave so many questions behind you?'

'There's no time!'

'Tell me the truth about your wife, Robin. Tell me the truth about Alice.'

'What does it matter? They're dead! Finished. Gone.'

'Not one word of sorrow? Remorse?'

'I thought she was bringing money with her! She said her parents would come round. Set us up in life. Instead she was a millstone round my neck. She's dead, and she drowned the child, and good riddance to the pair of them.'

'How can you speak so?'

The slim, shaking silhouette stiffened suddenly.

'Did you hear something?' Robin asked in a low murmur.

'Nothing.'

His son listened intently for a few moments, then returned his attention to Armstrong. 'If he's not here yet, he soon will be. Give me the money and let me go.'

'What about the child from the Swan? The one you neither claimed nor relinquished. That charade at the summer fair. Tell me about that.'

'The same thing as always! Don't you know me by now? The same thing that is hanging from your belt in the leather pouch.'

'You expected to make money out of her?'

'From the Vaughans. It was plain from the minute I walked into the Swan that night that Vaughan knew the girl wasn't his. She couldn't have been. I knew it, and he knew it. I knew there was money to be made if I only had the time to think it through – I fainted, or they thought I did, and worked it all out there and then, flat out on the floorboards. They wanted the girl and had money. I wanted money and could claim the girl.'

'You meant to *pretend* a claim and then *sell* it?'

'Vaughan was on the brink of paying up, but once Mother had sent the girl back, he had no need. I was in debt, thanks to her.'

'Do not speak ill of your mother. She taught you right from wrong. If you had listened better to her you might be a better man today.'

'But she did not do right, did she? She only talked of doing so! I'd have been a better man if she'd been a better woman. I place the responsibility at her door.'

'Watch what you say, Robin.'

'Look at the three of us! She so white and you so black! And look at me! I know you are not my father. I have known from a child that I was not your son.'

Armstrong took a moment to find his words.

'I have loved you as a father loves his child.'

'She tricked you, didn't she? She was with child by another man and desperate for someone to marry her, but who'd want a lame and boss-eyed woman for a wife? Not the baby's father, that's for sure. But then you came along. The black farmer. And she set her cap at you, didn't she? What a trade that was. A white bride for a black farmer – and me, eight months later.'

'You are wrong.'

'You are not my father! I have always known it. And I know who my true father is.'

Armstrong flinched. 'You know?'

'You remember when I forced the bureau drawer and stole that money?'

'I would prefer to forget it.'

'That is when I saw the letter.'

Armstrong was puzzled, and then his confusion cleared. 'The letter from Lord Embury?'

'The letter from my father. That says what is to come to his natural son. Money that you and my mother have kept from me and that I have taken from you by stealth.'

'*Your* father . . . ?'

'That's right. I know Lord Embury is my father. I have known it since I was eight.'

Armstrong shook his head. 'He is not your father.'

'I have read the letter.'

Armstrong shook his head again. 'He is not your father.'

'I have *got* the letter!'

Armstrong shook his head a third time and opened his mouth to repeat himself again. The words sounded in the wet air – '*He is not your father!*' – but it was not his own voice that spoke them.

The voice struck Robert Armstrong as being distantly familiar.

Robin's face twisted in despair.

'He's here!' he moaned under his breath.

Armstrong turned and looked all around, but his eyes could not penetrate the darkness. Every tree trunk and every shrub might conceal a figure, and a throng of phantoms hovered mistily in the black dampness. At last, by dint of staring, his eyes made out a shape. Half-water, half-night, it waded towards them, a stunted form whose wide garment trailed in the water and whose hat sat low and concealed its features.

Splash by splash it came closer to Robin.

The young man took a step back. He could not draw his fearful eyes from the approaching figure, but at the same time he shrank from it.

When the man – for man it was – came to a spot five feet from Robin, he stopped and the moonlight suddenly illuminated his face.

'*I* am your father.'

Robin shook his head.

'Do you not know me, son?'

'I know you.' Robin's voice shook. 'I know you are a low-born villain, a base man who lives by the knife and by crime. I know you are a charlatan and a thief and a liar, and worse besides.'

The man's face creased into a proud smile.

'He knows me!' he said to Armstrong. 'And I see you know me too.'

'Victor Nash,' said Armstrong heavily. 'I had hoped never to see you again after I threw you off my farm so long ago. Like the bad penny you are, you came back, and I wasn't sorry to think you'd drowned off Brandy Island.'

Victor bowed. 'Drowned? It was not my time. I live to claim what's mine. I owe you thanks, Armstrong, for raising my son and educating him. Don't he speak fine, after all his teaching? Listen to what comes out of his mouth – why sometimes I can hardly understand him, when he gets going with his Latin and his Greek and his long words nobody knows. And he can write so nice. See him with a pen and watch how quick he takes the notions from your tongue and sets them down in ink, and never a blot! All curls and twiddles and it looks a picture, it does. And his manners! Nobody can say a word against his manners – he is like the finest lord of the land. I am proud of my son, truly I am. For in him the best of me – all my cunning and all my guile – is mixed with the best of your missus – ain't he fair, with his soft hair and his white skin? And you have played your part, Armstrong. You have polished him over with the best of you too.'

Robin shuddered.

'It's not true!' he told Victor and, turning to Armstrong, 'It's not true, is it? Tell him! Tell him who my father is!'

Victor sniggered.

'It is true,' Armstrong told Robin. 'This man is your father.'

Robin stared. 'But Lord Embury!'

'Lord Embury!' echoed the man, with a snigger. 'Lord Embury! He be somebody's father all right, eh, Armstrong? Why don't you tell him?'

'Lord Embury is *my* father, Robin. He fell in love with my mother when he was a very young man and she a servant girl. That is what the letter in the bureau referred to. It is the agreement he made to assure my financial future before he died. *I* am the Robert Armstrong mentioned in the letter.'

Robin looked, stricken, into Armstrong's face.

'Then my mother . . .'

'Her innocence was taken advantage of in the vilest manner by this scoundrel, and I did my utmost to make things right for her. And to make things right for you.'

'Yes, well, enough of that. I have come to claim him. It is time to give him up to me. You have had him for twenty-three years and now he must come to his true father. Mustn't you, Rob?'

'Come to you? You think I will come to you?' Robin laughed. 'You're mad.'

'Ah, but you must, boy. Family is family. We are kin, you and me. With my base plotting and your fine looks, with my low knowledge and your high manners, think what we can do! We have only just begun! We must continue what we have started! Together, my boy, we can work wonders! After all the waiting, our time has come!'

'I'll have nothing to do with you!' Robin snarled. 'I tell you now, leave me alone! I'll not have it said that I'm your son. If you tell a soul of this, I'll . . . I'll . . .'

'What will you, Robin, my boy? What, eh?'

Robin panted.

'What is it I know, Robin? Tell me that. What is it I know about you that nobody else knows?'

Robin froze. 'Whatever you say brings you down with me!'

Victor nodded slowly. 'So be it.'

'You would not incriminate yourself.'

Victor looked at the water. 'Who's to say what a man would or wouldn't do when his own son denies him? It's about family, my boy. I lost my mother in the days before I can remember. My father taught me everything I know, but he was hanged before I was grown to manhood. I had a sister once – at least, I called her sister – but even she betrayed me. You are all I have, my Robin with the soft hair and the silky words and the lordly ways . . . You are all the world to me, and if I cannot have you, then what is the purpose of my life? No, our future is one, Robin, and it is up to you which way you will have it. We can go into business together, as we have before, or you can deny me and I'll denounce you, and we will be chained together in the cells and will go to the gallows, father and son together, as is the natural way of things.'

Robin wept.

'What is the hold this man has over you?' Armstrong asked. 'What conspiracy is it that binds you to him?'

'Shall I tell him?' Victor asked.

'No!'

'I think I will. This is one refuge I will close and when it is gone the only succour left will be at my side.' He turned to Armstrong. 'I knew this fine young man liked to drink in a place on the edge of Oxford and I got to know him there, slow and gradual. I sowed a plot in his mind and let him think it was his own invention. He thought I was following behind his every step, when in fact the route was all mine. We stole your pig together, Armstrong – that was the first thing! How I laughed in my sleeve that night, thinking that you had told me twenty-three years before to stay away and not come within twelve miles of you and your Bess, and there I was, being let into your yard to steal your favourite pig, and it was my own son unlatching the gate and tempting her with raspberries to help me do it! He ran off with me and we had a good little business for a while. I knew how to set it up, the trickery of a fortune-telling pig. The fairs brought us in some good money – we was well off, for low-down types, only your son wasn't satisfied. He wanted more. So we used what we had – the pig and the fair – and we leapt to greater things. Didn't we, Rob, my son?'

Robin shuddered.

'The Vaughan child . . .' Armstrong murmured, aghast. 'The kidnap . . .'

'Well done! Rob used all his inveigling words to draw that foolish girl Ruby into parting with a shilling. Your ginger pig looked with soft eyes into that girl's silly round ones, and from behind a curtain Robin here in his sweetest piggy voice told her where to go to see the face of her one true love in the night river. Didn't you, my son?'

Robin put his face in his hands and turned to Armstrong, but Armstrong took him by the wrists and forced him to look him in the eye.

'Is this true?'

Robin cringed and his face crumpled.

'And there is more, isn't there, Rob, my lad?'

'Don't listen to him!' Robin wailed.

'Yes, for that was only the beginning. Whose idea was it, Rob, at the start? Whose idea to take the little girl from the Vaughans, and how to do it?'

'That was your idea!'

'Aye, it was too, but whose idea did you think it was, at the outset?'

Robin turned his face away.

'Who was it who crowed at his own cleverness? Who was it who gave orders to the men in the boat, who wrote out the ransom note, who set each man his hiding place? Who was it who strutted about on the night itself, checking each man had his instructions clear? I was proud of you then! When I saw you, only a stripling, yet sure of yourself and your villainy. *He's my boy*, I thought. *He's got my blood in his veins and my wickedness in his heart, and there's nothing Armstrong can do to clean it out. He's mine, body and soul.*'

'Give him the money,' Robin whispered into Armstrong's ear, but not quietly enough, for the words carried over the rising water and the man laughed. 'The money? Yes, we'll take the money all right, won't we, son? Share and share alike. I'll share it with you, Rob, my boy, fifty–fifty!'

The water had risen to reach the knees of the three, and the rain soaked into their hats and ran down their necks and into their shirts, and before long their top halves were as wet as their bottom halves and it made no difference whether they were in or out of the water.

'And the rest, Rob,' Victor went on. 'The rest!'

'Don't . . .' Robin moaned, but his voice scarcely sounded above the rain that fell torrentially on the water.

'Yes, the rest . . . We had the little lass, didn't we, Rob? We had her in our grip. Out the window and down the ladder and sprinting down the garden to the river, where our boat was waiting.'

He turned to Armstrong. 'Canny he was! Did he trespass in the garden? Did he climb the ladder? Did he break an entry? Not he! Others did all that dangerous work. He waited in the boat. Too great an organizational mind to be risked in action, you see. Got a head on his shoulders, eh?' He turned back to Robin. 'So down the garden we came and the child with us, chloroformed, in a sack. I had her, for though I am slight my strength is formidable, and I tossed her like a bag of cress into the arms of Rob here.'

Robin sobbed.

'I chucked her over the water to my son, waiting in the boat. And what happened, Rob?'

Robin shook his head while his shoulders shook.

'No!' exclaimed Armstrong.

'Yes!' said Victor. 'Yes! The boat tilted and he half dropped her. There was a crack against the side of the boat and in his grasping to clutch her back again he lost his grip again, and in she went. Down like a sack of stones she sunk. He set the men to prodding with their oars, and how we did it I don't know, but we found her at last. How long was it, Robin? Five minutes? Ten?'

Robin, a white face in the dark, did not answer.

'We found her, anyway. And off we went. Back to Brandy Island. There we set her down and opened up the sack, didn't we, Rob, son?

All might have been lost,' he said with gravity and a sombre shaking of the head. 'It could have been the end of everything. But Rob here, with his clear head, saved the day. "It matters not whether she be alive or dead," said he, "for the Vaughans won't know it till the money is passed over!" And he wrote out the note – a prettier note I never did see – and it was sent, and though we had not the goods, not in a fit state anyhow, we sent the invoice all the same. And why not, he said, for we had had the labour and the risk of it, eh Rob? I knew he was my son then too.'

Armstrong all the while had edged up the slope and away from the swirling water, but Robin stood still. The water eddied around him, and he seemed not to feel it.

'So we had the ransom from Vaughan. We had it, and we gave him back his girl too, didn't we, though he made out we hadn't. Lasted a good long while, that money. Lovely house, Rob got. I've seen it. Didn't my heart swell with pride, a son of mine in a fine white house in the city of Oxford. Mind you, he has never invited me there. Not once. After everything we had gone through together. Pig rustling and fairground trickery and kidnap and murder – you might think as they was pastimes would bind one man to another in comradeship, mightn't you? That pained me, that did, Rob. And when the money ran out – he is a gambler, Armstrong, this child of ours, did you know that? I've warned him, but he won't listen – yes, after that money ran out, I've been the one to keep him afloat. Every penny I've got has gone into his pocket. I've worked myself to the bone to keep him in his finery, my boy, so that now, you might say as he belongs to me.

'Now that you know I'm your father, you wouldn't be so unkind again, would you? With all those IOUs, that fine white house is my house now, but there is nothing of mine I will not share with you, my son.'

Rob looked at the man. His eyes were dark and quiet and his shivering had ceased.

'Look at him,' Victor sighed. 'See how fine a figure he cuts, that's my lad. Come, we'll take the money, Armstrong, and be on our way. Are you ready to go, Rob?'

He stepped towards Robin, hand outstretched. Robin sliced the air with his hand, and Victor took an awkward step back, stumbling. He held his hand up to stare at it in surprise and saw that it was running with dark liquid.

'Son?' he said uncertainly.

Robin took a step towards him. He raised his hand again and this time the light caught the blade of Armstrong's slaughter knife.

'No!' came Armstrong's roar, but again Robin's hand came down, a swift line in the air, and Victor stepped back again. This time the ground was not where he expected it to be. He teetered on the brink, clasped the coat of his son, who slashed at him – one, two, three – with the knife. They were on the very edge of the riverbank and it was into the running river that they fell – together.

'*Father!*' Robin cried as he fell, and in the moment before the river swept him away, he reached a desperate arm towards Armstrong, and cried out once again: '*Save me, Father!*'

'*Robin!*' Armstrong waded to the point where he had seen his son enter the water. He felt the current tug at his legs. He saw Robin go under, scanned the water frantically to see him re-emerge, and when he saw the flailing limbs was shocked at how far the current had already carried his boy downstream. He had been readying himself to launch into the wild stream but, recognizing his own powerlessness, refrained.

A punt appeared from out of the rain. A tall figure raised a pole towards the sky, and when it descended and found the riverbed, the long narrow vessel moved with remarkable force through the water, slicing through it with effortless grace. The ferryman reached into the water and with thin, bare arms and easy strength drew out the body of a man in a long sodden coat. He laid the body in the bottom of the punt.

'My son!' cried Armstrong. 'For God's sake, where is my son?'

The ferryman reached in again, and with the same ease he pulled a second body from the water. As he hauled it in, Armstrong caught a glimpse of Robin's face, still and lifeless and like – so very like – the other man's.

He cried out, a painful cry, and knew what it was to feel your heart break.

The ferryman launched his pole into the air and let it fall through his fingers.

'Quietly!' called Armstrong, after him. 'Give him back to me! Please!'

The ferryman did not appear to hear him. The punt disappeared swiftly into the rain.

Armstrong did not mount Fleet but they walked, man and beast, out of the water through the torrential rain towards the shelter of the Swan. They went their way in silence for the most part, Armstrong weighed down by the intolerable weight of his grief. But from time to time, he spoke a few words to Fleet, and Fleet softly whinnied a reply.

'Who would have thought it?' he murmured. 'I know the stories about Quietly, but I have never believed them. To think the human mind is capable of producing visions like that. It seemed real at the time. Didn't you think so?'

And later: 'There must be more to stories than you think.'

And much later, when they were nearly there: 'I could swear I also saw . . . In the punt – behind the ferryman . . . Am I mad? What did you see, Fleet?'

Fleet whinnied, an unsettled and nervous sound.

'Impossible!' Armstrong shook his head to dispel the image. 'My mind is playing tricks on me. These visions must be the ravings of despair.'

Lily and the River

COLD. IT WAS cold. And if Lily knew she was cold then she was awake. Darkness was ebbing from the room, dawn was coming and – surely – something else too. She opened her eyes to the sting of cold on her eyeballs. What wasn't right?

Was it him? Returned from the river?

'Victor?'

No reply.

That left one thing. Her throat tightened.

This afternoon she had noticed that one of the floor tiles in the kitchen was sticking up. Tile edges had always protruded here and there. She was used to them shifting a little when she walked about. But this tile had seemed *more* uneven than before. She had nudged the high edge with her toe to straighten it; as it sank, a silvery line of water appeared round its edges. Prising up the tile, Lily had seen water underneath. She had hurried to forget it. Now she remembered.

Lily raised herself on one elbow and peered down to the kitchen.

In the weak light, her first impression was that everything had shrunk. The table was shorter than it ought to be and the sink was nearer the floor. The chair was stunted. Then she caught a movement: the tin bath rocked gently, like a cradle. The dull terracotta floor tiles had disappeared and over them lay a broad flatness that shifted and shimmered like a thing making up its mind.

Though she could not see it grow, it *was* growing: at first it was inches from the bottom rung of the ladder, then it reached it, and then it swallowed it altogether. It crept slowly but persistently up the walls and pressed against the door.

It occurred to Lily that the thing was perhaps not looking for her, after all. 'It wants the way out,' she thought. When it was nearing the second rung, her fear of action was overtaken by her fear of inaction.

'It'll be no different from standing in a bath tub,' she told herself as she descended the ladder, 'only colder, that's all.'

Three-quarters of the way down, she gathered up her chemise into a bundle and tucked it in her armpit. Another step and then, with the next one – *in*!

It came above her knees and, as she waded, resisted her. She pressed on, and her movement roused it into swirls and eddies around her body.

The door was reluctant to open. The wood swelled in the wet, it warped the door and made it stick in the jamb. She put all her weight on it, but nothing happened. In a panic she rammed it with her shoulder; it loosened from the frame to stand ajar, but still was stiff. Lily let go of her chemise, which trailed in the water, and gave the door a great double-handed shove. Against resistance she pushed it wide open – on to a new world.

The sky had fallen into Lily's yard. Its dawn-grey had come to earth and lain itself over grass, rocks, paths and weeds. Clouds floated at knee height. Lily stared in bewilderment. Where was the basketman's flood post? Where was the new flood post? She lifted her gaze automatically to the river, but it was gone. A flat silver stillness lay over everything. Here and there a tree emerged out of it and was reflected in its polished finish along with the sky. Every dip and crevice in the landscape was flattened out, every detail concealed, every incline erased. All was simple and bare and flat, and the air was luminous.

Lily swallowed. Tears welled in her. She hadn't thought it would be like this. She had expected heaving masses of water, violent currents and murderous waves, not this serenity without end. Motionless, she stood in her doorway, staring at the fearful loveliness. It barely moved, just shimmered at times, peacefully alive. A swan came gliding across the water; the trail it left in the clouds settled into flatness.

Were there fish? she wondered.

She stepped carefully out from her cottage, trying to disturb the water as little as possible. Her nightdress hem was already sodden; now the water crept up, plastering it to her legs.

She took two more steps down the slope and the water rose to her thighs.

Onwards. The water came to her waist.

You could see shapes down there, flickering movements of things alive under the surface. Once your eye had worked out what to look for, you saw the slivers of motion everywhere, and with a thrill Lily felt it too in her own veins. Another step. Another. She came to a place and thought, *This is where the old post is.* You could just see it, under the water. How strangely marvellous to be here on the bank, with the water higher than it had ever been in the entire lifetime of the old post. Was this fear? She was in the grip of a great feeling, something many times vaster than fear – but she was not afraid.

How odd I must look, she thought. *A chest and a head above water, reflected upside down beneath my own chin.*

Grass and plants waved dreamily in their new world beneath the surface. Ahead of her the silver gave way to a darker, shadowy place. This was where the bank fell away more steeply. This was where the current would be, still there, under the surface. *I won't go any further*, she thought. *I'll stop here.*

There were lots more fish here, and also – *Oh!* – something larger, pinkly fleshy. It floated slowly and heavily in the water, was coming her way, but just out of reach.

Lily stretched out an arm for the body. If she could just catch a limb with one hand and draw it to her . . .

Was it too far? The little body drifted closer. In a moment it would be at its nearest point, but still out of reach.

Without thought, without fear, Lily launched forwards.

Her fingers closed on the pink limb.

There was nothing beneath her feet but water.

Jonathan Tells a Story

'MY OWN SON!' Armstrong groaned, with a distraught shake of the head, when he had finished his story.

'Not your son, though,' Margot reminded him. 'He had his true father in him, I'm sad to say.'

'I must make amends. How it can be done I do not know, but I must find a way. And before that, there is a task I dread but must not put off. I must tell the Vaughans what happened to their daughter, and my son's part in it.'

'It is not the time to tell Mrs Vaughan about it now,' Rita told him gently. 'When Mr Vaughan returns, we will tell them together.'

'Why is he not here?'

'He is out with the other men, searching for the child. She is missing.'

'*Missing?* Then I must search with them.'

Seeing his dazed face and his trembling hands, the women tried to dissuade him, but he would not be stopped. 'At this moment it is the only thing I can do to help them, so I must do it.'

Rita returned to Helena, who was nursing her baby.

'Is there any news?' she asked.

'Nothing yet. Mr Armstrong has joined the search. Try not to worry, Helena.'

The young mother looked down at her newborn and some of the worry melted from her face as she lay her smallest finger against his cheek and stroked it. She smiled. 'I can see my own dear father in him, Rita! Isn't that a gift!'

When no answer came, Helena glanced up. 'Rita! Whatever's the matter?'

'I don't know what my father looked like. Nor my mother, even.'

'Don't cry! Rita, dearest!'

Rita sat down next to her friend on the bed.

'You can't bear that she's gone, can you?'

'No. Before you came to claim her – that night a year ago – and before Armstrong turned up – and before Lily White – during that long night, when Daunt was unconscious in this very bed and I was in that chair, over there – I took her on my lap. We fell asleep together. I thought then that if it turned out she wasn't Daunt's, and if she had nobody in the world, that I . . .'

'I know.'

'You know? How?'

'I saw you with her. You felt the same way we all did. Daunt feels it too.'

'Does he? I just want to know where she is. I can't bear her not being here.'

'Nor can I. But it's harder for you.'

'Harder for me? But you—'

'I thought I was her mother? I also thought I'd invented her. Do you remember I told you I sometimes wondered whether she was real?'

'I do. Why do you think it's harder for me?'

'Because I have him.' Helena nodded at her baby. 'My own real baby. Here. Hold him.'

Rita put out her arms and Helena placed the baby into them.

'Not like that. Not like a nurse. Hold him like I do. Like a mother.'

Rita settled the infant in her arms. He fell asleep.

'There,' whispered Helena after a silence. 'How does that feel now?'

The flood water lapped around the Swan. It came to the very door, but no further.

When *Collodion* returned, and Armstrong soon after, the men shook their heads, grim-faced. Vaughan went directly to see his wife and the baby. Both were asleep. He found Rita there.

'Anything?' she whispered.

He shook his head.

When he had gazed long enough in careful silence so as not to wake his son, and kissed his wife's sleeping head, he went with Rita to the winter room. Wet boots had been prised off, feet were stretched towards the fire and socks steamed. The Little Margots had put more logs on the fire and brought hot drinks for everyone.

'Joe?' Vaughan asked, though he could guess the answer.

'Gone,' one of his daughters said.

Then nobody spoke, and they breathed the minutes in and out till they made an hour.

The door opened.

Whoever it was did not rush to come in. The cold air made the candles flicker and brought the tang of the river more powerfully into the room. All looked up.

Every eye saw, yet none reacted. They were trying to understand what it was they were seeing, framed by the open doorway.

'Lily!' Rita exclaimed. She was a figure from a dream. Her white nightgown ran with water, her hair was flat to her scalp, her eyes were wide with shock. In her arms she clutched a body.

All those who had been there at solstice night a year ago were struck by the sight of her. First Daunt had arrived at that door with a corpse in his arms. Later that same night it was Rita who came in, clutching the girl in her arms. Now for a third time the scene replayed itself.

Lily swayed on the threshold and her eyelids flickered. This time it was Daunt and Vaughan who leapt up to catch the new arrival as she fell, and it was Armstrong who stretched out his arms and received into them the wriggling body of a half-drowned piglet.

'Good Lord!' Armstrong exclaimed. 'It's Maisie!'

And so it was – the sweetest piglet from Maud's litter, the one he had given to Lily, according to his promise, when he'd come to fetch Maud and take her back to the farm.

The Little Margots took kind charge of Lily, helping her into dry clothes and making hot drinks to stop the shivers, and when she came back to the winter room, Armstrong complimented her on her courage in rescuing the little pig from the flood water.

On Armstrong's lap the piglet warmed up, and when it had recovered its good spirits, it squealed and squirmed in lively fashion.

The noisy surprise brought Jonathan out of the room where he had been keeping watch over the body of his father. Yawning, one of his sisters followed him.

'You haven't found her?' the Little Margot asked.

Daunt shook his head.

'Found who?' Jonathan wondered.

'The little girl who is lost,' Rita reminded him. *It is late*, she thought, *he is too tired to remember, we must get him to sleep.*

'But she has been found,' he said, surprised. 'Didn't you know?'

'Found?' They looked at each other quizzically. 'No, Jonathan, we don't think so.'

'Yes.' He gave a nod that was quite certain. 'I saw her.'

They stared.

'She came just now.'

'Here?'

'Outside the window.'

Rita sprang up and ran to the room he had just come from, and she looked in agitation from the window, this way and that. 'Where, Jonathan? Where was she?'

'In the punt. That came for Father.'

'Oh, Jonathan.' Despondently she led him back to the winter room. 'Tell us just what you thought you saw, in order, from the start.'

'Well, Father died and he was waiting for Quietly, and Quietly came. Like Mother said he would. He came right up to the window, in his punt, to take Father to the other side of the river, and when I looked out, there she was. In the punt. I said, "Everybody's out looking for you," and she said, "Tell them my father came to fetch me." And then they went away. He's very powerful, her father. I've never seen a punt go so fast.'

There was a lengthy pause.

'The child doesn't speak, Jonathan. Do you remember that?' Daunt asked kindly.

'She does now,' Jonathan said. 'As they were leaving, I said, "Don't go yet," and she said, "I'll come back, Jonathan. Not for a long time, but I'll come back, and I'll see you then." And they went.'

'I think you might have fallen asleep . . . Perhaps you were dreaming?'

He thought about it hard for a moment, then firmly shook his head. '*She* was sleeping,' – indicating his sister. 'I wasn't.'

'This is too serious a thing for a boy to be telling stories about,' suggested Vaughan.

Everybody present opened their mouths and spoke as one: 'But Jonathan can't tell stories.'

In the corner, Armstrong shook his head in quiet wonderment. He'd seen her too. Sitting behind her ferryman father as he propelled the punt so powerfully between the worlds of the living and the dead, between reality and a story.

A Tale of Two Children

AT KELMSCOTT FARMHOUSE the flames burnt bright in the hearth, yet nothing they did could warm the pair of sitters, each in an armchair, one each side of the fireplace.

They had dried their eyes and now gazed into the flames with gravest sorrow.

'You tried,' Bess said. 'You could have done no more.'

'At the river, do you mean? Or his whole life?'

'Both.'

He stared where she was staring, into the flames. 'Would it have been different if I had been harsher with him at the beginning? Should I have whipped him when he stole for the first time?'

'Things might have been different. Or they might not. You can never know. And if they were different, there is no telling whether they would have been better or worse.'

'How could things be worse?'

She turned towards him the face that had been hidden in shadow.

'I Saw him, you know.'

He looked up from the fire, wondering.

'After the time with the bureau. I know we agreed I wouldn't, but I couldn't help it. I'd had the other boys by then, and I knew what kind of children they were by just looking at them with my ordinary eye. Their baby faces were open; it was plain who they were. But Robin was different. He was not like the other babies. He always kept himself concealed. He was not kind to the little ones. You remember how he pinched and bullied them? There were always tears when Robin was there, but without him they played as good as gold. So I often thought of it, but I had said I would not use my eye, and I thought it better to abide by that. Until the day of the bureau. I knew he had done it – he was not such a good liar then as he is now. As he became later, I should say – and I did not believe him when he said he'd seen a fellow running off down the lane and found the bureau forced open. So I took off my patch and I held him by the shoulders and I Saw him.'

'What did you See?'

'No more and no less than you saw tonight. That he was a liar and a cheat. That he had not one jot of care for any person in this world other than himself. That his first and last thought in life would be for his own comfort and his own ease, and that he would hurt anybody, whether it be his own brothers and sisters or his own father, if it brought some small advantage to himself.'

'And so none of this has ever surprised you.'

'No.'

'You said there is no telling if things would have been better or worse . . . Nothing could be worse than this.'

'I did not like you following him tonight. Knowing he had the knife. After what he did to Susan, I was afraid of what he might do to you – and though he was my own flesh and blood, and though I was bound to love him no matter what, I tell you the truth when I say, losing you would have been worse.'

They sat then for a while in silence. Each pursued their own thoughts, and their thoughts were not so very different.

There then came a faint noise, a light tap some distance away. Lost in their own reflections, they at first ignored it, but it came again.

Bess looked up at her husband. 'Was that the door?'

He shrugged. 'Nobody would come knocking at this time of night.'

They returned to their ruminations, but then it came again, no louder, but lasting longer.

'It *is* the door,' he said, rising. 'What a night for it. I shall send them away, whoever they are.'

He took the candle, crossed the hall to the great oak door and slid back the bolts. Opening the door a fraction, he looked out. There was nobody there, and he was just about to close the door again when a small voice stopped him.

'Please, Mr Armstrong . . .'

He looked down. There at waist height was a pair of boys.

'Not tonight, children,' he began. 'This is a house of mourning . . .' And then he looked closer. He raised his candle and peered at the larger of the two boys. He was dressed in rags, shivering and thin, but he knew him. 'Ben? Is it Ben, the butcher's boy?'

'Yes, Sir.'

'Come in.' He opened the door wide. 'It is not the best of nights for visitors, but come, I cannot have you out of doors when it is so cold.'

Ben carefully ushered in the second child ahead of him, and as the smaller boy passed into the candlelight, Armstrong's breath caught in his chest.

'Robin!' he exclaimed.

He bent and held the candle so that its light fell on the boy's face. It was a fine-boned face, made thin by hunger; it had Robin's slenderness; the nostrils had Robin's delicate flare.

'Robin?' Armstrong's voice trembled.

How many times impossible was it? Robin was a grown man. Robin had died tonight, this very night, and he had seen it happen. This child could not be Robin, and yet . . .

The eyes blinked, and Armstrong saw that the child looking out of Robin's face was not Robin, but some other boy. His eyes were gentle and timid – and grey. In the midst of his astonishment, Armstrong heard a half-murmur from Ben and turned to see him falter and sway. He caught Ben as he fell, and called out for Bessie.

'It is the butcher's boy who went missing from Bampton,' he explained. 'He's overcome by the warmth after being out so long.'

'And he has gone short of food lately, by the look of him,' Bessie said, kneeling to support the child, who was returning to his senses after his faint.

Armstrong stood aside so that his wife could see Ben's companion and gestured with his hand. 'He has brought this little fellow with him.'

'Robin! But—' Bessie stared at the child. She could hardly drag her eyes away, but when she did, it was to turn to her husband. 'How . . . ?'

'It is not Robin.' Ben's voice was feeble, but had not lost its habit of delivering words all in a rush with no pauses. 'Sir, it is the little child you were looking for, it is Alice, and I cut her hair – forgive me, I didn't want to do it but we were on the road so long and it seemed safer to be two brothers than to be a boy and a girl and if I did wrong I'm sorry.'

Armstrong stared. Robin's features rearranged themselves in his eyes. He reached out a hand and laid it trembling on the child's shorn head.

'Alice,' he breathed.

Bessie came to stand beside him. 'Alice?'

The child looked at Ben. He nodded. 'It's all right here. You can be Alice again.'

She turned her face to the Armstrongs. Halfway into a smile, her mouth stretched instead into a large exhausted yawn. Her grandfather gathered her into his arms.

Later, after a midnight feast of soup and cheese and apple pie, they sat in the kitchen. Alice slept in her grandmother's arms, while her aunts and uncles, roused from their beds by the excitement in the house, clustered in their nightgowns around the kitchen hearth, and they all listened to Ben's account of how he found the child.

'Soon after I last saw Mr Armstrong, my father took a strap to me and beat me so long and so hard that the world went black and when I came round again I was sure I must be in heaven, but no, I was on the floor of the kitchen and I hurt to my bones and my mother crept to me and said she wondered I wasn't dead and surely I would be next time, and I decided it was time to follow my plan of running away, which I had worked out a long time since, thinking it best to be prepared, and I did everything accordingly, which was to go to the bridge and climb on to the parapet and wait there for a boat, though in the dark a boat is not always easy to spot but you can always hear it, and so there

I stood and never sat for fear of falling asleep, and I shook because a beating like that always sets up a trembling in a body, and at last there came a boat downstream in the darkness, and I clambered on top of the parapet and I lowered myself over it, dangling from my fingertips, and my shoulders and arms that were black and blue from the beating were aching terrible bad and I thought I might fall in the water, but I didn't, for I clung on till the boat was right under me and then I let myself fall and hoped to fall on to something soft like fleeces and not on to something hard like barrels of liquor, and in the end it was neither so good nor so bad as it might have been for I fell on to cheeses, which are between soft and hard, but still they jolted my bones and hurt me where I was already hurting, but I didn't cry out for fear of giving away that I had stowed away, but instead cried quietly and hid as best I could and tried not to fall asleep, but fall asleep I did and woke up, being roughly shaken, and a boatman standing over me was in a fury and he cried out over and over the same words, "Orphanage! Who do they take me for? I'm not a bloody orphanage!" and at first I couldn't understand what he was saying, being so dull with sleep, but then his words came clear as a bell into my ears and from there into my thinking where they met up with some other words already there about Alice who disappeared into the river and I asked the man, was it a little girl who dropped into his boat last time and what happened to her, and he was too furious to answer me or to listen to my questions and threatened to drop me overboard and let me swim for my life and I thought, *Is that what happened to Alice?* and I asked him and he went on being furious for some while yet and then all of a sudden he got hungry and opened a cheese and ate some, but he didn't give any to me, and when he had eaten he was quiet and I asked him all over again and this time he told me that yes, last time it was a little girl, and no, he didn't make her swim for her life, but when he got to London he left her in the care of some orphanage where they take the unwanted children, so I said, "What is the name of this place?" and he didn't know, but he told me the part of town where it was and I stayed with him and I helped him with the unloading and the loading and he gave me cheese for the help, but not much, and when we got to London

I scarpered from his boat and asked directions from a dozen people who sent me here and there and in all directions and eventually I came to the place and asked for Alice and they said they had no Alice and besides orphans weren't there to be taken by anybody, and in the end they closed the door on me, so the next day at a different time I knocked again and it was a different person answered the door and I told them I was hungry and homeless and had no mother and no father and they took me in and set me to work, and all the time I kept my eye out for Alice and asked all the other boys, but the boys were kept separate from the girls so I never saw her until one day I was sent to paint the office of the director of the orphanage, and from the window I saw over the wall into the girls' courtyard and that's when I saw her and knew I was in the right place, and was glad it hadn't all been a waste of time, not so far anyway, and I thought and thought how to get to her and in the end it was as simple as pie because a fine lady took a fancy for doing something good for the orphans and she sent in a great hamper of food to be shared out, and it was, but only the director and his fellows tasted it, and we never got none, but afterwards we was all taken to church to give thanks for the great goodness that was done to us, and when we had sat and stood and sat again and prayed for the virtuous lady, we was all marched out again, the girls from the pews on their side and we boys on the other, and there she was, Alice, right by my side, and I whispered to her, "Do you remember me?" and she nodded, and so I said, "When I say run, run, all right?" and I took her hand and when I ran she ran with me, but not for long for we hid behind a statue and nobody noticed then that we was gone, and after everybody had passed out of the church we set off on our own, walking every day, following the river, and I did a bit of loading and unloading when I could and we ate what we could get, and I cut her hair when a bad lady tried to steal her away from me, thinking to be two boys together was safer, and it took a long time to get here because the boatmen wouldn't take the two of us aboard because only I was big enough to work but the two of us would want feeding, so our feet were sore and we got hungry sometimes and cold others and sometimes hungry and cold together, and now . . .'

He paused to yawn and at the end of the yawn they suddenly saw how dazed his eyes were and that he was on the verge of sleep.

Mr Armstrong wiped a tear from his eye.

'You have done well, Ben. You couldn't have done better.'

'Thank you, Sir, and thank you for the soup and the cheese and the apple pie, it was most excellent.' He slipped from his chair and saluted the family. 'Now I had better be getting along.'

'But where will you go?' asked Mrs Armstrong. 'Where is your home?'

'I set out to run away, and run away I must.'

Robert put both hands on the table. 'We can't have that, Ben. You must stay here and be one of the family.'

Ben looked at the girls and boys around the hearth. 'But you have plenty here eating your profits already, Sir. And now Alice too. Profits don't grow on trees, you know.'

'I know. But if we all work together we make extra profit, and I can see you are a hardworking boy who will pull his weight. Bess, is there a bed for the child?'

'He will sleep with the middle boys. He looks about the same age as Joe and Nelson.'

'There, you see? And you will help with the pigs. All right?'

And so it was settled.

Once Upon a Time, a Long Time Ago

AFTERWARDS, BUT BEFORE the flood had entirely retreated, Daunt took Rita on *Collodion* back to her flooded cottage. They used the little row boat to get to the door, and when Daunt stepped out of it to push the warped door with all his might, the water was up to his knees. Inside there was a line around the walls that showed the water had been three feet high here. All around the room the paint was peeling away from the walls. The receding water had left on the seat of Rita's writing chair, as if there were some meaning in it, an arrangement of twigs, pebbles and other less identifiable matter. She had had the forethought to raise the blue armchair on boxes; its feet had been in water, but the cushions were sound. The red rug could not make up its mind whether to float or sink; every motion of the water caused it to shift with weighty indecision. A dank and unpleasant smell was everywhere.

Daunt stepped aside to let Rita see in. She waded through her front door and into the living room. He watched her face as she surveyed her home, admiring her impassivity as she contemplated the damage.

'It will take weeks to dry out. Months, even,' he said.

'Yes.'

'Where will you go? To the Swan? Margot and Jonathan might be glad of your company when the girls go home. Or the Vaughans? They would be pleased to have you.'

She shrugged. Her thoughts were on other more fundamental matters. This devastation of her home was a trivial detail.

'The books first,' she said.

He waded to the bookcase and saw that the lower shelves were empty. Above the water line the upper shelves were double-stacked.

'You were prepared.'

She shrugged. 'When you live by the river . . .'

He handed her the books a few at a time; she passed them out of the window and placed them in the boat that bobbed just below the level of the sill. They worked in silence. One volume she put aside, on the cushion of the blue armchair.

When the first bookcase was empty and the boat was low in the water, Daunt rowed it back to *Collodion* and unloaded there. On his return to the cottage, he found Rita in the blue chair, still on its boxes. The water from her skirt was darkening the fabric.

'I always wanted to photograph you in that chair.'

She lifted her eyes from the book. 'They've called off the search, haven't they?'

'Yes.'

'She's not coming back.'

'No.' He knew it was true. He had the feeling that the world might easily stop turning without the girl in it. Every hour was arduous, and when it was over, you had to start again with a new one, no better. He wondered how long he would be able to keep going.

'Look,' he said, 'you went to all that trouble to save the blue chair and now your dress is making it wet.'

'It doesn't matter. The thing is, the world seemed complete before she came. And then she was here. And now she's gone, there's something missing.'

'I found her in the river. I feel as if I should be able to find her again.'

Rita nodded. 'When I thought she was dead, I wanted so much for her to live. Instead of leaving her alone there, I stayed. I held her wrist. And she lived. I want to do the same now. I keep thinking about the story of Quietly and what he did to save his child. I understand it now. I would go anywhere, Daunt, I would suffer any pain, to have my child in my arms again.'

She sat in her wet skirt on the blue chair over the water, and he stood motionless in the water. They did not know what to do with their grief. Then wordlessly they set to packing books again.

They emptied the second bookcase, and he rowed again to *Collodion* to unpack.

On his return, Rita was reading the book that she had separated from the rest.

Although the sky was dismal and cast an indifferent light, the greyness was enlivened, even indoors, by the silvery shimmer of reflections from the endless water, which cast ripples of light over Rita. Daunt watched her face lighten and darken in the shifting illumination. Then he looked beyond the ever-changing surface to study the stillness of her expression beneath. He knew his camera could not capture this, that some things were only truly seen by a human eye. This was one of the images of his lifetime. He simply exposed his retina and let love burn her flickering, shimmering, absorbed face on to his soul.

Slowly Rita brought the book down to her side. She continued to stare at the place where the book had been, as if the text continued there, written on the watery light.

'What is it?' he said. 'What are you thinking?'

She did not move. 'The cressmen.' She still stared at nothing.

He was nonplussed. He wouldn't have thought cressmen capable of inspiring intensity like this. 'From the Swan?'

'Yes.' She turned her eyes to his. 'I remembered it the other night. The baby was born in its caul.'

'What's a caul?'

'It's a sack of fluid. The baby grows inside it for the entire pregnancy. Usually it ruptures during labour, but sometimes – rarely – it survives labour and the baby emerges with the caul intact. I cut it open last night and out he swam on a wave.'

'But what has that to do with cressmen?'

'Because of a strange thing I heard them say at the Swan. They were talking about Darwin and man being born of apes, and one of the cressmen reckoned he'd heard a story about men once being underwater creatures.'

'Ridiculous.'

She shook her head, raised the book and tapped it. 'It's in here. Once upon a time, a long time ago, an ape became human. And once upon a time, long before that, an aquatic creature came out of the water and breathed air.'

'Really?'

'Really.'

'And?'

'And once upon a time, twelve months ago, a little girl who should have drowned, didn't. She entered the water and seemed to die there. You pulled her out; I found she had no pulse, no breath, her pupils were dilated. Every sign told me she was dead. And then she wasn't. How can that be? Dead people do not return to life.

Immersing the face in cold water slows the heart dramatically. Is it possible that sudden immersion in very cold water might slow the heart and constrict the blood flow so radically that a person might appear to be dead? It sounds too strange to be true. But if you remember that every one of us spent the first nine months of our existence suspended in liquid, perhaps that makes it a little less incredible. Remember next that our land-going, oxygen-breathing selves derive from underwater life – that we once lived in water as we now live in air – think of *that* and doesn't the impossible start to edge closer to the conceivable?'

She tucked the book into her pocket and put out a hand for Daunt to help her down from the chair. 'I'll get no further, I think. I've come as far as I can go. Ideas, notions, theories.'

Rita packed her medicines, a bundle of clothes and linen, her Sunday shoes, and they left without attempting to close the door. They rowed to *Collodion*.

'Where now?' he said.

'Nowhere.' She flung herself on the bench and closed her eyes.

'Which side of the river is that?'

'It's right here, Daunt. I'd like to stay here.'

Later, on *Collodion*'s narrow bed and with the river cradling the boat, Daunt and Rita loved each other. In the dark his hands saw what his eyes could not: the curl of her loosened hair, the curve and point of her breasts, the shallow dip at the small of her back, the outward flare of her hips. They saw the smoothness of her thighs and the complicated fleshiness between them. He touched her and she touched him and when he entered her he felt a river rise in him. For a little while he mastered the river, then it grew and he abandoned himself to it. There was only the river then, nothing but the river, and the river was everything – until the current at last surged and broke and ebbed.

Afterwards they lay together, and spoke quietly of mysterious things: they wondered how Daunt had got from Devil's Weir to the Swan, and why everybody had thought the girl a puppet or a doll when they first saw her. They asked why her feet were so perfect it was as if they had never put foot to earth, and how a father could cross to other worlds and bring his daughter home, and they realized there are no stories of children crossing into other worlds to find their parents, and wondered why. They puzzled over what exactly Jonathan had seen from the window of the room where his father lay dead. They talked of the strange stories Joe brought back from his sinking spells and all the other stories at the Swan, and they wondered what the solstice had to do with all or any of it. More than once they came back to two questions: where had the girl come from? And where had she gone to? They came to no conclusion. They thought too about other things both inconsequential and significant. The river swelled and subsided without insistence.

All the time, Daunt's hand lay on Rita's belly, and she had her hand over his.

Beneath their hands, in the damp vessels of her abdomen, life was swimming urgently upstream.

Something, they both thought, *is going to happen*.

Happily Ever After

IN THE MONTHS that followed, Ruby Wheeler married Ernest; at the church, her grandmother took Daunt and Rita by the hands and said, 'Bless you both. I wish you every happiness together.'

At Kelmscott farmhouse, Alice grew her hair. She began to look less like her father when he was a child and more like the little girl she was. Bess took off her patch and declared, 'There's not much of Robin in her at all. That girl he married must have been a good woman. This is a lovely child.' And Armstrong said, 'I think in some ways she takes after you, dearest.'

Basketman's Cottage was uninhabitable after the flood and would always be so. Lily moved to the parsonage. She looked about the housekeeper's room in awe, touched the bedhead and the night table and the mahogany chest of drawers and reminded herself that the days when she had said about even the smallest possession, 'I shall only lose it,' were over. The puppy slept in a basket in the kitchen and the parson grew as fond of it as Lily was. In fact, when she came to think about it, she wondered whether it hadn't perhaps been her who was so keen on puppies as a girl – or perhaps she and her sister both were.

The water, when it eventually receded, left behind a small skeleton on the floodplain. A gold chain was around its neck and an anchor hung between the bones of its ribcage. The Vaughans buried their daughter and grieved for her, and rejoiced in their son. They went together to a house in Oxford, where Mrs Constantine listened to them talk about everything that had happened and they wept in her tranquil room and washed their faces afterwards, and soon afterwards Buscot Lodge and all its farmland and Brandy Island were put on the market. Helena and Anthony said goodbye to their friends and departed with their baby son to new rivers in New Zealand.

With Joe gone, Margot decided it was time for another generation to take the helm at the Swan. Her eldest daughter moved to the inn with her husband and her children and they made a great success of it. Margot was still as present as ever in the bar, mulling her cider, though she let her son-in-law – a strong fellow – chop the logs and carry the barrels. Jonathan helped his sister, as he had helped his mother, and often told a story about the child who was taken from the river one solstice night, first drowned then alive again, who spoke not a word, until the river came up the banks to take her back, a year to the day later, and she was reunited with her father the ferryman. But if you asked him to tell any other story, he couldn't.

Joe the storyteller was remembered at the Swan for a long, long time. And though eventually there came a time when the man himself was forgotten, his stories lived on.

Daunt finished his book of photographs and it enjoyed a modest success. He had intended to create a fine volume that would include every town and every village, every myth and every folk tale, every jetty and every water wheel, every turn and twist of the river, but inevitably the book fell short of its ambition. Still he had sold over a hundred copies already, enough to order a reprint, and the book pleased many, including Rita.

Standing at the helm as *Collodion* powered along, Daunt had to acknowledge that the river was too vast a thing to be contained in any book. Majestic, powerful, unknowable, it lends itself tolerantly to the doings of men until it doesn't, and then anything can happen. One day the river helpfully turns a wheel to grind your barley, the next it drowns your crop. He watched the water slide tantalizingly past the boat, seeming in its flashes of reflected light to contain fragments of the past and of the future. It has meant many things to many people over the years – he put a little essay into the book about that.

He wondered, fancifully, whether there was a way of appeasing the spirit of the river. A way of encouraging it to be on your side and not dangerously against you. Along with the dead dogs, illegal liquor, rashly flung wedding rings and stolen goods that litter the riverbed, there are pieces of gold and silver down there. Ritualistic offerings whose meanings are hard to fathom so many centuries later. He might throw something in himself. His book? He considered it. The book was worth five shillings, and there was Rita now. There was a home to maintain, and a boat, and a business, and a nursery to be decorated. Five shillings was too much to sacrifice to appease a deity in which he didn't really believe. He would take photographs of it. How many photographs could a man take in a lifetime? A hundred thousand? About that. A hundred thousand slivers of life – ten or fifteen seconds long – captured by light on glass. Somehow, in all that photography, he would figure out how to capture the river.

Rita grew round as the months passed and the baby inside her grew. She and Daunt discussed names for their child. Iris, they thought, like the flowers that bloomed on the riverbank.

'What if it's a boy?' Margot asked.

They shook their heads. It was a girl. They knew.

Rita thought sometimes of the women who'd lost their lives giving birth and she thought often of her own mother. When she felt the baby turn in her underwater world she thought of Quietly. There were times when God, who had once disappeared, seemed not so very far away. The future was unfathomable, but with every heartbeat she carried her daughter towards it.

And the girl? What of her? Accounts emerged of sightings of her in the company of the river gypsies. She was quite at ease there, apparently. She had fallen overboard in the dark that first solstice night, it was said, and her parents hadn't realized she was gone until the next day. They gave her up for dead, until word reached them of a child being looked after by wealthy people at Buscot. It sounded as if she'd be all right. No need to hurry back. They'd be passing that way the same time next year. She seemed happy to be back in her gypsy life, so it was said, after her year of being lost.

These stories came late in the day, from far afield, one- and two-line reports, lacking detail, without colour or interest. They were taken up briefly by the regulars at the Swan, considered and discarded. It wasn't much of a story, they felt, but then they never liked other people's stories as much as their own. Jonathan's was the version they preferred by far.

There are those who see her still, on the river, in good and bad weather, when the current is treacherous or slow, when mist obscures the view and when the surface glitters. The drinkers see her when they mistake their footing, the worse for wear after one glass too many. Rash boys see her when they jump from the bridge on a fine summer's day and discover how the serene surface stillness belies the pull of the current underneath. They see her when they find themselves out after twilight, and when they cannot bail as fast as they thought. For a time these reports were of a man and a child together in the punt. With the years the child grew until she did the punting herself, and then came the time – nobody can remember when exactly – when it was no longer the two of them, but she alone. Majestic, they say; strong as three men; insubstantial as the mist. She handles the punt with smooth grace and has all her father's mastery over the water. If you ask where she lives, they will blow their cheeks out and shake their heads in mystification. 'At Radcot, perhaps,' they suggest at Buscot, but at Radcot they shrug and wonder if it's not at Buscot.

At the Swan, if you press them, they will tell you she lives on the other side of the river, though they don't know exactly where. But wherever she lives – if she does live anywhere, and I am inclined to doubt it – she is never far away, and when a soul is in danger she is always there. When it is not time to cross that border she will see that you keep on the right side of it. And when it *is* time, why, she will see you just as surely to that other destination, the one you didn't know you were headed for, at least, not today.

And now, dear reader, the story is over. It is time for you to cross the bridge once more and return to the world you came from. This river, which is and is not the Thames, must continue flowing without you. You have haunted here long enough, and besides, surely you have rivers of your own to attend to?

Author's Note

THE RIVER THAMES irrigates not only the landscape but also the imagination, and as it does so, it alters. At times the demands of the story have called upon me to tinker with travel times and nudge locations up- or downstream by a few furlongs. If reading my book inspires you to go on a river walk (something I wholeheartedly recommend), by all means take this book with you – but you might want to take a map or guidebook too.

The character of Henry Daunt is inspired by the magnificent real-life photographer of the Thames, Henry Taunt. Like my Henry, he had a houseboat kitted out as a darkroom. During the course of his lifetime he took some 53,000 photographs using the wet collodion process. His work came close to being destroyed when, after his death, his house was sold and his garden workshop dismantled. On learning that many thousands of the glass plates stored there had already been smashed or wiped clean for use as greenhouse glass, a local historian, Harry Paintin, alerted E. E. Skuse, the city librarian in Oxford. Skuse was able to stop the work and arrange removal of the surviving plates for safekeeping. I note their names here out of gratitude for their swift actions. It is thanks to them that I have been able to explore the Victorian Thames visually and weave this story around Taunt's images.

Do people really drown and come to life again? Well, not really, but it can seem so. The mammalian dive reflex is triggered when a person is suddenly submerged, face and body, into very cold water. The body's metabolism slows as the reflex redirects circulation away from the limbs and routes blood between the heart, brain and lungs only. The heart beats more slowly and oxygen is conserved for essential bodily processes, so as to maintain life for as long as possible. Once recovered from the water, the near-drowned person will appear dead. This physiological phenomenon was first written up in the medical journals in the middle of the twentieth century. The dive reflex is thought to occur in all mammals, both terrestrial and aquatic. It has been observed in adult humans, but is believed to be most dramatic in small children.

Acknowledgements

THERE ARE TIMES when friends make all the difference. Helen Potts, this book owes you an enormous debt of gratitude. Julie Summers, our writerly walks along the Thames have been invaluable. Thank you both.

Graham Diprose provided helpful pointers relating to the history of photography, and John Brewer talked me very patiently through the wet collodion process of photographic development.

Nick Reynard of the Centre for Ecology and Hydrology in Wallingford put me right about flooding in language that proves how close science is to poetry.

Captain Cliff Colborne from the Thames Traditional Boat Society helped figure out how an accident such as Daunt's might have happened.

Dr Susan Hawkins of Kingston University provided valuable information about nurses and their use of thermometers in the nineteenth century.

Professor Joshua Getzler and Professor Rebecca Probert made useful suggestions relating to legal claims to found children in the nineteenth century.

Simon Steele was illuminating on the subject of distilling.

Nathan Franklin knows everything a man can possibly know about pigs.

A great many people explained aspects of rowing to me; despite their best efforts, I still don't really understand it. Simon, Will, Julie, Naomi, thank you anyway.

Thank you also to Mary and John Acton, Jo Powell Anson, Mike Anson, Margot Arendse, Jane Bailey, Gaia Banks, Alison Barrow, Toppen Bech, Emily Bestler, Kari Bolin, Valerie Borchardt, Will Bourne Taylor, Maggie Budden, Emma Burton, Erin, Fergus, Paula and Ross Catley, Mark Cocker, Emma Darwin, Jane Darwin, Philip del Nevo, Margaret Denman, Assly Elvins, Lucy Fawcett, Anna Franklin, Vivien Green, Douglas Gurr, Claudia Hammer-Hewstone, Christine Harland-Lang, Ursula Harrison, Peter Hawkins, Philip Hull, Jenny Jacobs, Maggie Ju, Mary and Robert Julier, Håkon Langballe, Eunice Martin, Gary McGibbon, Mary Muir, Kate Samano, Mandy Setterfield, Jeffrey and Pauline Setterfield, Jo Smith, Bernadete Soares de Andrade, Caroline Stüwe Lemarechal, Rachel Phipps of the Woodstock Bookshop, Chris Steele, Greg Thomas, Marianne Velmans, Sarah Whittaker, Anna Withers.

Sources Consulted

Peter Ackroyd, *Thames: Sacred River*
Graham Diprose and Jeff Robins, *The Thames Revisited*
Robert Gibbings, *Sweet Thames Run Softly*
Malcolm Graham, *Henry Taunt of Oxford: a Victorian Photographer*
Susan Read, *The Thames of Henry Taunt*
Henry Taunt, *A New Map of the Thames*
Alfred Williams, *Round About the Upper Thames*

There is one website I navigated a thousand times while writing this book and which was invaluable to me. It takes you on a journey through space and time, along the river. Where Thames Smooth Waters Glide (www.thames.me.uk) was created by John Eade and he maintains it with dedication. If you can't get to the Thames itself, this website is the next best thing.

Diane Setterfield's bestselling novel *The Thirteenth Tale* was published in thirty-eight countries, sold more than three million copies, and was made into a television drama scripted by Christopher Hampton, starring Olivia Colman and Vanessa Redgrave. Her second novel was *Bellman & Black*, and her new novel is *Once Upon a River*. Born in rural Berkshire, she now lives near Oxford, by the Thames.